DOWNBURST

DOWNBURST

KATIE ROBISON

QUIL BOOKS, INC

For my family and friends
who made this possible

STAGE ONE: GATHERING

A thunderstorm develops when two converging winds force air to rise into the atmosphere.

The Cowichan and Ojibwa tribes teach their children about the Thunderbirds—giant, many-colored birds with great powers. When they fly, they bring together the clouds and control the rain. When they beat their wings, they send thunder rolling across the sky. And when they blink their eyes, they shoot lightning through the heavens.

We must treat the Thunderbirds with great reverence so as to not incur their wrath.

I

When I was two, the wind tried to kill me.

At least, that's what my mom told me. My real mom, the one whose voice slips into my dreams at night. We were playing at the park and eating ice cream sandwiches. I can almost remember that day—sitting on an apple-colored swing, dabs of chocolate crust sticking to my fingers.

Mom said I wanted to see the waterfall, so Dad walked me over to the edge and hoisted me onto the stone retaining wall. I gripped his hand and leaned bravely over the cliff, peering at the churning water beneath my feet. My father, the photographer, saw something he liked and let go of me so he could grab his camera. At that moment, a gust of wind came barreling through the trees and shoved me on the back. I shrieked as I reeled forward, about to tumble to the rocks below, but Dad grabbed my shirt just before I fell. Mom was furious, of course. She was furious when she repeated the story too, that blue vein on her forehead bulging beneath her smooth, brown skin. It's one of the last things I remember her telling me.

She may have been right about the wind. Even now, a lifetime later, it seems bent on my destruction. As I lean out of my hiding spot, the gale pulls my hair free of the limp elastic that's holding it back in some semblance of a ponytail, and grime and cigarette butts fly into my face. *Kava*, I curse, using one of Mom's favorite words. *Stupid Canadian squall.* I spit out the dirt and shield my eyes with my arm so I can continue to watch the road.

They're late.

I step back into the protection of the alcove, really an enclosed driveway for the food equipment company that owns this building, though it's so narrow I can't imagine the delivery truck can be anything impressive. Piles of trash have collected in the corners, another gift of the wind, and beer cans and crushed cartons mingle with the mounds of dirt. I'm careful not to brush against the walls.

Joe was impressed when I staked this spot out on my own. "Not bad for a rookie," he said. The store itself, with its faded paint and soot-caked bricks, is ready to go under. One of the upper windows is broken, and I can hear the wind whistle its way through the jagged glass. But it's the location that's the sweet part—the shop is on a curving one-way street, and the two nearest streetlamps have both burned out. Across the road are dirt parking lots surrounded by chain link fences, empty now that business hours are over. There are more empty lots on either side of the store, and the nearest buildings are either abandoned or closed for the night. All in all, it's the perfect place to make some cash.

Assuming the person bringing the cash actually shows up.

I hazard another look down the road, fingers kneading the frayed corner of my jacket. Nothing. They must have lost their nerve. Joe will be wild, but I can't risk waiting here any longer. Looking carefully in both directions, I step onto the sidewalk.

Staggeringly bright xenon headlamps suddenly whip around the corner as a red BMW hurtles down the street toward me. I shuffle backward, ducking into the niche and smacking my heel on the corner of a brick. I curse at the driver and rub my foot.

Before I poke my head back out of the recess, I count to ten, giving the car plenty of time to pass. But when I peer around the wall, I curse again. The BMW is still there, and now it's backing up, moving slowly, as if the people inside are looking for an address. It must be them. *Idiots.* They're going to get us all arrested—or worse.

Deciding not to chance it, I retreat further into the shadows of the alcove. I'll just tell Joe they never showed. But then the driver's window rolls down, and a girl sticks her head out into the night. She checks the number on the store sign against the paper in her hand, looks up and down the street, and as I feel the weight of the envelope in my pocket, I remind myself what it will mean if I do this job. Clenching my trembling fingers, I step back onto the sidewalk.

When the girl sees me, I gesture for her to turn down the lamps. Her head disappears inside. A second later, the lights go dark.

"Do you have the money?" I ask when I reach the car. My voice doesn't quaver. I'm getting better at this.

A heavy fragrance escapes through the window and drenches the air, the combination of thickly applied perfumes and hairspray. Synthetic vanilla and jasmine. I fight the urge to cover my nose.

"Here." The girl extends her hand, a stack of crisp twenties pinned under her neon blue fingernails. The polish on her thumb is chipped, and I wonder if she's been biting her nails, like I have.

I take the bills and count them quickly. One hundred … three hundred … five hundred … it's all there. Where do they come up with this money? Probably their rich parents. The things I could do with five hundred dollars.

I pull the envelope out of my pocket and hand it to the blue fingernails. As I look up at the girl's face, I feel my eyes widen, and I'm glad her attention is on the envelope so she doesn't notice. It's like I'm watching my reflection, maybe even my twin. We have the same jawline, the same hard angles that suddenly swoop into a rounded point beneath our big lips, the same flat spot on the tips of our long noses. Same straight eyebrows, same cocoa-colored skin with thick, espresso hair.

I remember now. Joe said the girl could have been me when he was putting the license together. I thought he was just taunting me. I had no idea he was being so literal.

The girl hands one of the I.D.s to a person in the passenger seat before putting her own license in her purse. As she bends down, a neon blue highlight slips from behind her ear and onto her cheek. Then she looks up, and I meet her gaze for the first time. Her almond eyes narrow, and suddenly I see myself the way she does, not as her twin but as a nobody. I lower my own oval eyes to the curb.

"Are we done here?" she asks. I nod, stepping back. Joe was wrong. That girl could never be me. I could never be her.

She must have been waiting with her foot on the accelerator because the headlamps immediately flare to full power, and I have to jump backward to keep my feet from being crushed. The tires squeal as they fight for traction on the curving road, the sudden clamor fracturing the cultivated silence of the neighborhood.

Spinning around, I shove the money down the tattered lining of my windbreaker and book it in the opposite direction. The girl's reckless exit could have signaled anyone within half a mile. *Great.* Now I'm not going to be able to use this spot again.

The cash feels heavy against my ribs. Obvious. Like anyone who looked at me would know how much I'm carrying. I realize I'm practically running and force myself to slow down. I try not to look around too much, but it's hard to keep my eyes from flicking toward every movement in the dark streets and alleyways. *How in the world did I get into this mess?* I ask myself yet again. Selling fake identification wasn't exactly the kind of work I imagined finding when I ran away from home.

The cops aren't the only ones I have to worry about. There are the gangs too. I'm an easy target for a mugging, a skinny girl on my own, carrying a cool five hundred. And just a few streets away is the train yard, the entrance to the North End. Shredder territory.

It's the Shredders I'm worried about the most. Another gang would probably just take the money and let me go, but the Shredders enjoy hurting people, torturing people. They didn't earn their name for nothing. I reach for the switchblade tucked in my jean pocket, a souvenir from my one and only excursion to the North End. The cold steel makes my fingertips tingle.

It happened the first week I was working for Joe. He got a big client, a desperate client, and desperate people always mean good money. The man and his family needed to leave the country. Passports are a lot harder to make than driver's licenses, but Joe's the best in the business and he said he'd do it—for a price, of course. The man's only stipulation was that the trade had to be done north of the city center. He knew a good place.

As the new delivery girl, I was given the job. Joe didn't trust me yet, so he made me wear a tracker and told me that if I ran he would find me and kill me. I wondered why he didn't just get the money himself, but once I entered the North End, I understood: he didn't want to risk his own neck.

Upheaved pavement, broken glass, graffiti-smudged doors, overturned dumpsters, charred houses, trashed yards, gutted stores, splintered fences, hostile stares, that was the North End. I'd never seen anything like it. By the time I reached the rendezvous point I was visibly trembling.

When the man handed me the money, I didn't want to count it; I just wanted to get out of there. But I knew Joe would accuse me of stealing if I came back with less than the promised ten grand, so I flipped through the bills. Quickly. Then I stuffed the money in my windbreaker, gave the man his passports, and took off.

I was ten yards from the train tracks, ten yards from safety, when they found me—five of them. For a moment, all I saw were the shaved heads and the red tattoos that covered their arms and necks, the drooping cargo pants and the stained wife beaters. But the worst were the scars. All of them had burned the letter *S* somewhere on their body. Their forearms, their heads, their cheeks.

I hesitated for only a second before I started to cross the street, but then one of them crossed as well. I turned to go back and found that another one had circled behind me, a puffy red *S* curving around his eye. He smiled and revealed a knife.

"What's a chick like you doing around here?" he asked.

"Visiting a friend." I prayed he couldn't see the cash through my jacket.

"Didn't your friend warn you we don't dig strangers?" He flicked the knife across his fingertips, drawing his own blood.

"Maybe we can have a little fun with her first," another one chimed in. The other gang members whistled.

Suddenly, I wasn't so worried about the money. I looked around frantically, but the streets were deserted. The gang tightened the circle.

And then, incredibly, a police car rounded the corner. I'd never been so happy to see the cops in my entire life. As I jumped up and down and screamed for help, the Shredders bolted. The one with the scar over his eye tripped on a pothole and dropped his knife. He growled but didn't stop to pick it up, and by the time the police reached me, he had hurtled a fence and disappeared.

"Are you okay, miss?" one of the officers asked while his partner gave chase. I nodded, dry-mouthed, amazed at how lucky I had been. But with my relief came a new worry. One false move on my part could give away the ten thousand dollars stashed not so carefully in my jacket, could get me sent back home.

The cop got on the radio to notify another policeman in the area, and when he wasn't looking, I stooped down to grab the Shredder's knife. The other officer returned soon afterward, panting from his brief exertion.

"Can we give you a ride?" he asked. I opened my mouth to say no then reconsidered. I wasn't out of Shredder territory yet, I had a long walk ahead of me, and I could barely stand. So I accepted.

Joe about had a heart attack when he watched the cop car drive down our street and saw me climb out. I led the officers to believe I lived in one of the houses—it would have been stupid to reveal my actual address—but I wanted Joe to see me. I wanted him to be scared.

"Don't ever send me to the North End again!" I shouted when I got back to the apartment, throwing the plastic bag onto the table and storming over to the living room corner where I slept.

It was then that I first examined the knife and discovered it was a switchblade, something else the cops could have arrested me for.

I got a lucky break that day, I think as I quicken my pace and run my finger along the closed blade. The thought of stabbing someone makes me sick, but if a Shredder showed up, it would be my only chance. Too bad I don't have a handgun, or, even better, my old Remington 798. That would definitely keep the gangs at bay.

After a few blocks, I hit Main Street, and the scene changes dramatically. The shops here are clean, and there's lots of traffic. I'm still not used to the city—the throng of people makes my pulse rise—but at least the crowds lower my chance of being robbed. That doesn't mean it's safe, exactly. Walking anywhere downtown after dark is a risk, but I'll take Main Street over the North End alleyways any day.

As I wait at the light, I steal a glance at the brunette to my left and notice she's carrying a flute case. *Melody*, I name her.

I peek at the two men on my right. Brothers, judging by their dark hair and identical goatees. One is wearing scrubs, whistling under his breath as he checks out Melody. The other is sporting a shirt that's unbuttoned to his navel like he's ready to hit up Republic Nightclub. *Dr. Heckle and Mr. Jive.*

By the time the light changes, I'm breathing more normally. I cross the street and pass the Manitoba Museum. The museum is something I've never had the desire, or the money, to go inside, but I'd love to step foot in the domed building next to it—that's the planetarium. Physics and astronomy were the only classes I did well in, maybe because our science teacher didn't assign homework, but they were also the subjects that interested me the most.

I keep walking, and soon I see the red street lamps and pagoda-like gates of China Town, reminding me of my first taste of Chinese food, three days ago. The wind teases me with the smell of fried rice and spicy-sweet sauces, but I don't stop.

I speed up slightly as I pass City Hall. Hiding in the back, behind the flowerbeds and statues, is the police station. My wrists grow moist, and I wipe them against the inside of my sleeves. *I can't keep doing this*, I think. If only I had another choice.

Before long, I reach the heart of downtown Winnipeg. The skyscrapers here aren't as tall as the ones in Minneapolis or St. Paul, but they're worlds bigger than anything we have in Williams. My eyes roam up the lofty glass business towers and pillared banks, taking in the lights. Millions of yellow stars against the black sky.

Things grow less glamorous as I near the railway again. The city's full of tracks, and even Main Street has to give way to the trains' endless chugging and shaking. The wind picks up, carrying a hint of rain, and I pull the hood of my jacket over my head. The fabric blocks most of my peripheral vision, but it doesn't matter. There isn't much to see on this stretch.

I take the two bridges over the Forks—the place where the Assiniboine River meets the Red—and enter an older part of town. A plump woman in a brown coat crosses the street in front of me, keeping a tight grip on her two children and hopping her way around a pile of garbage, like a bird. *Mother Wren*, I decide.

In her wake, a boy, probably only ten or eleven, struggles to push a stroller, a cowlick on the back of his head bobbing up and down. I look away before I feel the familiar throbbing in my throat, before I think about the twins.

Now I've reached our neighborhood, where the streets are lined with giant trees, the swaying silhouettes only hinting at their true size. They block the pale light coming from the tiny windows in the tiny houses. A dog barks in the distance. In someone's living room, a TV flickers, blue and white.

I turn onto the next block, knowing exactly where to lift my feet so I don't trip on the large roots that push through the concrete. When I reach the old brick apartment building that I've called home for a month, I walk into the dimly lit foyer and press the button for apartment three. After about four seconds, the lock buzzes, and I pull open the door and go inside. Holding my breath out of habit, I walk down the dingy hallway to the last apartment, turn the knob, and enter Joe's smoke-filled living room.

I flinch, like I always do when I smell smoke, but this is just cigar smoke, so my heartbeat calms down quickly.

"Hey, Joe," I call into the empty room, throwing the five hundred dollars on the counter and walking toward the stove. I should really hang onto the money, use it as a bargaining chip, but I don't want to risk making him angry. Not today.

Through the smoke I can detect a hint of baked beans, our typical dinner, and my stomach growls. Joe does well for himself in his line of work, but you'd never know it from the canned cuisine or the outdated apartment—stained orange carpet, pale green countertops, worn brown couch. I wonder again what he does with his money. *Probably all goes to his bookie.*

I grab a spoon from a rickety drawer and scoop some beans from the pot.

"Thief," Joe mumbles around the cigar in his mouth as he walks out of the bedroom and into the kitchen.

"Whatever," I say, carefully holding the hot beans on my tongue so I don't burn the roof of my mouth. I swallow and take another spoonful.

"The deal came off?" Joe asks, taking a long drag.

"Yep." I point to the cash on the counter.

Joe sits down heavily on a stool and counts the money, like he always does. A short man, with oversized ears and a tuft of white hair on the back of his head, Joe looks harmless, but there's a calculating brain inside that head. And a lot of fight. Some of his clients have made the mistake of thinking they can push him around. It's a mistake I wouldn't recommend.

Joe found me on my tenth day in Winnipeg, huddled on a park bench, half-crazy with starvation. He didn't ask me if I had a place to go. He didn't ask if there was someone looking for me either. He just said he could give me room and board and a job to boot. I told him to bug off, but he said he wasn't interested in taking advantage of hungry girls. His work was legitimate. More or less.

As it turns out, Joe's been true to his word: he's fed me, given me a place to sleep, and put me to work. He just hasn't been so great about paying me.

"So," I begin, hesitating a moment, "today's pay day, right?"

Joe looks up sharply then barks his hoarse laugh. "I guess you're right, doll. What did we say? Fifty bones a drop. So that's what, three hundred?"

Don't react, I think, picking up a shoelace on the counter and casually tying a square knot, imagining all the things I could do if I had a full length of rope—lasso him maybe, tie him up, leave him like that until he agreed to pay me what he owed.

"I think it's more like six."

He coughs. "You hosing me?" He takes another puff then leans forward, exhaling a cloud of smoke.

I don't say anything, just stare back at him and grip the shoelace, trying not to choke on the fumes. Finally, he sighs. "All right. I'll cut you a check."

"No checks, Joe. I need cash."

"Babe, I don't keep my paper here, you know that."

Liar. But I can't say I didn't see this coming. "Well, I can take this five hundred now, and you can pay me the difference later."

Suddenly, the door bursts open, and the unnaturally blond hair and gangly arms of Joe's assistant Troy fill the entryway. "Cops," he pants. "Outside." He darts back into the hall.

Joe knocks over the stool as he runs for the bedroom where he keeps his equipment. "Ball out, Kit!" he growls.

For a full three heartbeats, I don't move. Then his words sink in, and I spin around. The back door is right in front of me. I turn the knob, yank the door open. But then I pause and look back at the five hundred dollars still sitting on the counter, not six feet away. I can't leave without it.

As I take a step toward the money, the front door flies open again and five uniformed officers storm into the room. "Police!" one of them yells.

I turn around and leap out the open door, crossing the tiny patio in two steps before dashing across the lawn. I know they'll probably call other cops on their radios—there may even be someone stationed outside the building—so I don't go toward the street. Instead, I jump over a hedge and cut through the backyards behind us.

My heart rocks in my chest as I run close to the fence lines, keeping away from the windows and porch lights of the small houses. I imagine I can hear the police calling after me. Dogs barking. Sirens shrieking. I knock over a trash can, stumble, and keep running.

When I reach the end of the backyards, I sprint across the street and head east, away from the river. I'm a fast runner, and it doesn't take me long to leave the residential area. Once I get to the main road, I race across the lanes, narrowly avoiding a car. The driver honks, but I don't stop until I reach the other side of the street and cross into the next neighborhood.

I survey the unfamiliar homes around me and try to calm my rough panting so I can listen. No cops, no dogs, no sirens, just the sound of chirping crickets. I'm out of danger, for now. I fight the urge to start running again, my feet shuffling quickly forward, involuntary bursts of speed making my pace jerky and erratic.

As I move from shadow to shadow, I try to think of a plan—I can't work without a plan—but I have absolutely no idea what to do. I have no money, no job, no place to live, and, to top it off, the police are after me. They saw my face, they'll get my fingerprints from the apartment, and if they catch me and find out I'm in the country illegally … *Why wasn't I faster?* If I hadn't hesitated, I could have grabbed the money and gotten out of there before they arrived.

If only I had that fake I.D. Joe kept promising me. I'd borrow bus fare from one of his friends, get out of Winnipeg—maybe go to Calgary or Edmonton—and start over. But without it, without money, I'm screwed.

It's mid-September now, and it won't be long before the snow comes. The winter doesn't really bother me, but even I can't sleep outside in one of the coldest countries in the world. If I don't figure something out soon, I might be forced to turn myself in and go back to Williams.

I've come to a dead end. An imposing country club blocks the street and continues south for what looks like a long way. To get around it, I'll need to backtrack and go north, unless …

Looking around to make sure no one's watching, I cross the parking lot. There's a wrought iron fence, but it only takes me five seconds to climb it and disappear into the hundreds of trees surrounding the green. I walk through the man-made forest and plop to the ground under the protective branches of a willow.

Leaning my head against the knobby trunk, I reach under my shirt and pull out the necklace my parents gave me when I was a baby. The pendant is made of some kind of animal bone, polished as smooth as glass and carved into an indistinct pattern of swirling lines. I used to try to follow the twists and turns to see how they all connected, but I've long given that up. I still don't know what it is. Whenever I asked my father, he would only say, "Yours."

Maybe I should sell it.

No, it wouldn't be worth anything. I tuck it back under my shirt.

Just then, a crack of thunder announces the storm has finally arrived, and in moments the rain is cascading on my head. Cursing, I rise to my feet. I'll have to look for shelter.

I run out into the torrent, dodging trees and sloshing through mud puddles. When I reach the other side of the green, I clamber up the iron fence, but I lose my footing on the wet metal and fall to the ground. Grimacing, I stand up and stumble forward, slipping on the wet grass, searching for something that will keep me dry. I continue to lurch through the neighborhoods until at last I stagger into a train yard.

I baulk at the sight of the tracks but force myself to keep going. *This isn't the North End*, I remind myself. *Even if it were, no one's going to be out in this rain.* And there's something else that makes me feel better. Boxcars. Lots and lots of boxcars.

I walk toward the first car and pull the handle, but it doesn't move. I try another one. Also locked. I move toward the third, wondering if I'll actually have to sleep under the train. I tug on the door. It slides open easily—too easily—and I slip on the wet rocks. Only my grip on the handle keeps me from falling.

I pull myself up and look at the bolt. Apparently, someone had the same idea and busted the lock. I push the door the rest of the way open.

"Hello?" I call warily, not eager to deal with a bum. But no one answers. Deciding to risk it, I climb inside and close the door behind me, wedging myself against the hard planks, wrapping my arms around my chest.

I pull the switchblade out of my pocket, thumb poised on the button, ready to flip the knife out if anyone opens the door. I try to think clearly, but my skin and clothes are caked in mud, my empty stomach gnaws on its own lining, and my head thrums as if someone were keeping time for a marching band inside my brain. Shivering, I hug myself more tightly and press my other hand against my temple. *What do I do now?*

Above my head, the wind slips through a crack in the wood and hisses in my ear. I stare at the boards in front of me, barely making out the shape of the warped planks in the darkness. *Why can't I think of a plan? I need a plan, need a plan, a plan …*

My body tenses when I wake, slits of light bearing down on me like prison bars, the air too musty. Then I remember where I am, and I groan and sit up, feeling the ache in my back. My clothes are still damp, and I'm shaking. I run my fingers through my hair, snarled hopelessly by the wind and rain. It takes me a minute to work the elastic out of the knots. Then I do what I can to keep the mess pulled away from my face.

My belly throbs, and I remember that I haven't eaten anything since lunch the day before except for that spoonful of beans. I need a plan, or I'm a goner. *Start with something simple: food.* Maybe I can beg a free breakfast at Joe's favorite diner. The owner is a friend of ours. He might help me.

I reach for the door, but just as I'm about to pull it open, I hear voices—deep, male voices. My hand pauses on the handle, and I put my eye up to a crack in the side of the car. Peering through the hole, I make out the shapes of two large men against the gray sky. They're both wearing dark leather jackets with matching gloves, and their black hair is knotted above their collars. I can't see their faces, but I do see tattoos. Black ink crawling along their skin, disappearing under the leather. My heart shoots rapid-fire against my chest.

After a moment, I see a third person. A girl. They say something to her, but the wind carries off their words, and I can't hear what it is. Suddenly, one of them grabs her shoulders and shoves her against the side of a boxcar.

Then, before I can think of a plan, the thug pulls a knife from his belt and slides it through the girl's throat.

2

I smother my scream in my hands. A strangled noise escapes, but it's not enough to attract their attention. The man releases the girl, and her lifeless body slumps onto the tracks. The second man picks up her purse and spills its contents onto the wet ballast, scattering them across the hard rocks. A bottle of nail polish bounces close to the girl's side. Her keys skid under a rail, and her wallet and cell phone land a few feet away. The first man picks up the phone, sets it on the tracks, and crushes it with his heel, while the second man grabs the wallet and removes the cash. Once he's taken everything, he tosses the empty billfold back by the body. It hits the girl's foot, making it twitch. Bile rises in my throat.

Then they walk away without saying a word, leaving me rocking back and forth in my boxcar, taking deep, shuddering breaths, trying not to throw up. Finally my brain snaps back on. *Get out of here, Kit!* I stagger to my feet and slide open the door, lower myself to the ground. I know I should run for all I'm worth, but I can't move. Instead, I look at the girl.

She's lying unnaturally on one arm, her torso twisted, legs curled together, head flopped back under the car. A steady stream of blood flows from her throat, making its way down her chest and onto the gravel. Neon blue paint, leaking from the cracked handle of the nail polish, mixes with the blood and washes the rocks in a hideous purple. My stomach lurches.

Blue nail polish. I stumble a few steps back as realization sets in. Hands shaking, I crouch down to get a glimpse of the girl's face under the boxcar. Her blank eyes are partially covered by her hair—thick, black hair with a blue highlight.

This time I don't hesitate. I turn and run. Run and run and run. The girl's sightless eyes hover before me, and I blink violently, but they don't go away. I stumble on a rail. My ankle rolls, and I fall forward, catching myself with my hands. The rocks scrape slices of skin from my palms, but I don't feel it. Everything around me is sliding out of focus. I find a pebble under my face, slimmer than the others, and stare at it until the ground stops revolving. It's coated in mud, the ends tapered. Brown. Oval. Like my eyes. Like *her* eyes. *No!* The mutilated image returns, her vacant gaze, that blue highlight dipped in blood.

I dig my hands wildly under the rocks, into the drenched earth, searching for something solid to stop the spinning. Only ten hours ago, I had a conversation with this girl. I took her money; I gave her a fake I.D.

Fake I.D.

My hands stop digging as a lump forms in my stomach. The driver's license, the one that looks like it could be mine, is it still with her? The ground remains unsteady, but for the moment I push the gory specter to the side. I think about the wallet the men pulled out of the girl's purse, see it landing by her body. The I.D. would be in there. If I could just get it, I might still have a chance. I could find work. I wouldn't have to go back to Williams.

All I have to do is take it.

But taking it means going back there, seeing her again, and I can't do it, not that. *I'll find another solution*, I think as I struggle to my feet. Right now I've got to get out of here before the police show up.

I take a step forward and then stop. *Sweet kava—the police!* When they go through the girl's stuff, they'll find the license. *I* touched that thing! They might connect me to the murder. I could get sent home, maybe even to prison. Unless ... *Unless I remove the evidence.*

I squeeze my fingers against my brow, try to think. But I know I don't have a choice anymore, not if I want to be sure. I breathe in again, a deep, raspy breath, and force my legs to turn around, to walk back. *Just a few steps, that's all it is.*

I don't look at her face, at her contorted body, at the pool of purple blood. I just stare at the ground and focus on the wallet, a patch of white against the awful backdrop of blue and red. I waver for a moment, the nausea returning. *You can do this!* I take a step toward it. And another. And another. Then, when I'm a foot away, I leap forward, snatch it up, and run.

I run faster than before, leaping over tracks, dodging boxcars, keeping my eyes on the distant highway that marks the end of the train yard. My ankle throbs, but I ignore it. I can't let anyone see me.

I churn my legs harder. My feet only just skim the ground. I block out everything—the soreness in my body, the pit in my stomach, the bloody corpse. The only thing I allow myself to think about is the road.

Soon I can see the asphalt that means my freedom, and something else I wasn't expecting: a chain link fence. Unlike the railing at the golf course, this fence has barbed wire strung along the top, and one look tells me I'll have to find another way out. I run beside it, moving south, ever aware of how close I'm getting to the operating buildings. *Please don't let them notice me*, I pray to whatever god might be feeling merciful today. *Please don't let them see.*

I scramble down a ditch and around a mountain of wet dirt, past piles of scrap metal and spare parts scattered around the yard. I dash from one to the other, squeezing by rusted bulldozers and giant PVC pipes until, finally, I can see a parking lot and the end of the fence.

I unsteadily survey the final stretch of yard. Not a soul in sight. *Now!* As I bolt for the parking lot, the ground tips away from me, and it's all I can do to keep the asphalt in my field of vision. Finally, my feet touch the blacktop, and I run toward a large patch of bushes and trees on the other side, not even trying to be cautious. I duck behind the tightly grown shrubs and drop to my knees on the grass, sucking in air with wheezing gasps.

When I've caught my breath again, I slowly unclench my fist and look down at the wallet in my hand. It's made of faux alligator skin, edges worn to a dirty gray, and it smells faintly of vanilla. Fingers shaking, I flip it over to open the latch and immediately drop it on the ground. The front flap is stained with blood. Big splotches of brown and purple.

This time I can't hold it down. I bend over and retch whatever was left in my stomach. Even after my belly is emptied, I continue to heave. Acid burns my throat, and I stay doubled over, convulsing. Whenever I think I'm about to stop, I see the girl's pallid face, smell the vanilla and toluene, and my middle seizes up.

At last the spasms subside, and I clutch a tree for support, try to clear my brain, remember my plan. I can't stay here. I've got to keep moving. That's it. Keep moving. Where should I go? The diner, to see Joe's friend. Ask for food. Maybe bus money. But I need to do something first. What is it? Think! Right, the I.D.—I need to make sure I have the I.D.

Holding my breath, I open the wallet and remove the cards tucked inside. My hands are shaking uncontrollably, and I have to close my eyes for a moment. When I open them again, the first thing I see is the license. I slump against the tree and utter a prayer of thanks to my divine guardian.

My eyes find the picture, and I brace myself for another wave of nausea, but the girl staring back at me looks nothing like the girl in the train yard. Joe was right. She looks like *me*—a cleaner, wealthier version of me.

I continue to stare at the photo, scrutinizing the details of the girl's face, confirming the resemblance. It really is like I'm looking at my own picture, except … the smile's not quite right. When I smile, I get dimples. Her cheeks are smooth. Still, that's not something anyone's going to notice, particularly since I hardly ever smile.

Flor Garcia is the name on the I.D., my new name. I take a deep breath. I should be able to pull that off—most people think I'm

Latina anyway. I glance at the date of birth. I'm eighteen now, two years older than I really am.

Flipping the license to the back of the stack, I take a look at the next card. It's the girl's real license, and now I know three more things about her. She's five feet six inches, she weighs one hundred and fifteen pounds, and her name is Aura Torres.

Aura Torres. I press my fist against my forehead. Without meaning to, I picture her from the night before—her scornful gaze and strong perfume, chipped nails and made-up face. And then I think of her body, lying crumpled on the tracks. I exhale slowly. Then I cram the cards back in the wallet and shove the whole thing in my pocket. It's time to go.

Staggering out of the bushes, I blink away the haze and try to get my bearings. The diner is west of here, so I'll need to cross the street.

I turn to leave the lot, but as I walk past the cars, I catch sight of something that makes me stop. Parked between a faded blue pickup and a gold sedan is a red BMW.

Her red BMW.

The vertigo returns, and I steady myself on the bumper of the car next to me. What was Aura doing here? Had she actually come to *meet* those men?

A blur of movement is the only warning I get before something dark whips over my head, blocking out the air and light. I scream and strike out with my fists, but a hand clamps over my mouth. "Shut up, or I'll kill you," a man says in a deep voice. I feel something sharp jab into my back.

I stop struggling. The man grabs my arms and pulls them behind me, lashing my wrists together with a zip tie then pushing me forward. I'm dumped onto a back seat of a car, buckled in, and then the car's starting and we're backing out of the parking stall, moving out of the lot.

Rivers of cold sweat flow down the back of my neck. In my mind, I see the enormous black-haired men with their awful tattoos, see the flash of the knife before it drives into Aura's throat, and my heart thunders in my ears. Is that who abducted me, one of those men? Do they know I saw them—did they see me run with her wallet? It's so hard to breathe inside this bag.

Suddenly, the radio roars to life at full volume, overpowering the noise of the road, suffocating me even further. I press my hands against the seat, but it doesn't help. I'm completely disconnected from the world—I can't hear anything except the music. At any moment he might attack me, and I'd have no warning. My stomach is cramping itself into stone, and pellets of salty water drip into my eyes. I rub my face against the seat, but the bag just drives the sweat in further, making my eyes sting more.

I have no idea how long we've been driving when a bump in the road jolts me to the side, and I feel something in my right pocket dig into my leg. My switchblade. I hold perfectly still. Would it be possible for me to get it? I deliberate for several minutes. I have no way of knowing if the man is watching me or not, and if he sees me get my knife, he'll take it away. But if I wait, I might not get another chance. I'll just have to hope he's focusing on the road.

Moving as slowly as possible, I shift my arms so that they're resting on my right hip. And then, slowly, slowly, I dig my fingers into my pocket. The knife is shoved down deep, and it takes some concerted twisting to reach it. I try to keep my body still, but soon my back is twitching, my arms shaking.

Finally, my fingers latch onto the metal. I slide the blade up my pocket and slip it into my palm. Readjusting my arms so that they're behind my back again, I aim the knife away from my body and push the button. I feel rather than hear the quiet swish as the blade pops out. I wait for ten seconds, but there's no sign that the man heard anything.

Carefully, I rotate the knife in my fingers and place the sharp edge on the plastic tie, moving the blade in a sawing motion, exerting as much pressure as I can. The loud music has turned out to be a blessing—even I can't hear the sound of the knife. But it's taking a long time, and it's getting hard to hold the blade in my increasingly sweaty hands.

Abruptly, the zip tie snaps, and I feel the blade nick the back of the seat. I freeze, hold my breath. But the music continues to blare, and the car keeps moving. I quietly exhale then wriggle my wrists out of the broken plastic and shut the knife.

The sweat is still in my eyes, and I want more than anything to tear the bag from my head, but I can't give myself away. So I wait, heart thumping, back dripping, fingers twitching on the blade.

After an eternity, the car slows down, and we turn off the road and come to a stop. The radio dies, but the silence is somehow more stifling than the music had been.

"All right, we're here," my captor says, his voice not as deep as I remember.

Suddenly, the bag is yanked off my head, and I duck to the side, muscles tense, ready to spring if he attacks me. But nothing happens. As I blink against the bright light, I gradually see the person in the front seat looking back at me, and I blink again. He isn't big or burly, and he doesn't have any tattoos. He's young, maybe early twenties, and tall, judging by how close his head is to the roof of the car.

The man grins and opens his mouth to say something, but I don't wait to hear what it is. I unbuckle my belt and lunge for the door, dashing outside onto a parking lot. In front of me is a gas station, and I sprint toward it.

I've only gone five steps when I feel the man's hand grab my arm. In desperation, I pop open the switchblade and thrust it at his heart. But the man is fast. He leaps out of the way, and I barely cut his shoulder. Before I can strike again, his arm whips out, and he seizes my wrist, twisting it hard behind my back so that I'm forced to drop the knife. Then he kicks my feet out from under me, and I crash onto the asphalt, bracing myself for another blow.

It doesn't come. Instead he says, "Holy crap, Aura! Your dad warned me you weren't excited about going to camp, but this is nuts. What are you trying to do, kill me?" He inspects the nick on his shoulder then bends down to pick up my blade. "A switchblade? Yikes, you really are a piece of work."

"*I'm* a piece of work?" I shout, scrambling to my feet. "You're the one who threw a bag over my head and threatened to kill me! Are you out of your mind?"

He takes a step toward me, but I scramble backward. "Don't touch me!"

"Now just calm down."

"Don't tell me to calm down!"

"Okay, okay. I'm sorry I scared you. I'm not going to hurt you. I promise."

"Get away from me."

"Aura, listen, I'm sorry. But we have to—"

"Look, I don't know who you are or what's going on, but I'm not Aura. You've made a mistake. Now leave me alone!"

He frowns, and I notice for the first time that his disheveled brown hair is restrained by a red bandana, that there's a large mole on his left cheek. "You must have had quite the night," he says, hitching up his eyebrows as his sharp eyes study the mud on my clothes. "Hope you got it out of your system, because there won't be that kind of partying where we're going. Come on, we need to go meet up with the others."

"I'm sorry, maybe you didn't hear me," I snap. "I'm. Not. Aura."

"Maybe you didn't hear *me*," he returns. "Your dad already warned me you would try to pull something. And honestly, I'm not that impressed. If you really didn't want to come, why were you at the meeting spot at the exact time you were supposed to be? Besides, you look just like your picture—even with all the mud."

"That's a coincidence," I begin then hesitate. How am I going to tell him that Aura was murdered, that I saw it happen?

"Sure it is," the man says, rolling his eyes. "I bet I know a way to settle this." All of a sudden, he leaps toward me and thrusts his fingers into my jacket pocket.

I jump back. "What are you doing?" And then I see the wallet in his hand. "Give me that!" I yell, reaching for it.

But it's too late—he's already opened it, already seen both licenses. His eyebrows rise even higher as he pulls out the Flor Garcia I.D., and he whistles. "Wow, you're worse than I thought. So that explains all this." He waves his hand in my general direction.

I don't say anything. There's nothing I *can* say. If I convince him I'm not Aura, he'll wonder what I'm doing with her license. I swear under my breath.

The man hears me, but he just smiles, probably taking it as my admission. "It's not going to be that bad," he says. "Yeah, you have to kayak for a bit, but the rest will be fun. It's only for a week, and then you can come back and roll around in your pigsty."

I glare at him. I need to buy time, need to figure this out. "Why did you kidnap me?"

"It's part of the tradition, just some harmless hazing. Though I have to say I've never had anyone try to knife me before."

"Well, it's a stupid idea." I say as I back away slowly. *I'll get him to lower his guard, and then I'll run.*

"Nah," he grins. "It's lots of fun. And anyway, you know you're not allowed to know where the camp is. If you saw which way I left town, you might be able to figure it out." He looks at a watch on his wrist. "C'mon, lets go meet the others. Your hissy fit has made us late."

Suddenly, the man jumps forward again and seizes my arm. I struggle to free myself, but his grip is too strong. He pulls me behind him, making me stumble forward. I try punching the shoulder I cut, but he twists my arm again, and the pain forces me to give in. *I need a plan,* I think frantically as he drags me across the parking lot. *I can't let him take me to some camp in the middle of nowhere!*

Or can I?

The thought makes me pause, and I trip again as he wrenches me forward. My mind whirls, but the more I think about it, the more I see its advantages. It's an easy way to get out of Winnipeg and lie low for a week, I'll be given food and somewhere to sleep, and it sounds like the camp is in a remote location where no one will think to look for me. Plus, it involves kayaking, something I'm actually good at. Once I'm at the camp, or maybe on the way back, I can figure out a way to go to another city. It's a perfect solution.

Well, almost perfect. There is one thing standing in my way: I have to pretend to be somebody else, somebody who's dead.

By now we've reached the gas station—a lone building on the side of the highway. Parked at a pump is a blue fifteen-passenger van, and standing next to it are several teens and two young adults. They wave when they see us.

"There you are!" says one of the adults, a woman with dreadlocks and a stud on her upper lip. "I was just about to call you."

"Sorry to keep you waiting," my captor replies. "We had a little knife fight." He bounces my switchblade in his hand.

I scowl. Pretending to be Aura also means I'm going to have to put up with *him* the entire time.

I look at the other teens. They're gaping at me, probably trying to figure out if I really attempted to stab the moron holding my arm. I run my hand through my hair, but my fingers catch on the sweat-drenched tangles. I guess there might be other reasons they're staring.

"This is Jeremy," the woman says, introducing my abductor to the group then looking at me. "I'm Aponi, and this is Damon." She gestures to the dark-haired man standing beside her. "We're your counselors."

"And now that everyone's here, we can start our road trip," Damon says. "I hope you all ate big breakfasts!" He grins, and suddenly I'm aware of the aching emptiness that's squeezing my gut. I bite down on my lip.

"We want to go as quickly as possible," Jeremy adds, "so there will only be one bathroom break. If you need to perform your necessaries, as I suspect many of you do"—the counselors chuckle, making me guess the other teens were hazing victims too—"you should do that now. There's a washroom in the gas station. Feel free to, you know, freshen up." He looks pointedly down at me as he says it, and I imagine myself punching him in the nose.

"We'll meet back here in ten minutes," Aponi inserts.

Jeremy pinches my arm as he lowers his face toward mine. "No funny business, okay?" he says sternly.

I pull my arm free. "Yeah, yeah, don't worry. You win."

As I approach the gas station, several paces behind the others, I catch my reflection in the glass door and stop walking. I look worse than I thought. Cuts and bruises on my cheeks and arms. Mud in my ratted hair. A split and swollen lip. *How did that happen?* I wonder as I touch my mouth.

When I finally move to open the door, I stumble on the step and, as I catch myself, hear my heartbeat pulsing in my ears. Everything looks unnaturally white, and it's hard to focus.

I pull open the door and walk toward the snack aisle, glancing dizzily at the mirrors in the corners of the room. It's a risk, I know, but if I don't get something in me soon, I'll pass out. I settle on a granola bar, slip it up my sleeve, and try not to trip again as I walk toward the door.

"You gonna pay for that?"

"What?" I look up. A middle-aged salesclerk is watching me and chewing on a pen.

"That candy bar you lifted," she says.

"I didn't take a candy bar."

"I saw you do it."

"Oh, you mean this *granola* bar?" I ask, dropping the snack into my palm. "I was going to ask my friend for some money, that's all."

"Uh huh. Well, you can leave that here while you ask."

"Um, sure, okay." I take a step toward the counter, trying to decide if it would be worth it to run.

"Here you go," someone says behind me. I turn around and see a girl from the group. She's tiny, with wispy, honey-colored hair floating around her face, and she's holding a five-dollar bill.

"Er, thanks," I say after a moment, taking the money.

The girl smiles quickly and ducks outside. I watch her disappear around the corner then turn back to the clerk. "I also want some water and a hot dog," I say.

The clerk grunts and studies her nails.

I carry the food outside, gobbling the hot dog in three bites, not caring that it's probably been sitting in the warmer for days. I drain the entire water bottle, but I can still taste acid in my throat, and Aura's bloodied face pops into my mind. I push her away and look around for the girl who gave me the money. She's by the van, talking to Aponi.

I sit down on the curb. To distract myself, I look down at my battered hands and try to remove flecks of mud from the damaged skin, but after a few minutes I start shaking and have to fold my arms.

A boy crouches down a few feet away from me. He has a large, pink nose, and as he takes a tissue of his pocket and blows into it, the pink deepens into fire engine red. It stands out against his fair skin and pale eyes, making his face look like a target. *Bullseye*, I name him, and my muscles relax a titch.

I look around at the others. Leaning against the van are two siblings, a brother and sister, twins probably. The girl has long black hair that hangs in a straight ponytail down her back, and the boy's glossy locks, which swoop across his forehead, slide back and forth as he struggles to open a packet of gummy bears. *Dee and Dum*. Dee for the girl. Dum for the boy.

A boy with reddish-blond hair sits on the van's back bumper. He catches me looking and turns to sneer at me, his long neck curving unpleasantly, fat lips squished together. *Gander*, I decide.

I look away from him as another boy joins the group. He's big, with arms three or four times the size of mine. He has light brown hair, deep brown eyes, and wide shoulders. He's also eating four hot dogs. *Titan*.

Then there's the girl next to him, the one who gave me the money. Her wrists are like the legs of a sparrow, and as her feathery hair falls into her eyes, she brushes it away with quick swipes of her tiny hand. I think about naming her after a bird, but I can't forget the five dollars. *Charity*.

The last person to join the group is a girl with glaringly blonde hair and thickly applied mascara. Before I've had a chance to name her, Jeremy whistles to get our attention.

"Okay, initiates, it's time to get in the van," he announces. "This is when your period of silence begins—you will not be allowed to speak again until you arrive at the camp. Use this time to prepare mentally. Damon, Aponi, and I will instruct you as needed. Otherwise, we too will uphold the silence. Ready? Let's do this!"

Period of silence? I can't believe my luck. My benign god must still be looking out for me.

I jump when something prods me in the arm. Looking up, I see Jeremy pushing a finger into my flesh. "You first," he smiles. I glare at him. Taking my time, I stand up and walk over to the van. *He's probably putting me in the back so I don't try to escape.*

But when Gander, who's assigned to sit next to me, makes a face and scoots as far away as possible, I realize Jeremy may have other reasons for confining me to the back seat: I might, well, smell bad … just a little. I catch the other initiates wrinkling their noses, but I don't really care. Making friends was never my forte anyway.

As we pull out of the gas station, I lean against the window and immediately feel a hard object press into my side. Aura's wallet. I grimace and pull it out. But as I'm moving it to the other pocket, a piece of beige paper falls onto my lap. I pick it up. It's small, about half the size of an index card, and on its otherwise blank surface is printed a place and a time. *Symington Yards. 7:00 am.* So Aura was at the tracks to meet Jeremy.

I flip the paper over. There's a design on the back, so faint it's only visible when I hold it up to the sunlight. An eagle, traced in glittering red, clutching an axe. It must be the symbol for this camp we're going to. Hopefully, it will be a high adventure camp, somewhere I can blend in. Because if I can't …

I shake my shoulders and stick the paper back in the wallet before dropping the whole thing into my pocket. Then I rest my head against the back of the seat and close my eyes, reaching for my necklace. Instantly, Aura's face fills my vision, and I have to look outside again. I try to think about something else, but I can't keep my mind away from this morning, from all that blood.

Who were those men that killed her? They looked like they belonged to a gang, but not any gang I'd seen around Winnipeg. Their heads weren't shaved, and they were too far east to be Shredders. What did they want—were they trying to rob her? No, they took her money *after* they slit her throat. *They wanted it to look like a robbery,* I realize. *That's why they dumped her purse and broke her cell phone.* A chill settles in my chest. Will the police figure it out, or will they just assume what the men wanted them to, that it was a mugging gone wrong?

The answer makes me squirm in my seat. They're not going to figure it out. The men were too careful, the whole thing too calculated. There's only one person who can identify them, and that's me. But, of course, I never will, so they'll get off scot-free, and I'm the one who has to worry about being blamed for it.

Gripping my pendant more tightly, I look out the window, stare at the highway rolling away beneath me, and think about all of the reasons I absolutely cannot go to the police.

The rest of the day goes by in a sluggish blur, marked by the rumbling whir of the engine and the monotonous vibrations of the wheels, broken up only by our single pit stop. I continue to ignore the glares of the initiates next to me, continue to watch the road, trying anything not to think about Aura, about what will happen if I mess up and they find out I'm not her.

Finally, we reach our stopping point for the night and check in to our hotel. I've only stayed at a hotel once—on my school trip to the Twin Cities—but even I can tell this place is nothing to brag about. Torn carpet. Weak lighting. Peeling paint. Still, compared to Joe's, it's not half bad.

"We'll meet in the lobby tomorrow morning at six," Jeremy tells us as he hands out the keys to our rooms. "Don't be late. We want to make an early start."

As soon as I get to my room, I head straight for the shower. Without pausing to take off my clothes, I turn on the handle and step under the warm spray, vigorously washing away all the mud, scrubbing my skin hard, forcing her face to go away. When I emerge an hour later, I discover my roommate, the blonde girl with lots of makeup, tapping her foot on the chipped tile and waiting with a towel draped over her arm.

"Took you long enough," she says.

I raise an eyebrow. I thought we weren't allowed to say anything until we got to the camp. I don't really care if she speaks or not, but I'm certainly not going to apologize, especially since she's been scrunching her nose at me all day. Leaning forward, I snatch the towel from the rack directly behind her head and, ignoring her sputters of indignation, wring out my hair. Then I walk over to the bed, peel off my clothes, and burrow into what I hope are clean sheets, throwing the wet towel on the floor and instantly closing my eyes.

I wake up a few hours later, gasping for air. I'm used to nightmares, but this one was especially bloody, and it takes me a while to go back to sleep.

Around four o'clock in the morning, my roommate's alarm clock goes off. Not quite comprehending, I squint at her as she gets out of bed, flips on the light, and walks over to the counter. None of the initiates have any luggage—probably another reason Jeremy mistook me for Aura—but this girl has found a way around that, and I watch, eyes slowly widening, as she removes makeup, travel-sized body spray, hair gel, and even a miniature straightening iron from her pockets.

After watching for a few minutes, I roll over and pull the blankets above my head. But not before I've decided on her name—*Diva*.

At ten to six, I crawl reluctantly out of bed. I splash cold water on my face, tie back my dense hair, kinked more than usual from lying in bed, and pull on my wrinkled clothes. The jeans are still damp, but at least they're not coated in mud.

By this time, Diva's blindingly blonde locks have been perfectly straightened and smoothed. She adds yet another layer of mascara to her lashes and then checks herself out in the mirror. When she sees me looking at her, she scowls. I blow her a kiss and leave the room.

Once we've all gathered in the musty lobby, our counselors lead us back out to the van. This time they assign me to the middle row, though for some reason Gander and I are punished with sitting next to each other for another eight hours.

Damon takes us to a drive-through for breakfast, and as we return to the highway, Jeremy passes back limp egg sandwiches and watery orange juice.

Just as I'm handing a tray of cups to the people behind me, Damon hits a pothole, and the juice flies from my grasp, dousing the neck and shirt of the person in the back seat. That person happens to be Diva.

"Idiot!" Diva screams. "Freak! What's wrong with you?"

Aponi whips her head around. "That's enough," she scolds. "You shame yourself." It's the first time I've seen her frown. Usually the stud on her lip is rising with the curves of her mouth. Diva's face grows dark red, and she wipes furiously at her shirt with a pile of napkins.

I look away, meticulously unwrapping my egg sandwich. *Good thing I didn't get her hair wet. She might have clawed my eyes out.* But it's hard to forget that second thing she called me, hard to push down the memories, and I feel my back stiffen.

Around me, the other initiatives are shifting in their seats and staring fixedly at their sandwiches, the compulsory silence heightening the tension in the van. *It's not because of what she said,* I realize. *It's because she* said *something.* And for the first time I wonder why we aren't allowed to speak, why it's so important.

I look at the people sitting in the row in front of me—Titan, Charity, and Bullseye. All of them have their heads bowed low, like athletes in a locker room before a game, hands clasped between knees, lips rolling under teeth, and as I watch their hunched shoulders, my stomach clenches. I remember now. Jeremy said the period of silence was for mental preparation.

That leaves just one question.

What exactly are we preparing for?

3

I am running.

I pass lightly over twigs and branches, landing on the rich moss. The trees keep the black path moist and the air heavy. It's dark, quiet. Only the soft thudding of my feet and the whisper of my breath. Tiny swirls of cotton dance around my head. One of the puffs lands on my eyebrow, and I swish it away. To my left, the sun pierces the thick canopy, soaking a section of leaves in light. They shimmer, iridescent, green.

Up ahead, the trees end. The world beyond is golden and welcoming, and I run faster, springing off the balls of my feet, bursting from the cover of the forest, vaulting onto the dirt road. Fat, splotchy clouds break up the glare above, and the new blades on the cornstalks whish as I go by.

A redwing blackbird springs from the grass by my feet and charges at my head, protecting his nest. I raise my arms in defense and shoot more power into my legs. The bird follows me for several paces then flies to a watchful post above. I see his proud silhouette against the bright sky.

I turn onto a new road, following my usual route, and the corn gives way to softer crops. The tall grasses bend easily in the breeze, the strong wind nudges the small of my back, and ahead of me, the dirt path extends forever. On both sides, fields follow fields. A collapsed barn. Trees waving in the distance. Small towers of gray wooden beehives. A congregation of horses. These are my only companions.

The wind dies, and the sweat drips into my eyes, down my back. The air is suddenly scalding. Each blistering breath smothers my lungs, and my feet pound the taupe dirt while my mind directs my panting. *In. Out. In. Out.* My legs shine, and I can feel the heat radiating from my cheeks.

In the field to my right, a long smear of vibrant yellow leaps out against the green crops. The color of July. I leave the road and enter the meadow, slowing to a walk as I'm surrounded by lemon and goldenrod. My sweat attracts the flies, but I wave them away and brush the flowering crops with my fingertips. I drink in the dandelion sunshine, the hum of the bees. Pure serenity. The wind picks up again, and I welcome the coolness against my flushed cheeks, breathing deeply.

Smoke burns my throat.

I snap my head behind me and see a column of swirling slate. Immediately, I turn and run in the opposite direction. Around me, the mustard flowers begin to fade, their gray stalks crumbling as I rush past. I run faster, but the smoke stays with me. The wind drives the fumes into my mouth and nose. I splutter and wheeze and keep running as everything grows gray and hazy. I can't even see the dead field. All I hear is the crunch of the dry, withered plants beneath my feet.

At last I reach the forest and plunge into the trees. The light is even grayer and dimmer under the leaves, but the shade offers no relief from the heat—or the smoke. My shirt clings stickily to my skin. My hair is stiff and wet. I want to stop and rest, but I can't. I have to keep moving. I run until my feet throb.

It's no use. The dark plumes find me. They swallow the trees, curl around my feet, entwine themselves about my torso. Hideous black tattoos appear in the mist, twisting the smoke into a giant snake. The tattoos slither up the gray scales, coiling together to form the monster's eyes and teeth, and then the snake opens its mouth and digs its fangs into my flesh.

"No!" I scream. But my blood is already flowing, purple torrents pulsing down my chest and onto the ground, the only color against the gray.

And now I'm just like them.

41

I jolt forward, almost hitting the back of the seat in front of me, and gape at the faded blue fabric until relief slowly oozes into my veins. I'm in the van. It was only a dream.

I glance at the other passengers, wondering if I screamed out loud, but none of them are looking in my direction, and I lean back against the seat. No one noticed. Well, almost no one. A peek to my right confirms Gander's smirking face—he probably felt me start awake. I scowl at him and turn my attention back to the view from my window.

Outside, the forest continues to roll bumpily past, just as it has for the past five hours since we left civilization and took to the back roads. As I peer through the glass at the endless pines, I think of my dream and shudder, tell myself to breathe deeply. Then I see something and sit up straight. It's a house. I crane my neck to look ahead. I think there are more of them.

"We're here!" Jeremy calls from the front.

I keep my forehead glued to the window as more and more homes come into view and we enter a town. The town is small, but it's still bigger than Williams with its population of barely two hundred. And unlike Williams, there's no flat farmland here. Just dense, suffocating forest.

In a matter of minutes, we drive straight through the village and stop at the edge of a lake. Jeremy orders everyone out of the van, and Damon and Aponi usher us toward a small convenience store to use the bathroom. My legs feel like goo, and I have to stretch them slowly.

While I wait my turn in line, I see two men talking by the coolers. I strain to make out what they're saying, but they're not speaking English, or even French. Instead, it sounds like some kind of Indian dialect. We're further out in the boonies than I thought.

When I walk back outside, Aponi is handing out energy bars. I wonder why our counselors are giving us such exorbitant snacks, but I'm hungry, so I rip it open quickly.

"Alrighty," Damon pronounces, "the fun is about to begin!" He motions grandly behind him at a line of backpacks and forest green one-man kayaks.

"Everyone grab a pack and kayak," Jeremy directs, "and walk it over to the beach here."

Finally. Shoving the half-eaten energy bar into my pocket, I join the group and pick out a kayak. Then I hoist a pack onto my shoulders, pick up a paddle and a lifejacket, and carry the vessel down to the water. It's not as heavy as a canoe, but it's not exactly lightweight either. That means we probably won't be going on a long trip, just paddling out to a campsite. I've done that scores of times on 4-H excursions to Voyageurs National Park.

I admire the kayak as I set it down next to the others. Our counselors may have fed us fast food and booked a cheap hotel room, but they aren't holding back here. These are good quality watercraft, not sea kayaks by any means, but certainly worth upwards of seven hundred dollars. Slick design, equipped with skegs, they look like they're built to handle some surf, maybe even some whitewater. I want to see what's inside the backpack, but none of the other initiates are opening theirs, so I don't either.

"Okay, everyone, load 'em up," Jeremy instructs.

One glance tells me the compartment in the stern won't be big enough to hold the large backpack, so instead I slide it into the space for my legs. I'll just have to hope the gear inside has been waterproofed. I lower myself into the seat, adjust the foot braces, and grab the paddle.

When I look up, I discover that I'm the only one in my kayak. Most of the others are still struggling to find a spot for their backpacks—Dum is attempting to shove the remaining two-thirds of his pack inside the hatch even though it's in as far as it can go.

"All right," Jeremy says when the others are finally ready. "In your backpacks you'll find a topographic map, a compass, and the coordinates for the campsite. It's approximately sixty-four kilometers northeast of here. You have until tomorrow night to arrive."

Sixty-four kilometers? I feel a pinch in my gut. That's got to be around forty miles.

"You can work together if you wish," Jeremy continues, "but remember, you are still observing the period of silence and you *must* arrive with your kayaks. Once you reach the island there"—he points across the lake—"you may look inside your packs."

I squint at the speck of land and estimate it will take a good thirty minutes to reach it. Maybe more. The water looks choppy.

"Okay, then," he concludes, "I think that does it. Oh, one more thing—remember, if you show up late, you'll be sent home. If you don't show up, well … " His voice trails off. "Let's just hope we see you tomorrow night."

I stare at him. *What does he mean? What will happen if we don't show up?*

As Aponi and Damon begin pushing the kayaks into the lake, Jeremy walks over to me. "It's probably against the rules," he says, "but I thought you might like your knife." He holds out my switchblade, and I take it from him numbly, putting it in my pocket, wanting desperately to ask.

"Don't get lost," he winks. Before I can react, he walks behind my kayak and shoves it into the water. "Happy sailing!"

I automatically begin to paddle, aiming the bow for the island, but all I'm thinking about is what will happen if I run into trouble. Would they actually leave me out here? I'm a good kayaker, but forty miles is a long way to go.

I force the thought out of my head and concentrate on catching up with the others. After a few minutes, I finally connect to the tail end of the small armada. Surprisingly, it takes some strenuous paddling to match their pace. Somehow, all of the initiates, even Diva, know how to kayak, the steady strokes of their paddles belying their earlier clumsiness. And they're fast. It's all I can do to keep up with them, and in ten minutes, I won't even be able to do that, not at this speed.

Ten minutes was too generous. In two minutes, I've dropped five feet behind the group. In four minutes, it's twenty feet. I take deep, thrashing cuts at the water as I fall further and further behind and as the pressure bubbles higher and higher inside of me.

Seriously, what is going on? One minute these kids have no idea what they're doing, and the next they're kayaking like pros. It doesn't make any sense—even Dum is making this look easy. Aren't any of them worried about what Jeremy said? We're traveling into the Canadian wilderness, and there's a chance no one will come looking for us if something goes wrong!

When the closest person is a good hundred feet in front of me, the pressure suddenly surges up my chest, and I thump my paddle hard against the water. It makes a satisfying smacking sound, and I do it again, letting the shuddering sensation run up my arm as I swat the oar again and again on the water. My kayak rocks back and forth, but I keep thrashing as the frustration froths out of me.

This is all Aura's fault. Suddenly, I see her face in the lake, and I whack at it with my paddle. The images from yesterday spin fast around my head. I whack at each one, but another just takes its place. Black tattoos. Blood-stained knives. Blank brown eyes. Blotchy wallets. The dark cyclone swirls to include Diva and Gander and Jeremy and Joe and the police and …

I stop and double over, struggling to shove it back down, my breathing uneven, my whole body tight. A choking sound escapes my lips, and I sit up and jab my spine against the backrest. This isn't getting me anywhere. It never does.

Taking a deep breath, I pick up the paddle again, this time using it the way it was intended, and with each dip in the lake, I do what I do best. I push it all away from me, bury their faces under the waves. I can't think about Aura or why this doesn't make sense. I can't think about anything except moving forward. I paddle on the right and then on the left. Right, left, right, left. All I know is the movement of my arms and the tossing swell beneath me.

45

I'm the last one to reach the island. I paddle around it until I find a small bay with a nicely sloping beach. I don't see anyone else. Either they're on another side, or they've already moved on. I slide up the wet sand and step out of the kayak, pulling it up on the shore behind me. It's time to see what's in my pack.

I drag the backpack out—luckily, it isn't too wet—unlatch the flap, and loosen the cords. At the top of the pack, as promised, is a waterproof topographic map, and below that sits a compass, a ruler, and the paper with the coordinates. I pull out the rest of the equipment: a sleeping bag, water purifying tablets and a water bottle, soup mix, granola, two freeze-dried meals, a mess kit with a small pot, a pocketknife, a flashlight, toilet paper, matches, and a bivy shelter.

I put everything back in the pack except for the map, compass, ruler, and coordinates, which I lay out on a rock. Then I study the map and try to get my bearings. It takes me a minute because it's not a USGS topographic map, like the kind I learned to read in 4-H. It's a 1/250,000-scale map, issued by the National Topographic System of Canada. I look at the scale bar at the bottom of the map and read, "1 cm = 2 ½ km."

After I locate the town, I find my island and the coordinates Jeremy gave us. He wasn't kidding when he said sixty-four kilometers. Using the ruler, I match the orienting arrow on the compass with the lines on the map then pick up the compass and turn my body. When the needle lands on the arrow, I know which way I need to go.

I look out across the lake. The slanting sunlight hits the crests of the waves, blurring the details in the glare and turning the shaded troughs an even darker blue. I probably have three good hours of daylight left—I'll need to make as much progress today as I can.

As I return the ruler and coordinates to my backpack, I run the calculations in my head. A three-mile-an hour pace will get me there if I plan to kayak for twelve straight hours tomorrow, which I don't. So I have to go faster than that. Six miles an hour will have me arriving around early afternoon. I hope that speed is doable. I've never kayaked that long before.

I hang the compass around my neck and slide the backpack into its spot under the bow. Then, walking the kayak halfway into the water, I get in and push off with my paddle. As I'm working my way out of the bay, I hear voices on the shore.

"Did you see how slow she was?" a familiar voice says. "I knew she was a wimp, even though she tried to impress Jeremy by showing off with that knife. And she was so gross!"

"Yeah, super bad B.O.," a boy answers. "Bet you twenty bucks she doesn't make it to the camp."

When I round the corner, I'm not surprised to see Diva and Gander. They're standing on some rocks on the island, holding their maps and compasses but not doing anything with them. Dee and Dum are also on the rocks, huddled around a map and talking over each other as they argue about the right way to go. I guess I *should* be surprised that they're talking, but I'm not.

It's obvious that they've been discussing me. Their words sting, but I try to brush them off. After all, I'm already back in the water even though I got to the island long after they did.

"So wait, what do I do with this ruler?" Dum asks.

"You could try paddling with it!" I call.

All of them jump, and the shock on their faces almost makes me smile. I wave and then paddle quickly away. *Would Aura have broken the silence?* Maybe, maybe not, but it's not like *they're* going to tell on me. We'll just see who makes it to the camp now.

The temperature is pleasant as I make my way across the lake, the heat of the day trapped in a lingering goodbye, and the muscles in my back begin to relax. It feels good to be out of the city, away from the crowds and railways, the gangs and police. Overhead, I see a large bird, maybe an eagle. It swoops over the water and snatches a fish in its talons.

Before long, I near a sizeable peninsula and have to choose between kayaking around it or getting out and hiking over it. I consult the map and decide it's not worth getting out of the kayak yet. I'll have plenty of trekking to do later, and I'm not eager to get started—I got more than my fill last month when I hiked over the Canadian border, walking three full days to get to Winnipeg.

I'm just rounding the peninsula when the waves begin to grow more turbulent. In a matter of moments, the water turns black. Not a good sign. I look up at the sky and see big storm clouds hovering in the near distance. I set my sights on the stretch of land ahead of me, maybe a mile out, and paddle fiercely. The wind is behind me, bringing the clouds closer, but at least I'm not fighting it.

Out of the corner of my eye I see a dash of green. Someone—I think it's Bullseye—is zooming forward at an incredible speed. *How is he freaking doing that?* I paddle faster, but my arms are already growing tired.

"Kava," I spit, some of my earlier frustration returning. The rain starts to fall, and I pull the hood of my jacket over my head and keep going. The kayak rocks dangerously as I rise and sink with the waves. Water splashes onto my feet, and I hope the backpack isn't getting soaked. The raindrops plop into the lake, leaving dark pinholes that are quickly covered up and then punctured again by other drops. I feel them pelt my back, trying to make pinholes in me too.

At last, I make it to land. There are no smooth beaches here, so I find a slab of rock, aim my kayak directly at it, and paddle as fast as I can. I glide up the stone and stick. I climb quickly out, pulling the kayak the rest of the way with me, then reach inside and haul out the backpack, swinging it over my shoulders and buckling it around my waist. Finally, I turn around and take in my surroundings.

There's a clearing at the edge of the rocks. After that, a thick wall of trees marks the beginning of the forest. Reflexively, I name the species I can identify: Black Spruce, White Spruce, Balsam Fir, Tamarack Larch, Jack Pine, Trembling Aspen, White Birch. Not much else.

I eye the long grasses in the dell. There will probably be ticks in there. I tuck the bottom of my jeans into my socks and zip my jacket all the way up, tying the hood securely. Then, getting a firm hold on the kayak, I stomp through the clearing and plunge into the trees.

There are millions of trees, and they grow unbelievably close together. The forests are dense in Minnesota too, but when I ran from Williams, I was able to follow the train tracks all the way to Winnipeg. Here, I have no such luxury, as a thwack from a branch confirms. I quickly realize there's no way I'm going to be able to make even a two- or three-mile-an-hour pace, especially with a ten-foot hunk of plastic in tow. Fortunately, there's water everywhere. I just need to get back to it.

The thick trees block most of the rain—I can hear the droplets tap dancing on the leaves above my head—but they also block out the light, and I continue to trip over rocks and scrape my cheeks on pine needles. After an hour or so of agonizingly slow progress, I decide to give up and make camp. Mercifully, I reach the edge of a small lake and find another clearing along the shore. As I step into the glade, it stops raining.

I clear a place for a fire pit and gather some wood. Thanks to the dense forest, I'm able to find plenty of dry branches. In no time at all, I have a fire going, and I fill up the water bottle in the lake and add a purifying tablet. While I wait for the tablet to work its magic, I eat the rest of my energy bar, set up the bivy, and pull out the soup mix and mess kit.

Too bad I don't have my Remington; I'd get myself some real dinner. When I ran, I took the rifle with me, and it kept me alive—in the forest. But in the city, there was nothing to shoot. So I sold it. The worst part is that I didn't get even close to what it was worth. A model 798 like that should have earned me a few hundred dollars. The jackass storeowner gave me fifty. I argued for more, but he accused me of having stolen it and threatened to call the police. Since the cops were the last people I wanted to talk to, I had to give in.

Thinking about it just makes me angry, so I pull out the map and try to gauge the day's progress while I wait for the soup to warm up. I didn't go nearly as far as I had hoped to. Tomorrow I'll have to hit it hard if I want to reach the camp before dark—and if I want to beat Diva and company. At least now I know my strategy: I'll kayak the whole way, or as much as I'm able to anyway.

I groan and roll my aching shoulders. By tomorrow night, my arms will be dead. Thanks to my scraped-up palms, my hands are already blistering. I'll have to wrap them in something or I won't be able to paddle.

As I eat the soup out of the pot, I listen to the birds. There must be thousands of them, each one maxing out its vocal cords, their shrieks and whistles overlapping in a deafening cacophony. I wonder what this would be like in the middle of summer, before migration.

Across the lake, the sun begins to set. The sky is yellow at first, the sections furthest from the hazy orb the color of a ripe peach. Then the soft orange morphs into a rosy pink and veils the water in velvet lavender. The lavender grows darker, bursting into layers of magenta, plum, and amethyst, highlighted with streaks of tangerine. I breathe it in, admiring even the dancing silhouettes of insects above the water. I didn't see any sunsets when I was in Winnipeg.

Then the light is gone for good, and midnight blue spreads across the heavens as the birds stop their chattering. It's time for some shuteye. I return my food supplies to the backpack and hang it from a tall tree branch, four feet from the trunk. Next, I take advantage of the toilet paper, put out the fire, and scoot into the bivy. I zip the cover closed and curl up in the sleeping bag.

I close my eyes, but the crickets and frogs have picked up where the birds left off, and their chirps and croaks are ten times louder than anything I heard back home, each cadence filling in the gaps of another so that there is no break in the noise. I clap my hands over my ears and try to block out the interminable droning. At length, however, I give up and hope my fatigue will prove stronger than the tumult.

And then, as I'm finally drifting off, I hear something—not a chirp, not a croak—something the wind carries across the water.

Someone is crying.

I unzip the corner of my bivy and listen. For a moment, all I hear is the insistent *chirr chirr* of the amphibians and insects. Was I imagining things? No, there it is again. A wheezing, spluttering sob. It must be one of the initiates—no one else would be out here. Rolling over on my side, I plug my ears and hope the person will grow a backbone so I can get some sleep.

But the crying doesn't stop. It only gets louder. I press my palms against my ears more forcefully, but I can still hear it. The truncated rhythm forces its way into my brain, and I know I won't be able to fall asleep.

Muttering under my breath, I fish for my flashlight and shoes. I crawl out of my bivy and, switching on the light, walk in the direction of the sound. I step carefully over the rocks and logs, spotting low-hanging branches just in time to stoop down. Well, almost in time. I hit my forehead on one and curse. This had better be worth the trouble.

I march forward, swinging my flashlight in a large arc, and then I glimpse something gleaming dully behind a tree. I walk toward it, giving the tree a wide berth and keeping the light fixed on that spot. It's what I thought it was. A kayak, identical to my own, tipped over on its side.

As I raise the light again, I catch sight of a backpack, not five feet away, its contents strewn across the ground. The sleeping bag is unraveled halfway, and the box of matches lies open, the cardboard box warped and soft. I bend down to pick up a match. It's wet. I reach out and experimentally touch the sleeping bag. Soaked through.

A sniff to my right makes me swing the lamp into the trees. I peer into the shadows, and then I see them: two puckered eyes staring back at me.

"Hey—" I say before remembering I'm not supposed to talk. I don't know if this is one of the rule breakers or not, so I just motion for him or her to come out from behind the tree. The person hesitates, but after a moment, she steps into the beam of my flashlight.

My lips form an "oh," but I keep the sound from coming out. The girl is sopping wet and shivering violently. Water drips from her clothes and makes her wispy hair almost unrecognizable, but I would know that tiny frame anywhere. It's Charity.

Stepping forward quickly, I take off my jacket and wrap it around her. Then I hurry over to her gear and scoop it into the pack. I swing the water-soaked thing over my shoulders then grasp her kayak handle with one hand. My other hand still holds the flashlight. I wave the light in the direction of my camp and walk toward it, dragging the kayak behind me. I look over my shoulder to make sure she's following. She is.

When we get back to my campsite, I start a fire while Charity watches me, snuffling and quivering. I sit her down on a rock, search through her bag for her water bottle and purifying tablets, and treat some water from the lake. She hasn't said anything, so, using hand gestures, I instruct her to take off her wet clothing and lay it on the rocks. When she's shaking in her underwear, I check her for ticks. She has three, and I remove them with the tweezers from my pocketknife.

After I've disposed of the parasites, I wrap Charity in my jacket and push her into my sleeping bag. She's shivering even more now, enough to worry me. Moving swiftly, I turn her bag inside out and lay it by the fire next to her clothes, along with the matches and other gear.

I find the soup packet and mess kit and repeat my earlier dinner preparations. Once the soup's ready, I force Charity to eat it, holding the spoon to her lips. When she's finished, I put the utensils and rest of the food in the backpack and hang it up, near mine.

It's only then that I realize I haven't seen her map or compass. I look by the clothes to see if she put them out to dry as well, but they aren't there. I frown. Without her compass, she would have had no way of knowing where the camp was. Maybe she could have made her way back to the town, but if she was even the slightest bit disoriented … if I hadn't been there …

I recall Jeremy's words. No one would have come looking for her.

They wouldn't really *have left her out here, would they?* But I think about the initiates' sober faces, the mysterious nature of this whole trip, and my throat tightens.

When I've taken care of everything, I climb into the sleeping bag with Charity and wrap my arms around her tiny body. She's still trembling, and her wet hair numbs my cheek, but as I continue to hold her, her shaking eventually subsides. When her breathing is no longer ragged, I relax my grip and slip gratefully into sleep.

I wake to the smell of smoke. I scurry hastily out of the bivy, panic mounting my throat, but then I see Charity sitting by a small, contained blaze. She's dressed again, and perched on the rock next to her are our newly filled water bottles and the two packets of granola. She smiles shyly up at me, and I cough and dig my shoe into the dirt.

We eat breakfast in silence, listening to the water lap gently against the shore and the cheerful singing of the birds, less aggravating now than they were last night. When we finish eating, we pack up the gear.

Charity may know how to light a fire, but camping is clearly unfamiliar territory for her. She follows my example, watching me to figure out how to fold up the bivy and packing her bag the way I do. But she's a quick study, and it doesn't take us long to finish.

When everything's ready, she takes off my jacket and hands it back to me. As I put it on, my hands move automatically to my pockets, and my fingers bump against an unfamiliar object, something square. I yank my hand back out. The wallet—I had almost forgotten.

I raise a finger to let Charity know I need a moment. Grabbing the toilet paper to make it seem convincing, I walk a little way into the trees. When I'm out of sight, I reach into my pocket and, pinching the wallet between two fingers, pull it out of my windbreaker. I open it and remove the two licenses. Then I dig a hole in the ground with my foot and drop the bloodstained plastic inside, covering it with an ample pile of dirt and a large boulder. No one will ever find it—or my fingerprints—here, but I'm not in the clear yet. *I'll have to ditch Aura's real I.D. later, after I leave the camp.*

I walk back to Charity, and we drag the kayaks to the lake and get situated. After I look at my compass and point toward the direction we need to go, she nods, and we both shove off into the water.

The next few hours are peaceful, our pace quick and easy. The lakes and rivers we follow aren't large enough for the waves that troubled the water around the town where we got the kayaks, and, even if they were, there isn't any wind to stir them up. The trees are more verdant in the full light of day, more welcoming. Their images glisten in the water, making it seem as if we're actually kayaking through the treetops. Occasionally, yellow leaves drop from the sky, landing on our heads and in our satiny reflections, sparking tiny ripples, releasing the smell of autumn. At one point, I see a black bear, fishing by the bank, and when I point it out to Charity, her face warms into an enormous smile.

I have to admit it's nice having a companion. There's a strange confidence that comes from traveling in numbers, and my worries about finding the camp have lessened considerably, which is odd when I consider that the responsibility for locating it rests on my shoulders alone.

We continue to make steady progress, stopping occasionally to pick away at our freeze-dried meals or to carry our kayaks across a strip of land. By early afternoon, however, my arms are stiff and heavy, and I'm starting to slow down. My hands, even though they're wrapped in a strip of cloth cut from my shirt, are bleeding.

A breeze swipes the sweat from the back of my neck. Thank goodness for that. It's gotten hot over the last hour, and it looks like the sun's going to keep beating down on us. The extra heat won't help things at all. As best as I can tell from the map, we still have about twenty kilometers to go. Four hours at a good pace—twice that long if I keep slowing down.

I'm trying to figure out how to communicate my concerns to Charity when I look up and see she's fifty feet ahead of me and moving still further away. A moment ago, she was right by my side. I splash my paddle on the water to get her attention. She slows down and looks over her shoulder at me then gestures excitedly with her arm. I paddle as quickly as I can, which doesn't feel very fast, and when I'm fifteen feet away, she points vigorously skyward.

I look up, afraid we might be in for another storm, but the sky is clear. There's not even a cloud. Nothing except the bright sun. I look back at her and discover she's moved forward yet again.

"Ah, c'mon," I mutter. "Stop doing that. I can't go that fast." I paddle awkwardly after her.

After a few minutes, she notices I'm not keeping up and waits for me. When I finally catch up, huffing from the effort, she looks at me, forehead wrinkled. I want to ask how's she able to go so quickly, but I don't want to offend her by breaking the silence. So I meet her perplexed gaze with my own.

She frowns. Then she paddles the kayak backward until her stern touches my bow and, reaching back, loops our toggled handles together. I stare at her, not even trying to hide my incredulity. Does she really think she's going to be able to paddle for both of us?

Apparently, she does. As soon as the kayaks are linked, she dips the oar back into the water. I skeptically raise my paddle to join her, but before it even touches the water, we're moving forward, not as quickly as she had been before, but certainly faster than I was going on my own. I gape at the back of her lifejacket, at her scrawny arms. How is this possible?

Finally, I decide to be more than a dead weight and add my paddling to hers. I can't tell that it makes any difference, but at least I don't feel like such a loser. We cruise through the water, covering more distance in the next fifteen minutes than we had in the previous hour.

Countless questions ricochet inside my head. How does Charity have such amazing upper body strength? Why did she wait until now to go this fast? How do *any* of the kids from the van know how to kayak so quickly and yet know nothing about camping? But soon the ache in my arms and back drown out everything else. I don't want to stop paddling, but keeping up with Charity's pace is beyond exhausting.

The next hour goes by in a throbbing haze, and I lose feeling in my arms long before the end of it. Just as I'm about to give up, we reach a fork in the river, and Charity stops, looking at me for direction. Gratefully, I bend down to retrieve the map from my pack. I move slowly, afraid the break will be over as soon as I give her our heading. But it turns out there's no need for my dawdling—it legitimately takes me several minutes to figure out where we are. I can't believe how much ground we've covered. It seems impossible, but we're only a kilometer or two away from our destination.

I show Charity the location of the camp on the map and point to the stream branching to the right. She nods and, to my simultaneous relief and disappointment, unhooks the kayaks. I see the fatigue in her face. If I'm tired, she must be ready to drop.

We paddle leisurely down the river, resting our arms often since there's enough of a current to do the work for us. As I wonder again what lies ahead, I feel that twist in my stomach. What kind of a camp abandons its campers in the wilderness? I jiggle my shoulders, trying to shake out the tension.

The river shrinks drastically, and as we come around the bend, it grows so narrow the tree branches on either side of the bank entwine above the water. We sit low in our kayaks as we travel through the tunnel of leaves and pine needles. It's quiet. Just the lapping of our paddles and the whistle of a bird.

Suddenly, the tunnel widens, and we enter a bay the size of several football fields, fed by at least twenty other tunnels like the one from which we just emerged. I look up at the trees, astonished at the way they've all grown together to create a natural canopy. But something about it seems strange. The tree trunks don't curve. It's as if the limbs have extended outward, merging with their neighbors even though there's nothing underneath to support them. I continue to stare, and then I figure it out—there aren't really pine boughs and aspen leaves above us. It's some kind of netting.

Frowning, I paddle after Charity toward a beach on our right where metal racks hold at least fifty green kayaks. Two people are arriving just ahead of us, but no one I recognize. A man in a baseball cap approaches them, says something, and then helps them carry their kayaks to the stands. By the time we reach the shore, the two initiates have disappeared over a small hill.

The man in the baseball hat greets us as we get out of our kayaks. "*Manewa*. Welcome to the testing grounds!" he says. "Your period of silence is honorably ended. I'll take your backpacks. Please stack your kayaks on the frames and go to the *wakenu* to check in."

The kink in my stomach tightens. Testing grounds—what does that mean? And what language is he speaking?

Taking deep breaths and hoping Charity understands what he's talking about, I drag my kayak up the beach and follow her over the hill. *Stay calm*, I remind myself. *Act natural.*

"Thanks for helping me last night." Charity looks over at me and smiles softly, her voice cracking.

"What?" I cough. "Oh, that—don't mention it." I open my mouth to ask her about the kayaking, but then I see the camp and the words don't come out.

At first it seems like we could be anywhere in the forest. Pine trees extend in all directions for as far as I can see, separated now and then by patches of deciduous gold. But after a moment I see the same camouflaged netting overhead and spot rope walkways strung between the trees. And, just ahead of us, a spiral staircase wraps around a large pine. I follow it with my eyes until it disappears halfway up the trunk.

I squint. Where did it go? I take a few steps to the right, and the branches shift. I step back to the left, and the trunks bend again. And then I see why: they're not trees at all. They're reflections. Hanging in the forest is an enormous mirror.

As we get closer, I discover there are actually four enormous mirrors—each one forming the side of a large rectangular building. The mirrors reflect the trees around them, making the building blend in almost perfectly with the surrounding forest. The entire structure is supported by a dozen pine trees and stands halfway between the ground and the pine boughs at the top.

Charity walks toward the staircase, and I trail after her. The stairs lead us up through the floor of the building, depositing us in a wide corridor made entirely of steel. Not just the floor—the walls too.

At the other end of the hallway is a second staircase leading to an upper level, and to the right of us are two rooms. A steel table is stationed between the doorways to the two rooms, a large flag draped across its front. Embroidered on the flag is a red eagle grasping an axe. *No, not an axe*, I think, noting the feathers on the handle and the shape of the blade. *A tomahawk.*

The only person in sight is a middle-aged woman sitting behind the table. Charity and I walk toward her.

"*Tanaka*," the woman says.

"*Tanaka*," Charity replies. I echo her awkwardly.

"What was your base city?" the woman asks, twitching a narrow, pointed eyebrow. Her back is rigidly straight, and her black hair, slashed with gray, is pleated behind her in a long braid.

"Winnipeg," Charity says.

The woman picks up a sleek walkie-talkie. "Jeremy!" she barks into the device. A few moments later, our counselor comes bounding down the staircase from the floor above.

"Yo, Naira," he answers. Then he sees us, and a smile fans out across his lips. "Hey, hey! You made it! Come with me."

As I follow Charity toward the other staircase, the woman at the table stands up and walks over to the door that's closest to me. I glance to my right in time to see her enter the room. The door swings back, and as I get a brief glimpse inside, I stumble forward, bumping into Charity.

"Sorry," I mumble, my mind spinning.

The room was filled with machine guns.

4

I curl one sweaty hand around my switchblade as I ascend the stairs, my mind fixed on the long rows of polished automatic rifles. Military weapons.

When we step onto the next level, I can feel the vein on my neck twitching, the blood pounding behind my ears. But then I look around me, and just for a moment, the guns fade from my mind. The room up here couldn't be more different from the one below. Instead of bare, angular walls, there is shape and color. Curved black beams support the ceiling and round out the corners. Crescent chairs and circular gray tables, some of them built around the tree trunks that shoot up through the floor, are positioned comfortably around the room, and curvy red couches are clustered around white globes that actually contain small fires. Wavy black and gray tiles spiral outward from the largest tree trunk in the center of the room. I've never seen anything so elegant or spacious. There's enough seating to accommodate hundreds of people.

Colossal windows stretch from the floor to the ceiling on every side, but the world outside is slightly darkened. These must be one-way windows—windows on the inside, mirrors on the outside.

Several counselors lounge comfortably on the couches and chairs, chatting and laughing. I see Aponi among them. She leaves the group and joins us.

Jeremy takes us to a table at the far side of the room, behind which sit three more counselors. On the table are laptops and scanners and other pieces of equipment I don't recognize. Aponi puts a hand on Charity's shoulder and leads her to the person on the far right, leaving me with Jeremy.

"Nice work, kid," he says as takes me to the person on the left. "I had fifty bucks riding on you. Thanks for pulling through."

I wonder hazily who was betting against me.

"What's the name?" the counselor asks when we're standing in front of him.

"Aura Torres," I answer. My stomach cramps further when I hear how hoarse my voice sounds. What will happen if they find out I'm not her? An icy sweat breaks out at the base of my neck, and suddenly I'm thinking about the rifles downstairs, about the bets my counselors placed on who would make it here alive, about the camouflaged netting and tinted windows and Naira's harsh eyes.

The man finds the name on his computer. "Do you have your I.D.?" he asks.

His question slowly pushes through the sludge in my brain. I plunge a clammy hand into my coat pocket and pull out Aura's license. My fingers shake slightly as I hand it to him.

"Will this work?"

The man slips the I.D. underneath the scanner attached to the laptop. Then he carefully studies the image on the screen. *He's going to realize it's not me.* I find my switchblade again.

"Put your thumb on this," the man says, pushing a small electronic pad toward me.

I place my sweaty thumb on the screen, wait for the words of accusation.

But the man just nods his head and types something into the computer before grabbing a thin gray instrument from a stack on the table and plugging it into the laptop. More typing. Then he removes Aura's I.D. from the scanner and returns it to me. He unplugs the gray device.

"Give me your hand," he says. I extend my arm, trying to keep it steady. "This is your Quil." He takes the gray rectangle and snaps it around my wrist. My eyes widen. A second ago, this thing was solid. As I look at the gadget, numbers appear on the smooth band and rotate around my wrist. *2:30.*

"Your number is two hundred and seventy-three," the man says, handing me a sack lunch he retrieves from the floor. "You're in *wakemo* fourteen. Dinner's at seven." I nod and turn dizzily away from the table, clutching the paper bag.

"Where's *wakemo* fourteen?" I ask Jeremy as we walk away from the table. *What's wakemo fourteen?*

"I'll show you," he says. Then he stops and scrutinizes my face. "Hey, are you okay? You look really pale."

"Speak for yourself," I say. "You must not get outside much."

"Are you kidding? I totally bronzed this summer."

"Could have fooled me."

He leads me to a circular doorway near the stairs, and I softly release my breath. *Keep it together, Kit.*

The doorway opens into a spherical glass tunnel that leads us out of the building. We're still suspended above the ground, and I gape through what must also be one-way windows at the forest floor below, a good twenty feet beneath my shoes.

"What's the matter, kid?" Jeremy asks. "Need me to carry you?"

I snort. "Yeah right."

"Well, c'mon then." He grabs my hand to pull me down the tunnel, and my breath escapes in a hiss. He looks at the bloody cloth wrapped around my palm then drops my hand. "You should probably put something on that," he says.

"Thanks, Mom," I reply, shoving my hand in my pocket.

A screen door marks the end of the tunnel, and we step through it onto a large wooden porch. Branching out from the porch are five rope bridges—the ones I noticed from the ground—each going in a different direction. Jeremy chooses the fourth bridge. The swaying motion doesn't help my lurching stomach, so I grip the rope railing and stare at a damp spot on his back.

The bridge takes us a hundred feet or so to a wood cylindrical building propped in the trees. Pine boughs shade its circular windows, and a rope ladder extends from the platform on which we stand to the ground below. A sign by the door reads, "13."

Three more bridges extend from the platform, and Jeremy leads me past the treehouse onto the first bridge. We stop at another treehouse, this one with a "14" on its sign.

"Clean up, get some rest, and we'll see you at dinner," Jeremy says. "And seriously, I mean it. Clean up."

I make a face, but he just grins and walks back across the bridge. I watch him for a moment before turning to face the entrance. Then, breathing in deeply through my nose, I push the door open with my shoulder and enter the building.

The interior walls are also made of wood—seamless, smooth panels that mimic the inside of a tree. There are only two things in the room: a door and a ramp. Peeking through the door, I find a bathroom, complete with showers, sinks, and toilet stalls. I breathe out and return to the foyer.

Straight ahead, the floor meets the ramp and curves up and around the perimeter of the building, like the spiral staircase at the *wakenu* but without the stairs. In the center of the spiral is a metal pole that extends from the floor all the way to the ceiling. I walk over to the ramp and begin my ascent, running my fingers along the polished wood. Square panels on the ceiling glow warmly, adding their light to the dappled beams that enter through the windows.

Every few feet, a niche is carved into the outside wall, forming a space for some shelves and a bed. A sign on the first mattress says it's reserved for the *wakemo* counselor, but the rest of the beds are free game. On the mattresses sit piles of folded clothing, towels, and travel-sized toiletries.

I go all the way to the top of the ramp. Twenty bunks in all, and none of them touched. Apparently, I'm the first person to be sent to *wakemo* fourteen. I decide to take the uppermost bed—there's something secure about the way the mattress is nestled into the corner where the wall meets the ceiling; plus, this way people won't be walking past me all the time.

I sit on the edge of my mattress for a moment, stare at a knot in the wood, force my mind to stay empty. When the pressure in my chest has returned to its usual level of tightness, I gather up the towel and toiletries, get off the bed, and walk toward the pole. I wrap my towel around the metal so the friction won't hurt my hands then take a deep breath and slide down, putting the weight in my legs. It's a long drop, longer than I thought it would be, but when I get to the bottom, I decide I enjoyed it.

In the bathroom, I remove everything except for my necklace and the strange watch—I can't figure out how to take it off my wrist—and step into one of the showers. Instead of a perforated spray, the water spills onto the beige tiles like a small waterfall. I wash my dizziness away with the sweat and dirt, concentrating on the drops that spring off my skin as the flow splashes onto my arms. The water stings my hands, but I make sure the wounds are thoroughly cleaned.

The warm drizzle runs over the pendant resting on my chest, and I rub my thumb across the swirling design. The bone was white when my father gave it to me. Now it's yellow with age. For a second, I can remember his face, but, as always, the memory wilts, and I can't summon it back.

I return to my bunk clean but barely able to place one foot in front of the other. On one of the shelves I find a small first aid kit, and I generously apply ointment and bandages to my palms. Then I investigate the clothing on my mattress. There are three khaki-colored pants, six tee shirts—two tan, two green, and two brown—and plenty of undergarments, including bras. The clothes look small, but when I try them on, they stretch to fit my body exactly. The fabric is lightweight and cool and, surprisingly, not very tight. I pull off the shirt I'm wearing and try another one. Same thing, a perfect fit.

Somewhere in my mind I know that this doesn't make sense, but when I realize that I've been staring blankly at the shirt in my hand for a good thirty seconds, I push the clothes off the bed and onto the shelves. That's something to figure out another time.

Time. I look at the watch. Three o'clock. How did we do it? How did *Charity* do it?

Charity! I never finished thanking her, never found out her real name. Maybe I'll see her at dinner.

Dinner. My stomach rumbles, and I reach for the paper sack the counselor gave me. Inside I find a sandwich, an apple, a granola bar, and a water bottle. In no time at all, I've devoured the food and emptied the bottle. I yawn. Now it's time to sleep.

As I crumple my trash into the paper bag, I notice a piece of paper inside. I pull it out. The words along the top read, "*Maitanga Tura*." I glance at the first line. It's also in the strange language, but there's an English translation: "Rule 1: Fires after dark are strictly prohibited." *That's weird.* Why wouldn't they want to light fires? I think about the netting and mirrors, the fact that the location of the camp is a secret. *Why?* What are they hiding?

I hold my stomach and look back at the paper. Perhaps there's more information in here, something that will clue me in to what's going on. I keep reading the rules, but my eyes have trouble focusing. I squint at the words. There's something about curfew, making too much noise at night, proper waste disposal, wildlife … As I read the same sentence again and again, the words begin to warp and blur. I set the paper down and lean back into the pillows. I'll just close my eyes for one second. Then I'll figure it out.

I blink and stare at the wooden boards above my head until I remember where I am. I sit up. There are other girls in the bunkhouse now—I can hear water running through the pipes in the bathroom below, footsteps on the ramp, two people laughing. I blink again and look at my watch. I've been asleep for three and a half hours. It's almost time for dinner. I yawn and stretch.

A pretty girl pokes her head around the curve in the wall. Her hair is curly and brown and slightly damp, probably from a recent shower. Her hazel eyes crinkle.

"*Tanaka*! You're awake!" she says. "I was just about to come get you. I didn't want you to be late for dinner."

I stare at her, my brain struggling to process. "Thanks," I finally stammer.

"No prob. We're going to be neighbors for the next week, so I thought I'd better start the relationship off on good terms. Although to be honest, I wasn't sure what was going to be the best way to wake you. I figured maybe I'd throw a pillow or something." She laughs. "My name's Lila."

"I'm Kit." And then I remember. I'm not Kit anymore. *Kava!*

"Where are you from?" she asks.

"Winnipeg," I answer, getting something right.

"A Canadian, *eh?* That's cool. I'm from Seattle. What's your number?"

"I don't have a cell phone."

Lila laughs. "Good one." She waits expectantly, and when I say nothing, she asks, "What number did they assign you?"

Number? Now I remember. *What number* was *that?* "Um … "

"Did you forget?" she asks.

"Yeah."

"Well, check your Quil."

"What?"

She walks toward me and grabs my wrist. Then she slides her finger over the screen of my watch. Suddenly, the *6:34* is replaced by something else. The temperature. Then the date. Then my bunk assignment. Finally, a *273* appears on the band.

"Two-seventy-three. That's too bad," Lila says. "I'm one-fifty-eight."

I don't know what to say. What exactly *is* this thing on my wrist? And why is my number bad?

"Should we go to dinner?" Lila asks.

"Sure," I stutter. I climb out of bed and twirl my hair into a bun. I can tell without looking that I didn't do a good job.

When she sees my bandaged hands, Lila suggests we walk instead of use the pole. As we plod down the ramp, I notice that most of the bunks have received occupants while I've been asleep. Not all of them though.

Lila points to one of the empty beds. "Guess my sister was right," she says. "She told me there's at least one person from every group who doesn't make it."

I purse my lips together and breathe out slowly. There must be a logical explanation—Lila doesn't seem concerned. *But neither did Jeremy when he said no one would come looking for us.*

"All part of keeping the testing grounds hidden," Lila chirps. "The year my grandfather came to the camp was the year they caught the spy. He got to watch them torture her until she broke. The whole camp did!"

What! The floor dips away from me, and I almost trip.

"Torture?" I stutter.

"Yeah, you know—when someone impersonated an initiate? They started with her fingers."

This time I do trip.

"Are you okay?" Lila asks as I scramble back up.

"Yeah, I'm fine." I try to swallow, but my throat is too dry. *Will they torture me if they find out I'm not Aura?* I blink rapidly to control the dizziness, and when we walk across the rope bridge from *wakemo* fourteen to *wakemo* thirteen, I have to fight to keep my lunch down.

As I stagger across the wooden slats, I notice a gleam on the forest floor. I peer over the rope railing at a boy standing on the ground below. He raises his hand, and all I see is a blur of metal whirring through the air before a tomahawk sinks into the tree in front of him. He walks over to the trunk and yanks the weapon free then runs his finger across the blade. Suddenly, I see the switchblade in the Shredder's hand, see my fingers being chopped off, and the boy and the ground whirl away from me. A blend of sandwich and apple leaps into my throat.

I clamp my teeth together and straighten up quickly. Lila's curls bounce in and out of focus as I stumble after her. I turn my head to the right and then the left, taking in the wilderness that rolls out on all sides of the camp for hundreds of miles. If they decide to torture and kill me, no one would ever know about it.

I make it to the dining hall without throwing up, but the pressure in my stomach tells me I won't be able to eat a thing. I look around the room, full of initiates now, all of them wearing brown, beige, or green, laughing and joking just like the counselors had been. Some of them have wet, recently showered hair. Others are still dusty and sweaty, as if they've only just arrived. I notice dimly that the check-in tables have been moved elsewhere, probably so that late arrivals won't have to fight their way through the crowd.

The mob is gathered around a large buffet table brimming with food. While we wait in line, my eyes dart rapidly in all directions, refusing to focus on any one object. It's then that I detect the retractable metal curtains along the tops of the windows. *This room can become like the steel room downstairs.* I scoop some mashed potatoes onto my plate and attempt to ignore the buzzing in my ears.

There are hundreds of people, and as we look for a seat, I try to invent names for some of them, but I can't concentrate long enough. Instead, I scan the faces of the initiates around me and look for Charity. I don't see her, but I do spot Gander—and Dee and Dum. *So they did make it.* I lower my head as Dee turns in my direction.

"Do you see anyone you know?" Lila asks.

I shake my head. "You?"

She looks around. "A couple. The girl with the black hair over there, that's my friend Holly. And that boy getting a slice of cake is Lester. Oh, and there's Rye. We go to the same school. Knowing him, he was probably one of the first ones here."

I glance to where she's pointing, at a table not far from us. A boy with brown hair is talking with his friends.

"He's something, huh?" Lila sighs. "I spent the whole trip ogling him. Too bad he's taken."

"Too bad," I say, but I'm not sure I even saw his face.

We've just found a seat when the sound of a whistle makes the room go silent. Everyone looks toward the stairs as Naira, the lady with the gray-flecked braid, steps onto the floor and climbs a small platform.

"*Manewa*, initiates!" she says. "And congratulations. You've passed the first stage of your *maitanga*." Everyone cheers. "My name is Naira," she continues. "I'm this year's *Takaito*, and I'm pleased to inform you that so far two hundred and eighty-four of our anticipated three hundred and three have arrived. That's a new record!" More cheering.

I furrow my brow, press my back against the chair, look up at the ceiling. But the room is spinning there too, so I look back down at my plate.

"Anyone who arrives after midnight will be sent home, as the rules dictate," Naira says. "In the morning, we'll send out search parties for the stragglers."

I raise my eyes. Search parties? Did I hear her right? But I thought … *Idiot!* Of course they weren't going to let those kids die! *C'mon, Kit, really? You believed Jeremy—the guy whose idea of harmless hazing means throwing a bag over someone's head and threatening to kill them?* But that still doesn't answer my other questions. What about the strange language? The guns? The torture?

I'm missing Naira's speech, so I try to pay attention. "On Day Six," she continues, "we will celebrate your success and announce your recommended placement among the Yakone. The seventh day you will return home—more comfortably than the way you arrived, of course." The crowd chuckles.

Yakone. Maybe these people belong to a tribe. That would explain the language.

"Tomorrow, you will have the morning to rest and relax," Naira concludes. "Breakfast will be served from seven to nine; lunch, from eleven to one. Our first competition will be held at two o'clock in the Aerie. Enjoy the rest of your evening." She places a fist over her heart. Everyone in the room mimics the gesture, so I do as well. Then Naira steps down from the platform, and the conversations resume.

Even though the cramp in my gut hasn't disappeared entirely, some of the tautness begins to evaporate, and I can feel color returning to my face. The guns must be for the competitions, the tomahawk too. *See, there's a logical explanation for everything.* That means there's one for the torture as well. No need to panic. I'll just pretend I know what's going on, get through the next six days, and everything will be fine. Then they'll take me back to civilization, and I'll get on with my fresh start. I regard the food on my plate. Maybe I will be able to eat something after all.

I'm working on a piece of cake when a girl with flawless dark skin and five piercings on her left ear comes over to our table. It's Lila's friend, Holly.

"Lila!" she says. "The kids from Billings brought marshmallows! We're going to make a campfire and roast them as soon as it gets dark. Out past number twenty."

"Sweet," Lila answers. "Kit, do you want to go?"

Finally, something normal. I open my mouth to say yes then remember the rule. "I thought fires weren't allowed."

"Well, obviously," Holly says. "So we have to be careful."

As much as I would love some s'mores, I can't risk getting in trouble and drawing attention to myself. "I'm really tired," I tell them. "I think I'll just go to bed."

"Suit yourself," she replies.

When we've finished eating, we take our trays to a conveyor belt at the edge of the room and exit through the tunnel. Holly and Lila walk me back to the bunkhouse then head to *wakemo* twenty for the campfire, leaving me standing on the porch listening to the crickets, wondering what I'm going to do for the rest of the night.

Suddenly, I hear singing. A group of initiates is walking through the forest below, their clear voices bouncing off the trees. The song is in that Yakone language. I close my eyes, and for a moment it's like I'm a child again, trying to decipher fragments of French music on the radio.

I enter the bunkhouse—there's nothing for me to do out here. There's nothing to do inside either, so I brush my teeth and get ready for bed.

When I return to my bunk, I push aside the pile of trash on my mattress then slip under the sheets. Before my eyes seal themselves shut, I look at the sturdy walls around me, grateful that at least I have somewhere to sleep, that I'm safe from the cops.

I wake up several times the next morning but only for brief intervals—my dreams have too firm a grasp. My nightmares, I should say. In one nightmare, I'm in a shooting contest, and Diva shoots me instead of the target. In another, a zombie version of Aura exposes me as an imposter, and Naira shoots me. In yet another, I get lost in the woods, and men in black tattoos shoot me. After eons of this, I finally force my eyes to open all the way and make myself sit up, exhaling as I lean against the wood panels, blinking in the sunlight, remembering that *no one* is going to shoot me.

I look at my Quil. My number, *273*, still circles the band. I slide my finger along the screen, the way Lila did, and the time appears in its place. *12:07*. I rub my head. *How did I manage to sleep for so long?* I climb out of bed and grab my towel.

On my way to the showers, I glance at Lila's bunk. It's empty. Most of the bunks are. Two of them contain sleeping occupants— late arrivals, probably—and one of them has never been touched, as the pile of clothes testifies.

When I return to my corner of the bunkhouse, I dress in a green shirt and a new pair of pants, and by the time I've plaited my hair and brushed my teeth, it's almost one.

I enter the dining hall through the glass tunnel again. The sun playing in the leaves makes the outside world shimmer, and I stop to admire the craftsmanship of the tunnel, the way it feels like I'm floating with the pine boughs and the birds.

Lila is inside. When she sees me, she waves me over to her table.

"There you are!" she exclaims. "You're quite the heavy sleeper. I threw a pillow at you this morning, but it didn't even faze you."

"I guess I was tired."

"I'll say," she agrees. "Don't worry though. You didn't miss anything."

We eat our lunch, making small talk about the weather, about how warm it is, how windy it is. I glance around, meaning to look for Charity, but instead, I find myself caught up in the design of the room. Last night I didn't fully appreciate how perfect the details were, how comfortable the furniture was. I relax into my curvy chair, listen to the popping fire by my feet, and stare out the window at the resplendent landscape. The ground slopes gradually downward from the meetinghouse, and everywhere I look I see trees. Endless evergreens beneath a sapphire sky.

We finish our meal much too quickly. "Ready to go to the Aerie?" Lila asks.

"All right," I say. *Let's see what this is all about.* We leave the meetinghouse, and Lila leads the way, breaking every now and then into a skip. We cross the first rope bridge, which leads to *wakemo* one, and take the next bridge to *wakemo* two.

As we walk, I begin to understand the layout of the camp. There are five clusters of bunkhouses, each with four buildings. The five bridges from the meetinghouse lead to the first bunkhouses in each grouping, and more bridges connect those bunkhouses to the other three in their set, like a star constellation.

Once we reach *wakemo* two, we follow yet another bridge, this time moving away from the bunkhouses altogether, and before long, I see it: a gigantic ball of sticks and branches propped up in the trees like an enormous bird's nest.

The bridge takes us straight there. We walk through the open double doors, and then we're standing in a narrow hallway that extends in both directions, following the curve of the structure. Directly in front of us are several bins. A counselor removes two facemasks and padded jackets from the containers and hands them to us. Lila puts hers on without question, so I do the same. The counselor points us to the left. We follow the hallway around the bend, and then the walls open up and I gawk at the sight before me.

The Aerie is a floating stadium. Tiered, metal seating is built into three-quarters of the arena's sides, but the segment directly across from me is open, covered only by a camouflaged net. Next to the net is a large scoreboard.

The Aerie roof stretches over the top of the stadium with large gaps in the sticks and branches revealing the sky above. The floor is overlaid with mats. It's flat where it meets the net, but as it reaches the opposite end of the stadium it curves up in a rounded quarter pipe, extending almost to the nest roof. Perched at the very top of the quarter pipe is an enclosed observation box. There are other doors on the perimeter of the stadium, but all of them are marked "Emergency Exit Only."

I follow Lila to a seat on the front row. Other people file in behind us, all wearing the masks and padding, all chattering loudly, and I feel my pulse match the buzz in the stadium. Within fifteen minutes, almost all of the seats are filled.

At two o'clock on the dot, a door underneath us opens, and a large group of initiates marches into the arena. All of them wear digitized camouflage—fitted gray body armor and full-face helmets. A blue stripe marks half of the players; a red stripe, the other half. As I watch, two large, glowing circles appear on their chests, one over the heart and one over the stomach.

A rack of automatic rifles emerges from both sides of the arena wall, and I grip the armrest on my seat as the contestants march toward the guns. The first person raises her Quil to a scanner attached to the rack. A metal latch pops open, and she takes one of the rifles and a belt containing clips of ammunition. The scoreboard displays the girl's face, along with her team color and the number "100."

"There's Rye!" Lila points at the board when a boy's face appears. I look at the screen and feel my eyes widen. For a split second all I see is sun-kissed chocolate hair, olive skin, and a pair of startling green eyes. Then he's gone, replaced by another image.

I look at the arena and watch Rye as he falls in line with the other blue players. He leans over and says something to one of his teammates, slings the belt around his chest, feels the weight of the gun. I realize I'm holding my breath.

Soon everyone has a rifle, and the empty racks return inside the walls. The words "*Kauna 1*" appear on the screen. Then someone hits a gong, and all sixty contestants turn. Almost as a single body, they run up the quarter pipe and leap into the air.

They don't come back down.

STAGE TWO: INSTABILITY

As the air reaches the condensation level, it forms a cloud. In unstable conditions, the air will continue to rise, and the clouds will grow to enormous sizes. Strong updrafts prevent the rain from falling.

Once a man wanted to locate the origin of thunder. He traveled north until he found a large plain and a gathering of wigwams. Nearby, some people were playing a ball game. When the game ended, they ducked into the wigwams and put on their feathered cloaks. The feathers turned into wings, and they flew away. This is how the Passamaquoddy found the home of the Thunderbirds.

5

I must have stood up, because when I come to my senses, I'm leaning over the railing, gaping at the people in the arena. At the people *flying* in the arena. Some of them are upside down, some of them are sideways, but all of them are in the air, whipping around the stadium. *How? How!* I want to scream. *How are you doing this?*

The scoreboard flashes wildly overhead as the players spin and lunge and soar around the Aerie. Guns fire in every direction, but the players aren't shooting bullets. They're shooting paintballs. The balls pelt the players in splashes of blue and red, the spectators too. I duck as a round streaks over our row. They're everywhere, whirring past my face and under my legs. Every time a contestant is hit, his or her face appears on the screen, and their number drops. A timer counts down from five minutes.

I stare at the blinking screen, at the whirling teenagers, at the hurtling shells. *This isn't possible.* There has to be an explanation. Their suits? Something in the arena? But I don't see any jetpacks or propellers, can't hear any motors. *What then?*

"Look out!" Lila yells. But it's too late. The barrage of pellets drives under my arm where there's no padding. *Ouch!* I grab my side and sit down with a thud.

"Oh man, that got you good!" Lila shouts over the bursting guns and screaming crowd. She laughs. "Sorry, I tried to warn you."

"I'm fine," I say hoarsely. I press my hand into my torso. Then I look down, prepared to see paint dripping from my fingers, but I don't see anything. I lift my hand to my nose. I can smell the fumes, but there's no color, just a clear substance sticking to my hand.

I look back at the mayhem below me, at the raging paintballs. The blue and red splatters are only showing up in one place: on the players' armor. The paint must be engineered to react to a certain type of fabric. *Or maybe it's the fabric that reacts to the paint.*

A girl on the red team zooms directly in front of me, and I follow her with my eyes, grateful to have something to focus on. She soars up the quarter pipe, nearly scraping the top of the nest, and dives back down near the netting. While diving, she aims her firearm at a boy in blue and pulls the trigger. The recoil makes her body twist slightly, but she recovers easily and loops around the ring. Her target is not so lucky. The ball hits him squarely in the circle over his heart, and his score drops by ten. He staggers back, clutching his chest, red trickling from his fingers. Even though I know it's paint, my stomach tenses.

I look for the girl again and see her pull a clip from her belt and load it into her rifle. Then, arcing and twisting around a series of bullets, she drops below the spray and fires directly up at her opponent, costing someone another ten points. She rockets into the sky, straight through one of the gaps in the roof.

When she's a full ten-story distance above the arena floor, she pulls herself up in a wide, graceful back flip. With her head pointing down, she drops back through the branches, plummeting in absolute free fall and spinning tightly, raining paint on red and blue players alike. Scores drop like crazy on the screen. With just ten feet to spare, she pulls up short, rotates her body, and pushes off the ground. *Tornado*, I name her.

A girl on the blue team zooms off the quarter pipe and flies along the Aerie roofline. Then she hurtles toward Tornado, coming from above and behind. Tornado doesn't see her. The blue girl takes aim.

All of a sudden, the blue girl falls. She screams until she lands on the ground with a sickening thwack.

"What happened?" I shout over the noise.

"Dead air," Lila shouts back. "The wind was weak up there. She should have seen it. It's her own fault."

The wind? I suddenly pay attention to the lusty breeze that's whipping around the arena, entering through the opening with the netting and channeling up the quarter pipe. I watch the movements of the contestants and realize they aren't just flying anywhere they want. There's a pattern. They're only going where the air is moving. My mouth drops open.

They're riding the wind.

I begin to remember all of the wind references I've heard this weekend, and everything starts to make sense. The kayaking, Charity pointing to the sky, her fast speeds only once a breeze was blowing—she was using the wind. All of those kids were. This is why Jeremy said we had to show up *with* our kayaks, why Lila wasn't concerned about the lost campers. They could fly out of trouble whenever they needed to. They just weren't allowed to fly to the testing grounds.

Who the heck are these people?

Around me, the initiates scream and pummel the metal bleachers with their fists while the paintballs explode in every direction. The noise is overwhelming, but I lean into it, soaking it all up. I have to know more.

When the timer runs out, the gong sounds again. The contestants stop firing and drop to the ground. The two teams line up, and the faces of about twenty-five players appear on the scoreboard, along with their scores. None of them has fewer than seventy points.

I see Rye again. His score is eighty-nine. Both red and blue paint stain his armor.

"They're allowed to shoot their teammates?" I ask Lila.

"That was the free-for-all round," she says. She gives me a funny look, and I remember I'm supposed to know the rules.

"Oh, right," I say quickly.

While the eliminated participants file off the field, the twenty-five contestants walk to their respective corners of the arena. Large showerheads spray them with a fine mist, and the paint almost instantly vanishes from their armor.

Doors open in the walls, and the weapon racks extend back into the ring. This time there are a variety of options. Assorted rifles and handguns. Knives. Tomahawks. Spears. As the players line up, scan their Quils, and select three items, the scoreboard displays their choices.

Tornado chooses a standard automatic rifle, a Carbon 15 Type 97S pistol, and a long-blade combat knife. The screen shows her serious face, blonde hair pulled back from her forehead—and something else. Her energy level. A green bar on the bottom indicates she's at eighty percent.

Rye's energy level is also at eighty. He selects an M16, a Glock 18, and a tomahawk. I want to ask Lila how they're going to play paintball with knives and tomahawks, but I've asked too much already.

After the players have chosen their weapons, the racks retract, and the two teams gather in huddles on opposite ends of the field, the red team outnumbering the blue team fifteen to ten. Then the arena begins to change. Trees and rocks rise out of the ground. Vines drop from the ceiling. Two large metal circles slide out from the wall by the net. There's a whirring sound, and suddenly converging streams of air are rushing down the center of the Aerie. *Bladeless fans*, I realize.

The scoreboard flashes two faces: Tornado and a boy with sandy hair from the blue team. Because they have the most points, they're the team captains.

"That's Buck," Lila says, nodding at the boy.

"Who?" I ask. I notice one of his weapons is a spear.

"Rye's cousin. They're best friends."

Looking down into the arena, I try to pick out Buck and Rye from among their teammates, but then my eyes snap to the players' armor. The circles are transforming. A small ring appears on each of the players' backs, and the two rings on their fronts shrink in size. The stripes of color also shrink until they're nothing but thin lines.

The players fan out on either side of the field, separated for now by the obstacles and blowing air. I watch as one of them raises his Quil to a tree. He lowers his arm again and pushes something on the tiny monitor. A second later, the gray camo on his armor becomes a mottled brown, an exact match of the tree's bark.

"Are you serious?" I gasp.

"What?" Lila says, turning to look at me. "Did you say something?"

I shake my head, and she looks back into the arena while I continue to gape at the players melting into the leaves and rocks. Ten seconds count down on the screen. Then the words, "*Kauna 2: Instant Elimination*," flash across the board.

When the gong sounds, the blue players catch a current that takes them up to the Aerie roof. They stay close to the trees, and for a moment I can't tell them apart from the trunks. Then, while four of them stay put, Rye and two other players catapult into the sky— their armor turning gray again—while Buck and another three dive into the crossing currents. The conflicting jets send them tumbling one way and then the next.

The red players open fire, but the blue players who remained behind shoot back, providing cover for their teammates. And a distraction. Rye and his wingmen dive down into the other side of the arena, bypassing the fans entirely and catching the red team off-guard. Rye and a short boy each get a kill. The two red contestants fall to the mats below. They lose ten points, and they're out of the game. But now Rye and Shorty's points go up by ten.

As the blue team keeps firing, Tornado and three other red players leap off the ground and land mid-air in a crouch. They zip around the curving arena walls. Tornado blasts a shot at the blue players crossing the wind currents. One of them is hit in the foot. Losing his balance, he fires his gun wildly. The kickback sends him into a tight spiral as he releases bullets in all directions. Then he slams into the mats and lies still.

By this time, Buck has made it across the dangerous current. He hurls a spear at a red player's back. The blunted tip hits the small circle, leaving a streak of blue, and Buck earns ten points.

Tornado scoops up an abandoned pistol and fires at Buck with a gun in each hand, grazing his arm. Because the paint didn't hit a circle, he's still in. Buck ducks behind a tree and answers Tornado's volley with his own. Tornado somersaults away from him, landing on the ground. She breaks into a sprint and runs right through the current. When she reaches the other side of the arena, she leaps back into the air and catches the other blue players by surprise. One of them goes down.

Suddenly, Rye launches off the quarter pipe and, grabbing a vine, swings over the dangerous blasts of air. He sends a shot at Tornado as he passes, and blue paint speckles her shoulder. The scoreboard takes three points from Tornado and gives them to Rye. He lands on the other side and helps Buck take out two red players.

Rye tosses aside his spent rifle and pulls out his Glock. Then he holds out an arm to Buck, and his cousin spins him around, releasing him into the air. Rye twists on his side and rolls past a player in red, firing bullets at both kill spots on her chest. The crowd screams as he earns twenty points.

Now the two teams are more evenly matched. The players whip around the arena in a frenzy, and I can't tell if they're using any kind of strategy or not. One thing is for sure—their energy levels are dropping dramatically. All of the indicator bars have changed from green to yellow.

One of the blue players gets caught by the fans and crashes into a tree. He isn't shot, but his helmet smacks the trunk hard, and he tumbles to the ground unconscious. Two medics run into the arena and carry him off the field, but the battle doesn't stop.

As Rye dives to the floor to retrieve his former teammate's rifle, a girl in red barrels down on him. From the ground, Rye does a backflip into the air and shoots the girl in the visor. But she's not out. She slams into a wall then spins away, clutching her arm.

The gong rings again, and the teams regroup, getting a two-minute respite to plan their next move. No new weapons this time.

One of the bladeless fans retracts, and the circles on their armor shrink even further while another shows up on their right thighs.

There are only ten players left, and each of them gets a bonus for making it to round three, putting most of their scores in the nineties. There are four people on the blue team: Rye, Buck, Shorty, and a girl with brown hair. The red team has six players: Tornado, a boy with glasses, a girl with blonde hair, a heavyset boy with dark hair, a tall boy with blue eyes, and the girl Rye shot in the helmet—the one who hurt her arm. From the way she's cradling it, it looks like it might be broken.

After two minutes, the gong sounds, and round three begins. Immediately, Tornado, the boy with glasses, and the girl with blonde hair whip around the arena wall and fire paint into the blue team. The blue players scatter, and the rest of the red team moves in to pick them off. The tall boy with blue eyes locks on Buck. Buck darts around the obstacles, but he can't shake him. Rye fires the Glock at his own pursuer then swoops down to help his cousin. He gets behind Blue Eyes and aims the pistol. Nothing comes out.

Rye lets the weapon fall and dives toward the ground. He snatches up an abandoned knife and leaps straight up, catching a wind current above his head and doing a gainer in the air. He lands directly in front of Blue Eyes. The blade slashes the spot on the boy's thigh, and a blue streak of paint marks the kill.

Blue Eyes starts to fall, but Rye suddenly grabs him by the arms and jerks him back up. A second later, a red bullet slams into Blue Eyes's spine. Rye pulls the tomahawk out of his belt and whirls the blade through the air. It hits the stomach of the person who was firing at him—the blonde girl. On the screen, Blondie's face goes dark, and she topples onto the mats. Rye pushes Blue Eyes aside and goes after the tomahawk.

Blondie was one of the last contestants to have any ammunition. Only one other person is still carrying a gun: Tornado. The brown-haired girl on the blue team goes after her with a spear. Tornado zigs her way to the nest roof, hops over one of the branches, and hooks her legs around it. She flips her body back and, hanging upside down, fires directly into the girl's chest. Eight players left.

Tornado unhooks her legs from her perch and dives headfirst for Buck, who is leaping for Brown Hair's spear. Tornado doesn't fire right away, probably because she only has a few bullets left. That gives Buck some time. He grabs the spear before it hits the ground, but then he accidentally drops into the wind current created by the fan. He manages to stay in the air, narrowly missing a tree, but the blast sweeps him away from Tornado.

Across the arena, the heavyset boy is grappling with Shorty, both of their knives poised directly over a kill spot. Only their shaking arms keep the blades at bay as they twirl in the air. It's simply a matter of time. I look at the scoreboard. Both of their energy levels are flashing red. Finally, Heavyset collapses and plunges toward the floor. Shorty barely stays aloft and gets the kill with his knife.

I look back at the board. It's down to six players: Rye, Buck, and Shorty, and Tornado, the boy with glasses, and the girl with the broken arm. Now almost all of the fighting is hand-to-hand. Rye contends with Glasses, while Buck tackles Broken Arm and Shorty takes his chances with Tornado. Rye's knife finds its target. So does Buck's spear. And Tornado's gun. Three left. Energy levels at fifteen percent and dropping.

The gong resonates again, and the screen flashes, "*Kauna 4.*" But this time, there's no break. They have to keep fighting. Buck finally catches up with Tornado and, twirling his spear, launches the weapon at her chest. Another blue mark slashes her gray armor, but it isn't a kill. And now Buck has no weapon. Tornado takes her shot, and Buck falls to the ground.

Rye watches his cousin plummet to the mats for only a moment, but it gives Tornado her edge. She somersaults toward him, finger on the trigger. I hear the pop.

Then Rye is falling. The crowd spouts a mixture of groans and cheers, and Tornado pumps her fists.

But just as Rye is about to the hit the arena floor, he catches a current and shoots forward, scooping up an M16 and skimming a foot above the ground. He zooms up the quarter pipe and launches through the roof high into the air, spinning tightly.

"I thought he was hit," I yell.

"He was faking it!" Lila claps her hands. "He fell before the ball hit him."

"Is there any ammo in that rifle?"

"I don't know!" she squeals, jumping up and down.

Rye soars far above the roof of the nest, so high, it's hard to see him. *He's going to hit dead air like that girl*, I think. And, sure enough, he's falling again. No, not falling. Diving. Rifle aimed directly for his opponent. Tornado hears the crowd scream and looks up. Into the barrel of his gun.

Rye gets the shot his cousin missed, and Tornado's legs flip up over her shoulders, sending her whirling backward. His gamble paid off. It's the win.

The crowd jumps to its feet, cheering wildly. Tornado regains control and comes out of the spin, yanking the helmet off her head and freeing long tresses of moist, blonde hair. She rubs her head, and I catch sight of a grimace. But then she's smiling, thumping her helmet with her hand and bowing to Rye.

He's removed his helmet as well. His hair sticks up in tufts, and a line of dirt traces his jawline. He pounds a fist on his chest. Then he sails over to Tornado and raises one of her arms. The crowd roars its approval.

A door on the observation box opens, and Naira steps onto a platform above the quarter pipe. Rye rides the wind up, landing next to her. She places a medal around his neck, and the spectators stamp their feet.

All of the players return to the field, and the scoreboard flashes the faces of the top scoring contestants. Buck earns third place with one hundred and six points, Tornado gets second with one hundred and twenty-seven, and Rye is named the *tooka* or winner, with one hundred and sixty-one. The screen changes to display a list of highest-ranking scores. Rye makes the top ten but falls short of the record two hundred and three.

The players thump their chests with their fists, everyone cheers, and then it's over. I sit in my seat and stare at the arena, at the exhausted but smiling players leaving the field, at the space in front of me where the whole world just changed.

"Come on, Kit," Lila says. "Let's go." I stand up, wincing when I feel the welt on my side. I had forgotten all about it.

I follow Lila toward the exit. As we leave, we drop our masks and jackets into the bins by the door. The kids around us jabber enthusiastically—about the types of weapons, about the winners, about the players' moves—but I'm not listening. I'm not paying attention to where I'm going either, and I mumble apologies as I bump into the people in front of me and step on someone's toes.

"It's too bad we're not allowed to windwalk back to the bunkhouse," Lila says as we shuffle our way across the crowded bridge.

"Yeah." So that's what it's called. Windwalking. I picture the players rocketing into the sky and whirling through the arena, all without parachutes or bungee cords. How did they do it? Are these people human?

I peek at Lila. She looks normal. All of the people around me look normal. Jeremy and the initiates from my van are normal, eccentric perhaps, but not alien. Jeremy can windwalk then. So can Aponi and Charity and even Diva. The whole idea is so crazy, so unbelievable.

I look up as the wind rustles the netting above me, and suddenly the camouflage and mirrors make perfect sense. I've just discovered the greatest secret in the universe.

"What do you think, Kit?" Lila asks.

"What?" I stammer. I look to my left and see that Holly has somehow found us in this throng of people.

"*Wakemo* ten is hosting a dance tonight," Holly repeats. "Wanna go?"

I try not to wrinkle my nose. In my experience, dances usually involve boys standing on one side of the gym and girls giggling in clumps on the other. I was rarely asked to dance, and when I was, it was only by boys with sweaty palms and bad breath.

"I guess," I say.

"What should we do now?" Lila asks.

"Let's go swimming!" Holly says.

We climb down from the platform, and I follow them to a lake on the other side of the camp. On the shore is a small cabin, built into the base of a large pine tree. It has two doors, one marked *Kama* and the other *Tamo*. We enter the first door.

The inside of the cabin looks a lot like the bunkhouse bathroom but with a row of shelves containing folded swimsuits and towels. We each grab a swimsuit and go into a changing stall. I take off my clothes and necklace, wadding them into a ball, then step into the suit. It fits perfectly—just like the other clothes. Frowning, I pinch the slick material and snap it against my skin.

"Last one in the lake is dead air," Lila yells.

I shove my clothes into one of the fancy wood lockers, grab a towel, and run outside. After kicking off my shoes and dropping the towel on a rock, I dive into the lake.

The water is cool and silky and gorgeously blue. And it's the perfect temperature. Most people would probably call it too cold, but I like that tiny nip on my skin. It makes me feel alive—and it feels great on my welt.

While Lila and Holly splash each other, I float on my back and look up at the clouds. Thick, fleecy things. Warm gray in the center and glowing white on the edges where the sun shines through more easily. They stand out against the ultramarine sky, and I watch them shift and move, propelled forward by the wind. How high can windwalkers go? Can they fly up there, into the clouds?

I took a 4-H class a few years ago where we learned how to observe and measure the wind, how to use it. We talked about windmills and wind turbines, wind power and wind farms. I was so fascinated I even memorized the Beaufort wind scale. But this, this blows it all away.

In my mind, I see Tornado diving and flipping, spinning off the Aerie roof and free falling without fear. I see Rye twisting and rolling, shooting upward until he vanishes into a pinprick. Just thinking about it makes my heart speed up. I close my eyes and try to imagine what it would be like to ride the wind. It makes me want to laugh. Really laugh.

"Cannonball!"

Large blobs of water suddenly douse my face. Blinking and sputtering, I flip around in time to see five boys jump into the lake. Catching my breath, I swim quickly for shore.

A head bursts out of the water in front of me, and I splash to a stop as the boy whips his neck around, his wet hair smacking his temples and spraying me again. He pushes the hair out of his face, and then I see the green eyes, the square jaw. It's Rye.

For a moment, we do nothing but tread water and look at each other. I try not to stare at his defined chest bobbing above the surface, try not to think about the fact that we're wearing next to nothing.

Then he grins. "Nice day for a swim."

My tongue feels thick. "Sure," I mumble as I duck my head and paddle past him. I'm shaking a little when I get to shore. Soon Lila and Holly join me.

"How lucky is this!" Holly says, openly eyeing the boys as she wrings out her hair. Some of them whistle at her.

"Was that Rye?" Lila asks me. "Did you talk to him?"

"Not exactly," I say as I yank my towel off the rock.

"That's too bad," Holly says. "You had him all to yourself."

"I wouldn't have known what to say either," Lila assures me, but we both know that's a lie.

I retrieve my clothes and tell them I want to go back to the bunkhouse. Holly opts to stay and watch the boys, but Lila says she'll go with me.

"*Taitai!*" Holly calls as we walk away. "Watch your back!"

"*Koka.* Watch yours," Lila replies. I raise an eyebrow. *Must be a windwalker thing.*

A windwalker thing. This morning I didn't even know such a thing existed. We return to the bunkhouse and I keep thinking about it, the way the contestants in the arena flowed with the wind, more graceful than figure skaters. I think about windwalking while I shower under the warm waterfall, while I comb out my snarled hair, while I put on clean clothes, while I apply fresh bandages to my hands, while I find ice for the bruise on my side, while I lean against the bunkhouse wall and gaze out the window.

Sometimes Rye's green eyes pop into my mind, his smooth chest, white teeth. But then I think of him windwalking, and he becomes one with the rest of the group. Elegant warriors in the sky.

Lila decides to take a nap, but I can't sit still so I leave the *wakemo* and stroll through the trees, breathe the rich forest air, look up at the pine needles, wishing I could fly to them. I've been walking for maybe twenty minutes when I hear voices up ahead. As I get closer, I discover that a group of people is gathered around a large canvas on the ground, each of them painting a section of it. Two counselors stand nearby, noting things on electronic tablets. A small crowd is watching off to the side. I see Holly, so I walk over to her.

"One of the guys from the lake is competing," she whispers when she sees me, pointing to a boy crouched over the canvas.

I peer over the shoulder of the person in front of me, and as I get a good look at the paintings, my hand goes to my mouth. The contestants are using the most vivid pigments I've ever seen—and they change colors. One moment a streak of paint is deep cerulean. The next, it sparkles into electric violet and then sea green.

The painters dip sculpted wooden sticks into a tray of paint and swirl long lines across the canvas. It's not in any logical order, a stroke here, a stroke there, but somehow the pictures come together.

I've never cared much about art before, but as I watch the initiates work, I feel something I can't explain. Something waking inside of me. I can't tear my eyes from the canvas. Stunning scenes of the heavens. Whirling waves in the sky.

Are they painting how they feel about the wind, or is this what it actually looks like? Maybe that's how they can ride it—because they can see it. I'd give anything to know their secret.

Time is called and a *tooka* chosen, but I continue to stare at the painting, losing myself in the streaks of iridescent jasmine and plum.

"Let's go," Holly says, dragging me away. "I'm starving!"

Mind buzzing, I follow her to the bunkhouse. We wake Lila up for dinner, and then the three of us walk together toward the *wakenu.* As we wait in line in the dining hall, I stare at the wall across from us where the counselors have hung the wind mural. The colors continue to change, making the wind look alive.

As I scoop food onto my plate, I glimpse Bullseye sitting at a nearby table. No sign of Charity though. The only other people from my van I haven't spotted yet are Titan and Diva. I think of Titan's immense arms and solemn face, the way he took the lead on the lake. He's definitely here. And Diva? *If Dee and Dum are here, she's here too.*

We sit down to eat, and I see Rye again. His chocolate hair is dry now, the clean locks reaching over his ears and swooping back from his forehead in a slight wave, as if he's been absently running his hands through them. He rests his arm on the back of the chair, and I see the strong outline of his biceps. My belly dips as I remember how close we were in the lake.

Not surprisingly, he's sitting in the middle of a crowd. Buck is on his right, and on his left is Tornado. I watch her for a few minutes. She laughs often and, at one point, reaches over to take something from Rye's plate.

"That's disgusting," Lila says. I look at her and see she's watching Tornado too. "She's all over him. I can't believe he's not telling her to back off."

"Yeah," I say carefully. "So, where is his girlfriend?"

"At home, I guess. It's probably not her year to come to the camp."

"You girls coming to the dance?" A boy with a huge smile suddenly leans across the table and winks at Holly.

"Oh, I don't know … " Holly says, twirling pasta with her fork.

"It'll be sick. Drums. Bonfire. We just need hot girls to show up."

Holly says something, but I don't pay attention because out of the corner of my eye, I see Rye and his entourage getting up from their table. They walk toward us, and I concentrate on my carrots as Rye good-humoredly punches the boy talking to Holly and then brushes past us. *Would he recognize me from the lake?* Probably not. But my eyes follow his back as he as walks out of the room.

It's dark when Lila and I make our way to the section of forest beyond bunkhouse ten, on the outer reaches of the camp. There's already a small crowd when we arrive, and they've lit a bonfire. I think about the rule I read, but I decide to stay—there are enough people that I won't be singled out if Naira does show up.

Someone starts beating a drum, not too loudly but forceful enough to provide a strong cadence. Another drummer joins the first, the tone slightly lower. Then another drum, a higher pitch. Someone adds a rattle, and now the rhythm is more complicated, more stimulating, and the initiates begin to dance.

At first, they move individually. They roll their shoulders, swivel their hips, dip their legs. They press against the other dancers, spin away, sway next to someone else. The bonfire burns more strongly, and some of the boys peel their shirts off. Their strong torsos gleam when they step near the flames. My eyes widen. This is nothing like the dances at Lake of the Woods School.

I spot Rye, and that prickle in my chest starts up again. He grabs a girl with black hair by the hand and twirls her one way then another, raising his arm up and whipping it back down. They dance close together for a moment. Then he swings her back into the ever-growing swarm of people.

Buck appears next to him. They circle to face each other and simultaneously jump apart. Buck drops to a crouch, and Rye leaps over him, spinning as he lands. Then he somersaults into a roll, and Buck jumps over his cousin's back. They flick their hands down and kick their legs up, laughing and bumping shoulders as they shimmy and bounce on their feet.

A crowd of girls surrounds them, and the boys play to the attention, stepping their legs out past shoulder length and bobbing low. They bring their hands out in front of them and hop with the beat. Rye raises his hands up to his head, elbows cocked, and pivots his hips suggestively. The girls squeal.

A brunette breaks out of the group and lifts her arms above her head, swaying her own hips as she moves close to Rye. A breeze whips through the trees, and suddenly the brunette vaults into the air, pirouetting into an aerial. Rye grins and rides the wind up to join her. Soon everyone is leaving the ground, some on their own, most in couples. Buck twirls two partners, one in each hand. The girls wind their arms around the boys' necks, and they press their foreheads close before they spin apart and then coil back together.

A boy swoops down and extends a hand to Lila. She giggles and rises into the air alongside him. I watch them rock in time to the intoxicating drumbeat. Then the rhythm changes. The girls converge in a whirling mass while the boys encircle them and clap their hands to the tempo, whooping and whistling as the girls show off their moves. Next, it's the boys' turn. They wheel and twist and dive while the girls cheer them on.

I step back under the cover of the trees as the dancers merge into couples once more. I wish someone would ask me to dance, but it will never happen. It *can't* happen. Because I can't windwalk.

I can't windwalk.

Instinctively, I bite the side of my lip, use the slight pain to keep myself in check. I wait a few long moments, memorizing everything. The pulsing drums. The pitching, spiraling dancers. The tiny sparks that run from the flames and vanish into the sable night. Like me.

My walk to the bunkhouse is slow. I play with my necklace and listen to the thrumming strain of the crickets, but my mind is in the sky. I look up at the glitter-tossed heavens, at the stars you can only see when there are no city lights, and suddenly I'm there again—back on the Johnson's farm. Back with the twins.

I was seven when Tom and Sue Johnson became my foster parents. The twins were two. The Johnsons volunteered to take us in, even though they had three children of their own. Tom was a farmer, and money was tight, especially when Sue had another baby a few years later, but somehow they made it work. Until a horse kicked Tom in the head and he died of a brain hemorrhage.

That was six months ago. Tom had no life insurance. The only money we got was from the government since we qualified for welfare. The community chipped in to pay for his coffin, and Sue sold most of the land and all of the livestock except for the cow and chickens. From that week on, I picked up extra shifts at the Northlake Café where I worked after school. I wasn't making good grades anyway, so I didn't care that I lost more homework time. But six dollars an hour doesn't go very far when there are seven mouths to feed, and it hardly offset my share of the expenses.

When summer arrived, I worked as many hours as I could and got a second job at the gas station, but it didn't seem to make much of a difference. That's when Sue's mother decided to come live with us and I decided to run away. There are few things I hate more than Williams, but Grandma Mildred is one of them. Her tight lips, shrill voice, and jabbing fingers terrorized me as a child. Fortunately, she loves the twins as much as everyone else does, or I could never have left them.

Jack and Maisy. I close my eyes as I picture their faces.

I felt bad about leaving, but I knew it was really the best thing I could do for them. My absence would mean one less mouth to feed, and since school was going to start again and I would go back to working part-time, they wouldn't suffer from the loss of my measly income. Besides, Sue was going to start a job at the high school library,

Grandma Mildred was going to contribute some of her retirement funds, and once I got set up in Winnipeg, I was going to send them part of my paycheck.

Right … my paycheck. I kick at a pile of dead leaves, sending them fluttering into the darkness. Well, they're just going to have to wait a little longer. Right now I've got to take care of myself.

A yellow glow falls on my head, and as I look up at my bunkhouse with its promise of a soft mattress and warm blankets, I reach for the ladder with a tiny boost of vigor. At least for the moment I have somewhere safe and comfortable to sleep.

I walk up the ramp to my bed, passing two girls leaning against the wall, talking. When I've rounded the bend, I hear one of the girls ask the other, "What day is your event?"

"Day Four," is the reply. "Yours?"

"Tomorrow. I'm so nervous!"

I pause. What are they talking about? And then it clicks. I rush back down the ramp.

"Hey," I say, trying not to talk too quickly. "Do you know where I can get a schedule?"

The girls stare at me for a moment. Then one of them raises a small gray object in her palm. "Your Quil?" she says.

"Oh, right. Thanks." I scuttle back to my bunk, sit down on the mattress, and look at the watch on my wrist, suddenly remembering all the crazy things I saw it do in the Aerie. *How do I get it off?* I turn it over and study the slick band. There's not even a seam.

I flip through the time, the date, all the display options, but I don't see anything useful. I shake it. I pull on it. Finally, I push the polished surface with my finger, and a small box appears. Inside are words I can't read, but to the right is a tiny vertical bar. I slide the bar up.

Suddenly, the watch falls off my wrist, and I catch it as it forms back into a rectangle. On the screen appears a picture of the red eagle with the tomahawk. Beneath the eagle is another box, a faded picture of a thumbprint in the background. Holding my breath, I press my thumb on the box.

The screen changes. Now it displays a series of triangular shaped images. I push the first one, and it pulls up a list of numbers, one through three hundred and three. Next to each number are two images: a telephone and a dark profile. This must allow me to call anyone in the camp. *I guess I have a phone after all.*

I go back to the main screen and scan the triangles. I find one with a picture that looks like a stack of papers and push it. Now the screen shows a schedule, with a day at the top and a list of times and events. There's a search box, so I select it and type in my number. The Quil pulls up two pages. I click on the first.

Ro 3
9:00 Raiwhapuhi
9:00 Muranga
10:00 Kohenrehi
11:00 Waerehi whawhai

I study the screen, looking for help. Then I see a small icon with a capital "E." I click it, and, suddenly, the words transform.

Day 3
9:00 Rifle shooting
9:00 Fire building
10:00 Windracing
11:00 Foot racing

I select each event and read the numbers. My pulse trips when I choose windracing. I read it twice, but there's no two hundred and seventy-three. I exhale fully. I did notice one hundred and fifty-eight, however. Lila's number.

Now the fourth contest. Foot racing. I read the numbers, and there I am. Eleven o'clock at the track. My heart rate grows steadier. A foot race I can handle, but what about the other event? I go back to the second page and change the screen into English.

Day 2
9:30 Kiipooyaq

9:45 Spear throwing
10:00 Basket weaving
10:00 Fishing

I hope for the fishing, but my number's not there. It's not in basket weaving or spear throwing either. I read the numbers for the first event, the only one that didn't translate.

I slump against my pillow and feel the blood drain from my cheeks. So much for lasting out the week. I now know the exact time and place where my life will end.

Tomorrow. Nine-thirty at the lake.

6

What in the world is a kiipooyaq? I wonder yet again as I push pieces of soggy waffle around on my plate.

Last night I couldn't sleep. I lay on my mattress, listening to the soft breathing of the girls in the bunkhouse and playing out the potential scenarios I would face the next day. Even though I knew it was ridiculous, implausible, irrational, Lila's talk about torture had surged to the top of my mind. I tried to ignore it, telling myself I'd just get sent back to Winnipeg, but that didn't help me feel any better, since going to Winnipeg would mean going to jail or maybe back to Williams, and that would be just as bad.

I decided to find a place to hide until my event was over. Running would have been safer, but I couldn't leave the camp, not without supplies. Since I couldn't do anything in the middle of the night, I slept for a few short hours, plummeting into my ever-worsening nightmares, then got up shortly before dawn and slid down the pole. I pushed open the door, stepped onto the porch, and walked right into Lila.

"Hey!" she said. "What are you doing up so early?"

"Oh, hi," I stammered. "I, um, couldn't sleep."

"Nervous about your event?"

"Yeah," I replied. Apparently, *she* had checked her Quil. "Why are you up?"

"Insomnia." She shrugged.

"Sorry. That sucks."

"Oh well. This way I get to see the sunrise."

I pressed the toe of my shoe into the wood and coughed. "Well, I'm just going to go for a walk. I'll see you—"

"A walk would be great! I'll come too."

So for the next hour I walked around the forest and struggled to make small talk while inside my guts roiled. Luckily, Lila did most of the talking. But she never left my side, and I couldn't figure out how to break away.

Now here I sit in the dining hall, unable to eat a thing, counting down the minutes until I'm tortured for being a spy.

"I can't wait to watch you," Lila declares as she takes a big bite of toast. "You're so brave to sign up for the *kiipooyaq*. I'm afraid I would crack my skull!" I press my fingers against my forehead and wait for her to finish eating.

When she's done, we leave the *wakenu* and walk to the lake. I glance at the Quil on my wrist—it took me half an hour last night to figure out how to put it back on—and see that it's a quarter after nine. Fifteen minutes left of freedom.

A tall female counselor with her hair pushed back by a headband is standing by the water's edge holding an electronic tablet. Behind her is a large wooden crate, and stretched out on the ground in front of her are several lengths of rope with fist-sized metal balls on the ends. Most of the contestants are already there, warming up.

I watch a girl pick up one of the ropes. The final third of the rope splits into three strands, and each of the strands is attached to a ball. The girl grasps the rope at the intersection of the three cords, and, twirling the metal spheres over her head, releases the contraption when her arm is extended in front of her. The balls wrap around a tree and stay put.

These must be *kiipooyaqs*. The tension in my abdomen drops down a notch. They're like lassoes. When I was ten, Tom taught me how to rope cattle, and I got so good at it, I even competed in the county fair, winning second place in my age group. Maybe this won't be a death sentence after all.

"I better go practice," I say to Lila.

She nods. "*Taitai!*"

While Lila strolls toward the seats set up for spectators, I walk over to the counselor. She holds out her tablet. I stare at it, but the display is blank.

"Help me out here," she says, grabbing my wrist and placing my Quil on her larger device. The screen beeps, checking me in.

I pick up one of the *kiipooyaqs* and bounce it experimentally. It's heavier than a lasso, which isn't surprising with these metal balls. Lila was serious when she said I could break my head open.

I don't want people watching my very first throw, so I walk along the lake's edge until I'm out of sight of the small crowd. I think about how the girl spun the *kiipooyaq*, using her whole arm. I raise the rope and try to mimic her, but my lasso training instinctively kicks in. My elbow remains level, and my wrist rotates as part of the forward swing. I go for a front and back loop, but the metal balls don't work quite the same way as a cattle rope.

When you throw a lasso, you want the knot to land behind the base of the cow's right horn. If you're just a fraction of a second late on your release, you'll rope the cow by its neck instead. I know exactly when I need to release a lasso. I hope it's the same for a *kiipooyaq*.

I let go of the rope, and my hand instinctively draws the slack. The problem is there's no slack to pull, and the balls fly straight back toward my face. I duck in time to avoid losing my nose, but one of the spheres grazes my temple. I press a hand over the bump on my skull, cursing myself for my stupidity.

My head pounds, but I make myself pick the weapon up again. There are only a few minutes before the competition. I have no delusions about winning, but I need to at least learn how to throw this thing, or they'll know something's wrong.

I try again, this time letting go of the rope entirely. And, like magic, the weapon snags the tree in front of me.

Exhaling deeply, I retrieve the *kiipooyaq* and get in a few more tries before I hear the whistle. *Here goes nothing.* I walk back to the check-in point and join the other contestants, noting that two staff members now accompany the counselor with the headband.

"Listen up, folks," says Headband. "We'll release the birds. When I blow the whistle, you're free to attack. You will be ranked according to how quickly you get your catch. Any questions?"

Ah, crap. I didn't give much thought to what the target was going to be, but I certainly wasn't expecting birds. This could be very bad. Still, even if I humiliate myself, at least I'll be able to throw the thing—I won't get in trouble for losing.

The ten of us stand behind a line Headband projects with a red laser light. As her helpers walk over to the crate, I position the *kiipooyaq* in my hand and lick my dry lips. The man whips the door open, and a dozen geese frantically escape. For a moment, all I can see is the cloud of gray feathers they leave behind as they fly out over the lake, and then I hear the whistle.

I dash forward, holding the *kiipooyaq* at the ready. One of the geese has landed not too far from the shore, and I pick her as my target, but since she's the closest one, I know the others will be after her too. It's a good thing I'm fast.

In a matter of seconds, I've splashed into the lake. The noise frightens the goose, and she flaps her wings to take off. I focus in on her shoulders. Unlike with a lasso, I'll only have one throw. I swing the rope forward, back, forward, back.

I release the *kiipooyaq.* The balls whirl in the air and hit the bird just as she's pulling in her wings to get some lift. It's a stroke of luck. The balls pin her wings to her side and yank her back into the shallow water.

Thank goodness. I hear Lila cheering behind me, and I breathe out slowly. No one will be torturing me today. I wade out to get the goose.

I brace myself for the bird's hissing and thrashing, but she doesn't move, and when I get closer, I see why. Her neck is broken, one of the balls wrapped tightly around it. I blink. Cattle don't die when you rope them unless you do something wrong, but I didn't do anything wrong here. This weapon is meant to kill. Cleanly too. Much tidier than the birds I would shoot with Tom.

I pick the goose up by her feet and carry her back to shore, but none of the other contestants are there. I look back at the lake. *Oh …*

No wonder I got to this one so easily. Everyone else is in the sky.

I watch as one person moves close to a goose. When the *kiipooyaq* flies from his grasp, it strangles the creature's neck, leaving the wings free. The bird flaps wildly, rising higher and higher into the air, but soon her wings begin to convulse and she dive bombs toward the water.

The three counselors are conversing together quietly when I reach the shore. I stand there awkwardly with my kill, waiting for the other contestants to return to land. Finally, Headband addresses us.

"It appears we've witnessed some unorthodox techniques this morning," she says. Everyone's eyes dart to me, so I find a twig on the ground and stare at it. "We've had to consult the rules," she continues, "but there is no stipulation that a competitor must windwalk. Therefore, the *tooka* of our contest is number two hundred and seventy-three."

The spectators applaud, and this time I'm certain I hear Lila hollering. I step forward to receive my medal.

"Nice form too," Headband smiles as she takes the goose. "I'll make sure Naira hears about that." I place my fist over my heart, give a short bow, and return to my place in line. I wish she wouldn't tell Naira. That won't help me keep a low profile.

I shift my weight between my feet while the other contestants are given their scores, bracing myself for their glares. Instead, all of them smile and, afterward, shake my hand.

"You were brilliant!" Lila raves upon joining me. "What a clever idea to stay on the ground and cut out all that time chasing a bird. And your wrist action was crazy. Where did you learn to throw like that?"

"On our farm," I say.

"You have a farm in Winnipeg?" she asks.

"Uh, no," I backpedal. "I mean my uncle has a farm, in the country—he taught me."

"That's awesome," she says before launching into a new subject.

I dodged that bullet. But only just.

We stay at the lake to watch the next event, the fishing contest, and as the contestants assemble, I decide it's a very good thing Aura did not sign up for this competition. There are no poles or tackle, no bait or line. Just knives and string.

After a moment, I see Rye among the participants. "Has he been here the whole time?" I ask Lila.

"Yep. He was watching your event."

I look down at my medal, feeling my face grow warm. "Oh," I say.

When the whistle blows, the contestants each grab a knife and run, not toward the lake, but toward the trees. With their blades, they hastily whack off a branch then lash their knives onto the ends of the sticks and race into the water. They spread out across the shore, each of them with his or her arms raised, motionless, poised to strike.

A boy with red hair shoots his arm down first, but when his spear comes back up, the tip is empty—he missed. A girl with her hair in braids and a boy with long legs hit the water at the same time. Braids pulls her spear up just before Longlegs does. Her knife has a fish, and so does his. A girl in a green shirt gets the third fish, Rye gets the fourth, and Redhead finally gets the fifth. The rest of the contestants aren't far behind.

While I watch the presentation of awards, my eyes seek Rye's face. He looks up, I think at me, but I turn away quickly, so I'm not sure if I imagined it or not.

"What should we do now?" Lila asks.

"I need something for this bruise on my head," I tell her, feeling the growing lump with my fingers and consciously keeping my gaze away from the contestants.

"Ew, yikes. Okay, let's go to the *wakenu*. They'll have stuff there."

We leave the lake and walk to the meetinghouse where a counselor gets me an ice pack. Since they're serving lunch, we stay in the dining hall to eat, and I load up my tray. Now that the *kiipooyaq* contest is behind me, I can feel the canyon in my stomach. We find a table and sit down.

I'm halfway through my sandwich when Naira enters the cafeteria and steps onto her platform. Everyone looks up.

"I'm pleased to inform you," she begins, "that this evening we will have a dance. At eight o'clock, here in the *wakenu*."

All of the initiates turn to their neighbors, and whispers fly around the room. Naira continues, "I would like to impress upon everyone the importance of following the camp rules. I know discipline has been slack in the past, but this year violations will not be tolerated. I don't think I need to remind anyone of the Incident." That's all she says. Then she pounds a fist on her chest and steps down from the platform.

"Drat," Lila mutters. "This dance won't be any fun, not if we can't ride."

"Lila! Kit!" Holly drops into a chair next to us. "I can't believe it—all of the guys from ten have been suspended!"

"What?" Lila and I say at the same time.

"Naira found out about the fire. Now none of them are allowed to compete. They can stay the rest of the week if they want, but they won't get an assignment."

"That's crazy," Lila exclaims. "The Incident was like a bajillion years ago. Why is Naira freaking out?"

Holly shrugs. "Maybe it's a power trip."

"She needs to take a chill pill," Lila says, biting into her sandwich. "No one's going to spy on us."

"What would happen if someone did?" I ask, holding my breath.

Holly snorts. "Knowing Naira, she'd probably give it to them slowly."

"Yeah," Lila says. "The old-fashioned way."

Holly makes a face. "Ugh. Decortication is super nasty."

"What's decortication?" I ask.

Lila turns to me. "You know, it's like when you peel the skin off an orange."

"Hey ladies!" a skinny boy yells as he passes our table. "We're starting a game of volleyball!"

"Sweet!" Holly jumps out of her chair.

"I'm totally there." Lila scoops up her tray. "You coming, Kit?"

"Sure," I mumble. I'm not going to be able to finish my sandwich anyway. As I follow Lila and Holly out of the dining hall, the hammering in my brain threatens to split my skull.

Outside, we find the initiates playing volleyball, or at least something that resembles volleyball. There's a net and a ball, but the net is really a laser projection between two trees, the ball is small and black, and their Quils keep score.

I sit down on a tree stump, telling Lila I'll just watch. The players are too good, and I don't know all the rules. Besides, I wouldn't be able to concentrate enough to play even if I wanted to. For a while, I watch the initiates send the ball sailing back and forth above the laser. That extra high jump. Last-second save. Powerful spike. The wind's behind all of it.

After a few minutes, I can't even focus enough to be a spectator and instead turn to my Quil, hoping for a better diversion. Now that I know how it works, I slip it easily off my wrist, press my thumb on the box, and experiment with the options on the screen. Most of the buttons are locked, but I investigate the ones I can open. One of them tells me how fast the wind is blowing and in what direction, one offers me an option to link to another device, and another gives me a list of stats about my body: my pulse, weight, blood pressure, height.

A girl sitting next to me shows me how to customize the Quil's display when it's in watch mode. I can remove something, like my bunkhouse assignment, or I can add something, like the schedule for the day or someone's number. I do both of these, assigning Lila's information to my favorites, since hers is the only number I know. When I'm done, I put the Quil back on my wrist and flip to the abbreviated schedule, set in English. It tells me another battle is at two o'clock, and I count down the time, tapping my foot and trying not to think about decortication.

Shortly before two, the ball players finally pack up their game, and we head to the Aerie. We grab jackets and masks from the bins and find seats as close to the front as we can get. Soon the gong rings, and when the contestants enter the field below us, I lean forward, eager for the distraction.

"*Kauna 1*" begins, and a thrill runs through my chest as the contestants zoom around the arena. I try to see what they see, to find the wind currents, imagining I know which ones will be stable, which ones will take me in the direction I want. I see myself leaping from one to another, soaring beside the other players, dodging bullets, firing my own. Flipping and spinning and wheeling. And then I imagine leaving the Aerie altogether. Gliding with the birds above the trees, free from all dangers and fears.

I lean back in my seat, feeling the sun on my face through the mask, and realize the pounding in my head has faded. *See? I just needed to relax.* Even if they did catch a spy a long time ago, I don't have to worry about it because, for one thing, I'm not a spy and, for another, they're not going to catch me. So far, everything has been going perfectly, far better than I had hoped. I survived the *kiipooyaq* contest, and tomorrow I'll run a race. Easy enough. The rest of the week, I'll continue to hide out from the cops, eat good food, and, best of all, watch the windwalking. There's nothing to worry about.

I turn my attention back to the battle as the first round ends and two-thirds of the players leave the field. Looking at the scoreboard, I do a double take when I see a familiar face on the blue team. It's Diva.

Then the obstacles rise out of the floor—in different places than last time—the fans turn on, and the teams plan their attacks. As the battle begins again, I glance at Lila. She's pulled her Quil off her wrist and is studying the screen.

"What are you looking at?" I ask.

"I know someone down there. I'm tracking her score." Lila whistles. "Oh man, she just caught some sweet surf."

Just then a blue player zooms in front of us. A second later, a member of the red team pelts him directly on the circle on his back, sending him flying into the netting. The tightly woven mesh springs him back into the arena, and he lands face up on the mats.

Lila cups her hands together. "*Taitai!*" she yells, laughing. "Watch your back!"

Taitai, I repeat as I look at the blue player struggling to get back on his feet. I think I'm beginning to understand what the expression means, where it comes from. It's not just "good luck" or "take care." It's more like "good luck taking care." A cynical kind of well-wishing.

The round ends, and I look at the screen. Diva is still in. "Someone tell me how that's possible," I mutter.

Lila leans toward me. "I'm so nervous!" she says. "I can't believe I'm going to be down there tomorrow."

I wrinkle my brow as I turn to look at her. I didn't know she would be fighting in the arena. "You'll do great," I say.

"Probably not as well as you will. The way you threw the *kiipooyaq* this morning, I know you'll be awesome." I stare at her as she keeps talking. "I wonder who will be fighting with me. You haven't met anyone with a number between one-twenty and one-eighty, have you?"

I'm glad I'm wearing the mask. It hides my creased forehead, the sweat on my hairline. When I don't answer, Lila points to her Quil, and then I get it.

"No, I haven't," I manage to gasp.

Our numbers. Naira said there were approximately three hundred trainees, and there are five days of testing ... that's sixty people in the arena each day. I recall how Lila said my number was bad, and now I know why: it puts me in the very last group. I fight on Day Five.

Quickly, I take off my Quil and open the schedule of events, search for my number. It pulls up the two pages with the *kiipooyaq* contest and foot race. Hand shaking, I slide my finger across the screen. A third page appears. There it is.

Day 5. 2:00. Aerie Challenge.

I lower the Quil. *This is bad. Very bad.* I'm not going to be able to pull this off. I can't even get out on purpose, like I did when we'd play dodge ball at school. You aren't eliminated automatically in the first round. I'll be the only one standing on the arena floor, and then everyone will know that I don't belong here, that I'm an imposter. They'll think I'm a spy.

And then they'll peel my skin off.

No, no, no! Everything was going so well—I killed my goose. I'm going to run in their race. This isn't fair. I bounce my knee up and down, rub my fingers along my forehead, but I can't think of any solutions.

The gong sounds, and the contestants return to the air. They twirl and flip, launch themselves up, nosedive back down, but I'm not watching anymore. *What do I do? I need a plan.* I could try hiding again, but missing the Challenge would draw as much attention to myself as not being able to windwalk. I look out through the netting on the far side of the arena, at the endless stretch of trees and lakes, and then I know my only option. I'm going to have to run away.

The clouds cover the sun, and the white jackets of the spectators around me turn ashen. I can hardly bear to watch the contestants now. Each drop and lunge makes my chest tighten. Fortunately, the battle ends quickly.

Diva earns eighth place, and it's another boy who wins first. He wasn't quite as dazzling as Rye, but he does score one hundred and thirty points. I don't pay much attention until he removes his helmet, and I recognize the thick neck and stern eyes. It's Titan.

"He was in my van," I mumble.

"Really?" Lila asks. "What's his name?"

"Ti—I mean, I don't know."

"He's cute," Lila says. "Do you know if he's single?"

"No idea."

"I wonder how he'll match up with Rye," she muses.

"What do you mean?" I ask.

"You know, when all the winners fight in front of the tribe. For the title of *Tookapuna.*"

"Of course," I mutter. Well, I certainly won't be there to see it. I slide my lips back and forth under my teeth, jab my fingernails into my palms. *Concentrate. What do I need in order to get away from here?* Camping gear—I won't survive long without some basic supplies. I'll have to figure out where to find them.

As we leave the Aerie, I look back into the field, at the obstacles sinking into the floor and the weapons littered across the mats. The billboard is turned off now, its blank surface glinting dully in the sun. I drop my facemask and jacket in a bin and walk out the door.

Lila and I are shuffling along with the rest of the crowd when a single gesture in the horde of people grabs my attention. The quick swipe of a tiny hand to brush back fine, honey blonde bangs. Charity.

"I'll be right back," I say as I push my way through the mob. I almost call out to her but then remember I don't know her real name. "Excuse me," I say, squeezing past the people in front of me. "I need to get through."

But I'm too late. When I get to the bridge, I catch a glimpse of her feathery hair more than halfway across it. I won't be able to catch up. Instead, I wait for Lila.

"See someone you know?" Lila asks.

"Yeah, but I couldn't get her attention," I say.

"Oh well, I'm sure you'll see her later."

"Probably." I watch Charity's head melt into the throng, not sure why I'm feeling so disappointed.

Lila and I use the rope ladder to get to the ground so we don't have to fight the crowds crossing the bridge, and I ask her what she plans to do for the rest of the afternoon.

"I'm going to go down to the course," she says. "I need to practice for my race. What are you going to do?"

"I think I'll go practice too," I lie.

"Wanna meet at the *wakemo* before dinner?"

"Sure."

As she tromps off through the pine needles, I turn and walk in the opposite direction, toward the bay.

It doesn't take me long to reach the kayaks. Hundreds of them are stacked along the beach. *Probably three hundred and three*, I think. *If they found all the stragglers.* No one will notice if one is missing.

I walk toward the watercraft to make sure they aren't tied down, sinking to a crouch to investigate the kayaks on the first stand. No ropes, no chains, no locks. Free for the taking.

But there is one setback: I don't see any paddles. I traipse further along the shore, wondering if they might be at the far end, but there's nothing. I scramble back up the beach and stride toward the *wakenu*. I only know one place to look.

I climb the spiral staircase and enter the first level of the meetinghouse. The hallway is empty. As I walk toward the doors by the table, I hear my pulse in my ears.

I pause briefly at the first door. In the center of the steel panel is a porthole window, and I peek inside at what must be the kitchen. Several people mill around large stoves, preparing dinner. I won't find what I'm looking for in there.

I move to the second room, the one where I saw the paintball guns. A plaque on the door reads, "Staff Only." I turn the knob and step inside.

7

The room is large—a storage area, like I thought. Shelving units run along the walls and down the middle of the floor, creating several aisles. Some of the shelves are built into the tree trunks that support the building. On them are piled heaps of equipment, mostly materials for the contests: spears, tomahawks, axes, knives, *kiipooyaqs*, rope.

I see buckets of paintballs but no guns, which means I need to be quick. The staff could bring them back from the arena at any moment. I walk swiftly up and down the aisles, but I can't find any kayak paddles or camping gear. I turn a corner, and there, in front of me, are the backpacks.

"Yes!" I whisper. But a look inside one makes me curse. They're empty. "The gear must be around here somewhere," I mutter.

I try another aisle and find several big steel containers, but the doors are bolted and there's no way to open them, not without a key. I turn down the center walkway, the only area I haven't checked yet. As I pass the really large tree trunk, the one that bears most of the building's weight, I see something that makes me stop. In the center of the trunk is a door. And it's ajar.

A sign on the door says, "Restricted Access." Built into the frame is a scanner, probably to read people's Quils. I peer through the crack, hoping to find a closet of camping supplies, but instead I find another spiral staircase, leading down inside the trunk. I frown. The interior of the trunk is plated with steel. I tap the bole with my fist, and a dull clang answers me. This isn't a tree at all. It's a steel pylon made to look like a tree.

Where do these stairs go? My guess is somewhere underground, perhaps to another storage area.

Holding my breath, I open the door all the way and place my foot on the first step. But then I hear voices echoing inside the steel trunk, ascending the stairs, and I turn back and scamper toward the storage room entrance. I can't let them see me. I burst across the threshold … and run headlong into Jeremy.

"Whoa!" he says, grabbing me by the arms. "What's going on here?"

"Hi," I say, breathlessly. "I was, uh, just looking for you."

He lifts an eyebrow. "Really."

"Or any counselor."

"Why?"

I think quickly. "I lost my toothbrush. I need another one."

"Lost your toothbrush. I see. How did you do that?"

My throat is dry. "I left it in the bathroom by accident. When I went back, it wasn't there."

"Okay, tell you what. You go back to your *wakemo*, and I'll bring you a new toothbrush."

"Thanks." I try to smile but can't quite do it. "Or I could come with you."

He leans toward me. "I'll bring it to you."

By now, the people are entering the storage room, so I nod and back away from the door. As I walk across the hallway, I have to force myself not to run.

That was close, I think as I climb the stairs and enter the dining area. I'll have to be careful. Jeremy will be wary from now on, if he wasn't already. Unfortunately, I'm no nearer now to forming an escape plan than I was this morning. If I could just see where those stairs go …

I don't see Diva until she's right in front of me. I stop short. Dum and Gander join her, and all three block my path.

"Please tell me you've showered today," Diva says. Her hair is smooth and shiny, despite the fact that she just competed in the arena.

"I see your straightener made it with you," I counter. I try to step around them, but Dum moves to prevent me. "Did you find a use for that ruler?" I ask.

His face flushes, and he folds his arms. I keep my own face calm, but my whole body is tensed to run. My only comfort is that we're in the dining hall with other people. They won't try anything here.

"You better watch your back," Diva hisses, as she pushes past me. There's no way she meant that to be friendly.

"*Koka*," I call cheerfully, mimicking Lila. Diva glowers at me over her shoulder then tromps off, Dum and Gander in tow. I turn away and release my breath, shooting air up along my nose and forehead. Just one more reason I need to get out of here.

I spend the next hour walking around the camp, running escape plans through my head. Since I can't survive in the wild without supplies, I keep coming back to the door with the stairs. That *must* be where they store the camping equipment—there's nowhere else it could be. I finally decide that I'll investigate during the battle tomorrow when everyone will be at the Aerie. In the meantime, I should start sneaking food out of the dining hall.

I return to the bunkhouse to wait for Lila. When I get to my bed, I push aside the pile of junk that's accumulated on the blankets, and as I shove it onto the shelves, something crinkles beneath a shirt. I lift the shirt up and discover the paper with the rules, the one I was reading my first day here. I pick it up and scan its contents, blinking when I see rule number six: "Windwalking outside of a competition is prohibited." How did I miss that?

No windwalking, no fires, and no noise at night. That's three strikes against the dance. No wonder Naira was upset.

Thinking about Naira's announcement makes me think about decortication, and I quickly toss the paper onto the rest of the stuff. Then I pull the *kiipooyaq* medal out of my pocket and clear a space on one of the shelves. I look at the shiny gold surface, amazed at how I managed to get through that event. If only it could be enough.

Lila shows up a few minutes later, sweaty from practicing. She showers, and then we walk together to the *wakenu*. I consider asking her if she knows about the door in the storage room, but I don't. If she doesn't know, she'll just ask how I do.

We get to the dining hall a little early, in time to see the buffet tables rise up through the floor on a type of elevator. It looks like the main course tonight is turkey. I add stuffing and green beans to my plate before finding a seat with Lila. The meat is good. Rich and gamey. Much better than the birds we eat every year at Thanksgiving. I spear another piece with my fork.

"Thanks for dinner," Lila teases.

"What do you mean?"

"Well, you killed one of these," she says.

I lower my fork then glance over at the buffet tables, counting ten birds. She's right. "Cooked my goose," I mutter. How fitting.

"What?" she asks.

"Nothing—just talking to myself." I ask how her practice went. While she answers, I surreptitiously look for Rye, but I don't see him.

After dinner, Lila goes to play more volleyball, and I return to the bunkhouse. I pause before going inside and lean against one of the railings on the deck. It's a beautiful evening, the sky just getting ready to slip into its gown of amber and vermillion. Too bad I can't enjoy it.

If I can't find the camping gear, I won't be able to leave. I'll have to come up with a back-up plan. Could I force myself to get sick? Maybe eat something bad? Could I break a bone, jump off this platform? Would it be worth it? I eye the ground twenty feet or so below me. No, even if I were that desperate, people would just want to know why I hadn't windwalked.

I'm going back to the getting sick idea when I hear the bridge sway as one of the girls returns to the bunkhouse. I raise my eyes to acknowledge her arrival then stand up taller. It's not one of my roommates. It's Jeremy. The setting sun outlines his strong shoulders.

"Hi," I say.

"Howdy." He stands next to me, leaning his elbow on the railing. "I brought you this." He holds up a toothbrush. "Thought you might need it before the dance tonight."

I roll my eyes and take it from him as he turns around and rests his forearms next to mine. We both watch the sun. "I heard about your win with the *kiipooyaq*," he says. "Congratulations."

"It was a lucky shot," I reply, telling the truth.

He shrugs. "How are your hands?"

I look at the bandages, wrinkled and stretched from the day's activities. "They're doing much better."

"I'm glad." He turns his gaze to me now, and I notice again how sharp his eyes are. He stares at me steadily, and I worry he might really be onto my plans to run away. I focus on making my face look innocent.

"You have a bruise on your head," he says.

"Yeah, I know."

The sun makes his light brown hair and gossamer whiskers glow gold. And his eyes ... his eyes, I can't figure out. It's the sun's fault probably. For a moment, they look blue-gray; then, a second later, they seem to be muted green or teal, less harsh, less experienced. *He's young*, I realize. Not much older than I am.

He leans close, and I jump when I register that his face is only inches from mine. "I'll be at the dance," he says, "to make sure you're on your best behavior." He thrums my nose with his finger and straightens back up.

"Great, you're going to ruin all my fun," I say, rubbing my nose. He laughs and walks back down the bridge, lifting an arm in farewell.

I shake my head, try to clear my mind, then look at the toothbrush. He got this from somewhere. I just have to find out where.

When Lila returns from her game, we get ready for the dance. She pins her hair up easily, and her brown curls cascade becomingly around her face. I brush my own hair out and stare hopelessly at the puffy tresses that greet me in the mirror. Then I sigh and start to pull my half-Afro back into a ponytail.

"Wait," Lila says. "Here, let me help you." She takes my hair between her deft fingers and plaits it slackly in a French braid along one side of my head and then twists the braid back up, working it into a loose up-do. She pulls strands out of the braid and wraps them around her fingers so that gentle curls hang around my cheeks and at the base of my neck.

"Done!" she pronounces, stepping back.

I look in the glass. "Whoa," I whisper. Somehow, my nose looks less prominent, my neck more supple, my jaw softer. "How did you do that?"

"Years of practice," she says. "I have five sisters, and we're always doing each other's hair."

"I have one sister, and I've never done hers." I think of Maisy, her silky brown pigtails, and I splash some water on my face. "Ready to go?" I ask as I dry myself off with my towel.

We walk toward the meetinghouse. Along the way, we run into Holly. "It's going to be so boring," she complains. "No riding! And counselors everywhere. Probably none of the cute guys will even show up."

"So why are we going?" I ask. I notice her hair has been done up too.

"Well, there might be one or two," she admits. "It's worth checking."

I wonder briefly if Rye will be at the dance but then shrug off the thought. What will it matter if he is? He's got a girlfriend, and soon I'll be leaving.

When we enter the glass tunnel, we hear the music. Not contemporary pop, like they play at school dances. Drumming, like we had last night, but even more frenzied and up-tempo, if such a thing is possible. Lila does a little spin, and Holly whoops and sways her hips.

All of the furniture in the dining hall has been pushed against the walls, and a single buffet table stands at the back of the room, laden with cookies and other refreshments. Five counselors sit near the front, playing the drums, their accustomed hands flying across the taut leather. The steel screens have been pulled down over the windows, and the only light comes from the globe fireplaces, now placed around the sides of the room. For an indoor dance, it looks a lot like the outdoor one last night.

The hall is already crowded, with more people streaming in behind us, and everyone is dancing. No clumps of girls giggling nervously on the sidelines. No one waiting for an invitation. All of the initiates whirl and sway in time with the drums. The dancing isn't as gritty as it was the night before, but it's just as invigorating.

Lila and Holly plunge into the throng. I want to join them, to feel the drumbeat, but I don't know how to dance like that, even if it is on the ground. So instead of dancing, I move to the edge of the room.

The dancers twirl and leap. Their glistening bodies surge together, and their legs thump with the drums. As I move along the wall, I see Rye. He's dancing close to a girl, hands on her hips. Then he spins her away and turns to meet a different girl. He pulls her in then wheels her back out before grabbing yet another partner. I can see his grin, his white teeth.

Just then the drums cease their frenzy. A single drummer takes up a soft, rhythmic beat, and one of the musicians reaches for a flute. She plays a slow, stirring melody, and the dancing changes. The initiates merge into gently twirling couples, their swelling chests easing back to a normal rise and fall.

I turn to face the crowd, and I notice Rye again. He's not dancing with anyone. Instead, he's looking straight at me. And he's walking in my direction. I look down at the floor as my pulse flickers through my veins. Is he really going to ask me to dance?

"Excuse me."

I look up, heart fluttering. But the words came from behind me. I turn around—and see Jeremy.

"Hi," I say, trying to hide the strain in my voice. I glance over my shoulder to see if Rye's still there. He's stopped walking and is watching us. *Go away, Jeremy!*

Instead, he asks, "Would you like to dance?"

I search frantically for an excuse. "Are counselors allowed to dance with the initiates?"

He grabs my hand. "Why not?" As he leads me onto the floor, I watch Rye head toward a brunette. I try not to glare at my counselor, but I'm not sure how well I succeed.

We step among the couples and into a deluge of heat. The sweat glands in my armpits prick, and I haven't even started dancing yet. Jeremy takes my arms and places them around his neck while his own hands slide around my waist. Then he leads me in a rhythmic forward and back step, nothing at all like the confined, monotonous swaying I experienced at school dances. He spins me gracefully to the right then to the left before bringing me in close and looping my arm back over his head. I have no idea where to place my feet, but he steers me effortlessly through the complex moves.

When he brings me in from another spin, I catch a whiff of a crisp scent on his neck. Lemongrass. I look at his face. The bandana around his disheveled hair doesn't quite keep the perspiration from dripping down his cheeks, and his skin glows a pale pink. His light facial hair hides the mole above his lip. The color of his eyes still eludes me, though. They're even harder to see in here, where they reflect the carmine flames.

"Something wrong?" he asks, and I realize I've been staring.

"No," I stammer. "It's just that you're such a good dancer."

"And you're surprised?"

"I guess."

He wheels me around then places a hand firmly on the small of my back. "I have an important question to ask you."

"Okay … " Something in his tone makes my stomach quiver. Or maybe it's just the way he's standing so close.

He tips his face toward mine and says in a serious voice, "Did you use the toothbrush?"

I stick out my tongue. "Yes."

"That's a relief." He spins me back out. "I don't like dancing with people who have bad breath."

"Good thing you're not dancing with yourself," I retort.

"Your hair looks nice," he says.

"Thank you."

"Much better than it usually does."

"Gee, thanks." I scowl at him then notice that the corners of his mouth are twitching.

"You're too easy to tease," he declares. "Probably because you're so serious all the time."

"I am not!"

"Trust me. You are. You need to lighten up, learn to have some fun, take a joke. Remember how you tried to stab me with a switchblade?"

"You said you were going to kill me!"

"Yeah, but you had to know I was kidding."

"Well, I didn't," I mumble.

"Because you're too serious," he says, lowering his face so his eyes are level with mine. I look away, and we dance for a few moments in silence.

He's the first to speak again. "So, are you scared?" he asks.

"About what?"

"Running."

"What?" I stumble forward, and he catches me.

"Careful," he says gently.

He continues to hold me as I look up at him. "I'm confused," I say at last.

"Your race tomorrow." He crooks his eyebrow. "Are you nervous?"

"Oh." My heart beats normally again. "A little."

"You'll do great. I'll come watch you." Could that be a threat, a warning that he'll be following my every move? I realize he's still holding me closely, that we're not dancing anymore. His sharp eyes drill into mine, and, somehow, I find it impossible to look away.

The song ends. There's a lingering second of stillness—of Jeremy's slight panting, of his lemongrass skin, of his ever-changing eyes—and then the music returns to a faster tempo.

"Thanks for the dance," he says. He leans forward and whispers in my ear, so close his lips brush my cheek. "Don't let me down, kid." After that, he slips away and melts into the crowd.

I'm still standing right where he left me when Lila bounds over to my side. "Who was that?" she asks, nudging me with her shoulder. "He was hot!"

Hot? I'd never thought of Jeremy as hot, just officious and aggravating. But for some reason I can't stop thinking about the pressure of his hand on my back or his breath against my cheek.

"One of my counselors," I tell her.

"Ooh, that's lucky. That means you're from the same area, so you can see him when you go home."

Only it doesn't, because I won't be going back to Winnipeg. I ignore the sudden pinch in my chest.

Someone asks Lila to dance. They walk toward the middle of the floor, and she widens her eyes at me over her shoulder. Then they're swallowed by the sweaty mass of whirling bodies. I look around for Rye. He's dancing with a blonde girl, closely too.

As I turn around, I see someone else I know: Diva. She narrows her eyes and mouths something, but the dancers spin between us before I can make it out.

The fiery dancers, the pulsing heat, Diva's glower, Jeremy's eyes, it all beats down on me to the frenzied cadence of the drums. I push through the crowd and escape into the glass tunnel. As soon as I get to the deck and the cool air, I climb down to the forest floor, and, on a whim, remove my shoes, walking barefoot through the soft dirt.

After several minutes, I find a log and sit down. I can faintly hear the drums back at the meetinghouse, but more immediately present are the calls of the birds and the buzzing of the flies.

Don't let me down, Jeremy said. What is that supposed to mean? Is he betting on me again? Or does he suspect I'm going to leave? Maybe neither. It probably has something to do with Aura. He thought she didn't want to come to the camp. But what would she have done that would have disappointed him?

It doesn't matter what Aura would have done. I still don't have a plan. I'll be thrown into the Aerie where I won't be able to windwalk, and then Jeremy will know what it is to be let down.

I rub my head, but the smell of the lemongrass stays with me. I'm too serious, he says. If only he knew.

I run my hands through my hair, and my fingers get caught in the braid. I drop my hand. I guess I did look good tonight, like Jeremy said. After all, wasn't Rye going to ask me to dance? If Jeremy hadn't been there, it might have been my body pressing close to his, instead of that other girl's—but only because Lila worked her magic on my hair. He never would have noticed me otherwise.

Lila. I've known her scarcely three days, but I feel like it's been much longer than that. What made her want to be my friend? I'm not talented or interesting, and I've never had a friend who was so pretty or popular. Actually, I've never really had friends at all, not that I ever wanted any. The kids at school were nice enough when my parents died; I just didn't want to talk to anyone, and, eventually, people got used to the fact that I never spoke, so they stopped trying to make me. Instead, they invented another game—who can make Kit cry?

I kick the log with my heel. No one ever could, and then they started calling me a freak, a robot. And when you stay in the same school with the same people your whole life, there's no changing your reputation.

I get up and keep walking. Jack and Maisy didn't have the same problem. They were too young when it happened, and they don't even remember our parents. By the time they went to school, they were just like the other children, and I think people forgot they weren't actually Tom and Sue's. They looked like they could be Johnsons, with their light brown hair and blue eyes. But not me.

My gut feels hollow. Do they miss me? Maybe, but they'll get over it. Probably already have. They're happy where they are, and I never knew how to take care of them anyway. My plan to send them money seems like a distant dream, but soon enough I'll be back on-track. Far away from all this.

I pause halfway up the rope ladder and survey the starlit forest and softly glowing bunkhouses. Catch the sighing of the trees in the pine-drenched wind. If I were completely honest … but no, there isn't any point in indulging idle fantasies. I climb the rest of the way up.

In the bathroom, I undo the braid and brush out my hair, clean my teeth, wash my face, and then walk back up the ramp. As I climb into bed, I try to forget about running away, leave it for the morning. Instead, my mind drifts to Diva. I remember she was mouthing something at me across the room. What was it?

I'm almost asleep when I figure it out. My eyes fly open, and I sit up. Diva knows I'm not Aura.

8

Poser. That's what she called me. I can see it now, every detail of her glare, the shape of her mouth as she formed the "p" and "o" sounds and then the final syllable.

How much time do I have—how long before she turns me in? Has she *already* turned me in? Are they on their way to get me right now, to chain me up in front of the entire camp and cut off my fingers, shred my skin? *I need to leave immediately!*

I jump out of bed, snap my head back and forth, try to decide what to do. *Get dressed, leave the bunkhouse, walk as far and as fast as I can.*

In the dark? With no compass? No food? *I don't have a choice. It's that or stay and be tortured.* I frantically pull on some pants, but then I pause as another thought strikes me: maybe I misread Diva's lips. It was dark. She was far away. She could have said something entirely different.

I stand uncertainly beside my bunk, a shirt in one hand. Then I look out the nearest window at the black sky. Walking into the forest unprepared would be suicide. If I stay here, at least there's the chance that I'm wrong about Diva. Slowly, I pull off the khakis and climb back into bed.

But it's impossible to fall asleep now, and I toss and turn as I try unsuccessfully to push her out of my mind. An hour or two goes by, and gradually I hear other girls returning to the bunkhouse. More time passes, maybe another hour, before Lila sticks her head around the bend.

"There you are!" she exclaims. "Where did you go?"

"I had a headache, so I came back early."

"That's too bad. The dance was actually pretty cool." She leans against the wall and intently examines her nails, clears her throat. "So, you know that guy from your van?"

Titan? "Yeah … "

A sly grin tugs on her lips. "He's a good kisser." She laughs at my expression then declares, "Well, better go to bed. Got my race tomorrow." She disappears down the pole, leaving me to a long, restless night alone with my thoughts.

The morning finally comes, and Lila and I drag ourselves to breakfast, neither of us eating anything. Lila obsessively recounts all the rules and strategies for her event while I struggle to listen. But as we head to the course and I take a seat on the stands, my stomach relaxes its self-mangling. No one's come to take me, which means I probably misunderstood. Diva must have said something else.

Either that, or she's just biding her time, hoping to make me sweat.

I tug hard on my ponytail. I can't think about this anymore. It's making me too jumpy, and I might slip up, give myself away. All I can do is stay alert and move forward with my plan.

I lower my hand to the bench, forcing myself not to tap my fingers against the metal. The *Kohenrehi* track—a big loop built into the forest—is directly below me. But unlike the track I ran on at school, the starting line is not on the ground. It's on a raised platform.

From what I recall from Lila's explanation, the contestants begin on the platform and go around the loop three times. Each time, the course changes. Placed along the route are electronic signs displaying large arrows, and the racers go in the direction the arrows point— up, down, right, left—dodging whatever obstacles are in their way. Then, once the racers have passed the signs, the arrows change in preparation for the next lap. According to Lila, the trick is not just to go fast but also to pick the right air current. If you don't choose well, you could end up going backward or falling a bone-breaking distance.

I look at the racers. They're wearing helmets and kneepads, and I think I see mouth guards too. Among them are some faces I recognize: Gander, Bullseye, Dee, Buck … and Rye.

At the chirp of a whistle, the contestants take their marks, the counselor in charge sounds a gong, and the race begins. My stomach jumps as the initiates leap off the thirty-foot platform and soar toward the first arrow. It's pointing up.

Suddenly, the ground opens beneath the sign, revealing five giant fans. Rye is the first to dive into one of the vertical currents, and he shoots into the sky. Lila isn't far behind. Nor are Buck and Bullseye.

A broken tree trunk stretches across the course above them, blocking their path. The front racers somersault easily over it, but a girl in the middle of the pack rockets slightly to the right of the others and smacks into the thick bark. She hits her shoulder hard and tumbles out of the sky, crashing on the ground.

I look at her crumpled body lying in the dirt then over at the fans. And that's when I see that the humming metal circles are pointed in slightly different directions. *So that's what Lila meant about choosing the right current.* The racers have to look ahead, have to know which stream of wind will get them where they need to go. Otherwise they might smash into a tree.

The contestants keep moving, following the arrows that point them first one way and then another. They dodge pine trees, dip into ditches, twist to avoid tree stumps, and swerve through sprinkler systems, always looking for the right surf.

When the initiates speed around the turn, I look down at my Quil where their images appear on my screen, courtesy of cameras placed along the track. Lila's doing well. Rye is still ahead of her, and Buck, but she's in the top five.

Seconds later, they're back in view. Rye is a streak of beige as he bursts around the bend, swerving left, following the next arrow. Lila is right on his heels. They zoom across the platform.

On to lap two.

Suddenly, Lila catches a fast-moving current and shoots past Rye. But when the next arrow sends her into a stand of trees, her foot catches on a camouflaged net, and Rye and Buck zip past her again.

I see a glint of metal as Lila cuts herself free. In moments, she's rejoined the others. She's not a leader anymore, but she's still ahead of most of the group. And she's fast. She overtakes two people before getting to the next arrow.

I lean to the side in order to see as much as possible, watching as her curls vanish around the bend, but I lean too far, and my Quil slips off my lap and skids across the metal floor. I have to crawl past several people before I find it. When I pick it up, I discover the screen has gone dark. *I hope that's not a problem.*

I look up as the racers cross the platform and the final pass begins. Buck is the leader with Rye right behind him. Bullseye has the third spot. And fourth—it's Lila!

They're in the same positions as they disappear around the curve. The spectators are on their feet now, looking back and forth between their Quils and the track, waiting for the racers to come around the final bend. Since my Quil is still off, I stand up with them and strain to see through the trees.

They burst into view. Rye's taken the lead, Buck is in second, and Lila is in third, Bullseye not far behind. There's a sizeable gap between them and the rest of the contestants and only two more arrows before the finish line. The first one points up; the second, back to the finish platform. The four racers rise into the sky.

And then the fans turn off.

The crowd shouts as all four initiates plummet toward the ground. Rye and Buck find a natural breeze on their way down and stop falling ten feet above the earth. They whisk toward the finish.

But Bullseye and Lila keep dropping. Then Bullseye gets hold of a current, and as he scoots forward, he throws out a hand to grasp Lila's arm. It slows her fall, but her feet slam into the dirt, and she pulls him down with her. The two of them tumble onto the ground.

The fans turn back on, but now the other contestants are within striking range. Bullseye shoots Lila a glance and then leaps into the sky. She staggers after him.

Up ahead, Buck gets a burst of speed and crosses the finish line milliseconds before Rye. Bullseye follows a few seconds later, claiming the third spot. Lila takes fourth. The rest of the pack is just moments behind.

The racers soar over the platform and drop to the ground on the other side where they stand, doubled over, panting. I run down to the course with some of the other spectators.

"Are you okay?" I ask Lila.

She shows her teeth. "I'm fine. A few bruises, nothing bad."

"You did really well."

She shrugs. "Fourth's not terrible, I guess."

I look at Bullseye. His forehead is damp, his nose crimson. *I wonder why he helped her.*

I glance over to where Buck and Rye are leaning against a tree trunk, exchanging some winded banter. After a moment, they stand up and walk toward us.

"Nice racing," Rye says to Lila and Bullseye.

"Yeah, that was some crazy surf today," Buck adds. All of them shake hands.

Then Rye looks at me, his eyes scanning my face, and as he tips his head slightly to one side, my pulse speeds up. He opens his mouth to say something, but a whistle from the counselor cuts him off. It's time for the awards.

Lila stands to the side with the rest of the contestants—I see Gander and Dee again—while Buck, Rye, and Bullseye receive their medals. She smiles and applauds with the others.

"At least *that's* over," she says when she joins me afterward. "Now I just have the battle this afternoon, and I can finally relax. But it's almost time for your race."

Right. My race. "How do I turn this back on?" I ask, holding up my Quil.

"It's not off. It's just dormant." She taps the screen three times, and the eagle with the tomahawk reappears, along with the box for my thumbprint.

"Thanks," I say, selecting watch mode and slipping it back on my wrist.

We walk to the track. It's not far from the windwalking course, about halfway between it and the lake, and when we arrive, I'm only faintly surprised to see it's not paved. In fact, it looks almost the same as Lila's course, only with no arrows and no loop. We'll run straight through the forest to a designated spot and turn around. No lanes, no real path, just there and back.

I look at the other contestants and raise an eyebrow. All of them are girls. As I scan their faces, I catch sight of glossy blonde hair and my stomach clenches. Diva's lips twist into a scowl, and I glare back, curling my fingers into a fist as I imagine pulling out her perfect ponytail. But the queasiness remains. *Does she know?*

There's only one other person in the group I recognize, and that's Tornado.

"Watch your back," Lila winks at me before she goes to find a seat.

Great. I find a place in line that's as far away from Diva as I can get and start stretching. It's not a warm day, but I can feel the sweat dripping through my ponytail. *I'll hang back*, I decide, *finish somewhere in the middle.* That will keep the spotlight away.

A male counselor steps onto a platform, and as I turn to look at him, I notice someone in the crowd watching me. My face grows warm when I see the familiar pair of green eyes, and I jerk my own eyes back to the counselor. But the entire time he's speaking, I'm conscious only of Rye's gaze on my blushing cheeks.

"All right, girls," the counselor says, "looks like we're ready to start. Remember there's absolutely no windwalking allowed. You must stay on the ground at all times. Any questions?" No one says anything. "Okay, on my mark." He raises an arm. "Get set ... go!"

He brings his hand down, and I pound away at the dirt, forgetting all about my resolution to hold back. The first stretch is flat and clear, an easy distance to cover, and I whisk across the earth, vaulting quickly from the balls of my feet. A girl shoves her elbow into my side, trying to cut me off, but I push her back and hold my ground. *I guess this is what happens when there are no lanes.* As I run, I feel that heat in my blood, that drive to compete, and I have to admit that even if Rye weren't watching, I probably wouldn't have been able to make myself slow down.

Soon we enter the forest, and a log, about three feet off the ground, blocks our path. Most of the girls hurdle the obstacle effortlessly—Tornado, who is just ahead of me, somersaults over it—while I swerve slightly off-course to jump over the lowest part.

My small detour forces me to lose ground to two other racers, but I plot a diagonal course through the trees and cut them off again, shooting ahead. *Oh, it feels good to run.* My legs are pumping so quickly, I can't even feel the rocks underfoot. I pass one and then two girls. Dodge a branch. Leap over a bush. The rush is incredible. The forest scent fills my lungs. I could do this forever.

Whack! Something hard bashes into my lower back, and I stumble forward and crash onto the ground. Gasping for breath, I look up ... and see Diva. She sneers as she runs by me, a large staff in her hands. I lurch to my feet, muttering my strongest expletives.

But just as I've stood up, another girl rushes past and shoves me down hard. I fall back on the ground, stunned. Diva, I can understand, but what did I ever do to this girl? Sitting up cautiously, I gawk at the scene around me. All of the runners are hitting and smacking each other. Some of them have branches, like Diva. Others are using blunted tomahawks. A few are whirling what I hope are fake *kiipooyaqs*. And some are just throwing punches with their bare fists.

Where did they get weapons? No one had any of these at the starting line, I'm sure of it. I stand up and quickly survey the forest. Then, in the leaves above my head, I notice a bunch of red feathers hanging from a twig. I follow the feathers up and see a large wooden paddle resting in a branch, six inches above me.

A wild shriek makes me look back down. A girl has broken a stick off a tree and is charging toward me. Without stopping to think, I jump up and tug on the feathers. The paddle falls, and I grab it. I leap to the side and swing the paddle at my opponent as she turns to face me, catching her behind her knees. She goes down, and I take off.

I scan the trees ahead and get just a glimpse of Diva's bleached hair before she's gone too far for me to see. *Oh no you don't, sister.* I charge after her, but one look at the frenzy ahead makes me slow down. It'll take too long to force my way through.

Turning, I plunge into the trees to my left. No one said I *had* to go in a straight line. Under normal circumstances, this would probably cost me the race, but there's no way those girls will make better time than me with all their shrieking and slapping. Besides, at this point, I don't care about winning. My only goal is to take down Diva.

I circle back gradually, giving the wildcats a wide berth and catching up to a brunette just ahead of me. I'm moving to pass her when, all of a sudden, she wheels around and attacks me with a javelin. I jump back, barely blocking the blade with my paddle. She pulls it back to strike again, and I take a whack at her legs. She dodges my blow and jabs me in the shoulder. Swearing, I spring to the left and run harder. As I glance up, I see a huge tree in our path and jump even further to the left to avoid it. The girl moves to pursue me. She's taking aim, so she doesn't see the tree. *Bam!* She plows right into it.

I keep running as she slams onto her back. *Serves her right.* But now I know that I can't play nice if I want to catch Diva. So I push down the next girl before she sees me, and I shove another to the side, remembering to look behind me so I don't fall victim to my own tactics—to watch my back.

I feel like I'm running extra fast, and I wonder if it's because of the adrenaline pumping through my veins. But then I notice that my body is tilting slightly forward. The ground is steadily sloping down, which means it'll be an uphill climb on the way back.

Twenty feet in front of me, I see a thin, black podium sticking out of the ground. On top of the stand is a small screen. I run toward it and hold my Quil up to the monitor. After an electronic chime tells me my information has been recorded, I whirl around, ready to charge back.

And then I realize that I haven't seen Diva, that I didn't pass her on the way down. Whipping my head from side to side, I see a flash of blonde in the trees to the right. She's doing what I did—taking a detour to avoid the girls who will be stampeding down the hill.

I make a beeline for the trees. The diagonal approach helps with the hill. I hardly notice the incline. My foot slips on a rock, and I feel a throb in my ankle. But I don't stop. I can't lose Diva.

In moments, I'm barreling through the bushes after her. I can just make out the sheen of her hair, forty feet or so ahead. That's a lot of ground to cover, but I won't give up. I'm not going to let her beat me. I throw my paddle to the side. It's slowing me down.

I fly through the trees. I don't care about bushes or pine boughs; I smash through them. I don't feel the stab in my ankle or the burn in my chest, don't pause to pick up the staffs and tomahawks hidden in the trees. I don't even look behind me. The only thing I see is that blonde ponytail.

And then I'm only fifteen feet away. Ten. Five. She hears me coming and looks over her shoulder, and I almost stumble. It's not Diva. It's Tornado. I scan the forest past her. *There she is.* Maybe twenty feet ahead.

But what do I do about Tornado? I recall her viciousness in the Aerie. If I try to fight her, I won't stand a chance.

"Not. After. You," I pant, holding up my hands as she wheels to face me. "Her." I point at Diva. "Please … it's personal."

She studies me carefully, lowers the knife she's drawn. Then she nods. "I'll help." I don't have time to decide if she's tricking me or not, so I nod in turn and continue running. She keeps pace beside me. We bound over logs, slip between trees, and Diva grows steadily closer.

But I'm feeling the hill now. My thighs are blazing, my breath comes out in punctured gasps, and the back of my throat is like sandpaper. It's only the diminishing gap between me and my goal that keeps me going. Only a few more feet …

A punch on my arm makes me leap to the side, fists raised, but Tornado is just trying to get my attention. She holds up a length of rope and extends one of the ends to me, tilting her head toward Diva. I grasp my end tightly. I was right not to mess with her.

Tornado counts to three on her free hand. On three, we burst forward, running even faster than before. Diva looks over her shoulder, but it's too late. We catch the rope under her knees and flip her onto her back. She slams onto the ground and lies still.

"*Taitai!*" I yell as I run past.

I hand the rope back to Tornado. "Go ahead," I wheeze. I have no desire to compete with her, and she did me a good turn.

"Thanks," she huffs.

I fall back a few paces and let her take the lead. Then I glance back at Diva. She's still not moving.

I keep running, focusing on Tornado's swinging ponytail, feeling the deep, deep throbbing in my legs. The sweat dripping behind my knees, the fire in my lungs, the tension in my gut. It's suddenly too much, and I stagger forward.

But then we break out of the trees, and there's the stretch of flat ground and, beyond that, the finish line. I see the crowd standing up, cheering, and then I see why. There are only two girls in front of us, and they're not very far away.

Tornado switches into turbo and charges for the nearer of the two girls. I feel that familiar buzz in my blood. The end is so close.

A hard yank on my ponytail sends me shrieking backward. Pain squeezes my vision, and I skid onto my rear. When I open my eyes, the first thing I see is Diva's livid face. The next is her foot. I roll to the side, and she misses my head. I grab her leg with both hands and jerk it forward. She trips over me, sprawling in the dirt, but she kicks at me again and nails my stomach. I gasp, choking for breath, while she jumps up and darts after Tornado.

I scramble to my feet. Ahead, Tornado has immobilized her target and is racing toward the last girl—and the finish line. Diva is close behind. I charge after them, the wind buffeting my loose hair. When I'm about twenty yards away, Diva leaps for Tornado.

Tornado must have heard her, because she whirls around just before Diva knocks her to the ground. She keeps a firm grip on her opponent's hair, and the two of them tumble across the dirt.

Suddenly, Tornado yelps and releases her hold as Diva springs away from her and dashes toward the finish line, vying for second place. But Tornado jumps up a second later, sprinting hard, blood seeping from her arm.

I tear down the track behind them, the wind at my back urging me onward. The end is close. Fifteen yards. Ten. Suddenly, I hear shoes hammering the dirt, catch the sound of heavy breathing. I risk a look over my shoulder and see a girl behind me, raising a paddle. *My* paddle—I see the red feathers.

I spin to the side. She misses, and I hurtle forward. Now we're neck and neck. My thick, black hair blows into my face, blocking my vision, but I don't slow down or even brush it away. I must be five yards from the line, maybe less.

The roar from the spectators tells me it's over. I sweep my hair aside and discover I've crossed the finish. But so has the girl.

Panting hard, I look at a monitor where the rankings are displayed, sensors picking up the information from our Quils when we cross the line. I blink and stare at the numbers.

1. *194*
2. *88*
3. *36*
4. *273*

I nod. It's not a medal, but at least she didn't pass me.

Walking to the side of the track, I sink into a crouch, my heart pummeling the sides of my chest, my lungs heaving. That was by far the craziest race I've ever run.

I look back at the course. The girl who used to be in second place is limping across the finish—what did Tornado do to her?—and the other racers are finally emerging from the trees. Our detour really did pay off.

I glance around for Tornado and see her speaking with a medic. Her arm is still gushing blood, the skin torn right off her bicep. I puzzle over the strange shape of the injury, and then it dawns on me. Teeth marks. Diva must have bitten her. No wonder Tornado let her go.

Gradually, my pulse calms down, and I stand back up to watch the others finish the race. All of the girls look terrible. Welts, cuts, swollen eyes. *I probably don't look much better*, I realize as I touch the bruises on my back and shoulder, massage my ankle. At least I wasn't caught in the thick of it.

I notice that my shirt is not as sweat-stained as I thought I would be. The fabric must repel moisture. Too bad it can't do anything for my hair.

When all of the racers have returned, the counselor climbs back on the platform, and we line up. "It has come to my attention," he announces, "that there was some cheating on the course and that one of the contestants will have to be disqualified." I look down the line of battered girls and wonder what could possibly constitute cheating in a race like this.

"That makes our third place winner … number two hundred and seventy-three." I look up. Did he just call my number? Hesitantly, I walk toward the counselor and scan my Quil on the screen in his hand. It beeps in confirmation, and he places a medal around my neck. That means the cheater was one of the girls ahead of me.

As I take my spot on the small dais, he announces the next winner. "Second place goes to number thirty-six." Tornado walks forward to receive her prize, and I hold my breath. Who was it? Diva or one-ninety-four?

"And our *tooka* is … number one hundred and ninety-four."

While the girl comes up to receive her medal, I look for Diva. She's standing at the end of the line, little spasms running down her neck onto her shoulders. Her skin has turned a purplish color, and her eyes are spitting poison. I quickly shift my gaze.

We hold up our medals for the cheering crowd, and I see Lila, standing by Holly, hollering and clapping. My eyes continue to wander until they settle on the next familiar face: Jeremy. He's sitting beside Damon, applauding politely. The strange expression in his keen eyes makes my skin tingle.

The people in the bleachers are starting to leave, but as I turn away, my eyes lock onto the one person who's still sitting, and my pulse jumps. His elbows are on his knees, hands clasped together, and he's staring at me, just like he was at the beginning of the race. The wind brushes the chocolate hair back from his forehead. His green eyes don't blink. I glance to the side to check if he's actually looking at Tornado, but she's no longer there.

"Hooray!" Lila pounces me. "You got a medal."

I wince as she hits my sore shoulder. "Barely." I glance back at the bleachers, but he's slipped away into the crowd.

"I can't believe that girl cheated," Lila says.

"What happened?" I ask.

"I heard that she windwalked when she was back in the forest. Someone saw her and reported it."

That must be how she caught up so fast, after we knocked her down.

"She was off the course, so the cameras didn't catch it," Lila continues. "Oh man, *waerehi whawhai* is definitely one of the most exciting events. You were crazy with that paddle. And so fast."

"You mean you saw everything?" My face turns red. Of course, she did. She probably watched it on her Quil. *That means Jeremy saw everything too. And Rye.*

"Almost. Except for that part when the cameras couldn't find you. You're a wild woman, Kit."

"Terrific," I mutter. So much for a low profile. I avoid making eye contact with the people around us as we return to our *wakemo*.

Inside the treehouse, I shower and apply bandages to the scrapes on my arms and neck. *I guess they gave us these first aid kits for a reason.* My ankle is slightly swollen, but it doesn't seem to be too serious.

After we clean up, we walk to the meetinghouse for lunch. As I eat, I only half-listen to the conversation of Lila's friends around us. Mostly, I think about Diva and how she's got to loathe me now. *What will she do?* No one has accused me yet of pretending to be Aura, so I'm still hoping that means she doesn't really know the truth, but I can't be sure. And not being sure means there's still a chance, still a possibility they might … I shudder and cram my sandwich in my mouth.

Lila needs to be at the Aerie half an hour early to get ready for the battle, but I tell her I'm not done eating and I'll see her there. After she leaves, I casually grab two apples from the buffet table and munch on one as I find a seat at the far end of the dining hall. I look out of the large windows and try to think about my plan, about what I'll do when I get to the nearest city, but instead my thoughts keep drifting to the race. First to Diva. But then to Rye.

Why was he staring at me? I remember the way he almost said something after the windwalking race, remember how he was going to ask me to dance, remember his head popping out of the lake and spraying me with water. His grin, his bare chest, not an arm's length away.

And then for some reason, Jeremy's face replaces Rye's, and I see teal eyes instead of emerald ones. Feel his breath, his hands. Smell his lemongrass skin … I jerk my head back. Why am I thinking about Jeremy? I need to focus on getting out of here.

When the clock says five to two and everyone except the staff has left the dining hall, I toss out the apple core, stick the other apple in my pocket, and go down the stairs. The first level is empty, so I walk over to the storage room door and peek inside. The paintball guns are gone, and there's no one around.

Slipping inside the room, I make my way toward the backpacks, picking one up and creeping toward the door with the stairs. It's still propped open—does that mean someone's inside? I poke my head through the doorway and listen.

Nothing. It's now or never. I step onto the first stair, careful to ease the door behind me and rest the latch lightly against the frame. Dim lights illuminate the staircase just enough for me to see the steps in front of me. I slide my hand along the cool, steel walls as I wind around and down, pausing occasionally to listen. I walk for what must be several minutes—the battle will have started by now. I wish Lila luck, and then I wish some for myself.

At last I reach the bottom and, turning the corner, enter an enormous underground room with five small tunnels branching off the sides. The chamber itself is made entirely of cement, the walls, ceiling, floor, pylons, everything. To my right, U-shaped metal pipes stick out of the ground, adorned with shut-off valves and pressure gauges. A natural gas well. We had one like it in Williams. Some of the pipes continue up the wall and travel along the ceiling where they fan out and disappear down the various tunnels, probably carrying gas and water to the *wakemos*.

Like the storage room above, this room also has steel shelves stacked with supplies. I look at one of the racks nearest me and jump back. *Kava!* It's packed with guns, and they aren't the paintball guns that scared me the first day. They're real guns. M16s. There must be a hundred of them.

My knees are shaking and I have to squeeze my eyes shut for a moment, but then I brave another look. I pause, lean forward. The rifles are covered in a thick layer of dust. That means they haven't been used in months, years, maybe. I exhale slowly. *Focus so you don't screw this up.*

I look at the next shelf. It's heaped with toiletries and supplies for the bunkhouses, including the toothbrushes. *So Jeremy did get it down here after all.* Nice to finally be right about something.

I continue searching, and then I find what I'm looking for. The camping equipment—compasses, pocketknives, mess kits, water purifiers, sleeping bags—it's all here. Moving swiftly, I grab one of everything, including a bivy shelter, and shove the supplies into the pack along with my apple. Then I see the piles of freeze-dried meals and snatch up a handful of those too. The only thing I can't find is a kayak paddle. *Guess it will be a backpacking trip.* I take a few more dried meals.

Once I've filled my pack, I don't waste any time running back to the stairs. I've got to stash this away before anyone sees me. The jog up is hard on my tired thighs and feet, but I don't slow down. I can't believe my luck. I just hope it holds out.

It doesn't. When I reach the top of the stairs, the door is no longer propped open, and no matter how many times I turn the handle, it doesn't budge. I'm locked in.

9

I try the knob again. And again. It doesn't move. The sweat on my forehead increases, and I wipe at it with equally damp hands. What do I do? I could wait for someone to come back and open it, but then I'd be in trouble for sure. Unable to help myself, I think of the guns, of the Incident, and a tremor runs through my body. *There must be another way out.*

And then I remember the tunnels. I run back down the stairs, enter the cavern, and try to get my bearings. The staircase is on the south side of the *wakenu*. The five tunnels are in front of me, aimed north. I think about the layout of the camp, the five clusters of bunkhouses.

I grab a flashlight from one of the shelves and shine it down the fifth tunnel. If my theory is correct, the tunnel will lead to the easternmost cluster of bunkhouses, the one furthest from the Aerie. That's where I need to go if I don't want anyone to see me when I come out the other side. *If* I come out the other side.

I enter the passageway. The air is cool and dank, and pale lights are mounted every ten feet or so along the cement walls. They don't reveal much of the tunnel, so I'm glad I have my flashlight. The metal pipes run above my head, and I catch the faint smell of sulfur.

Before long, the shaft widens slightly and branches into four new tunnels. I frown. Three I can understand—they would lead to *wakemos* eighteen, nineteen, and twenty, which would put me below *wakemo* seventeen. But if there are four tunnels, maybe I've completely miscalculated. Maybe I'm not at a bunkhouse yet.

I look up at the ductwork, and the pressure in my chest ebbs. Some of the pipes above my head split off from the others and ascend a tube in the ceiling. More importantly, mounted on the wall next to the pipes are the steel rungs of a ladder. I wipe my forehead with my sleeve. It doesn't matter if I'm under a bunkhouse or not. I've found a way out.

I pull out my flashlight and shine it up the tube. It looks like the ladder continues for at least twenty-five feet, maybe more. I reach out and touch the closest rung. It's slick, so I take off my shoes and socks and stuff them in the backpack. The tread on my sneakers has long worn away, and I don't want to take any chances. I grasp a rung by my head with one hand, the torch still in the other.

As I'm placing my foot on the bottom rung, I hear something from the direction of the room. I hold my breath and listen. Voices. And they're coming my way. I turn off the flashlight and scramble up the ladder, smacking my injured ankle on one of the rungs. Pain shoots up my calf, but I keep climbing. The voices are getting closer.

I reach the ceiling, but I can't fit inside the tube—not with the backpack on my shoulders. The sweat moistens my palms again as I tuck the flashlight under my chin and shimmy out of the straps. Propping the bag between me and the ladder, I drop the flashlight inside the pouch. Then I swing the pack down with one hand so it hovers below my knees.

I've just gotten inside the tube when the voices grow much louder, accompanied by echoing footsteps. I pull the backpack up as high as I can so it doesn't hang through the ceiling. A small stream of sweat trickles down my elbow.

"Everything looks normal down here," one of the voices says. It belongs to a man.

"Where do you want to go next?" asks another voice, female this time.

"Let's take the cross tunnel to the next set."

"Sounds good."

The footsteps recede, and I allow myself to start breathing again. *That fourth tunnel must lead to another cluster of bunkhouses. A shortcut, instead of going all the way back to the main room.*

Suddenly, the Quil begins to flash on my wrist. Someone is calling me. I cover the screen with my hand and pray it doesn't make any noise.

"Hang on," I hear the man say. "I see something." The footsteps return, and my heart pumps blood ferociously through my veins.

"Look at this," he says. He's standing right below me. The sweat is pouring off my brow.

"What?" the woman asks.

"There's a leak in this pipe. We'll have to get Keith to come fix it."

"I'll let him know when we go back up."

And then they're walking away. I wait until I can no longer hear their footfalls, their voices, and then I gasp for air, lean my head back against the cement. My arms are shaking.

I give myself a moment to recover and then continue to scale the ladder. There's no light at all in the tube, and, before long, the faint glow from the tunnel disappears completely, blocked by the backpack. I continue to climb blindly for what seems like eons until I smack my head on a metal grate in the ceiling.

"Ouch!" I pull the backpack up, leaning it against my chest. I rub my head with my hand then raise my fingers cautiously toward the grating. After tracing the metal latticework for a moment, I push against it with my palm.

Nothing happens, so I press harder. And then, slowly, the grate begins to open. The metal grille groans as it swings upward, hinging back away from me. I give it a final shove, and it clangs against the floor. *I hope no one was around to hear that.*

Grabbing the backpack, I hoist it through the opening and toss it away from the hole. Then I reach my arms through and prop my elbows on the floor above me. More cement greets my skin, and I wonder where I am. It's warm and dark, and I can't see a thing. Pushing off the rungs with my feet, I press down with my arms and then my hands until I've lifted myself through the hole. My arms jiggle, but I manage to slide onto the floor. I rest there for a moment, catching my breath.

Suddenly, something hisses behind me. I jump forward, and my arm smacks a metal pipe. I hear more hissing. Now a gurgling sound. I touch the pipe carefully then draw back my hand. It's hot. I follow it gingerly with my fingers until I find a flat metal surface, the source of the noises. I'm inside a utility closet.

Ahead, I see the crack of light on the floor that tells me where the door is. Reaching into the darkness, I find the doorknob and swing the door open.

I'm in a bathroom. A boys' bathroom. If the urinals weren't there to give it away, that smell would. The stale odor of sweat. I listen carefully, but I don't hear anything. Hopefully, everyone is at the Aerie.

I turn around and lower the grate back onto the floor. The hinge is rusted terribly, which must be why it was so hard to open. Next to the grate are all the pipes—and the water heater and furnace. Grabbing my backpack, I shut the closet door behind me.

I put my socks and shoes back on and hold my nose as I tiptoe through the bathroom. I'm halfway across the floor when I hear a toilet flush. Stifling a yelp, I scuttle toward the door, run through the foyer, and burst out of the bunkhouse. I hurry down the rope ladder and slip beneath the *wakemo*, crouching behind one of the trunks. I wait, but no one pokes a head out of the treehouse to look for me.

I lean against the tree. No more dank tunnels or stuffy closets or pungent bathrooms. Just clean, fresh air.

My hair catches on the bark, and I turn around, tap the trunk with my fist. The surface feels like a real tree, but now I know it's not. All of the other bunkhouse trees must also be made of cement and steel, like that one in the *wakenu*. Probably the trees at the windrace course too, the ones that hid the bladeless fans. I look around the forest and wonder if any of the pines I see are actually real.

This whole place is man-made—you'd just never know it. Peering down at the ground, imagining I can see the tunnels below me, I think about how close I was to being caught, and a shudder zaps my shoulders. I push it from my mind and, rising to my feet, trek into the trees. The first thing I need to do is hide the backpack. After breakfast tomorrow, I'll retrieve it and make my escape. One day to spare.

I walk for a few minutes until I come to a large river. An enormous tree trunk stretches from one bank to the other, providing a convenient bridge. I tread cautiously across the slippery bark.

Not long after I've reached the other side, I find the perfect spot: a tree with a long, thick branch, hidden by the surrounding pines. It's an effort to scale it, but I finally succeed in hanging the backpack from the branch. Then I return to the ground and admire my work. Bears won't be able to get to it, and people won't be able to see it unless they walk right underneath the tree, which isn't likely with all these bushes and pines, and the river. I think it will do nicely.

Wiping the sap on my hands onto my pants, I turn around and head back across the bridge. I need to get to the Aerie—I promised Lila I would watch her. For the first time, it occurs to me that I'll never see her again, that'll she'll never know why I ran away or what happened to me.

I could leave her a message on her Quil. And say what? That I was impersonating a dead girl and had to leave before Naira found out and tortured me? No. It will be better for both of us if I just disappear.

I hear the screaming crowd long before I reach the stadium. That's good. It means they're still fighting. I climb up the ladder and enter the double doors. The bins with the padded jackets and facemasks are in their usual place, but there's no counselor. He or she is probably watching the match. I put on a jacket, grab a mask, and walk down the hall.

When I reach the spot where the hall opens into the arena, I see the counselor leaning against the wall, watching the flying paintballs from a safe distance. I hesitate. Will he ask me why I'm only just arriving? Maybe I should go back.

But it's too late; he's already heard me. The counselor turns his head, and I feel a surge of blood in my chest. It's Jeremy.

Oddly, a ruddy color spreads across his cheeks as well, but it disappears quickly. "You're late," he says.

I shrug. "I was asleep. My race made me tired."

He angles his head, piercing eyes taking in every detail of my appearance, and I'm suddenly conscious of my moist hairline, the sap on my face.

"Well, Sleeping Beauty," he says, "next time you might want to check a mirror before you leave the house. You skipped the Beauty part."

"And you skipped Charming," I say, my blood relaxing slightly.

"I'll take that as a compliment—as least I'm still a prince."

"Sure. Among thieves and paupers maybe."

"Don't mix your allusions," Jeremy scolds, but he's grinning. "By the way, you almost slept through the entire thing. We're on the third round now. Only eight people left."

I look past him into the arena. Eight paint-splattered contestants careen around the stadium, pelting each other with bullets. Lila's face is on the scoreboard. I pull on my mask and make my way to a seat on the second row where I see Holly waving at me.

"I tried calling you," she shouts as I sit down. *So that's who that was.*

"I was asleep," I yell back. It's a good thing the sound on my Quil was silenced.

In the arena, the contestants have divided into four pairs. Lila's current adversary is a stocky boy with broad shoulders. Lila reaches for a clip to reload her rifle, and so does Stocky. But his belt is empty. He looks at her, sees her prepare to load, and dives for her throat.

She fends him off, swinging her gun at his shoulder and pulling out a knife, but Stocky kicks the blade out of her grasp. When she tries to catch it, he stabs at her chest. The tip of his rifle catches the belt strung across her torso, and as he twists the gun, the belt breaks loose, tumbling to the arena floor below. Stocky leaps after it.

Lila isn't far behind. She dives beneath him, legs spread in a full split, and hammers his stomach with the butt of her rifle. He stumbles back. Moving swiftly, she grabs a clip from the belt lying on the ground and loads it into her gun. Still in the splits, she fires.

It's a kill.

A girl above has just dispatched her own opponent. She sees Lila and charges. Lila leaps to her feet, spraying the girl with paint, but none of the balls hits a circle. The girl raises her gun. Nothing. She's out of ammo too.

Suddenly, she hurls her weapon at Lila. Caught off guard, Lila totters back a step, and the girl zooms forward and snaps the rifle out of her hands. Defenseless, Lila jumps into the air, pivoting into a back aerial and landing on the ground near her knife. She throws it at her adversary just before the girl fires.

The knife swipes the circle over the girl's heart, but a ball from Lila's own gun splatters on her right thigh. They're both out.

I watch as my friend leaves the field, wondering how she learned to fight like that, how any of the initiates learned.

The battle ends not long after Lila's defeat, but her score puts her in seventh place. I find her after the brief ceremony.

"You were great," I tell her.

"Nah, my score sucked."

"You still did better than fifty-three other people. Plus, you had a race this morning. It wasn't fair of them to put you in two events on the same day."

She shrugs. "Well, in the real world, we don't always have the luxury of being well-rested, do we?"

What is that supposed to mean? I wonder.

We walk back to the bunkhouse. I look around at the camp—the artificial trees that blend in so perfectly with the rest of the forest, the nearly invisible meetinghouse, the swaying bridges. I think of the splendor of the matches in the arena, the power behind the windwalkers' movements, the way they coast elegantly through the air.

Tomorrow, it will all be a memory.

If only I were Aura for real. Then I wouldn't have to leave. I could finish out the week, fight in the Aerie. Dance with Rye. See Jeremy again. That last one brings me up short.

I keep walking. *Don't be a fool.* If I were Aura, I'd be dead.

We enter the bunkhouse and circle up the ramp. *I don't belong here, remember?* It's no use living in a dream world, because at some point I'll have to wake up. At some point, they'll catch me.

While Lila showers, I brush my hair and wash my face. I look so sullied it's a wonder Jeremy didn't press me any further than he did. I think about his face when he saw me in the Aerie, the color that spilled across his fair skin, the way he was studying me after my event. What was he thinking? Was he impressed? Disappointed? "Don't let me down," he said. Did I let him down? Will I?

Stop it! It doesn't matter. After tomorrow, I'll never see him again. I'll never see any of them again. But do I have to leave? Is there an option I haven't considered yet, an alternative? *Remember the Incident! Decortication! They'll torture me if they think I'm a spy.*

"Careful, Kit, don't drown yourself," Lila says behind me.

"What?" I look down at the sink. Apparently, I've been splashing water on my face. A lot of water.

"Are you okay?" she asks.

"Yeah, I'm fine. I'll be back in a little bit." Without saying anything else, I leave the bathroom, walk out of the bunkhouse, climb down to the forest floor. Trudging through the trees, I kick up twigs and pine needles, hurl the occasional stick. *Don't think about him, about windwalking. Just focus on the plan.*

I'm passing one of the bunkhouses when I hear voices, and as I look up, I slow my pace. Diva is standing on the platform. With her is Aponi.

"You have ten minutes to collect your things," Aponi says. "I'll be back to get you."

Aponi walks back along the bridge, and Diva turns to go inside. Then she stops and whirls on her heel. Her face blotches into a deep mahogany.

"You!" she spits. She leaps off the platform and flies through the air toward me. I stumble backward as she lands a mere foot away. "This is all your fault!"

"I didn't make you cheat," I insist, but I back up some more.

"You knocked me down," she hisses. "I was so close. Instead, you humiliated me in front of him."

"Who?" I back into a tree, and she brings her face an inch away from mine.

"You know who. You think you're so clever, pretending to be someone you're not."

My pulse thunders in my head. "I don't know what you're talking about."

"But I know what you really are. You're a fake."

I can't answer her. I can hardly breathe.

"You think your little act will impress him, when the truth is you don't know anything about being cool."

Being cool? I stare at her.

"So instead you have to embarrass the people who are. That's the only way you can get his attention."

"Seriously, what are you talking about?"

"You seemed to know just fine last night."

Last night? At the dance? I think about Diva's threat, her snarling eyes. Right after I danced with …

"Jeremy?"

"But you won't get him now. Not after going underground."

"What?" And then it comes together. "You were the one who shut the door!"

"That's right," she sneers. "And then I reported you. How did that feel?"

"There's no proof I was down there," I say, keeping my voice level.

She frowns. "What do you mean? Didn't they find you?"

"No one found me."

"That's impossible! How did you get out?"

146

She doesn't know about the tunnels, the utility closets. I smirk and take a step forward, forcing her back. Her face grows even darker as she realizes what this means, that she hasn't succeeded in shaming me at all, that she's only heaped further disgrace upon herself. Her eyes turn feral, bloodthirsty. She lunges for my hair.

I bat back her arms as she digs her fingers into my scalp. We fall to the ground, tumble across the dirt. I knee her in the chin, and her head snaps back. Then she elbows me in the stomach, the exact place she kicked me this morning. The breath leaves my body, and I curl up on my side, covering my head with my hands as she continues to strike with her fists.

"Stop!" The blows cease as someone pulls her off. I look up and see Damon pinning Diva's arms behind her back. Aponi is there too, and she crouches down next to me. "Are you okay?" she asks, extending a hand to help me up.

I stagger to my feet, cradling my gut. "Yeah." I look at Diva. Her face is almost black.

"You should go take care of those bruises," Aponi says to me. "Would you like me to come with you? There's a medical kit at the *wakenu.*"

"No, I'm fine."

As Damon and Aponi lead Diva away, I limp back through the woods. My shoulders are tight, scrunched up to my neck. I shake my arms, but I can't loosen the muscles, and the movement only makes me wince. I close my eyes, take deep breaths. Diva didn't know after all. No one is onto me, and I can escape as planned.

So why can't I relax?

It's because of him, isn't it? Jeremy. Diva was jealous of me. She thought he … *She thought he what? Liked me?* I stop walking. Does he like me?

I keep walking. No, that's ridiculous. Jeremy watches me to make sure I don't do anything I'm not supposed to. He's suspicious of me, at least, that's what I thought. I slow down. *Was I wrong about that too?*

147

A melodious jingling suddenly wafts through the forest, coming from my right. Grateful for the distraction, I wander toward it and in a few moments reach a clearing near the meetinghouse. Someone is hanging wind chimes from the branches of the aureolin Birch trees that surround the dell. The chimes are made of thin, iridescent pink shells, and as the breeze flows through them, it produces the dulcet music.

On one side of the clearing, four people are sitting on some folding chairs. It must be an event. I look at the schedule on my Quil—there it is. *Karikara.* There's no translation. I take a seat on the back row.

After about five minutes, a counselor stands up and begins the contest. There are only two participants, and they'll go one at a time. The first contestant gets up from her seat and walks into the clearing. She's wearing a shimmery coral dress that matches the shells on the chimes. In her hair are two black feathers. Additional pairs adorn each wrist and ankle.

The girl stands in the center of the glade, closes her eyes, and bows her head. For five long breaths, she stands still. Then, throwing her head back, she vaults into the sky and begins to dance. Not like the wild dancing by the campfire or at the *wakenu.* This dance is studied, formal.

The girl spins slowly in the air, stretching out her arms, wrapping them over her head, arching her back, twirling around the clearing— all to the honeyed peals of the chimes. There are no giant fans to provide the currents. She molds the dance to the wind that naturally exists, to the music it creates. It's like watching a rose petal pirouette in the breeze. For the duration of her dance, all I hear is the sweet pinging of the shells. All I see is the gossamer flower in the sky.

She ends with her arms thrown back over her head, the feathers on her hands joining the feathers on her feet, her toes coming to rest softly on the ground. Then she returns to her chair, and the other contestant takes her turn. The second dance is just as exquisite.

The event ends, ten minutes after it began. The first girl wins first place; the other girl gets second. There is no third.

My mind is revolving in a hundred directions as I leave the clearing to go to dinner. Everything about this place is so different, so baffling. I wish I had more time to figure these people out, to know what they know, but instead I'll just spend the rest of my life wondering. Wondering about their history, their secrets. Wondering about Jeremy. Wondering about what life might have been like if I had been born a windwalker.

When I approach the *wakenu*, I think about calling Lila to see if she wants to meet up but decide against it. No point in making things harder, and I don't feel like talking anyway.

At the salad bar, I take two extra packets of crackers and find a table in the corner of the dining hall. I slip the crackers in my pocket to add to my stash and eat my meal slowly, looking around the room, taking in the curve of the seats, the view of the sunset through the large windows.

After I've finished eating, I drop off my tray and leave the building, but it's too early to go to bed, so I pull up the schedule on my Quil. There's one more event for the day. A prayer ceremony, at the lake in half an hour. I was hoping my last event in the camp would be something a little more exciting, but I suppose this will have to do.

When I reach the lake, the sun has just dropped below the horizon, veiling the downy trees in soft pastels. The cornflower water is smooth and still, embraced in a lavender mist. I drink in the serenity and think again about the dancer and the wind chimes. I imagine that even now I can hear the soft clinking of the shells in the breeze.

"Beautiful, isn't it?"

I jump, whipping my head to the side. Jeremy is standing next to me, his arms crossed behind his back as he stares out across the water. "Makes you glad to be alive." He looks at me and smiles.

My heart beats faster. "Yeah," I say. "It's really pretty."

"I'm glad you finally showed up."

"What do you mean?"

"For the ceremony."

"Oh." I don't know what to say, and we stand there for a while in silence, regarding the lake. I peer at Jeremy from the corner of my eye. Could Diva be right? *Don't think about it.* I look back at the water.

When the shadows lengthen across the quiet ripples, we turn away and walk toward a group of tree stumps. Jeremy sits down next to me, and I try not to notice that our arms are touching.

One of the counselors gets up and recites something in Yakone. I act like I know what he's saying, but really my brain is drubbing against my skull. It's so hard to sit here and pretend, to be a poser, when all I want is for it to be real.

The counselor finishes and passes a bag around to the dozen or so people in attendance. When the bag gets to me, I reach inside and pull out a small handful of seeds, each one attached to a thin membranous wing. After everyone has taken some of the kernels, the counselor leads us to the edge of the darkening water.

"*Pualani ana.* May the cycle of life continue under the watchful eyes of First Parents," he says. Then he throws the seeds into the wind. The rest of us do the same.

I watch the small wings flutter and whirl as the breeze carries them away across the lake. I doubt any of them will actually turn into trees, but it's a nice gesture.

Next to me, Jeremy inhales deeply. "It's good to be reminded, you know? To take the time to remember what's really important."

I nod, wishing I knew what he was talking about.

When the seeds have vanished from sight, Jeremy walks me back to my bunkhouse. "Have a good night," he says. He waves at me and then fades into the trees.

I want to say something, make it last a little longer, but I don't. I just watch him walk away. Then I climb up the ladder.

Lila isn't inside the bunkhouse, but I still don't call her. Instead I clean myself up and get ready for bed. As I sink into my bunk, I feel the pressure of the mattress on my injuries, another good distraction—the graze on my head, the welt on my side, the scratches on my face, the cuts on my feet, the lumps on my back and shoulder, the bruises on my stomach. And that's not even counting my hands or my ankle. *But it was all worth it, just to see this place. Just to know.*

I don't cry as I close my eyes and rest my head against the pillow. I never cry.

The next morning, I get up early, take a good, long shower, and put on my windbreaker, making sure the switchblade is in my pocket. Luckily, the air has been growing cooler, so no one will think it's strange that I'm wearing a jacket.

I look at my medals for a moment but decide to leave them since they'll only weigh me down. Besides, I don't want to tip anyone off. If Lila saw they were missing, she might become curious. I bid a mental farewell to my sleeping friend, to my corner of the bunkhouse, to all of it, and slide down the pole for the last time.

As I walk to the *wakenu*, I breathe in deeply, soak up the crisp morning air. *It's a good day to begin a hiking trip.* I'll just eat a big breakfast and be on my way.

I enter the dining hall and pile a generous heaping of food on my plate. This is the last good meal I'm likely to have for several days, so I better make it count. I find an empty table and take a seat.

Not two minutes later, Holly plops her tray down next to mine. "Kit," she says, "You're not going to believe it! Some of the boys are having a free fall contest."

"Mm," I grunt, scooping some fried potatoes into my mouth.

"It's going to be at the lake. In fifteen minutes. Where's Lila?"

"Sleeping," I mumble around the food.

"Maybe I should call her. She'll be mad when she finds out she missed it."

"I have to miss it too," I say, swallowing.

"What! Why? You don't have another competition do you?"

"No, but a girl I know from home does. I told her I'd watch."

"What event?"

"It's the, um … " I search my brain. What events were listed today? "Drum making." I'm pretty sure that was one of them.

"Oh, you'll be fine then. Drum making isn't until eleven. The contest will be over long before that."

I frown. I can't think of any other excuses, and if I try too hard to get out of it, Holly will wonder why. *You win*, I sigh. I'll just have to leave after I watch the stupid contest. I hope it's quick.

After I finish eating, I walk with Holly down to the lake where a crowd of thirty or so has gathered along the shore, most of them girls. I notice there are no counselors.

Six boys are standing on the dock, and my stomach does a slight somersault when I see that familiar chocolate hair. Buck is there too, and he whistles to get everyone's attention.

"Let's start," he says. "You all know the rules. Hit the water, and you're out. Closest one to the lake wins. The prize is *tookakihi*."

A giggle sweeps through the crowd of girls. I peek at Rye, and my stomach jumps again. He's staring at me. I look away quickly.

"Okay," says Buck. "Take your marks. Then watch for my signal."

The five boys leap into the air, rising high above the lake. I watch them move back and forth, catching the right surf to travel higher and higher. They must be up at least five hundred feet—higher than even the tallest skyscraper in Winnipeg. I wonder briefly what will happen if Naira catches them, but my eyes are fixed on their shrinking bodies and the thought doesn't hold my attention for long.

At last, they stop moving and hover together in the clouds. Buck enters something on his Quil, and an instant later, the first contestant drops.

I choke back my yelp. The boy has his arms and legs spread wide as he plummets toward the earth at an alarming speed. I can't look away. In a matter of seconds, he's going to crash into the water. Now

152

I see why they're doing it above the lake. Landing on the ground could kill him. Heck, the water could kill him.

Suddenly, he stops falling. He grabs a current and rides it for a few yards before bobbing more or less in place, about the height of the nearest pine tree. Immediately, another boy drops. He stops a little closer to the water. Two-thirds of the way up the tree. Now the next boy falls. He catches the wind near the first.

It's down to Rye and one other person. I bite my tongue as I watch Rye drop past the other three. Then, not more than five feet above the water, he pulls up.

Now the final boy takes his turn. My eyes are glued to his plummeting body. He falls past the first and third boys … the second boy … Rye. When he's inches away from the surface, he grabs the wind. But his left arm keeps falling, hitting the water. He spins out of control and pitches into the lake, making Rye the winner.

All of the girls squeal as Rye grins and waves. The boys return to the dock, the last one wet and red-faced. They shake Rye's hand, and he pounds them on the back.

"Well done, lads," says Buck. "Rye, you may now claim your prize."

What is it? But I have a feeling I know, and I hold my breath as Rye looks into the crowd. His eyes roam thoughtfully over the eager girls, and he taps a finger against his chin. At last, however, his gaze settles on me. I inhale too quickly and choke on the air. *Don't cough,* I pray. *Not now.* Water beads up behind my eyes, and I know my face is turning maroon.

Rye steps down from the dock and walks toward me. The crowd parts slowly, each girl thinking he's coming for her, but his eyes never leave my face. *This can't be happening.*

When he's a foot away from me, he stops. "Will you oblige me?" he asks softly.

After a full ten seconds, I manage to whisper, "Okay."

He grins. Then he faces the horde of disappointed girls. "I would like to defer my reward until this evening." He turns back to me. "I'll come find you after dinner." He walks back to Buck and the other boys, leaving me glowing beet red. The other girls glare at me.

"Let's go," I say to Holly. Her eyes are wider than I've ever seen them, and for once she has nothing to say. After a few moments, however, she recovers from her speechlessness, and the entire walk back to the bunkhouse is filled with her continuous chatter.

We enter the *wakemo* and climb up the ramp—something I thought I'd never do again—and Holly shakes Lila awake. "Lila, you're not going to believe what happened! Rye chose Kit for his free fall prize."

"Huh?" Lila says groggily. Holly has to explain it to her three times before she understands.

"Rye's going to kiss Kit?" she asks as she rubs her eyes.

I close my eyes, wondering how this is happening. The cutest boy in the camp is going to kiss me. Only he won't, because after dinner, I won't be here. In my mind, I see Rye's eyes finding me in the crowd, hear him ask for my consent. Oh, why did he have to be so gorgeous?

"Kit?" Lila is asking me something.

"Sorry, what?"

"Are you okay?"

"I'm fine." But I know my face is pale.

"Don't worry," Holly says. "We can give you some kissing tips."

While Holly and Lila pummel me with friendly advice, I wage an inner war. Tomorrow I'll have to fight in the Aerie, and if I get talked into staying longer, they'll find out I can't windwalk. I'll be tortured as a spy. Tortured! No kiss is worth that. I've got to get out of here.

But he's so handsome, and I've never been kissed before. Maybe I could leave first thing in the morning, before breakfast. *No, something might come up. It's not worth the risk.* Or is it?

Before long, my head is throbbing.

Somehow I find myself being dragged to lunch. I pick at my food in a daze, struggling to make a decision. But delay is the easiest choice, and that's what I keep deciding. So when Lila and Holly set their course for the arena, I'm still in the camp, walking beside them. I know I should come up with an excuse to get away from them and leave, but I also know that they would quickly notice my absence. *Yes, that's right. If I were to leave today, before Rye kissed me, everyone would know I was missing.* Better to leave tonight, right after it happens.

I hope I know what I'm doing.

We don our masks and jackets and find seats. I'm grateful for the mask. It means people won't be whispering and pointing at me, like they were at lunch.

In the row in front of me, a little to my right, I notice unkempt hair sticking out from someone's mask. Light brown locks under a red bandana. Jeremy. I look away and hope he doesn't recognize me. For some reason, seeing him makes my chest hurt.

The battle begins with as much color and energy as usual. None of the contestants are particularly spectacular, however, not like Rye or Tornado or Lila, and I find myself preoccupied with my dilemma until, in the final round, a torrent of paint washes our section of the bleachers. I jerk back, flicking the clear liquid from my sleeves.

And then, directly in front of me, a boy in red takes his knife and slashes it across a girl's throat. The red paint oozes along her collar, and as the boy draws back his knife, black spots fuzz my vision. The girl's armor has been pummeled by paintballs from both teams, the blue and red pigments smearing together into a terrible purple hue, right under her neck. My seat tips, and the players shrink and twist away from me.

The acrylic smell on my hands. The knife. That ghastly color. Her gushing throat. I can't stand it.

"I'll be right back," I gasp. I rip off my mask and stumble past the spectators on our row, elbowing people on both sides of me. The smell is all over the stadium, inside my nose. It's like she's everywhere, suffocating me.

155

I reach the hallway that leads to the exit and collapse on the ground, clutch my legs, dig my face into my knees. *Get out!* I yell at the purple specter. *Get out!*

It's all coming back now. Her slumped body, twitching foot, stained wallet. The neon blue fingernails. Vanilla perfume. My feverish flight. Her face looking at me from her I.D. The face I've stolen. I'm here, being her. She was supposed to kill the goose, run the race, get Rye's kiss. Not me. I'm not her. I'm not—

"Aura?" someone says.

I shriek and smash my body against the wall. Two hands reach for my arms, and I slap at them blindly. But the hands are strong, and they press my arms down.

"Hey!" the voice commands. "Stop that. It's me!" I slowly raise my eyes.

"Jeremy." I fling myself at him.

"Hey now," he croons as he wraps one arm around me and strokes my hair with his other hand. "What's the matter?"

And that's when I decide I'm going to tell him everything. Jeremy won't let them torture me, not when he knows the full story. He'll make it right.

Only the words won't come out, just great, heaving gulps. He puts a finger over my mouth and rocks me gently, and I focus on the strength of his biceps, the way we're swaying back and forth, the faint citrus scent of his neck.

When I've finally calmed down, he brushes my hair behind my ears, and his fingers pause on my cheeks, the question on his lips.

The gong announces the end of the battle.

"Want to see who won?" he asks instead.

I nod, still not trusting myself to speak. We walk to the edge of the hall and look into the arena. Naira is standing on the platform with the winner, a girl this time. She places the medal around the girl's neck and bows.

Then she straightens back up. "Congratula—"A paintball splatters on her jacket, cutting her off mid-word.

The crowd gasps when they see the red blotch on Naira's chest. I gasp too, and then I frown. Something's wrong. I look down at the clear goop on my hands then back at Naira. She's not wearing any armor. That paint shouldn't have shown up.

Suddenly, Naira crumples onto the platform, the stream of red cascading down her body, and the spectators' gasps turn to screams. *That's not paint*, I realize. It's blood.

10

I don't have time to react—don't have time to think about Naira's dead body or her blood running down the quarter pipe—because as soon as she goes down, wild shouting overpowers the screams in the arena. I look up and see people dropping from the holes in the roof, their heads encased in helmets. They're dressed from the neck down in black leather, and the automatic rifles in their hands are not paintball guns. They dive into the Aerie and ride the wind around the stadium, training their weapons on the initiates standing in the field below and on the spectators in the stands.

And then everything explodes. The contestants in the arena vault into the air, some rushing over the bleachers to get to the exits, some trying to go over the net or through the roof, and some just hoping to dodge the deadly hailstorm. Few of them succeed. The bullets plow them down.

All around me, people are being blown out of their seats, off their feet as they run for the emergency exits. Some escape, bursting through the doors that lead to nothing but air, but as they ride the wind away from the Aerie, more assailants in black shoot them out of the sky. I stare at the bloodied faces and body parts and corpses, feel the gunshots resound inside my head. The crowd pins me against the wall as people flee toward the main doors.

Someone yanks me back behind the cover of the wall. It's Jeremy. He yells, I think at me, and whips off his jacket, pulling out a 9mm handgun tucked in the back of his pants.

"Stay close!" he shouts. But before we can go anywhere, gunfire shoots through the doors and into the panicked throng. The initiates nearest the exit drop to the floor, dead. Their bodies block the doorway. I look into the sightless eyes of a boy not five feet from me, his sneer gone forever. It's Gander.

I add my screams to the others. No one knows what to do. Some people charge over their dead peers and get shot in turn. Some run back inside the Aerie, searching for another exit, tripping and pushing and falling and howling.

Four of the leather-clad attackers burst through the front doors, stepping over and even on the corpses. Jeremy fires his gun, not at their chests, but at the tiny space between their helmets and their necklines. Two of them go down before firing a shot, but the third one gets Jeremy in the arm. He curses and switches hands, catching his adversary in the ankle and wrist. The fourth person backs out of the doors and disappears.

Jeremy sinks against the wall, gripping the wound on his arm. I stare at his bicep until the ruby gore fades to a muted pink and then ashy gray. Everything turns white and foggy, and I stagger forward. I don't hear Jeremy until he's yelling in my face.

"Come on!" he's saying. He pulls me after him, and I stumble over the bodies in our path.

We stop on the threshold. "I want you to hold onto me tight while I get us to cover," he says, lifting up the cuff of his pants to reveal a smaller gun, a .38 caliber pistol, strapped to his shin. He hands it to me. "Your job is to watch my back, got it?"

I clutch the warm metal and nod dizzily. I wait behind the door while he fires several rounds into the trees.

"Now!" he yells. I run forward, looping my arms and legs around his chest, looking over his shoulder. He sprints to the edge of the deck, and then we're sailing through the air.

I tighten my hold. Jeremy has his bad arm pressed against me, but it won't stop me from falling if I lose my grip. He zips right and left, and my stomach feels empty as I watch the trees whir by. My heart is lodged in my throat. I can feel my pulse reverberating on my tongue.

In the air around us, people are streaming out of the Aerie and into the sky. Some of the counselors have guns, like Jeremy, and are returning fire on the enemy, but none of the initiates do. The best they can hope for is to dodge the bullets and escape into the forest. I watch them get hit and fall, screaming, to the ground.

Stay focused, Kit. But I'm flying and my body is wrapped around Jeremy's and people are being shot and everything's bending funny. And then I see the dark, blurry shape behind us, catch the glint of a rifle.

Arms wobbling, I aim Jeremy's gun and fire. The shot splits my eardrums, and the kickback sends us dipping to the right. But I fired wide, and now our pursuer is raising his own weapon.

"Someone's behind us!" I scream.

"Gathered that," Jeremy grunts as he leaps to the side. The bullet just misses my arm. Shaking, I level the gun again, both hands this time. I'm not as accurate as Jeremy, but I'm a fair shot. I try for the neck, like he did.

I hit his stomach. The person flies backward and crashes toward the ground. But he recovers and catches the wind in time. *He must have a bulletproof vest.* He's still chasing us, but at least I've bought us some distance.

I'm turning my head to tell Jeremy when I hear the thunderclap of his gun. We plummet to a lower current, twirling from the force of the shot. I almost lose my grip and, shrieking, hold on tighter.

"Don't choke me," Jeremy wheezes.

"Sorry," I stammer.

And then a bullet finds its way into his thigh. Jeremy yells and suddenly we're diving into the trees. I mash my face into his shoulder as we crash through the branches and pine needles, hitting the ground hard. Jeremy takes the brunt of it, rolling to cushion my fall.

I tumble off him and lie shaking in the underbrush. We're still in the camp but hidden for the moment by a large log and some bushes. I turn to look at him. His face is pale, and I wonder if he broke his leg. Even if he hasn't, his other wounds will send him into shock soon.

"Listen," Jeremy grunts, "we only have a few seconds before they find us. I'm going to distract them so you can make a break for it." I shake my head. There's no way I'm going to leave his side.

"Count to ten," he continues, taking a clip out of his pocket and pressing into my palm, "and then go as fast as you can." He grimaces and sucks in his breath through his teeth.

"No, Jeremy, I won't let—"

He puts his hand on my mouth. "I can't protect you anymore," he says. "Promise me you'll run. Promise." His gaze holds mine without faltering. How did I ever think his eyes were sharp? They're warm and soft, softer than the sky.

My own eyes are burning as I nod my head. His hand slides from my mouth to my cheek. He holds my face close to his for one quiet moment, presses his lips against my forehead.

"Thanks for proving me wrong, kid," he says. And then he's gone.

I watch him stagger to his feet and limp out of our hiding spot. He rises shakily into the air.

One.

Immediately, the people in black find him, surround him. He fires three shots, moving higher, away from me.

Two.

Someone hits him in the shoulder. He spins to dodge another bullet and fires his own.

Three.

A backflip to get around yet another assailant. Climbing still higher.

Four.

It's working. He's leading them away. Heat swells behind my eyes.

Five.

One of the enemy falls out of the sky. Twirling in a death spiral.

Six.

But there are too many. He's hit again. And again.

Seven.

Someone drops down from behind him and empties a round of bullets into his torso. He arcs his back in pain, and I see his strong body tumble to the ground.

"Jeremy," I choke. I bite all the way through my lip, force the tears back before they have a chance to fall. I have to go now, or they'll find me.

Stumbling, I drop the clip into my pocket then push back the bushes and dash for the forest at the edge of camp, maybe a hundred yards away. Gunshots and screams ring through the trees. I clutch the handgun and swivel my head from side to side.

An explosion shakes the ground and sends me falling onto my face. I look over my shoulder at the black smoke devouring the trees. They've blown up the Aerie.

I climb to my feet, ears ringing, wondering who was still inside.

And then the *wakenu* bursts into a million pieces.

I hit the ground again. The glass shards blossom outward, reflecting the orange flames a billion times over, blinding my eyes. The top part of the meetinghouse is completely obliterated. The steel base and supports, warped and twisted, are the only things left. The beautiful dining hall, gone forever.

Run, you idiot! I get up and sprint for the woods.

A blast of searing hot air sends me flying forward. My head crashes into a tree, and I lie on the ground, stunned. I don't hear anything. No screams, no gunshots. I look back at the meetinghouse. The steel remnants have collapsed completely, sunken into a giant hole in the ground. The flames from the first explosion must have hit the natural gas well, causing the second explosion.

The fire has spread, running through the dry pine needles and latching onto the surrounding trees, but I don't hear the flames.

Suddenly, the ground in front of me starts to sink, and I hold onto my head, thinking it's the dizziness. But it's not. The dirt at my feet is literally slipping into the earth. I scramble backward, trying to get to higher ground. What's going on?

Around me the bunkhouses are swaying, tipping, smashing on the ground as everything collapses toward the center of the camp. A burst of fire shoots out of the earth fifty feet away from me. And then I know what's happening. The gas lines underground. The explosion must be spreading through the tunnels, weakening the cement—the entire infrastructure of the camp. The bunkhouses, the trees, the sticks on the ground, it's all going up in flames.

I run from the fire, from the tipping earth. The soil slides under my feet, and I have to scramble on all fours. I can't hear the flames, the exploding pipelines, but I can smell the gas-filled smoke. It scalds my throat and lungs. *Not this, please not this!*

I finally get clear of the landslide, enough to stand on my feet again, when I trip on the first body. The person is lying face up, her face blackened beyond recognition. I choke down bile and keep running. Past another body. And another. They're everywhere, emblems of the massacre.

And then I see her petite frame. Her feathery hair, plastered with blood. Charity. I can't hear myself screaming her name. I drop to my knees.

A second later, a bullet streaks above my head, and I feel the slice in the air, see it hit the tree in front of me. I look up. A man in black leather is riding the wind above me, his gun leveled at my head. He isn't wearing a helmet, and I can see his face. Black, coiling tattoos curve from his nose onto his cheeks and forehead, around his eyes and chin.

Frozen in place, I stare at the barrel of his rifle, knowing that it's all over, that I'm going to join the others. But then a tomahawk splits the man's face, and he drops to the ground. I turn away from the blood, gagging.

Someone bursts out of the forest and runs toward my dead assailant. He steps on the man's face, grabs the tomahawk by the handle, and yanks the blade free. My stomach heaves. Then the person strips the man of his weapons and turns to look at me, cheeks and hair smeared in black. If it weren't for the bright green eyes peering out through the ash, I wouldn't recognize him.

"Go!" I read the word in Rye's mouth rather than hear it. I lurch to my feet. Then he's at my side, grabbing my elbow, pushing me forward, and we run into the forest.

Rye drives me through the trees. I trip over the stumps and logs, but I keep going. Behind us, I can feel the smoke grow thicker, feel it creeping into my skull. I shake my head forcefully.

We reach the river. Rye pushes me, and I fall in, gasping as the cold water stings my burned skin. A second later, his arms reach around me and pull me out. He's windwalking, carrying me. We land on the opposite bank.

Rye says something, but I still can't hear him. I think he's asking why I didn't windwalk, so I point to my ears. He nods curtly and we keep running through the trees. We run for another hundred feet or so. Then he pulls me into a thick patch of bushes where we lie on our bellies under the leaves, panting. Rye grips his weapons—a tomahawk and the man's automatic rifle. I keep my hand wrapped around Jeremy's handgun.

The blood hammers in my head, the pain converging in the gash on my brow. My body shakes from my cold, wet clothes, from my galloping heartbeat. The only thing I can hear is the ringing in my ears. The screams of the dying. All I see are the blackened faces and twisting tattoos. Bulging, rolling gasps are working their way up my chest.

Rye raises a finger to his lips. I stuff the sleeve of my jacket into my mouth, and he peers through the bushes, his finger curving around the trigger of the rifle. I can't hear, but I can see. Dark shapes, stalking through the forest. Prowling on the ground. Hovering in the air. Moving aside branches with their automatic weapons.

I close my eyes and burrow my face in the dirt. I focus on lying perfectly still, try to stop shivering. A mosquito lands on my neck and drills its nose into my skin. The sweat drips into my ears. Something tickles my foot. But I don't move. My legs are rigid; my lungs burn. The ringing in my ears grows louder and louder, pounding me into the earth.

After an eternity, I feel Rye relax beside me. They must be gone. To be safe, we stay in the bushes for twenty minutes more. I stare at the yellowing leaves, at the tiny holes the bugs have left, at the quivering twigs. The ringing in my ears has morphed into a buzzing, and the thrumming noise pens me in more than the bushes do, pressing against every surface of my body until I think I'm going to collapse into myself like the camp.

The buzzing must be a good sign, however, because when Rye says, "I think we should go now," I can actually hear him. We climb cautiously out of our hiding spot, and, without a word, Rye begins walking north, parallel to the river. I follow him.

We move quietly, saying nothing. To our left, billowing clouds of charcoal cover the sky. The fire will have destroyed all signs of the testing grounds—and the carnage. Fortunately, the flames haven't spread to the trees over here. The river must have helped contain the blaze. A hollow, pulsing ache spreads throughout my chest. It's all gone. *They're* all gone. Rye and I could very well be the only survivors.

Soon we enter a section of forest that looks familiar. I recognize the clump of bushes, the tall pine. It's the place where I hid my backpack.

"Wait," I croak. Rye turns around and looks at me, eyebrow raised, as I walk over to the bushes, push past the branches, and stop under the tree. I look up. It's still there. I climb the trunk and remove the pack then drop back to the ground.

Rye widens his eyes slightly at the sight of the bag on my back, but he doesn't ask any questions. He just keeps walking, moving noiselessly through the trees, still heading north. I wonder where he's going. This isn't the way back to the town. Is he circling around the camp, taking a roundabout route so we aren't discovered? I don't want to say anything, don't want to make any noise, so I decide to just wait and see.

At first I look at the sky as I walk, keeping my hand on the gun. The people in black could still be around, and I focus on making my steps as quiet as possible. But after an hour of walking, I stop looking up and pay less attention to where I'm stepping.

I also give up trying to keep track of the direction we're going. Rye leads us on a circuitous path, twisting one way and then another, probably to confuse anyone who might come looking for us. I can only assume we're finally pointed toward the town. As I walk through the thickening forest, pushing the branches away from my face and wishing we had kayaks, I try to keep their images out of my head. I keep my eyes on Rye, on the sweat spots on his shirt. Damp circles on a strong back.

Jeremy. Despite my best efforts, his soft, blue eyes swim in my vision. I feel his breath on my face, his lips on my forehead, his strong, protective arms. *Why did he do it?*

I think back through the last week, replaying every interaction. The looks he sent me, the concern in his voice, the way he held me when we danced.

And now he's dead.

I smother my face in my hands. How can he be dead? His teasing smile, citrus skin, steady hands. It can't be real.

And what about Lila? Is she dead? Swallowed by flames. I never thanked her for being kind to me, for being my friend. Just like I never thanked Charity. Never even asked her real name.

All the others, are they dead too? Aponi and Damon and Holly. Titan and Bullseye, Dee and Dum. Tornado and Buck. I look at Rye's taut neck, his eyes focused on the forest. Did he lose his best friend today?

My whole body shakes, but I try to steady it, try not to make too much noise. I don't want the people in black to find us. Those men— who are they? Why were they killing unarmed kids, the way they killed Aura? I squeeze my nails into my palms, rub my forehead, but still those tortuous black tattoos stay with me. They're permanently etched in my brain, forever linked with death, with Aura's purple blood, Charity's scorched skin, Jeremy's lead-filled body.

I drop to the ground. How can he be gone? "Jeremy," I whisper.

The sound of a stick snapping makes me jerk my head up. Rye is standing there, looking down at me with steady eyes. He extends a hand, and I take it, weakly. He pulls me to my feet, places his other hand on my shoulder, says nothing, just continues to peer into my eyes while I shudder and gasp. Then he removes his hand and keeps walking.

I focus on putting one foot down after the other, concentrate on moving forward. I try to clear away the smoke, but the caustic smell stays with me, and so do the faces.

When the sun is heavy in the sky, Rye finally stops walking. It's hard to say how far we've traveled, but we've been hiking for several hours—long enough to cover a quarter of the distance to the town, I'd guess.

"We'll make camp for the night," Rye announces, the first thing he's said since we left our hiding spot. I set down my pack and take off my sweat-soaked jacket. "Got anything useful in that backpack?" he asks.

I show him the camping supplies. The crackers in my pocket are crushed, but the apple and the freeze-dried meals are fine, and when he sees the food and water purifying kit, the lines around his eyes soften. As we eat, I realize how famished I am, and how thirsty.

"How did you know this backpack was there?" Rye asks when his meal is finished.

"I put it there." I frown—I hadn't planned on telling him the truth.

"I guessed as much. But why?"

I hesitate. "For emergencies," I tell him.

"Your counselor let you keep your bag?" He looks skeptical.

"I didn't exactly ask permission," I admit.

"Good thing."

I nod, but I can't help thinking that if I had left this morning after breakfast, I would have been gone before the attack.

Suddenly, I remember why I didn't leave this morning, and I avoid looking at him. If our camp hadn't been attacked, it would have been Rye who kissed me today and not Jeremy. How long ago that seems, a different world. Even though we're together, alone in the wilderness, I feel no thrill in my veins. Kissing Rye is the last thing I want to do.

"How long do you think it will take us to get to the town?" I ask. I don't want to follow my train of thought any further.

"What town?" His forehead wrinkles.

"The town where we got the kayaks. Isn't that where we're going?"

"Definitely not. We can't afford to go near any cities. The Rangi would pick us off easily. Our only chance is to stay in the forest and go to the *Wakenunat*. As it is, the Rangi might still find us."

My brain aches, and I press my head into my hands. The Rangi— are those the people who attacked us? And what is the *Wakenunat*? More Yakone jargon I don't understand.

What I *do* understand is not good, that the killers could be looking for us, that I have to go to this place if I don't want to die.

"Are you okay?" he asks me.

"My head hurts," I mumble. "I think I need to go to bed." I stand up shakily and walk toward the backpack, pulling out the sleeping bag and bivy shelter, picking up my jacket to use as a pillow.

I'm walking toward a mostly flat piece of ground to spread out my sleeping bag when Rye calls after me. I turn around and see him crouching down, picking something off of the dirt. My heart drops when I see what's in his hand. An I.D. It must have slipped out of my pocket. *Please be the fake license*, I pray. *Please be Flor Garcia.*

Rye's face turns a shade paler. He looks at the I.D. then he looks at me. Back at the I.D., back at me. Finally, he narrows his eyes and says the words I've been dreading:

"You're not Aura Torres."

Stage Three: Descent

When the clouds reach higher altitudes, the raindrops finally fall. The cooled air sinks rapidly, and the skies become more turbulent and electrically charged. There is a significant drop in temperature.

From the Algonquian people, we know that the Thunderbirds helped to create the universe. They are the ancestors of the human race.

The Kwakwaka'wakw tell how the Thunderbirds, in their human form, lived by themselves on the northern tip of Vancouver Island. Some of them even married into human families. The people forgot the true nature of the Thunderbirds, and one time a neighboring tribe attempted to enslave them. But the Thunderbirds put on their feathered cloaks and destroyed every last person with their lightning and strong winds.

Unhappy with the human race, the Thunderbirds went away. Now they live in the furthest part of the earth, and we no longer see them.

11

"What?" I stammer, trying to form a plan. How do I convince him I'm not a threat, not a spy?

Before I can think of what to say, Rye strides toward me and points a finger at my face. "Are you Aura?"

"I ... um ... " I take a step back.

"Are you?" he presses.

"Yes ... " I falter. "I mean no." I shake my head, backing up some more. "I mean, maybe."

He steps forward and grabs me by the shoulders. I try to free myself, but his fingers dig into my skin. His frown deepens, and I hold my breath.

He points to the puffy cut on my brow. "Can you remember hitting your head?" he asks.

"Yes, I think so." The words come out in gasps. "The explosion."

"What day is it?"

I open my mouth to answer and then hesitate. What day *is* it? Wednesday? Thursday? How long have I been here? I lift up my Quil to check.

Rye stops me, pushing my arm back down. "Do you remember why you came to the *maitanga?*"

"Um ... "

"Can you remember your parents?"

My parents. Their faces are wrapped in haze. The thick, black smoke smothers my lungs, and I gnaw the inside of my cheek.

"Do you understand what's happened? Where we're going?"

"No!" I burst out, the pressure exploding in my chest. "I don't know who attacked us, or why, or what the *Wakenunat* is, or why we're going there because I'm not Aura!"

There I said it. I stumble back, keeping my eyes locked on his face.

Rye exhales slowly and runs his hands through his dirty hair. "Okay, why don't you sit down for a second?" He leads me over to a rock then crouches in front of me. "Aura"—he clears his throat—"I think you hit your head harder than you realize."

"What?" I stare at him.

He coughs again. "What I mean is, I think you might have had a concussion."

"No, that's not ... " My voice trails off as I finally process what's just happened. I don't say anything for a moment. I just try very hard to think. This could be it, my way out.

"Aura?" Rye says, watching me closely.

"I don't know what to do."

"Okay, let's start by figuring out what you do and don't remember. Do you recall anything before the attack?"

"Yes," I say slowly. *Now's my chance to figure things out, to ask questions.* "Bits and pieces," I tell him.

"Do you remember your contests?"

"I think so. Yes."

"Do you remember coming to the camp?"

I nod.

"What about before that? Do you remember your family? Your friends?"

"No," I pitch my voice higher and try to look panicked.

"Okay, all right, calm down. Do you remember that you're a member of the Yakone tribe?"

"That sounds familiar," I say.

He pushes his fingers back through his hair. "Do you remember what you ate for breakfast?"

I honestly don't, so I tell him no.

He exhales slowly. "My name is Rye Slade," he says, watching me sharply. "Do you remember me?"

"You won the Challenge on Day One."

"That's good." He closes his eyes for a moment then stands up. "Does your head hurt?" he asks. "Is your vision blurry?"

"It hurts a little, but I can see fine."

He nods. "Let's see how you're doing in the morning then. Maybe your memory will return. I'll stand watch. You get some rest." He turns away.

"Wait!" I say. He looks back at me. "Who were those people who attacked us?"

His gaze drops to the ground. "I'd rather not talk about it. Maybe you should be grateful you don't remember."

"Rye, please. I need to know."

He pauses for a long moment before answering. "They were from another tribe. The Rangi, our enemies. They're ruthless and savage, and they'll kill anyone, even children. They've never come this far north before, which means they're on the warpath. That's why we have to go to the *Wakenunat.*"

"What's the *Wakenunat?*"

"It's our fortress, the only place we'll be safe. The whole tribe will be gathering there. Or what's left of us anyway." He turns and walks into the trees.

I finish laying out my sleeping bag and setting up the bivy shelter. The work distracts me from my thoughts, but I get everything ready far too quickly, and as I slip between the slick polyester, my mind goes back to the camp.

The Rangi. That's what those people are called. Another tribe of windwalkers. How many tribes are there? And why were they attacking the Yakone teenagers—kids at a summer camp? *No, not a summer camp, a testing center.* Suddenly, I see the paintball matches in the Aerie, the arcing bodies and spraying bullets. Those mock battles weren't just for fun. The initiates' martial skills were being tested. They were preparing for a real battle.

I think of the tomahawk flying out of Rye's hands, the way he yanked the blade free of the Rangi's skull. He had been trained to do that. I shudder. What kind of a world have I entered? And how do I get out of it?

I can't. Not if there are Rangi prowling around the forest. If I leave Rye and try to make it back to the town on my own, I won't stand a chance. It doesn't matter that I'm not really a windwalker. I'm dressed like one, and they won't bother to ask questions before they kill me. I know that much.

But I can't go to the *Wakenunat* either—I'm still pretending to be Aura, and that won't last long once I get to the fortress where the whole tribe is gathered. Her family might be there, and when they find out I'm not her … *I'm screwed, big time.* If only I had left this morning, before the Rangi attacked.

I squeeze my hands around my sleeping bag and press the fabric against my ears. The night is so loud. The eerie cries of the loons, the incessant buzzing of the mosquitos, the interminable hissing, droning, warbling. What are those sounds, really? Could that rustling in the bushes be one of them, sneaking up on us? Suddenly, the echoing rings of gunshots and the stench of scorched flesh overwhelm my brain, and all I can see are warriors with swirling tattoos.

I slide further into my bag and shut my eyes, but the images and sounds only become more intense. The shots, the war cries, the blood. The air in my bivy grows hot and stuffy, and sweat runs down my neck. Will they find us? Swoop down on us in the middle of the night? Trapped in this little tent, I won't be able to run away. They'll shoot me before I know it's coming.

I jerk open the flap on the shelter and scoot out into the cool night air, breathing deeply for a few moments. Then I fold the tent up. I'm not going to be able to sleep in that thing again. I gather the sleeping bag around me like a blanket and walk over to the rocks. I'm not going to be able to sleep at all.

I sit down and stare into the darkening forest. It's not Aura who jumps out of the blackness now. It's Jeremy and Charity, Naira and Gander, and all the people I saw die I didn't even know. Their mangled faces crowd my head.

I'm glad I didn't see Jeremy's corpse. It's bad enough that I watch him perpetually being shot down in my mind, his back distorting in pain. I try instead to think about his eyes, his smile, the way he looked when he was alive. I reach out for the scent of lemongrass, but all I get is pine.

I don't know how long I stay like that, caught between waking nightmares and my attempted vigilance, but after a while I hear something. The quiet crunch of pine needles. I dig the .38 caliber out of my pocket and grip it tightly. A shape, outlined by the moon, moves out of the trees.

"Rye?" I whisper.

"Yeah, it's me," he says. His voice sounds thick, like he's been crying, but maybe I'm imagining it. He sits down on a nearby rock, and the lunar beams spill silver along his ears. Neither of us says anything further.

We stay like that, silent, tortured away from sleep, while the black clouds swallow the moon.

The morning is harsh and gray. My limbs are stiff, and the cut on my head is even more swollen and tender. We eat two of the freeze-dried meals without speaking. Only four left.

As we resume our march, tromping through the dripping grass and thick fog, I wonder how far away the *Wakenunat* is. Hopefully, it's within forty miles. Our food isn't going to last us very long. Through tomorrow, at most. After that, we'll have to hunt if we want to survive.

I rub the bump on my head, try to keep my mind on the food, on survival. That's easier to think about.

How long, I wonder. How long before the images fade? I can't handle one more night like the last, where every time I close my eyes, I see his face torn apart by tattooed monsters and when I keep them open I imagine I hear the creatures coming for me. I can't bear another morning like this, where everything I see or think reminds me of how empty the world is.

"Aura?"

I flinch then look around quickly. I don't see Rye—I must have fallen behind.

A branch ahead of me moves back, and he steps through the bushes. "There you are. The wind's back, and it's cleared up the fog. Time to get a move on."

What do you think we've been doing all morning? And then I understand.

"I'm not sure that's a good idea," I stammer.

"We'll stay low so the Rangi don't see us."

"That's not what I mean."

"What then?"

I hesitate. He studies my face for a moment and then frowns. "Don't tell me you've forgotten how to ride."

"Why don't we just stay on the ground?" I suggest.

He stares at me. "This isn't happening," he mutters. "Please say this isn't happening."

"What?" My throat is squeaking again.

"Aura," he says, his voice rising, "the *Wakenunat* is in the Rocky Mountains—in the Northwest Territories! That's close to eight hundred miles away! We can't make it there on foot."

I lean against a tree. *Eight hundred miles!*

"Aura," Rye barks. "Hello! Please focus."

I look up. "Sorry," I mumble.

"I don't think you've really forgotten how to windwalk," he says. "I just think you've forgotten that you *know* how to windwalk. It'll be fine once you try it."

I shake my head. "No. I won't be able to."

"You have to try! I can't carry you eight hundred miles, and the Rangi will find us if we don't get moving."

"Just leave me behind then," I snap. "You go to the *Wakenunat*. I'll figure something out."

"You have got to be joking," Rye says, more to himself than to me. "Look, I can't leave you behind. You'll be fine. You just have to trust me on this."

Before I can say anything, he grabs my hand and pulls me through the trees, stopping when we're standing on the shore of a lake. The breeze blows loose strands of hair across my face.

"Okay," Rye says. "Look across the water. Can you see it?"

"See what?"

"The wind!"

No, I can't see the wind! I remember a poem we memorized for that 4-H wind course. *Who has seen the wind? Neither I nor you: but when the leaves hang trembling, the wind is passing through.*

My eyes drift automatically to the pine boughs. The needles are quivering, and I still feel the air tickling my cheeks, though not quite enough to blow out a flag. I think of the Beaufort wind scale. *Light breeze. Four to seven miles per hour.*

"No, I don't," I say stiffly.

"C'mon," Rye retorts. "Of course you can. Your eyes still work. Try harder."

I want to punch him—how did I ever think he was attractive?— and yell that I can't see the wind because I'm not a windwalker, but, of course, I can't tell him that. So I scowl at the air above the lake.

A bird dives down from its perch on a nearby pine, and I watch it glide above the water, mark how the wind lifts its wings. As I stare at the space beneath those graceful feathers, I see something. A slight swirl in the air, a diaphanous ripple. I blink.

"You saw it, didn't you?" Rye asks. His eyes are fixed on my face.

I don't know what to say, so I stare harder. The faint movement comes gradually into focus. It flickers at first—I catch only a glimpse here and there. But then it sharpens, steadies, until I see gauzy waves billowing across the sky. I clutch a tree for support.

This can't be real. But it is. The nearly translucent streams of air stretch all the way across the lake, pushing back the pine trees and tugging gently at my hair. I look up and see more of them, thicker and more forceful the higher I cast my gaze. Most of the currents remain horizontal, but some rise sharply into the sky while others veer off in a different direction entirely.

I remember one summer evening, back in Williams, walking near the marsh by my house. Thick fog swooped over the cattails, curving up and down, surrounding me in its ethereal swells. It separated into various strands of opaque air, some denser than others. This is what the wind looks like, only not as gray, not as easy to see. But why can I see it now when I couldn't before?

"Now feel the pull," Rye says, "from in here." He points to his mid-section. "Open up and allow yourself to connect."

Do I dare? I can see the wind, but can I actually feel it, ride it? It's too much to hope for. What if I can't do it?

Rye takes the backpack from my shoulders then steps behind me and grabs my arms. I try to twist out of his grasp, but he's strong. "Relax," he says in my ear. "I'm going to help you." He places my hands on my abdomen. "Do you feel your emotions?" he asks.

My emotions? The debilitating fear and misery that swirl in my gut? Yes, I feel them all right.

"Now let the wind take them," he says.

"How?"

"Release whatever you're feeling. You have to remove yourself from your emotions before you can concentrate enough to create *honga*, your bond. You have to have control. So give them to the wind. Close your eyes if that helps."

I close my eyes and visualize the turmoil inside my chest, the dark pit that's eating me from the inside. It's been there for so long, how do I actually let it go?

The wind surrounds me, and I imagine I can hear it speaking to me, encouraging me.

I envision an opening forming under Rye's hands, see the black fog leak out of my torso, watch the breeze whisk it away. I feel the wind enter the void, fill it with light and air. Maybe, just for a moment, I can forget the pain.

And then it happens. I feel a tug in my chest, my feet want to step forward, my heels rise up, tipping me onto my toes. Rye moves his hands to my back and pushes me gently.

"What do I do now?" I ask, snapping my eyes open and halting at the edge of the water.

"Just do what comes naturally. I'll be right there with you."

Do what comes naturally. But there's nothing natural about thinking you can step off the ground and fly. Some of the dark fog returns, and I force it out, letting in the wind again. The tug grows stronger. The air in my stomach feels lighter, the light spreading down to my legs. My heels lift up again. The wind is everywhere in my body now, hovering, waiting. I just have to grab it. Become one.

"You've got it," he says. "Now go for it!"

So I do.

I jump into the air, and instantly, I'm zooming forward, gasping as a tingling shock rips through my nerves. I speed over the water, faster than I've ever run, the wind whipping up a spray beneath me. Knees slightly bent, I move along the barely visible currents, surrounded by the trees and the birds and the endless indigo. The moving air thrums in my veins.

Rye keeps pace beside me. I look at him, eyes round. I'm doing it. I'm windwalking.

"I told you," he shouts.

"I can't believe it." The wind hums even louder in my chest than before. The connection seems unbreakable. I can't separate my body from the rushing air. It's all the same. This is nothing like when Rye carried me across the river or when Jeremy flew me from the Aerie, maybe because I was merely a passenger.

Suddenly, I feel Jeremy's arms around me. The weight of the gun in my hand, the bullets ripping past my ears, the screaming weapons and people. They drown out the buzzing of the wind, and my body begins to feel heavy. *No, don't! Stay focused!*

Up ahead, the lake ends, and the wispy currents disappear into the trees. *Where do I go now?* The weight rapidly expands inside my chest. I don't know what to do. Can I fit between the trees? Should I look for another current? I see Jeremy's body assailed with bullets, twisting unnaturally, falling to the ground. Falling, falling.

I scream as I plunge into the lake. The cold water jolts my blood, and when my head breaks the surface again, my chest is aching. Rye lands on the shore and waits while I wade out.

"What happened?" he asks when I'm standing in front of him, shivering.

"I didn't know where to go," I say.

"So you chose the lake?"

I shrug and avoid his gaze. "I may have also gotten distracted." I don't like the way he's looking at me, like he can't believe a windwalker would have actually forgotten how to do this. I need to try harder. I rub my temple. It seems impossible, but I was doing it, I really was.

Rye clears his throat. "Ready when you are."

"Sorry."

"Okay, let's go over some basics. Apparently, it's not coming back to you like I thought it would. You know how to swim, right?"

"Clearly."

"Well, windwalking is a lot like swimming. Imagine you're in a fast-flowing river. You've got a few options. One, you can do nothing. Two, you can swim with the current. Three, you can swim against the current. Or four, you can tread water." He looks me in the eyes, and I nod.

"If you do nothing," he continues, "the river will carry you downstream. If you swim with the current, you'll move even faster downstream. If you swim against the current, you might be able to move upstream, depending on how fast the water is flowing. And if you tread water, you'll be able to stay more or less in place, again depending on how strong the current is. That makes sense, right?"

I nod again.

"Same with the wind. You can go with it or against it. If you move with it, you're able to go really fast. Moving against it *is* possible, but it's very difficult. You have to have a pretty weak breeze. It's easier to tread the air and hover, but that can wear you out too, and you'll still move forward a little bit. So the simplest thing, especially if you want to conserve energy, is to move *with* the wind. If the surf isn't going in a direction you like, you find a new current."

"Which is an option you didn't have in the river," I point out.

He blinks. "Right. So let's practice treading. That way you won't have to drop into the lake again."

He connects to the wind current we had been riding before and bobs in the air in front of me. "Remember, it's like treading water," he says, "but you've got to do it with your mind as well as with your body. Picture yourself moving against the wind and lean into it with your chest. You can even paddle with your hands and legs if that helps." He demonstrates, circling his limbs as if he were keeping himself afloat.

I close my eyes and open that spot in my mid-section, let the wind push away the images of Jeremy, the howls of the dying. Soon I feel the weight dissipate—more quickly than last time—and when I've made *honga*, I leap off the ground.

In my mind, I forbid the wind to move me, imagine I'm swimming in the air and pushing against the current. It's difficult. The breeze wants to whisk me away, but I manage to slow myself down to a crawl.

"Good," Rye says. "Now let's practice moving from one current to another." He frowns at the sky, probably worried that we haven't put enough distance between us and the Rangi.

"I'll do better this time," I promise. "I think it is coming back to me."

He nods. "You have to jump around a lot in order to move up, unless you can find a thermal—or an updraft, but that means you're windwalking in a storm, which isn't the smartest idea. When you locate the wind stream you want, reach out to it. As you jump, make *honga* again. Like this." He leaps from the wind current we're on to one that's about three feet above us.

A vertical jump of thirty-six inches? That's impossible. Then again, I'm doing the impossible right now.

I focus on the gaseous tendrils surging past my shoulders, on sending my energy into the flowing air, and I feel the bond shift. My hold on my present current weakens as my link to the one above me grows stronger. When my connection to the wind underneath my feet disappears almost entirely, I jump. My newly formed bond helps with the rest, pulling me into place, and I land on the higher wind stream. Immediately, I notice that it's stronger, denser even, than the wind below. And it's harder to hover. *Gentle breeze. Eight to twelve miles per hour.*

"Good work," Rye calls. "Now follow me. We'll weave through the treetops where the wind is a little bit faster and more reliable. Stay close, just in case."

I follow him as he leaps to a higher current. Now we're moving forward, zipping past the pine trees, and I keep my eyes locked on Rye and on the air. It's slightly more visible up here. The airy threads are thicker, woven together more tightly, which makes it easier to see my options. The wind bowls right into the trees, but it also splits into little paths that go around them. I follow Rye onto these diverging trails.

At first I'm too slow, and the needles scratch my arms. One branch clobbers me in the face, and I almost lose the connection, but I regain control in time to mimic Rye and leap onto a different current before I crash into a thick trunk. Before long, I get the hang of it, and I focus less on Rye and more on the forest below me, on the sky above.

I've left behind the gray haze that clouded the world this morning. Up here, everything is lush and brilliant. The sun shimmers on the lakes and rivers below, and the vivid pine boughs steep the air in their rich aroma. In every direction there are more of them. Billions and billions of glorious golden-green trees, far outshining the view from the dining hall. A hawk glides alongside me, screeching as it dives toward the earth. I watch it twist into the boughs below, and the sight of my feet skimming the peaks of the pines, dangling thirty feet above the ground, only makes me want to laugh.

As we move up even higher, the winds grow stronger, tossing the branches and shaking the seeds loose from the cones. The fragrant pollen twirls in the air beside me. *Moderate breeze. Thirteen to eighteen miles per hour.* I zoom ahead, extending my arms and tipping my face up to bathe in the saffron beams.

The lightness in my chest is like nothing in this world. The wind hums through every section of my skin. The sun, closer than it's ever been, melts into my face and mixes with my blood. The warmth seeps out of my fingers. My whole body must be glowing.

But riding the wind isn't exactly easy, and after an hour or so, the work catches up to me. My lungs are heaving, my legs burn from all the jumping, and my mind is fighting back.

In many ways, windwalking is like running. When I run, I have to consciously block out negative thoughts. Here, bad thoughts would be even more perilous. They could distract me, and if I lose *honga*, I could plummet to my death.

When Rye gestures for me to follow him to the ground, I'm starting to see fuzzy black spots in the clouds. I drop to the lower currents and then to the forest floor where I collapse gratefully against a tree. We break out more freeze-dried meals for lunch, and as we eat, Rye asks if I remember the hand signals.

"No," I say.

He runs his hands through his increasingly dirty hair then shows me the signs that mean go high, go low, north, south, east, and west, as well as the signals for danger and help. "We can use our Quils to communicate, but you should know the signals, just in case."

"Our Quils still work?"

"Yeah, they'll charge as long as they have enough exposure to the wind."

"I mean, will they work if we're not near a cell tower?"

"The Quils get their signals from a satellite, not cell towers. They'll work anywhere in the world."

"So, we can call for help?"

He shakes his head. "No. Ours are still in training mode. They would have given us full access at the end of the *maitanga*, but … anyway, right now, we can only call the people who were in our cohort. Hopefully, when the tribe realizes what's happened, someone will remove the locks remotely and try to contact us."

"We can't manually dial a number?" I ask.

"No. They're not like normal phones."

"Oh."

He pulls his Quil off his wrist. "What's your number?" he asks. I tell him, and he taps it into his screen.

"Mine's twenty-six," he says. I program it into my favorites. Then I see Lila's number next to his.

"Have … have you tried calling anyone?" I ask.

He tugs on his ear. "Yeah." My finger lingers over Lila's entry. "Try it," he says.

I take a deep breath then push her number. I hold the Quil up to my ear and wait, but there's not even a ring. Just silence, followed by a loud bleep. I lower the Quil and, hand trembling, delete the entry.

Rye looks down at his own screen. We sit there wordlessly for several minutes.

Then Rye coughs and looks up at the sky. "According to this, we've covered twenty-eight miles already. I'm hoping to go at least fifty more today. Unfortunately, we can't go very high because we don't have parachutes and the right equipment, and we don't want to be spotted."

I nod through my headache. How high do the windwalkers go?

"The jet stream wouldn't be of any help, anyway, since it's going against us."

Jet stream! I remember learning about those: air currents that form near the tropopause, more than five miles above the Earth. *I guess that answers that question.* I try to imagine what it would be like to go so high, but my head feels too heavy to think about it.

"Are the coordinates for the *Wakenunat* in our Quils?" I ask.

"Yeah. We've got that and a GPS, but, like I said, most of the good stuff is locked." He stands up. "We should keep going."

We return to the air, and the rest of the day blends together. My stomach still leaps when I soar above the trees, but I lose all feeling in my legs. My mind goes numb as well. I keep the darkness at bay, but all I can hear or feel is the thrumming of the wind.

At last, I give in. Unable to focus my eyes on the Quil's screen, I get Rye's attention and desperately make the signal for *go low* as I drop to the ground, almost hitting a tree on my way down.

We eat the last of the food for dinner. It's only four in the afternoon, but Rye agrees to let us stop for the night.

"We'll need to go further tomorrow, so get some rest. I'll take the first watch."

"It's my turn," I mumble.

"You can hardly keep your eyes open. I'll wake you when I need to switch."

I don't argue. I pull out the sleeping bag and fall asleep almost instantly.

I've fought off their faces all day, but in my dreams they find me. We're windwalking. Lila. Charity. Jeremy. Even Aura. Lila laughs, her curls blowing freely behind her, while Jeremy grins at me and takes my hand. We fly through the clouds. The trees shrink to tiny specks as we ascend higher and higher, up to the stratosphere. My chest is buoyant. I could keep climbing forever.

I look at Jeremy, and he smiles at me. But as he turns his head, a black tendril snakes across his cheek. It divides into more strands, spreading across his face, swallowing his lips and nose, carving his face into a serpentine stamp, until only his pale blue eyes remain.

I scream and drop his hand. But as I turn to flee, I realize I'm surrounded by the other windwalkers, all of them devoured by the tattoos, all of them—Lila, Charity, Jeremy—pointing guns at my head.

I lose my bond with the wind, spiraling down and down and down, through miles of empty air. The trees grow large again, their pointy tops rising up to spear me. I keep screaming as I drop into their prickly arms, as I hit the ground with a splat.

Panting, I sit up and reach for the cool lining of the sleeping bag, feel for broken bones. I let my heart rate slow down. Take deep breaths.

It's night now, and the full moon has an entourage of stars. I walk over to where Rye is sitting on a rock.

"I'll watch," I say.

He looks up, and I see only a dull gleam where his eyes should be. "Are you sure?" he asks.

"Yeah. Here's the sleeping bag."

"Thanks." He takes the bag and moves to a spot on the ground.

Taking his place on the rock, I pull my hood over my head and wrap my arms around my body, scrunching my shoulders against the cold that's slipping down my neck. Just like last night, the forest is alive with noise. The crickets and frogs compete for dominance, and the sky echoes with their monotonous clicks, punctuated every few moments by unearthly shrieks and whistles. I hug myself more tightly, try to listen around the metronomic insects, swivel my head every time there's a new sound. The wind rattles the dry Aspen and Tamarack leaves. Somewhere in the dark, a Great Horned Owl challenges the night. *Who Who Who Whoooo Who?* I train my eyes on the trees, glad at least that the sky is clear, the moon bright.

Gradually, the noises work themselves into a discernible pattern, and I force my arms to relax. But as the wind brushes my cheeks, the ache from my dream returns, hollowing out my chest. I tip back my head and stare relentlessly at the sky until the moon and the stars melt into a milky blur.

12

The smell of cooking fish wakes me up. I rub my eyes and then the back of my head where it's been resting against the rock, squint at the small fire, at Rye's body crouched over it. I jump to my feet.

"I'm really sorry! I didn't mean to fall asleep."

Rye looks at me. His hair is wet. "Ah, you're awake." He turns back to the fire. "It's a good thing we didn't have any visitors last night."

"I said I'm sorry." The smoky aroma makes my stomach rumble. "Where did you get the fish?"

"The frozen section."

Seriously? What's his deal? "How many times do you want me to apologize?"

"Oh, you don't have to apologize. I understand you need your beauty sleep."

I wheel around and march into the trees, forcing myself not to think about how much he sounded like … *Well, what does he want me to do, plead for forgiveness? It's not like I did it on purpose. And he could have woken me—I would have helped with breakfast.* I grip the .38 in my pocket. I don't need his stupid fish. I'll get my own food.

When I've reached a small meadow a good distance from our camp, I clear my mind and focus on the swirling air until the wind fills my breast. Then I jump into the surf. The air hums through me as I climb to a higher current and zip through the pines. I'll have a better chance hunting game from the sky.

I dodge a tree and duck under a branch. The whole day of practice served me well—I've improved a lot since yesterday morning. *How is it possible?* I wonder yet again. *I'm not a windwalker. Does that mean anyone can do this?* I couldn't see the wind until I looked for it, so maybe that's all it takes.

I bump into a pine bough, and suddenly, a furry shape leaps off the branch. "Whoa!" I tread air and watch as a flying squirrel jumps to the branch below me. *That'll work.* It's small, but I don't have time to find anything else. As it leaps to another bough, I raise my gun and fire at its head.

I miss, and the kickback knocks me against a branch. The thwack on my head makes me lose my concentration, and I slip to a lower current and another, hitting more branches on the way down until I crash on the ground. I groan as I stand up. I'll have another bruise to add to my collection. I feel my head. My hair is sticky with sap. *Great.* Now I'm sweaty and nasty and even hungrier. I slap at a mosquito.

A large branch is in my path. I kick it out of the way then jump back when I see what's beneath it. My squirrel. Dead. The bullet must have hit the branch, which in turn must have hit the rodent. I pick up the dead animal with a stick. Not much meat, but it will serve as breakfast, for one.

I return to camp, making sure Rye sees my catch.

"You wasted a bullet on that thing?" he asks. I notice he's eaten all the fish.

"I didn't want to lose time hunting for something bigger," I say.

"Good, because we're leaving."

"What—now?" And then I notice that he's also taken apart the fire pit.

"You've given away our location. We can't stay here any longer." As he walks over to the gear, I glare at his back, but I feel my chest constrict. Have I really just told the Rangi where we are?

"What do I do with this?" I hold up the squirrel, trying to keep my voice from shaking.

"Eat it raw or bring it with you."

Eat it raw or bring it with you, I mimic, but I can't quite pull the face I want.

We resume our journey, the dead squirrel strapped to the backpack, the backpack strapped to my shoulders, and just like yesterday, Rye takes the lead. He moves quickly, and I have to concentrate to keep up. His movements are tight, edgy, and soon I feel my neck muscles tense, find myself looking constantly over my shoulder, wondering how close the Rangi are. Rye continues to push us, and I try to stop thinking about it in order to maintain *honga* and match his pace.

It feels good to be off the ground, at least. The wind whisks away my sweat, the mosquitos can't catch me, and after an hour or so, the humming breeze drives away the majority of my fears. I even forget that I'm hungry and focus solely on the tingling air that fills my body.

The wind is strong, stronger than yesterday, and I feel it pulsing through my legs. My thighs are still tired, but I discover I can lean back slightly and use my grasp on the air to support my body, like a windsurfer holding onto her mast.

When we've gone for several hours with no sign of the Rangi, I allow myself to experiment with other tricks, like stretching out flat and riding the current, skimming just above the water, rolling in place. When we stop briefly for lunch—a lucky find: blueberries and wild leeks—I even try a front flip.

But my favorite is surfing with the current. Going really, really fast. Even when the wind isn't super powerful, I can still accelerate. It's like pulling myself forward with a rope or running on a moving sidewalk. It requires all of my attention, though. My mind has to be focused on that objective alone. But when I get it right, it's the most incredible feeling in the universe.

As we travel, I learn a few other things. That if the wind changes, I have to climb higher or return to the ground and walk. That I need to keep my eyes open for cross winds. And above all, that if the threads of air start to fade, I have to find a new current immediately or, at the very least, grab onto a branch.

We windwalk until the sky softens into amaranth and pumpkin and set up camp without speaking. We haven't spoken all day. While

Rye goes to look for dinner, lashing his pocketknife onto a branch like in the fishing contest, I finally skin the now reeking squirrel. It seems smaller than ever, and only my pride keeps me from throwing it into the forest.

Should I apologize again? I wonder as I skewer the tiny body on a stick. No, I did that enough already.

Rye returns, sopping wet, with two fish. We eat quietly, and then I break the silence by volunteering to take the first watch. "That way, I won't fall asleep on the job," I say. "I'll wake you when I get too tired." *There, that's the most he's going to get.*

"I'll plan to be woken up in a couple of hours then." A shade of a smile flicks across his lips then disappears.

I look down at my hands as a strange tickle surfaces in my chest.

We eat more fish for breakfast the next morning. Rye's still not very talkative, but he has nothing to complain about today: I kept watch for more than half the night.

"We've entered Alberta now," Rye says as we get ready to leave. "We're about a quarter of the way there."

Two hundred miles in three days—no one would believe it. But we still have six hundred miles to go. *Six hundred miles to figure out what I'm going to do.*

Rye allows us to go higher today, maybe ten or fifteen feet above the treetops. By the way my shirt beats against my back, I'd classify the wind up here as a strong breeze—twenty-five to thirty-one miles per hour. Small drops of water leak out of my eyes, making me understand why windwalkers need special equipment to reach even greater altitudes.

I mark the passing of the hours by the sun's steady movement, by the changing clouds, by our shadows on the pines. We cross paths with a flock of geese, honking and flapping in their rotating V. I think about the *kiipooyaq* contest, and it gives me an idea.

When we stop for the night, I cut some of the cords from the backpack and tie them together so I have a rope with three ends.

Then I find three rocks of equal weight and size and fasten them onto the tips. I practice throwing my crude weapon a few times to make sure it works. Amazingly, it does.

"I'll get dinner tonight," I tell Rye. He's been leaning against a tree, watching me. His face is hidden in the shadows, so I can't read his expression.

"I'll make a fire," he says.

I walk the short distance to a nearby lake and windwalk over the water. Earlier, when we came down, I saw some birds feeding on the far shore, and even now I can hear their loud calls. It doesn't take me long to find them. A flock of geese. Not Canadian geese, like the ones we passed earlier today. These are smaller, probably only half the size of the Canadians, and they're covered in bluish-gray plumage.

With so many to choose from, I have no difficulty catching one, and soon I return to camp with a five-pound bird under my arm. I think Rye is impressed when he sees me, but it's hard to tell because his expressions vanish so quickly, so different from the boy I first saw laughing in the dining hall, dancing around the fire, staring at me across the room.

I focus on plucking the bird. Honestly, I don't know where my thoughts come from sometimes.

After we've picked the bones clean, we linger around the fire, letting the warm food settle in our stomachs. Rye whittles something with the pocketknife, and I decide it's safe to ask a question.

"How many tribes are there?"

He looks at me. "You still can't remember?"

"No."

He tears a piece of dead skin from his lip. "Seven," he says. "There used to be hundreds, a long time ago, before we were born. But too many windwalkers died off, so the tribes merged together. The Yakone used to be just the windwalkers in Alaska and the Arctic regions of Canada. Now all the windwalkers in Canada, Greenland, Iceland, and the top third of the United States belong to our tribe."

I whistle. "That's a big area. How often does our tribe get together?"

"Not often." His eyebrows crease as he looks at me. "Once a year maybe, and even then not everyone comes. The youth who are ready to be tested—usually at age sixteen—gather every September and are assigned their place in the community. And then there's a celebration in the spring where the *tooka* of the competitions are honored and the victors of the battles fight for the title of grand champion, *Tookapuna*."

I remember Lila talking about that. "What places are we assigned?"

He breathes out through his lips. "You know, storyteller, artisan, builder, gardener, warrior. Mostly warrior."

"And these become our jobs?"

"No. Because we live among humans, we all get human jobs and live like humans. But these are our responsibilities within the tribe. The storytellers preserve our history, the warriors defend the tribe during war—"

"How often is there a war?"

"We haven't had one since my grandfather was alive."

"So, the warriors are like the National Guard, and now that there's been an attack they'll gather together to fight the Rangi?"

"Something like that." He studies me. "Funny that you remember what the National Guard is but nothing about our tribe."

"Not that funny," I say. He says nothing.

After a long pause, I speak again. "So the testing was supposed to tell us what our obligations would be to the tribe. But they're not a full-time job or anything."

"Right. The only exception is the *Riki* and the *Matoa*—the chief and the captain of the warriors. Everyone in the tribe contributes a small portion of their income to support them so they can devote their time to protecting the tribe."

"They didn't do a very good job, did they?"

Rye gives me a sharp look but doesn't respond.

"What will happen this year?" I ask quickly.

He shrugs. "I don't know.

We're both silent for a moment, and then I ask, "What tribe did your family belong to before the Yakone?"

"My great-grandfather was Okłumin, but they don't exist anymore."

"What happened?"

Rye resumes his whittling. "The usual. Killed by other windwalkers, killed by humans."

"How were they killed by humans?"

"On accident—by airplanes, power lines, disease. It became difficult to meet as a tribe, to windwalk without being noticed. Eventually, most of them decided it would be easier to live like humans instead of fight it."

"So, the tribes got so small, they joined with others?"

"Yes. To protect themselves and preserve their way of life, they needed allies. Then, a hundred years ago, there was a really bad war that decimated what was left of the windwalker population, so now the tribal territories are even more spread out."

"Where are the other tribes?"

"The Kaana cover the rest of the United States, Central America, and the top part of South America down to the equator—not many windwalkers live by the equator though. There's hardly any wind. The Kre have the rest of the continent. The Oya have Africa. The Biegga are in Europe and half of Russia, and the Cua take the rest of Russia, Asia, and Australia."

"What about the Rangi?"

"New Zealand."

"That's it?"

"And the South Pole."

"But that's nothing! No wonder they hate everyone."

"They earned it." He shrugs.

"What do you mean?"

"They rebelled, caused a war—it's kind of a long story."

"We have time … "

He deliberates for a second then says, "Sure, why not." He settles back against a tree trunk and clears his throat. "Back before there was an earth, we all lived in the sky. When things got too crowded up there, our first parents, the rulers, created the world and sent half of their children to live on it. Over time, the people spread out across the earth and forgot that they could ride the wind. They became human."

"Wait," I interrupt, "you're saying all humans started out as windwalkers?"

"Right."

"Okay … sorry, keep going."

"Some of the windwalkers were angry that they had not been chosen to go to the earth, so they made their own way down on a cloud. That cloud became the island of New Zealand. Immediately, the rebellious windwalkers started to torment the humans. These were the ancestors of the Rangi.

"The humans were defenseless against their attacks, so First Parents chose one of their children to lead the rest of the windwalkers down to earth to stop the havoc. They defeated the Rangi.

"At this point, all of First Parents' children were on the earth. The world was a beautiful place, so many of them decided to make their homes there permanently. The son who led the windwalkers against the Rangi settled in the North and established his own tribe."

"Let me guess," I say. "The Yakone."

"Close," Rye grins. "Okłumin. Anyway, the Rangi nursed their grudge and continued to wage war on the other windwalkers. They were continually defeated and eventually exiled to New Zealand, where they had first come to Earth.

"A century or so ago, when the tribes began joining together, the Rangi demanded they be given a larger territory. No one likes the Rangi, so they didn't get it. There was that massive war, and they were crushed. Things have been quiet since then, but now it seems they're at it again." Rye rubs his right temple then picks up his whittling. "The fact that they're this far north makes me think they've been having some success."

"So what will the Yakone do?"

"Kill them. They're like rabid animals. You can't reason with them, but you can make them pay. Make them suffer." He's whittling furiously now.

The screams and moans fill my ears again, the dead bodies, the smoke, the tattoos. "But you don't really believe that everyone started out as windwalkers, do you?" I ask. I need the conversation to keep going, need to keep them out of my head.

Rye raises an eyebrow, and I realize I've just questioned a tenet I'm supposed to share. "It's easy enough to prove," he says. "Think of almost any myth about the wind or the creation, and you can find traces of windwalkers in it—like the Muscogee people, who call themselves the Wind Family. And it's not just Native Americans. Look at basically any religion. Gods who fly through the air? That's us."

He leans forward, the reflection of the fire flickering in his eyes. "Why are humans so curious about what's up there, beyond this world? Why do they say things like 'I've had the wind knocked out of me,' or 'I caught my second wind'? Why do people have dreams about flying? Why have poets and artists, from the beginning of time, been obsessed with the wind? Take Percy Shelley, for example: 'If I were a dead leaf thou mightest bear; if I were a swift cloud to fly with thee; a wave to pant beneath thy power, and share the impulse of thy strength, only less free than thou, O Uncontrollable!'"

Rye looks beyond me, up at the stars, and continues quietly, "'Lift me as a wave, a leaf, a cloud. I fall upon the thorns of life. I bleed. A heavy weight of hours has chained and bowed one too like thee: tameless, and swift, and proud.'"

I stare at him as he finishes his recitation. Where did that come from?

"I'm sorry," he says. "I got carried away." He shuts the pocketknife then shoves it and the piece of wood in his pocket and walks into the trees.

I sit by the fire until it burns down to ash. Then I go to bed.

Rye wakes me for the second watch. I fidget in the darkness, waiting for the black sky to fade to gray, and think about what he said after dinner. Sue took us to church every week, but I was never particularly invested in her religion. Or any religion, for that matter. Maybe Rye's explanation is the correct one, I don't know—I guess I don't really care either—but it would explain how I was able to windwalk. Maybe one of my ancestors was a windwalker. Surely they intermarried with the humans.

I tug at a blade of grass. I can't figure that boy out. At the camp, he was the star athlete and flirtatious show-off all the girls were in love with. But after the attack, he became a different person. Withdrawn. Terse. Angry. I suppose there's nothing strange about his transformation. I've changed too.

But then tonight—that startling intensity. Stories and religion. Poetry declamations! At the testing grounds, I would have grouped him with the football players, but not now. I've never known any jocks who could recite poetry.

I wonder if Jeremy memorized poems. I snap the grass in half. There's so much about him I'll never know. His favorite food. Favorite color. What he wanted to do with his life. He hasn't even been dead three full days, and already the details of his face are slipping away from me.

I slide the delicate blade between my fingers. If only it were lemongrass. My eyes hurt, but I know I won't cry. And I know something else: that even if his image fades, I'll never forget him, the way he felt, smelled, laughed. The way he looked at me, the way no one ever has.

I lift my gaze to the moon and the billions of pinpricks encircling it. I try to lose myself in their endless spirals, hoping that, somewhere, in that eternal softness, I'll find him.

When streaks of mustard are pushing through the clouds, I hear something. A quiet crack, like a foot stepping on a twig. I sit up straight and peer into the dark forest. *Snap.* There it is again. A slight rustling in the bushes, more popping twigs—too many for one set of feet.

My heart is racing as I rush to Rye's side. "Wake up," I hiss. "They've found us."

In a second, he's on his feet, slipping the tomahawk into his belt and gripping the rifle with both hands. I dig out my pistol and switchblade. I can feel the pulse in my arm.

"Where?" he asks.

"There." I point toward the lake, and he moves forward. "Wait!" I whisper. "What are you doing? Shouldn't we run?"

"No more running," he says. "They're going to get what they deserve."

Two of us against all of them? Who knows how many there are? There could be twenty people. As Rye disappears into the forest, I take a step back, holding my breath.

"Aura!" I hear him call. He's laughing. I exhale and jog toward him.

"What is it?" I ask as I push through the bushes, but he doesn't have to answer. There, by the edge of the water, is a moose.

"Sound the alarm," Rye laughs. "The moose is out to get us."

"Rye … " I'm watching the moose. It's a bull, and I don't like the way he's peeling his ears back. He lowers his antlers and tosses his head back and forth. "Rye!" I yell. "Get back here."

"What's wrong?" He stops laughing and looks at the moose. But it's too late—the animal is already charging.

13

Rye backs up quickly, raising his rifle as the moose continues to rush him. But as he pulls the trigger, he slips and falls back in the lake, hitting his head on the rocks. The bullets skim the bull's shoulder, and instead of stopping, the infuriated animal runs even faster, antlers lowered, ready to crush Rye into the earth.

I scream and aim my gun with both hands, emptying the clip into the moose's flank. The animal thrashes its head and bellows. Then it turns and charges for me. I grab the wind and leap up to a branch, clinging to it shakily as the bull disappears into the forest, blood dripping from its sides.

When it's gone, I jump out of the tree and run to Rye. He's floating face down in the water.

"Rye!" I shriek, dropping the gun and pulling him onto the shore. "Rye, talk to me!" He lies still. His face is slightly purple, and there's a gash on his forehead, a stream of blood running down his cheek. I put my ear close to his mouth and listen. He's not breathing.

"Rye!" I drag him the rest of the way out of the water and shake his shoulders. Nothing. I slap his face. "Kava, Rye! Say something!" I pound him on the back. A shudder runs through his chest, and he coughs up water, but his eyes stay closed. I lower my face next to his and feel a tiny bit of air on my cheek, see his chest rise.

Trembling, I sit back up. Then I lean him against a tree, cut a strip of cloth from my shirt, and hold it against his head. I don't know what else to do, so I press on the wound with my hand, hoping to stop the bleeding. The blood seeps through the moisture-repellant fabric, onto my fingers, and I push harder. He still hasn't opened his eyes.

After a few minutes, he starts to shiver, so I pull him onto my lap and wrap one arm around his torso while my other hand continues to apply pressure to his head. We stay that way for a long time, me holding him tightly, straining to catch his faint breathing. There isn't a sound in the forest around us. No birds. No insects. Not even the wind. I bite my lip and continue to hold his head.

At last, I feel him stir in my arms, and I look down in time to see his eyes flutter open.

"Are you okay?" I ask shakily.

Rye frowns. "I think so. My head hurts." He tries to sit up, but I stop him.

"Careful," I say. "Just take it easy."

We sit there for a few moments, water dripping from his hair onto my lap. After a while, he nods. "I think I'm ready."

I help him stand up. "Thank you," he says, leaning against me. I'm relieved to see his head's stopped bleeding.

"I didn't do much."

"Hey," he grabs my arm. "You saved my life."

I meet his gaze for a brief moment. His eyes are different today. Deeper. Warmer. His whole face seems different, like I'm seeing him for the first time.

"Aura—"

"I'll get our stuff," I say quickly. "We should go as soon as you're ready. Our guns made a lot of noise."

Because Rye feels weak, we don't go as fast today. Instead, we stay close to the trees and take lots of breaks. When we stop for the night, I hunt for dinner. Grouse this time.

After we eat, Rye takes out the piece of wood he was whittling the day before and resumes his work. I sit across from him.

"What position were you hoping for?" I ask. Rye raises his eyes. "You know, in the *maitanga*? Did you want to be a storyteller?" I think of the poem he recited.

He gives a short laugh. "Storyteller? No. My dad would never allow it."

"Does your dad have a say?"

"Actually, he kind of does."

I wait for him to explain. When he doesn't, I ask, "So what does he want you to be?"

Rye makes a deep cut with the knife. "A warrior, like him."

"Oh. You'd be good at that."

He snorts. "Yeah, I guess I would be."

"But I don't get it. How could your dad have told Naira where to place you?"

Rye sighs. "My dad's the *Matoa*. He's second only to the chief."

"*Your* dad's the captain!" I try to remember the comment I made yesterday. "Look, what I said, I'm really sorry."

"Don't worry about it." He grins. "Just don't ever repeat it in front of him."

"I can promise you that." Rye continues moving his knife across the wood, and I watch the shuddering flames for a few minutes. But the silence is burdensome tonight. "What are you carving?" I ask.

He holds the piece out, and I take it in my hands. It's the head of a male deer. I run my fingers along the broad, rough strokes that form the face and antlers. It's rustic work but very pretty. I hand it back to him.

"It's beautiful," I say.

"Thanks."

"What's it for?"

"A memorial, I guess. For my cousin."

A buck, of course! How could I be so stupid? "It's beautiful," I repeat, wishing I knew what to say. The only noise is the soft whisking of the knife against the wood. I didn't know Buck, but I remember the way he flew around the arena, how he won the windrace. He was strong, like Rye.

"You must have trained a lot," I venture, thinking of their maneuvers in in the contests.

"My whole life. Just like you."

"Me?"

"Of course. You know how to throw a *kiipooyaq* and shoot a gun, don't you?"

"I guess. But you were so much better than the other kids in the Aerie." I wonder how much Aura had trained, how she would have done in the Challenge.

"Well," he muses, "I suppose some of us spent more time in training than others."

"You must like it then," I venture.

"Why do you say that?" His gaze is barbed.

"Well, because you've devoted so much time to it," I stammer.

"That was my dad's idea. Not mine."

"Oh." I listen to the wood crack. "So, what do you want to be?"

"It doesn't really matter what I want, does it?" The knife slips in his hand, slicing his finger. He curses and kicks one of the logs. The sparks swirl around our heads like a swarm of fireflies.

"You're tired," I say. "Get some sleep. I've got the first watch." He grunts his thanks and slips away into the darkness. After he's gone, I pull out my necklace and rub my thumb across the curving lines, gripping the pendant tightly as I listen to the crackling flames.

In the morning, we say nothing. We just rebuild the fire and eat the fish Rye caught for breakfast.

Finally, Rye speaks. "I'm sorry, Aura. I didn't mean to yell at you." His fingers rub the scab on his forehead.

I nod. "I know. It's okay." *I wish he'd call me Kit.* We both look at our hands.

"I think I want to be a farmer," Rye says, still looking down.

"A farmer?" I can't believe it. I spent my whole life dreaming about leaving the Johnsons' farm until I finally did. Why in the world would he want to live on one?

"It's weird, I know, but I think I'd like it. I like doing things with my hands. My mom comes from a farming family. They live in Whitman County, about four and a half hours from Seattle. They grow wheat and barley and have some livestock. We used to go there all the time when I was a kid."

"Is that why you're named Rye?"

"Yeah." He laughs quietly. "We all have names like that. My mom's name is Amaranth. My sisters are Chia and Maize, and my little brother is Teff."

"That's cool." I wish I could tell him Tom was a farmer, that he loved it, even if I didn't. We're both quiet for a moment, and then I blurt out, "I want to be an astronomer." I've never told anyone that before.

"Really?"

Kava. The words slipped out before I even thought about what I was saying. An astronomer isn't a position in the tribe, and I'm not supposed to be able to remember this kind of thing.

But Rye just smiles. "Stratosphere's not high enough for you?"

My pulse quickens, but I smile hesitantly back. "I guess not."

We pack up our things and keep going, ramping up our pace now that Rye's feeling better. The air is warm today, warmer than it has been in a while, but the winds are tricky. They keep pushing us south, and it's a lot of work to make any headway in the right direction.

For lunch, we stop near a lake to eat the leftover fish. Rye leans against the backpack and looks out across the water. Then he turns to me. "Have you ever gone waterskiing?" he asks. The right corner of his mouth is twitching.

"Once." We visited Tom's rich cousins two summers ago, and they took us out on their boat.

"How about barefoot waterskiing?"

"I've never even heard of it."

The twitching turns into a full smile. "Take off your shoes."

"What?"

"C'mon, just do it."

"I can't believe this," I say, but I take them off. My socks are gray and stiff. I peel them eagerly from my skin and wiggle my smelly, liberated toes.

"Okay, here's what we're going to do," Rye says. "We'll windwalk low over the lake, low enough to put our feet on the surface of the water. Keep your knees bent at first, and lean back, like you're sitting in a chair." He demonstrates, crouching with his legs shoulder distance apart. "Pull your toes up and angle them in."

"Why?"

"So they don't catch the water and shoot it into your face. When you're comfortable, you can slowly straighten your legs. But keep leaning back, and pretend the wind is a rope you're holding onto." He stands up. "If you feel like you're going to fall, lift yourself back into the air. It's simple."

"I don't know—" I begin, but he takes my hand and pulls me to the edge of the lake before I can finish making up an excuse.

Still holding my hand, he rises into the air. I join him, and we shoot out across the water. The winds are strong already, but Rye pushes us even faster. I grip his hand and try to keep up.

"Now!" he yells. He lowers his feet into the lake. I clench my teeth and follow suit, bending my legs like he told me to.

The water slaps the bottom of my feet hard, and I almost yank them out, but Rye is already crouching down, and he's still got my hand. I strengthen my hold on the wind and lean back. My feet bounce crazily, the spray flying into my eyes. I blink away the water and try to look at Rye's feet in order to mimic them. Toes pulled up, pointed in.

Eventually, my feet start to plane, and the water stays out of my eyes. Rye begins straightening his legs, so I do too. I tip dangerously to one side, but I pull myself upright. We lean back, holding hands, and glide across the top of the lake. The spray jets out behind us, soaking my clothes and hair. Everything is a blur of water and sky. And as the trees whiz by, I smile.

"Now for some tricks!" Rye shouts. He lets go of my hand and raises one leg in the air. Then he twists around so that he's facing backward. He twists again to face the front and does a flip, landing beside me, feet instantly skimming the water. Next, he drops onto his rump and twirls around. Then he's back on his feet.

"You're crazy!" I laugh.

"Try something!"

This is nuts, I think, but I slowly lift one of my legs out of the water, and, somehow, I keep my balance.

"Let's do a jump," Rye yells. "Reach for a higher wind current, and then drop into the water."

"Oh, no——" But he does it again, grabs my hand and pulls me up before I can argue. I shriek as I rise into the air, supported mostly by his grip, and then plunge back down. I lose *honga* and immediately crash through the water's surface.

"I'm gonna kill you," I gasp when I come back up.

Rye does a back flip, catapulting himself high into the air and dropping into the water. His head bursts out of the lake, and his hair sprays me with hundreds of droplets. And then he's bobbing next to me, the wet strands sticking to his forehead, those forest green eyes only a hand's length away.

Suddenly, I'm back at the camp, back to the first time he ever talked to me, and when he says, "Thought it was about time you took a bath!" my tongue doesn't work, and I have to look away.

"Hey, are you okay?" he asks. "Sorry, I should have given you more warning."

"I'm fine," I squeak. "Should we try it again?"

"You're game? All right, let's do it!" As he takes my hand, a shiver runs up my arm.

We grab the wind again, and I get up on my feet much more quickly. When I've got my balance, Rye looks at me and raises his fingers. *One. Two. Three.* This time, I'm on board. I jump with him to a higher current, and we hold the wind for a split-second until Rye yells, "Let go!" We drop, and I grab the wind just as my feet slam into the water. I tilt to the left, and Rye tightens his hold to keep me upright. We zoom forward in a rush of spray. I scream and laugh at the same time.

After a few more runs, we return to shore, stretching out on a large, flat rock to dry in the sun. "We're in the Northwest Territories now," Rye says, looking at his Quil.

"So we're close?"

"Probably two or three more days depending on the wind. We still have to go further west, into the mountains. The *Wakenunat* is almost in the Yukon."

Two or three more days. *What am I going to do?*

I look at Rye. The sun is pouring its rays onto his face, highlighting the stubble that has grown in along his strong, square jaw, and I find myself thinking about the free fall contest, about what might have happened if … He turns his head, and I jerk my gaze up to the sky.

"It's a nice day," I say lamely.

"Yeah. I think a storm's coming."

"Really?"

"The direction of the wind, the warm temperatures … I won't be surprised if we get some rain tomorrow."

"Will it be hard to windwalk?"

"Depends on how bad of a storm it is. The winds usually shift a lot."

"I see."

I close my eyes, and the heat sinks through my eyelids, filling my vision with embers. The water gently laps the shore. The wind swishes through the trees. Birds sing in the distance. I drink it all in, wishing I could lie here forever.

But I can't. Somehow, some way, I'm going to have to leave. In three days we'll be at the *Wakenunat*, and I absolutely can't go there, can't let them catch me. The GPS on my Quil will help me find my way back to civilization, and the *kiipooyaq* will feed me. The only thing I have to figure out is what to do about the Rangi. How do I avoid them?

I feel Rye's shoulder touching mine. *That's the other problem.* Maybe I should just tell him the truth.

No. It's too late for that. I can't be with him. We live in two different worlds, and he thinks I'm someone I'm not. When I get the chance, I *have* to go.

But I won't forget this—the warmth on my skin, the sound of Rye's breath beside me. I'll carry this moment with me for the rest of my life.

I open my eyes and turn my head to look at him, jumping a little when I see that he's staring at me.

"You're pretty when you're relaxed," he says.

"Thanks," I mumble, the heat on my cheeks from more than just the sun.

He laughs. "C'mon, it's time to go."

Our progress is as difficult as it was in the morning, and I wonder how hard it will be tomorrow when the storm breaks, if it will slow us down, buy me time.

When we stop for the night, my body is aching. I try looking for birds to kill, but I can't find any, so Rye goes fishing again. He only catches one.

"I'll be happy when I don't have to eat any more fish," I say.

"I'll be happy when I don't have to *catch* any more fish," Rye replies.

"Whose turn is it to take the first watch?" I yawn. "I can't remember."

"Actually, I don't think we need to keep watch anymore. We've been out here almost a week—if the Rangi were nearby, we would have met them by now. I highly doubt they'll be bold enough to attack the *Wakenunat*, and since we're getting close to it, we should be safe."

"Are you sure?" My pulse picks up.

"If all those bullets you've shot off haven't attracted them, I don't know what will."

"Hey! Some of those bullets were to save you from the moose!"

He laughs. "I know. I just have to give you a hard time." Then he looks at my face and stops laughing. "You okay?" he asks.

"Yeah, sorry. You just reminded me of someone I miss."

"Someone back home? Is your memory coming back?"

"No, someone, someone from the camp."

Rye scoots closer and puts his arms around me, and I rest my head against him. "I miss them too," he says.

I close my eyes against the pain, imagine Rye's strong arms keeping it away. He smells like pine and sweat and something else. Dirt? Lake water? Fish? All three? Certainly not lemon. But his scent keeps me grounded, and I don't slip into the dark hole that's formed inside my chest.

"Do we believe in an afterlife?" I ask.

"Of course." I feel his throat vibrate as he speaks. "When we die, we go back to live with First Parents. Their kingdom is high above this world, a land of warm winds and golden clouds, where the air smells like lilac, where there's no fighting or pain and you can windwalk forever."

"It sounds nice." I try to picture Jeremy and the others there, but I can't. "Do humans go there too?"

"Yes, that's when they'll realize they were once windwalkers."

"What about the Rangi?"

"Everyone has to be judged before they're admitted into the Eternal Sky." His voice grows hard. "The Rangi won't be judged well. They'll have to wander the winds on Earth until the world ends."

"When will that happen?"

He brushes the hair back from my forehead. "When there's no one left on the Earth who remembers how to windwalk."

We sit quietly for several minutes, and I focus on the way his fingers caress my skin. Eventually, the black pit seals back up, and I can breathe normally.

"Who gets the sleeping bag?" I ask, reluctantly pushing myself off his chest.

"You can have it," he says.

We kick out the fire, and I climb into the bag while Rye lies on his side a few feet away from me. As I trace the strong lines of his back with my eyes, I try to imagine the windwalkers' heaven, wishing I were in his arms again.

And then I think about what I've been pushing to the back of my mind all evening: if the Rangi aren't a threat anymore, that means I can leave. I scrunch up my forehead as Rye's outline blends into the darkness.

A raindrop splatters on my cheek, waking me. I sit up and look at the sky. Even though it's covered in thick clouds, I can tell that the sun is higher than it usually is. With no one keeping watch, we must have slept in. I stretch my arms. It feels good to have a full night's rest, even if my back is perpetually stiff from lying on the hard dirt and rocks.

I look to my right for Rye, but he's not there. *Probably went to catch some fish.* I start to stand up then stop, heart thudding. This is my chance. I should leave now before he comes back. I rise to my feet then quickly roll up the sleeping bag.

When I've tied it together, I carry it toward the backpack, and that's when I notice that the fire is cold—Rye usually starts it up before he goes fishing. Is he okay?

It's fine. Don't panic. Maybe he stepped into the trees. "Rye?" I call. No answer. *I'm sure he's just out of hearing range.*

Even though I'm losing precious time, I flip to the shortcut menu on my Quil and press his number. I have to know if he's all right. I wait, but the connection never forms, so I finish packing our gear then sit on a rock, trying to decide what to do. I should leave while I have this chance, but then I'd always wonder if he was hurt, if I abandoned him. *What if he met another moose? What if the Rangi found him?* I bounce my leg and tap my nails against the rock. The raindrops fall more frequently.

"Okay, I'm going to look for him," I say out loud. I grab the *kiipooyaq* and my switchblade and push through the trees. There's a stream about fifteen yards away. I'll check there first.

When I near the bank, I find his shirt, laid out on a rock, and then I find his shoes and pants, his boxers hanging from a branch.

I'm just putting two and two together when the top half of his body pops out of the river. I shield my eyes with my hand and turn my head away.

Rye laughs. "Well, good morning," he says.

"Sorry," I splutter. "I didn't know where you were and got worried."

"Just taking a bath. Although by the looks of things, I shouldn't have bothered taking my clothes off." I look up. The clouds are thicker, and the rain is falling faster now.

I hear splashing as Rye swims for the shore, and I back up, keeping my gaze averted.

"I'll wait for you at camp," I call. He laughs as I run back to our fire pit.

When Rye returns, I'm crouched under a pine tree. The boughs don't help very much, and my clothes are drenched.

He joins me. "I think we'll have to skip breakfast today. We should try to cover as much distance as possible before it gets really bad, and we wouldn't be able to light a fire anyway."

Rye leads the way, slinging the backpack over his shoulders, zigzagging up to the higher surf. The wind is blowing in all directions. One moment we're going west, and the next, we're going east. I concentrate on Rye's wet hair, the dark backpack.

The humming in my chest climbs to a high-pitched whine as the winds seethe inside my gut. It takes all of my energy to connect to one current and then another, and pretty soon I'm panting as if I've just sprinted a four hundred meter. My hair whips across my face. My jacket billows up behind me, catching the wind and slowing me down. The sun disappears entirely behind a wall of ugly gray.

When the thunder erupts above our heads, Rye gives the signal to go down, and the winds buffet my body as I drop behind him. We land in a clearing.

"We'll have to wait this out," Rye shouts. "It's too dangerous to windwalk."

"Fine with me!" I call back.

We jog toward the trees. A split-second later, I hear another crack of thunder. Something smashes into the tree next to me.

"Run!" Rye yells.

And then pain explodes in my left arm.

14

I think I scream. My feet stumble in the mud, and I drop to one knee, ready to fall forward. But then Rye is there, shouting, grabbing me by the jacket, wrenching me back up. He lifts the backpack to shield us, and we run toward the pines as the bullets fly around our legs.

Blood is gushing onto my hand. Warm. Thick. I try to fix my eyes on the forest ahead. It's taking us a lifetime to reach it. The blood is buzzing in my ears. The thunder echoes the cracking guns.

Then we reach the trees, and the guns stop firing. Rye hauls me along behind him until we find a thick spot of undergrowth. He pulls me to the ground, yanks off his shirt, and ties the cloth around my arm.

"We don't have much time," he says. "They'll find us in here soon enough."

"The Rangi?" I wheeze.

"Yeah. It's them all right."

"What do we do?"

"Fight." He pulls our weapons out of the now shredded backpack, shouldering the automatic rifle and gripping the tomahawk. He hands me the *kiipooyaq*.

I slide my good hand down the cords. There's no way this is going to do any damage, not against their automatics. "We're going to die, aren't we?"

"You're going to stay here. I'll draw them away, so you can escape."

"No!" I grab his arm. "No, there must be another way."

"There isn't. If we try to windwalk, we'll be sitting ducks."

"At least there's a chance. We have to risk it!"

"Can you windwalk with your injury? In these winds?" He flings the words at me.

"Yes." I lift my chin. "I can do it." But a heavy weight fills my chest. It was hard enough to windwalk before, and now the pain from my wound is hammering at the edges of my head, threatening to consume my whole mind.

I look up at the sky and try to spot the wind currents through the dense rain and the broiling clouds. My vision dims, and I have to blink rapidly. Finally, I see them, whipping back and forth, going every which way. It would be a nightmare to climb up, and it would take too long. Like Rye said, we'd be sitting ducks.

But then I see something, maybe ten yards away. A block of air shooting straight into the sky.

"Rye!" I point to the vertical current. "Over there. Is that an updraft?"

"Where?" He turns his head. "Yeah ... that might actually work." He looks back at me. "I need you to do exactly as I tell you, okay?"

"Okay." It comes out in a rasp. My whole body is shaking.

"Make a run for that updraft. Ride it as high as you can, and stay airborne. I'll follow behind you. Wait for me up there. But if anything happens to me, get out of here as fast as you can. Promise?"

"Don't make me promise," I whisper.

"Well, just don't do anything stupid then," he says.

"I won't."

"Leave the backpack behind. It will slow you down. Ready?" He looks me in the eyes. I nod. "Okay, on the count of three. One, two, three!"

I burst out of the bushes. The muddy ground wobbles, and the wet branches slap my face, blind my eyes, but I keep going. Behind me, I hear Rye release a few rounds. The Rangi must be close. Searing blasts shoot up my arm, but I shove the pain down, try to let in the wind.

When I'm in the middle of the updraft, I open myself to it fully, and the warm air rushes inside. I tighten the connection and rocket skyward. The rain stings my skin as I shoot towards the heavens, and I look down as the trees drop below me. Rye is keeping the Rangi at bay. I can see them clearly from up here. Helmets and black leather. There are three—not as many as I had feared, but they still outnumber us.

One of the Rangi sees me and immediately climbs into the sky, using another updraft. Rye fires at him, but he misses, and it gives the two on the ground a chance to move in. I pull on the wind and try to go faster.

The air carries me higher than I've ever gone before, right into the middle of the storm. As I enter the crackling clouds, the draft dissipates, blending in with the warm air around it. I grab a horizontal current and attempt to tread in place. *Where is he?* I clutch my arm, the *kiipooyaq* dangling from my hand, and peer into the gray, writhing mass of air and water.

I see a movement and immediately release my mental brakes. The wind hurtles me in the opposite direction.

Gunshots crack in my wake. *That was too close.* I grip the *kiipooyaq* more tightly. Rye's not going to be able to save me. I'll have to save myself. But what good will this thing be against a gun?

I keep moving, but my hold is weakening, and the currents knock me in all directions. At first I look constantly over my shoulder to make sure he's not in firing range, but soon it's all I can do to stay connected. My ragged breathing reverberates inside my throat. My drenched hair slips in front of my eyes. I feel cold. So very cold.

Another gunshot splinters the sky, and I spin around. The Rangi is speeding toward me, gun raised. I whirl my *kiipooyaq*.

The whole sky lights up, and a tremendous boom splits my eardrums as a shockwave plows through the air. The tremor jolts the Rangi forward, and he drops his rifle. The gun twirls toward the ground. When it's almost to the treetops, a blinding flash of heat incinerates the weapon. I don't even hear the crack this time.

Both of us are thrown across the sky. I somersault wildly, reaching out to regain my hold. My lungs burn. My chest is shaking. My whole body is shaking. I can't quite form *honga*. Finally, I find the connection, but my legs tremble violently, and I taste metal, want to vomit.

Just as I've steadied myself, the Rangi barrels into me, his fingers sliding around my throat. I scream and kick at his chest, but he grabs my foot and twists me back. Unable to concentrate, I lose the bond and tumble toward the ground. The Rangi follows.

He grabs me again, and this time his hand closes around my injured arm. The pain seizes up my entire body. I can't even scream. Desperately, I shove him away with both feet. He flips back around, and I raise the *kiipooyaq*. When he leaps, I throw the weapon, but I don't let go of the cord.

The metal balls wrap around his throat, and I yank it tight. Like a lasso. As we spin toward the ground, the Rangi kicks his legs and pulls at the cord around his neck, pushes off his helmet. It falls away, and I see his face.

It's not a man. It's a woman, and she doesn't have tattoos all over her cheeks and brow, like the others. She just has one, on her chin. Her skin is smooth and brown, her hair rich and black. She's beautiful. And I'm killing her.

Her lovely eyes, locked on mine, are popping out of her face, still lovely, lovely and hideous at the same time. Her skin is turning blue, and her lips part as she gasps for air. I stare at her for several long seconds until my senses return. Then I shriek and let go of the cord.

Somehow I manage to grab an air current just before we reach the trees. Then I watch her body plummet to the earth.

I clench my stomach and try to bob in place. The rain continues to soak my clothes as I heave nothing but air, gasping and shrieking and convulsing. I just killed someone. I just killed someone!

Where's Rye? I need Rye. I can't concentrate. The rain is getting in my eyes. The sky is too dark. How far has the wind taken me? What if I can't find him?

"Rye!" I scream, but I can barely hear myself. "Rye, where are you?" I find a current that's going east, back the way I came, at least I think it is—I'm so turned around, I really can't tell. I ride it anyway, searching the sky for any sign of him. Lightning fractures the clouds above me.

Suddenly, I hear the dim echo of a gunshot, and I race toward the sound. *Please don't be dead*, I pray to my guardian or God or First Parents or anyone that will listen. A few minutes later, I see him, below me, near another updraft, grappling with one of the Rangi. I scan the skies, but I only see one. He must have killed the other.

The rain slides off Rye's bare back as he wrestles with the taller man, both of their hands locked on the other's rifle. The tomahawk is gone, perhaps lodged somewhere in the first Rangi. *I have to help him.* But how? I reach inside my pocket. I still have my switchblade.

Grasping the knife, I pop the blade open, ignore my quivering fingers, the splintering ache in my other arm. I'll have to get close in order to use it. I dive toward them.

When I drop down behind the Rangi, knife raised, Rye sees me, and his eyes widen. Just then, the Rangi knees Rye in the gut. He gasps for air and doubles over, losing his hold on the man's rifle, and the Rangi pushes him back, aims the gun.

I dig my knife into the top of the man's arm and feel it hit the shoulder blade. The Rangi howls.

The rifle goes off.

Rye falls.

"No!" I scream as Rye's body vanishes into the trees.

The Rangi turns around, blood squirting from the protruding knife. He snarls and haltingly raises the gun.

I dive into the updraft. As the current whisks me up and away, a blistering wave of air skims my cheek. My hand flies to my face. The bullet just barely missed me, but it seared my skin.

More bullets blast past my feet, and I make myself go faster. Eventually I get out of range, but I know the Rangi can just follow me up here.

As I exit the updraft, my chest is ready to burst. Rye's dead. *And it's my fault. I distracted him.* I look below me, ready to meet the Rangi.

But he hasn't followed me yet—he's rocking unsteadily on the wind where I left him. The stab from my knife must have slowed him down. He's looking up though, probably deciding on the best way to catch me.

And then I see something shooting up the draft below him, and my cries stick in my throat. It's Rye.

He soars past the Rangi then somersaults out of the vertical current and dives back down toward his opponent. The Rangi still hasn't seen him. When he's practically at point-blank range, Rye empties his slugs into the man's neck, and the warrior falls out of the sky.

It's just like in the Aerie, when Rye defeated Tornado. He used the updraft like the quarter pipe. He only pretended to be shot.

When Rye looks around for me, I frantically wave my good hand and drop toward him. "Rye!" I choke.

He pulls me into his arms and holds me tightly. "Are you all right?" he yells.

I don't say anything. I just hide my face in his chest, feel his heartbeat.

"Let's get out of this." He keeps his arm around me as we descend to the ground and then huddle under a large spruce.

"I killed her," I whimper. "I strangled her. I watched her die."

"It's okay," he says, cradling my head. "It's okay."

"I watched her die," I repeat.

"It'll be okay." He rocks me back and forth.

My whole body is numb. I just keep seeing her discolored skin, her bulging eyes, her twitching lips. I stare at my hand. Did I really do it? Did I really pull on that cord, squeeze away her life? I close my eyes, but she won't leave me.

When the storm passes, Rye leans back and surveys my face. "Let's see what the damage is," he says. He frowns when he sees the burn on my cheek, touches it softly. Then he touches my eyebrows and hair. "You're a little singed," he says.

"I got pretty close to the lightning."

"How's your arm?"

"It hurts." That's an understatement. Every time I move, it's like I'm being stabbed. The adrenaline must have masked the pain. That, and the wind.

"Let me look at it." Rye carefully unties his makeshift bandage. The bleeding has stopped. He runs his hands along my arm, gently squeezing the muscles and ligaments. "The bullet went cleanly through," he announces, retying the shirt. "I don't think it hit a bone. That's lucky."

"Are *you* hurt?" I ask. He has a black eye, and I can see bruises forming on his chest and shoulders.

"Nothing bad. I did get cut on the leg a little bit." He shows me where something sharp ripped the cloth on his pants and the skin on his calf. The blood has congealed around it.

"I think we should clean ourselves up and keep moving," he says. "I know you're tired, but the winds are perfect right now. They're going directly northwest. It will be an easy ride, and they're fairly strong." My misery must have shown on my face, because his voice switches to a more persuasive tone. "We need to get to the *Wakenunat* as soon as possible so your wounds can be treated."

That's the wrong thing to say to try to convince me. But he's right. We should keep going. Just in case there are other Rangi around.

"How did they find us?" I grunt as I stagger to my feet.

Rye shrugs. "I don't think they were trackers. They were probably scouts that stumbled on us."

"So far north?"

He nods, his eyes grim. "That's what worries me. Another reason we need to get to the fortress."

It doesn't take us long to find a small river. Rye takes the shirt off my arm again, helps me wash my wound, then rinses out the shirt and turns it into a sling. I splash water on my face with my right hand while he cleans the cut on his leg. It's not very deep, so he doesn't bandage it.

After a few minutes, I have to sit down on the bank. The ground is spinning again, and I can feel my face going pale. On top of losing all the blood, I haven't eaten anything all day. Rye finds a few berries, and I gobble them greedily, but it barely takes the edge off.

I wonder how we're going to find food later. All of our weapons are gone, and so is the backpack, but Rye still has the pocketknife, so maybe he'll be able to catch something. My mouth waters. Right now even more fish sounds appetizing.

All too soon, it's time to go. Rye holds my hand as we climb into the sky. I struggle to make *honga*—I hurt everywhere, and I keep seeing her dying eyes—but once I get it, the wind blocks out some of the pain, and it gets better when we reach a higher altitude, like Rye promised. The winds are steady, and they're pointing in the direction we want. All I have to do is hang on. *Don't think about it. Just hang on.*

I keep my fingers curled around Rye's, pretend he's my link to the wind. He grips my hand just as tightly. *I almost lost him.* I wince whenever I think of his body tumbling toward the ground, like Jeremy, like the Rangi woman.

I can't do this, can't let him get this close. Twice I've delayed escaping because of him, and twice I've paid for it. I can't make that mistake again.

Rye looks at me and smiles encouragement, and I bite my cheek, remembering how badly I needed him after I killed the Rangi, how I almost collapsed when I found out he wasn't dead. *I have to be strong.*

But in about an hour, I'm anything but strong. I'm shaking uncontrollably, my cheeks are flushed, and I want to throw up the berries. I can barely keep *honga*, so Rye swings me onto his back, and I wrap my arm around his neck and release my hold on the wind. I press my burning cheek against his shoulder and close my eyes. I think I fall asleep.

The next thing I know, we're dropping to the ground. White flurries land on Rye's skin and dissolve into miniscule puddles.

"Snow?" I croak, looking up at the swirling flakes.

"Yeah," Rye pants. He sets me down and bends over, putting his hands on his knees.

"How far have we gone?" My voice is no more than a whisper.

"Hard to say. I'm hoping at least sixty miles. I just need a little break. Then we'll keep going." He looks up at the flaking sky. "Maybe I should catch some dinner, before it's impossible to find any." He bends down and unlaces his shoe then snaps a branch off a tree, pulls out the pocketknife. "Stay here," he says. "I'll be back in a few minutes."

I sit down and rest against a rock. The cold air feels good on my cheek, and I stare at the dancing flecks. The sky overhead is a milky gray. Calm, not at all like the incensed storm clouds. Everything is perfectly still. Silent. Peaceful. If I move or even breathe, I'll break the spell.

I watch the tiny designs land on my pants. They accumulate steadily, thickly, creating a soft blanket for my legs. I close my eyes and feel them kiss my scorched lids and lashes. It's like living in a dream. The snow will make it all go away.

There are people in this dream. I can feel it. People I know. I just have to find them. If I close my eyes more, they will come to me. They'll caress me like the snowflakes, make the hurt disappear, tell me everything is okay. I just have to go deeper …

"Aura." I hear them. But they've got my name wrong. I'm not Aura, I'm Kit. At least, I think I'm Kit. Didn't my mother call me Kit? Or maybe she called me Aura, and I've been pretending to be Kit. I can't quite remember. Somehow, it seems very important that I remember.

"Aura!" They're calling louder now. *I'm here! Come find me.* Why can't they find me? Are they confused too? They must be looking for the wrong person. *No, I'm over here! Don't go. Please come to me.*

The world lurches, and a man's face forms in the darkness. "Aura," he says insistently. It's Jeremy. He's come for me. We get to go into the dream now. But as he looks at me, I realize something's wrong.

His eyes aren't right. Jeremy didn't have green eyes. They were blue, or gray. I never could decide.

His face slips away. *Don't leave me! I'm coming. I'll be Aura if you want me to.* But he doesn't come back, and I call after him, begging him to wait. I reach blindly into the dark.

The cold night swallows me, and my body spins in the blackness. I keep calling for them, keep searching. They don't respond, but, in time, the darkness grows warmer. I can see light ahead. I urge myself toward it, crawl for that spot of brilliance.

I heave myself out of the darkness … and enter a jungle. It's hot, steamy, thick. I don't stop, pushing past the broad vibrant leaves and brightly colored flowers. Insects whirr around my ears. Monkeys screech in the distance. I'm getting closer. They're here somewhere. I remember.

Soon I see the house, my house. I wipe the sweat from my forehead. I forgot how hot it gets here. A parrot flies overhead, squawking at me. *I know. I'm hurrying.* I break into a run. I don't want to be late. The jungle fades around me, and when I reach my house, the Brazil nut trees are replaced with golden fields.

I burst through the doors. *Mom! Dad!* Where are they? I don't see them. Somewhere the twins are crying. Why is Mom letting them cry? Why is it so hot in here? I walk into the kitchen. A pot is boiling over on the stove. As I move into the living room, I almost walk past them. But then I see, and I stop. I turn. Their bodies are lying on the carpet, the new carpet, the carpet Mom ordered special for the house. It's stained now, a deep red stain around their heads.

I walk toward them. Slowly. Slowly. Slowly. I want to run, but I can't. My chest pounds. Mom? Dad? Why are they just lying there? And then I see their faces. Blank. Frightened. Dead.

Something explodes in the kitchen, and I hear the screaming flames and the crying twins. And something else: voices, deep voices, coming from the bedroom. I back away from the bodies, turn and run. The twins are in their cribs, and I snatch them up, burst out the back door. I run into the fields, run, run, run as the smoke billows behind us, until I collapse on the furrowed ground. We hide under the cornstalks, watch the roaring fire and the black waves as they devour our house—and our parents.

The twins are crying, and I try to hush them. We can't let them find us. I hush them, and I don't cry. We can't all cry. Someone has to be in charge. The smoke gets inside my lungs, and I choke on it, cough it out. They're looking for us. We can't let them find us. We're on our own.

Why in Hell is it so hot?

I sit up, drenched in sweat. I want to tear my clothes off, but my arm won't move, and pain shoots through my bones when I shift my weight. I look around frantically. *Where am I?* It looks like I'm inside a tree. *Back in wakemo fourteen?* No, I remember—that burned to the ground, burned like everything else.

The room is circular, the walls a patchy pattern of green and white. Next to me is a large wooden pole, and I follow it up with my eyes to where it's swallowed in pine boughs that hang low, surrounding everything. I'm not in a room at all, or even inside a tree. I'm *under* a tree. The pole is a trunk. I reach out to touch the walls. Pine needles and … ice?

A low fire is burning two feet to the right of me. The smoke mostly escapes out of a small opening in the snow, but some of it hovers in the air overhead. A cooked fish sits on a stone, and on the other side of the flames is Rye, stabbing the ground aimlessly with his pocketknife. He looks up.

"You're awake," he says.

"Where are we?" I ask, rubbing my temple.

"Take a look." He points to the opening.

I stick my head out through the hole, and the cold air freezes the sweat on my face. Everything is white. Deep drifts of snow extend for as far as I can see.

"The flurries turned into a blizzard," Rye continues as I pull my head back in. The heat rolls over me, and the beads of sweat melt, dribble down my neck. "Plus you were getting heavy, so I figured it was time to stop for the night. The snow had heaped up around this spruce, creating a perfect igloo-type shelter once I dug a way in."

"You carried me again?"

"Yeah, but you held the fish for me. In your sling."

"Gross." I look down and see I'm still wearing my jacket. No wonder I was hot.

"How's that fever?"

"I'm sweating like crazy," I say.

"Good. I kept the fire stoked, hoping it would break." His chest is glistening.

"You can put it out now, if you want," I tell him.

He grins. "You're my new favorite person." He smothers the flames with some snow and his shoe.

I look back at his chest, his bare skin. "Wait a second," I exclaim. "You were out in a blizzard—you dug out this shelter!—without a shirt on?"

"Here." He ignores my question and hands me a hollowed out piece of wood with water inside. "Melted snow. Drink up."

I guzzle down the liquid. It soothes my throat, but it only makes my stomach feel empty.

"That fish is yours," he says, as if reading my thoughts. "Sorry I didn't wait for you before eating mine."

"Thanks," I say, tearing into it.

Despite my hunger, I only manage to put a third of it away. I set the rest back down on the rock for later and wipe my fingers on my pants. "Are we going to stay here the night?" I ask.

"Depends." His mouth twitches. "Do you need more sleep?"

"More sleep?" I frown. "How long have I been out?"

"At least twenty-four hours," he says.

"What? It's tomorrow? I mean, the Rangi attacked us yesterday?"

"Yep. You fell asleep when I went to get the fish, and I couldn't wake you up. So I carried you until the snow got bad. We were here all of last night, and we're about two-thirds of the way through today."

"Oh, wow. I'm sorry."

"Your health is more important. Besides, we wouldn't have been able to windwalk in the blizzard anyway. I'm just glad you're feeling better."

"Thanks," I say. "For taking care of me. How are you feeling?"

"I'm fine. A little too much time to think maybe."

I know what he means. He stabs the knife in the ground again, and I notice his carving is resting by his foot.

"Are you still working on it?" I ask, nodding at the small figurine.

He picks up the deer and tosses it toward me. I barely catch it with my right hand. Bringing it into my chest, I look down at the tiny statue. It's destroyed—wood splintered, the antlers broken off. It must have happened in the fight.

"Oh," I breathe. We're both quiet.

"I just get so angry," Rye finally says, jabbing the blade back into the dirt. "I want to kill every last Rangi, make them die a slow death. But I can't windwalk and carry that hate at the same time. So it fades. And then I hate myself for letting it fade."

"I think I understand," I whisper. I wish I could tell him that I know what it's like, tell him about my parents, how I was so scared, I couldn't cry. I've never talked to anyone about it, not Tom or Sue, not the twins, not the school counselors. But I could tell Rye. He would understand.

But even if I could get my lips to form the words, I couldn't really tell him. Because Aura's parents didn't die when she was seven. And if I tell him who I am, I'll lose him.

"I think Buck would be proud of you," I say. It's not enough, not by a long shot, but it's all I can do.

Water wells in his deep eyes, and he sniffs and wrinkles his nose, trying to keep the tears from spilling over. I hate feeling so helpless, so utterly unable to make it better. *If I weren't such a coward* ... But I am. So I just reach across the dead fire and hold his hand.

15

We decide to spend the night under the tree after all. I'm still weak, and Rye isn't eager to carry me another hundred miles. Besides, he's not exactly in great shape either—apart from the fish, he hasn't eaten anything in over thirty-six hours. So for the rest of the day and into the evening, we rest in our hiding place, talking quietly, and I ask Rye to tell me about his family.

"Chia's fourteen," he says. "She's a brain. She gets good grades in school and is always winning awards. She can be kind of a brat sometimes though, and she takes forever to get ready in the morning. But most of the time she's pretty fun to hang out with. She's fast too. She can almost catch me in windracing.

"Maize is eleven," he continues. "She loves animals. I think she brings home a stray cat or dog every other week. Mom lets her take care of them for a few days until she can find them a home." He chuckles. "Once she came back from the pet store with a one-eyed fish. She bought it because she felt sorry for it."

"That's cute."

"Yeah, she's a sweetheart. And then there's Teff. He's nine, the youngest. He's always getting into trouble, but he's so oblivious, most of the time he doesn't realize that what he's doing is a problem. Like one time, we were at the park and someone's dog was tied to a lamp post. The dog was barking and tugging at the leash, and Teff figured that the dog didn't want to be tied up. So he walked over and let him loose. The dog's owner was furious! We had to chase the dog down for a half an hour until we finally caught him."

I smile, wishing I could tell him about all of Jack's crazy exploits and Maisy's obsession with horses. "What about your parents?" I ask.

"Mom's the best. She's always cooking something delicious or cracking us up with a joke. She's about the only person who can make Dad laugh."

"What's your dad's name?"

"Makya."

"What does it mean?"

"Eagle hunter."

"That's impressive."

"Yeah," Rye snorts, "especially compared to a grain."

It's quiet for a moment, and then I say, "So, does he actually hunt eagles, because that seems like something the Yakone wouldn't like."

Rye grins. "I guess my grandfather wasn't thinking about that when he named him, maybe because his parents were Okłumin."

"Is Makya an Okłumin word?"

His forehead wrinkles. "No, it's Kohangaere."

"Kohangaere? What's that?"

He sits up. "Aura, Kohangaere is our language."

I stare at him. *Crap.* "Our language?"

"Yeah, all windwalkers speak it."

"But we're speaking English now."

"Well, yeah, because we grew up speaking it, because we live in North America. We have to speak the language of the humans we live with, but we all learn Kohangaere. Otherwise, we wouldn't be able to communicate with each other."

"Is Kohangaere what the first windwalkers spoke?" I ask, hoping to distract him.

"Yes."

"And it hasn't changed, after all this time?"

"It has—just not among windwalkers. Pieces of it exist in languages all over the world."

"In human languages?"

"Right. When windwalkers became human, they continued to speak Kohangaere, but as they spread across the globe their language evolved into various dialects and eventually different languages."

"Oh." I fidget with my Quil, not sure what else to say.

"That's a good example, actually," Rye says, pointing to the device.

"This?"

"Yeah. *Quil* means eagle in Kohangaere, and as you've pointed out, our Yakone ancestors chose it as the symbol of our tribe and our ability to windwalk. The Latin word for eagle is *aquila*, and that's how you get *aigle* in French and eventually eagle in English." He leans forward. "But guess what the Romans called their wind god?"

"What?"

"Aquilo! See how it's all connected?"

I raise an eyebrow. "Are you sure you don't want to be a storyteller?"

"Nah. I'm just long-winded."

We look at each other and then burst out laughing.

After a moment, it grows quiet again, and Rye pushes the pine needles around with a twig then clears his throat. "So, when I came to get you—after I caught the fish—and I tried to wake you up, you called me Jeremy."

I look at my feet. "Oh."

"Is he your boyfriend?" Rye asks.

"No," I stammer quickly. "He was just a friend."

"Was?"

"He died. During the attack."

"I'm sorry." He pokes at the needles, pulls at his ear.

His question reminds me of something Lila told me a lifetime ago. "What about you?" I ask. "Do you have a girlfriend?"

"No." He snaps the twig in half. "There's someone my parents want me to marry, but I don't have a girlfriend."

"Who is she?"

"A family friend. It's not important."

"You don't think you'll marry her?"

"I don't know. I don't really want to talk about it."

"Okay. Sorry." I study the frozen pine boughs.

"I'll be right back," Rye says.

As he slips out through the opening, I punch my leg with my fist. *Stupid! Why did I have to keep asking questions?* I wish I could know who she is, what she's like.

A scraping noise against the hard snow makes me look up as Rye's head pops back through the gap. "You gotta come see this," he says, grinning.

I shimmy out through the opening, careful not to bump my arm on the ice, and step onto the smooth, crunchy snow. Then I look in the direction he's pointing and gasp.

Above the horizon, streaks of emerald and sapphire swirl against the black night. They snake above my head, pulsing larger and brighter, exploding to light up the entire sky, shrinking and flickering into oblivion, returning once more to resume their lambent dance.

"Aurora borealis," Rye says. "Aurora for the goddess of dawn. Boreas for the god of the north wind, like Aquilo."

"The god of the wind," I repeat. I can't tear my eyes away from the sea green waves cascading overhead.

"Speaking of stories," he says quietly, "do you know what the Inuit word is for aurora?"

"No. Should I?"

"It's Yakone."

"Really?"

He grins and, pitching his voice low, says, "The Eskimo say that the mannabai'wok, or giants, live in the direction of the north wind. They tell their children, 'The mannabai'wok are our friends, but we don't see them anymore. They are great hunters and fishermen, and whenever they are out with their torches to spear fish, we know it. For then the sky is bright in the place where they are.'"

I smile at his performance. "And we're supposed to be the mannabai'wok?"

"Yep."

"But we aren't up there." I point to the green heavens.

"Not yet."

I turn to look at him, at the hand he's holding out. His grin has faded to a soft smile, and his eyes match the color of the flickering lights. I hesitate only a moment, and then I entwine my fingers in his, and we leap into the night.

The breeze is gentle, and we scale the currents easily, climbing higher and higher into the darkness. The cold air whips around my arms, but it doesn't bother me. I keep my eyes fixed on the luminous beams twisting across the sky.

When we finally stop, I can't tell how far away the ground is. I'm suspended in the thick blackness, surrounded by stars and an ocean of viridian. The light spills across my hand, my arm, my clothes, as if I'm underwater, swimming in it.

I look at Rye. His whole face has become the color of his eyes, and the light flashes and shifts across his skin.

He leans close and speaks into my ear. "I know you don't remember, but the last day at the testing grounds, you promised me a kiss."

My sluggish blood suddenly surges through my veins. "I did?"

"Yeah, you did." He turns me to face him. Slides his arm around my waist, tips his head against mine, softly touches my neck, my cheek, my hair. The wind spins us in gentle circles.

A burst of rose and heliotrope shoots across the green sky, and suddenly everything is warm. His eyes are warm. His fingers are warm. His breath is warm. His lips, as they press against mine, are warm and warm and warm.

When the lights fade away, we return to our tree, still holding hands. Rye kisses me again and tells me to go to sleep. "I'll be back in a little bit," he says.

"Where are you going?"

"Just for a walk. I'll be back."

"But you're not even wearing a shirt."

He holds his arms out and laughs, "Do I look cold?"

I smile and let him go, watch his silhouette join the night. Then I duck into our snowy tent and curl up on my side on the pine needles. As I close my eyes and remember the sensation of his mouth on mine, the nerves in my chest buzz, sending tingling waves throughout my entire body.

Sleep is the furthest thing from my mind, but somehow it sneaks up on me, and I slip into its heady embrace. I wake up only once, opening my eyes to the dark and listening for Rye's steady breathing. When I hear it, I fall asleep for good.

In the morning, I wake to the sound of snapping flames and quiet singing. It's hard to open my eyes, hard to sit up. My body quivers from the lack of food, and my arm throbs. When I'm finally able to push myself off the pine needles, I see Rye. He's melting more snow and crooning softly to the fire. His face is pale, but his voice is deep and rich, almost husky. I can't make out the words.

"What song is that?" I ask.

He stops. "Good morning." His mouth sidles into an uncertain smile.

I feel similar spasms on my own lips and have trouble meeting his gaze. He looks down and pokes at the fire. "It's an old Yakone song. A song of farewell. Our people would sing it when their loved ones left for war."

"Can I hear the whole thing?"

He coughs. "I don't know."

"Please?"

"All right, maybe it will help you remember, but don't laugh at me. My voice is especially unreliable today."

"I won't," I promise.

He begins to sing.

The wind blows so sweetly, my love, through the night,
Crossing the distance that I cannot span;
Its gentle arms touch you, wherever you are
    So
Bridging the chasm as only love can.

The night is so still now, out under the moon—
Cascades of velvet, brief flashes of jade.
The cheek where you kissed me is cool to the touch.
     But
Stars shine inside me, born never to fade.

The wind sings so sweetly and speaks through the night
Saying the long wait will shortly be done;
I smile at the wind's song and sit by the door
     For
Lovers as we two forever are one.

He finishes and neither of us says a word. He was right. His voice wasn't perfect, but somehow it made the song better, more real. I see why he was embarrassed—the reference to the Northern Lights, what the song implies—and I look at my hands. If only it could be. If only I could have that kind of hope.

But soon I'll have to leave, and I'll never see him again.

"It's lovely," I say, the tears that won't fall gripping my throat.

"My voice doesn't do it justice," he says. "You should hear my mom sing it."

"I'd like to."

"Here." He hands me the cup of water. His hands are shaking. "Drink up. We probably won't find any more water today."

My hands shake too as I make myself drink. The liquid hits my stomach, and I feel more acutely the enormous, never-ending pit inside my body. I want to go back to sleep, make it go away.

We douse the fire and crawl out of the igloo, and when I stand up, a dark cloud dims my eyesight. I hold still for a moment, waiting for it to pass. It takes all my willpower not to collapse onto the snow.

I feel Rye's hand on my back. "Are you okay?" he asks. His face has grown paler.

I nod. "You?"

He doesn't answer my question. "I'll keep an eye out for food as we go, but the problem is we don't have any weapons."

"How close are we to the *Wakenunat*?"

"I think we can make it today, if we push ourselves."

My arm aches, and the emptiness in my legs makes me stumble, but it doesn't matter how tired or hungry or hurt I am—I *can't* go to the fortress. I'm going to have to make a break for it when Rye's ahead of me, not looking. I try not to think about what he'll feel, what it will do to him.

Just then, Rye slips on the ice and crashes onto the ground, scratching his bare skin on the jagged snow. I bend down to help him, and my chest tightens when I see how violently his limbs are trembling, how much he struggles to stand back up. Why is he so much weaker than I am?

"Did you really catch two fish?" I ask, suspicion dawning on me.

"It will be hard to connect to the wind," Rye says, "but it will help the pain once we do."

"Answer me," I demand. "Have you eaten anything in the past three days?"

He doesn't say anything, just looks away. *Oh no, Rye.*

"Why?" I whisper.

"I couldn't let you starve."

Suddenly, I see it all, see him taking off his shirt to bind my wound, leading the Rangi away so I could escape, carrying me countless miles while I was passed out, building a shelter in the middle of a blizzard, giving me all our food so my body would have strength to heal.

And I was going to leave him.

I close my eyes. If I go through with my plan, he won't be able to stop me. I can windwalk to the nearest city, stay alive. And Rye will die.

Or I can help him get to the fortress and give him a chance to live, which means they'll probably catch me. Torture me. Hand me over to the police—if I'm lucky.

I open my eyes and look at Rye, his shivering body, his gentle hands, arms, face. His kind, wonderful face.

I exhale slowly, my mind made up.

"Show me how to find the coordinates on my Quil," I say. *I have to come clean.* Not yet though. Soon. Before we get there.

He helps me find the screen with the GPS, and I move the map onto watch mode then loop my arm around his. "Ready?" I ask. He nods.

I reach for the airy swells. It's difficult to separate the mental opening I create from the gnawing I feel inside my stomach, and it takes me at least a minute to find *honga*. But I finally jump off the ground, and the bond keeps me steady.

Arms linked, we carefully work our way up the streams of air. It doesn't take us long to reach our normal altitude, and once we climb above the trees, I understand why, see what the snow had hidden from me. The landscape has changed, no more flat forest with thousands of lakes and tributaries. The earth has risen up to help propel us into the sky—these last two nights we were camped on top of a mountain.

We've entered the Rockies.

As we leave our hilltop, enormous peaks roll endlessly out in front of us. I've never seen anything like it. Some of the summits are higher than we are. They brush the fleecy clouds hovering overhead. Their rock faces are cut away in sharp, horizontal lines, plummeting into steep, swooping valleys. Huge drifts of snow cushion the stone ledges and climb up the canyon sides. In a gorge below us, a frosted river snakes its way through the range.

We pass over the ravine, and, for the first time, I'm frightened to windwalk. If I lose my connection now, I'll fall to my death. Rye must be thinking the same thing because he points down into the chasm, and we soar past the sheer crags, winding our way above the icy water.

I soon discover another reason for Rye's navigational choice. The canyon creates a natural wind tunnel. The air rushes between the cliffs at an accelerated rate, and we're able to go faster without putting forth any extra effort.

For the first few hours, the crisp mountain air and the phenomenal views keep me distracted. The wind numbs my injuries and hunger. By midday, however, the rock walls are blurring into the snow and sky, and when I look at the Quil, I can't read the screen. My wrist seems far away, like it's not connected to my body. My body starts to tip back, and I feel like I'm floating.

I realize I'm falling and scramble to stay connected.

"Rye," I mumble. "Pocketknife." When I feel him press it into my hand, I fumble to open the blade and then jab it into my skin.

The sharp pain jolts along my nerves, attacks my brain. I blink rapidly and stare at my palm until I see the bulbous drop of crimson form on the surface. More alert now, I rebuild my link to the wind, strengthening my grip on Rye's arm and pressing my palm hard into his skin, embracing the sting.

I steal a glance at Rye's face. His eyes are glazed over, and he's panting, but he's hanging in there. For now. I hold him tightly, willing him to stay strong.

But when long shadows fill the valleys, and the temperature drops even more, I'm ready to give in. I open my cracked lips to tell Rye I'm sorry, but I can't get the words to come out. I can't even salivate.

He saves me the effort. "Let's stop," he gasps. "Just for a few minutes."

The current we're on rises up at an incline, and we ride it until we see a flat ledge on the closest summit. We crash onto the slab, collapsing against the rocky mountainside.

Now that I don't have the wind to mask the pain, my arm is on fire, my head is splintering, and I can hardly support the weight of my skull. I close my eyes against the vertigo. The sharp breeze slaps my dry face. I lean into Rye, seeking his warmth, but his skin is as cold as mine.

I don't know how long we stay there, huddled against the wind's icy blows, struggling to keep our eyes from closing for good, but it's more than a few minutes. Before long, I can't move my fingers, nor do I want to. I peel my eyelids back one last time and see the blurry sun sinking behind the endless peaks.

And then, as the golden orb disappears beyond the distant crests, I see a tiny, beautiful spark of green light.

Green. Green like the pine trees. Green like Rye's eyes. Green like the Northern Lights. *Brief flashes of jade.*

Brief flashes of jade. Where have I heard that before? It has something to do with Rye. *Yes, his song. This morning.* So long ago. The Yakone sing it when their warriors leave. It's about the Aurora Borealis.

The green light is gone now, so fleeting, so brief. *Wait.* I blink slowly. *Brief. A brief flash.* Could it be? Maybe I was wrong. Maybe the song isn't about the Northern Lights. Maybe it's a song about home, about returning to that place high in the mountains, the only place where you can see a brief flash of green when the sun sets.

Maybe we're close.

I look at the Quil, and my heart begins to thud. It says we're here. I look around, but I don't see anything—just mountain peak after mountain peak.

"Rye?" My voice is so gravelly, so distant, it seems to be coming from someone else. "Rye, wake up." I shake him weakly.

He mutters something I can't make out, and I shake him again. "We're really close. The Quil says we're here, and I just saw the green flash, but I don't know where to go. You've got to help me."

"What?" he mumbles.

I try to clear my throat. "I saw the green flash. On the horizon. You know, the song."

He opens his eyes. "You did?" he croaks. "Where?"

I point ahead. "There."

"So close," he rasps. "But … can't do it."

"We have to. Come on, stand up." I try to climb to my feet but stumble and slam back into the cliff face. My injured arm hits the rock, and pain courses through my body, making me cry out.

Cringing, I tug on Rye's arm. "Stand up," I order again. At first I don't think he'll be able to do it, but after clutching my hand and the rocks, he manages to pull himself onto his feet. "Which way?" I ask.

"Northwest ... tallest peak to the northwest."

"Can you windwalk?"

He shakes his head. "I—I don't think so."

"Hold onto me," I say, and we stagger to the edge of the cliff. I don't know if I'll be strong enough to support us—this could very well be a jump to our deaths. But we don't have a choice.

"Hold onto me," I repeat, my voice dropping to a whisper. Rye wraps his arms around my shoulders, leans against my back. I open myself to the wind. *Help us*, I plead. I feel the air's strong threads entwine themselves within me.

We step off the ledge.

Immediately, Rye's weight sends us plummeting down. I scramble for a current and barely retain my hold on the wind. We shoot forward, but I don't know how long I'll be able to keep going with Rye dangling from my neck, nearly strangling me. I grasp his arms and search through the darkness for the mountain he described, praying it's nearby, but they all look the same. Enormous black shapes in the sunless sky.

I feel Rye's fingers slip and clutch his arm more tightly. I make myself go faster, ignoring everything else—the pain, the cold, the hunger. And then I see a tremendous mountain peak, taller than all its neighbors. That must be it.

My fingers start to slide off Rye's damp skin, and I dig my nails into his arm. *Don't let go of me*, I will him. *Don't let go.* If only the wind were faster.

As if it heard me, the breeze suddenly picks up speed, and we zoom directly toward the summit. I don't even have to change currents. *Don't let go. Don't let go*, I repeat in my mind, over and over. We're almost there. So close. *Don't let go.* It's difficult to think, to see, to breathe.

And then we're crashing onto the mount's sloping side, our weak feet slipping on the rocks, rolling down the incline. With my bad hand, I reach into the snow and curl my fingers around a rock. Rye's body tugs hard on my arm, sending tears to my eyes. The sharp stone rips blood from my skin, but we stop sliding, and I don't let go. I cling to him with my other hand.

I wait for the wave of pain to subside, make sure we won't fall any further. Then I sit up, slowly, haltingly, and check on Rye. "Are you okay?"

He groans. I touch his forehead and feel blood on my fingers. I can't tell how bad it is.

"Where's the *Wakenunat?*" I ask. "Do we have to climb up or down?"

"Hillside," he mumbles.

"What? We're on the hillside. I don't see anything."

"No. Inside." Slowly, he raises his head. Then he picks up a rock and throws it weakly against the mountain.

I watch the rock tumble down, listen to its long echoing clatter. Then I slump forward onto the snow. It's over now, for certain. Rye is delirious. He doesn't know where the *Wakenunat* is. He's trying to break into a mountain. By throwing rocks at it. The beckoning darkness seeps into my brain.

A mechanical groan makes me open my eyes. Above me, to the left, light spills into the dark night, and I hear voices. I try lifting my chin, calling out, but my tongue won't move. Then my head drops back into the icy rocks, and I know no more.

STAGE FOUR: COLLISION

When the downburst touches the ground, it spreads out in all directions, creating high-speed winds known as thundergusts. Thundergusts can cause as much damage as a tornado—and they produce deadly conditions for flying.

The Horned Serpents are our enemies. They are very dangerous, for they also control the skies. The Sioux call these monsters the Unktehila. In old times, the Thunderbirds fought the Unktehila on behalf of man. There was war on the earth for many years until finally the Thunderbirds won, and the Unktehila were destroyed. Now all that remains of their kind are the snakes that slither along the ground and strike at our feet.

16

I wake up surrounded by pale blue light. I stare at the ceiling until the rectangular lamp above me comes gradually into focus and I remember who I am. Slowly turning my head to the right, I see a long line of cots stretched out beside me, the mattresses wrapped in white sheets that reflect the glowing blue from above. Two of the beds have occupants, but most of them are empty.

The walls are strange. Black. Uneven. Like they're made of stone. As I reach out my hand to test them with my fingers, I feel a tug on my skin. There's an IV in my arm. I look down at the clear plastic tube pumping liquid into my veins, and then I know the rest. We made it. We're in the *Wakenunat*. I look back at the stone walls. *Rye wasn't delirious after all.* The *Wakenunat* is inside a mountain.

Rye! *Where is he? Is he alive?* I sit up, and a lightning bolt zips across my forehead. Gritting my teeth, I suck in my breath and press my temple with my fingers. When I can see again, I discover that my injured arm has been dressed in clean cloth, and a new sling is tied around my shoulders. My fingers are bandaged too, as is the burn on my face.

My clothes are gone—tattered jacket, shredded shirt and khakis, mud-caked shoes and socks, everything. Now I'm wearing soft gray pants and a matching gray shirt. I reach for my collar and feel the familiar shape of my necklace underneath the thick fabric. *Good, it's still there.* I look down at my wrist. I still have the Quil too, tucked underneath the bandage on my arm.

Turning my head, I reexamine the bunks on my right, the ones that were being used. One of the occupants is a small girl. The other is an elderly man. I look to my left. There are more bunks on this side, but they're all empty. *Where is Rye?*

In the center of the room, a woman dressed in gray sits at a table, sifting through papers.

"Hello?" I call. My voice comes out in a whisper, and I try again. "Hello?"

This time, the woman looks up. She pushes her chair back, walks toward me.

"Lie back down," she says, pressing my shoulders.

"Where's Rye?" I ask. "Is he okay?"

"It's important that you get your rest."

"Tell me where he is!"

She sighs. "Lie down. I'll be right back." She checks the IV then walks past the cots to an opening on the other side of the room.

I stare at the drip while I wait, at the slow stream of fluids entering my body. *What's taking her so long?*

Finally, she returns. Alone. She walks back to the table and sits down again, picks up her papers, says nothing to me.

I want to scream, but I know my voice won't be able to achieve the volume I require. Besides, I don't want to risk antagonizing her. She might never tell me what I want to know. So I make myself lie still, watch the liquid drip through the tube.

The soft thud of rubber soles on stone makes me look up, and my breath catches. "Rye," I whisper.

"Hey," he says, crouching next to me and taking my hand. "Are you okay?" A bandage is wrapped around his brow, but the color of his face looks good, and his black eye has faded to yellow. He's also wearing the soft gray clothes.

"Am I okay? What about you? The last time I saw you, you were passed out in the snow."

"And you were right there with me."

I cough. "How did they find us anyway?"

"There are security cameras and sensors on the outside of the mountain. I just had to attract their attention."

"When you threw that rock, I thought you had lost your mind."

"Me? Never." He smiles. "And now that I've had a good night's sleep and gotten some fluids in my body, I feel brand new. But you've slept for another whole day and night."

"I have? Again?"

"Yeah. You must be a really heavy sleeper."

That's what Lila told me. "Have you—do you know if any of the others made it, from the camp?"

His face darkens. "A few of them, but not very many. Most of the ones who did were counselors."

I nod, my throat tight. "Is your family here?"

"Yes, all but my dad. He's out with the chief. They've gone dark, so we haven't been able to contact them. No one's Quils are working either. My mom told me the Rangi hacked into our communications system, probably at the camp. They were using the Quils to track people, kill them, so the chief shut the system down. That's why the tribe couldn't find us, even though they sent out search parties."

"How did they learn about the attack?"

"The *Matoa* and *Riki* always attend the last day of the testing. When they showed up, well, you can imagine."

If Rye's family is here, Aura's might be too.

"Rye," I ask hesitantly. "Is Aur—is my family here?"

"No," he answers. "Not yet. Soon, I'm sure. Don't worry."

I feel my muscles relax. I'm safe, for now, but I don't have much time. They could show up at any moment. *I've got to tell him the truth. Before it's too late.*

I open my mouth, but instead of confessing I hear myself ask, "Do you think they'll let me get up?"

"I don't know. You were in pretty bad shape."

"I feel fine now."

"I'll talk to the doc," Rye says, "though I can't promise she'll go for it." Getting up, he walks over to the woman in gray. He says something to her, and they both return to my cot.

"I hear you want out of bed," the doctor says.

"Yeah. I feel much better."

"I'll tell you what. Stay here for another two hours, and show me that you can eat some food. If you're still feeling fine then, I'll release you."

"All right." *Two hours, and then I'll tell him.*

Rye stays with me as I eat some toast and chicken broth. I have to force my mouth to open at first—I can only take small sips of the broth, and I let the toast sit on my tongue until it dissolves—but soon I start to feel hungry, and I eat everything on my tray. When I'm done, Rye sets the tray on the floor, and I lean back into the pillows, enjoying the warm fullness in my stomach, ignoring for a moment what's to come.

"You almost cracked my skull back open, you know," Rye says, running his thumb over my fingers and grinning at me.

"That's what you get for not eating your fish," I retort, but I squeeze his hand.

He laughs. "I should let you sleep a little more."

"No, don't leave me," I beg when he stands up. *We only have two hours.*

"I'll be back soon. I promise."

Despite all my protests, he leaves. And despite my best intentions, I fall back asleep.

Rye wakes me by kissing my forehead. "How are you feeling?" he asks.

"I'm good," I yawn. "Will the doctor let me go?"

"I think so." He waves to the woman in gray, and she comes over and takes my temperature, listens to my heartbeat, feels my forehead. Then she removes the IV.

"Don't over do it," she warns, giving me some painkillers. "You have to take it easy on that arm, or it could start bleeding again."

"Sure thing." I swallow the pills. Then Rye helps me stand up. I'm a little wobbly on my feet at first, but by the time we've walked across the room, the dizziness has passed and I feel better than I have in weeks.

Now. I have to tell him now.

We reach the doorway. A large animal skin is draped across the threshold. Rye pushes the skin aside, and we exit the cavern. For a split-second, we're standing in darkness, but Rye takes a step forward, and suddenly the ceiling and walls directly around us are covered in thousands of tiny blue lights.

We're in a tunnel. The miniscule bulbs switch on in a wave until the entire passageway is covered in stars.

"Remember this?" Rye asks.

"No ... " I feel like I'm moving in slow motion, floating in space.

"LEDs," Rye says, pointing to the lights.

We walk through the corridor, and the bulbs continue to turn on, lighting up the passageway ahead of us. Then we round a bend, and the lights reveal other openings in the walls, also covered by rugs and animal skins.

"What's in the rooms?" I ask.

"See for yourself." We stop at the closest rug, and Rye raps on the wall then pushes back the woven fabric.

It's another cave. But instead of the LED stars, it has one central lighting panel on the ceiling—like the one over my cot. And it's filled with bunk beds. A group of children is playing with two gray and white Husky puppies in the center of the chamber, and sitting in a chair off to the side, watching them, is a woman with long white hair gathered in a braid.

"Hi, Sarah," Rye says.

The woman looks up. "Rye, my sweet boy! You've brought your friend."

She stands up and, with surprising alacrity, crosses the floor toward us, enveloping Rye in her arms, kissing his cheek. Then, before I know it's coming, she's wrapped her arms around me as well. She smells like lavender, and her hands are warm and soft. "I hope you're feeling better," she says.

"I am," I stammer. "Thank you."

The children who were playing on the floor suddenly surround Rye, pulling on his shirt and begging him to wrestle with them, while the dogs wiggle their tails and bound back and forth. Rye chases the kids around for a few minutes, tickling them whenever he catches them. They shriek with laughter, and the puppies yap. Finally, they all plop to the ground, breathing heavily.

"Would you like something to eat?" Sarah asks. "Your mother just sent me some grapes from the greenhouse. And we have bread and dried beef."

"Thanks, Sarah," Rye pants. "But I'm fine." He looks at me. "Do you want anything?"

"No," I say. "Thanks."

One of the children, a girl who looks like she's four or five, speaks up. "I want some bread, Auntie Sarah. With honey!"

"Me too!" the other children cry.

"All right," Sarah laughs. "Now I've done it. Line up, and I'll give you your snack."

"We've got to go," Rye says, standing up and pecking the old woman on the cheek. "But I'll see you again soon."

"Okay, dear." She tries to say goodbye to me, but the children are all over her now, dogs yelping again, and she turns to give them her full attention.

As we leave the room and return to the tunnel, Rye looks at me. "That's my mom's aunt," he says. "She's like my grandma."

"She was nice." *Nothing like Grandma Mildred.*

The stars light up again as we walk down the corridor, and when we come to a fork, Rye takes the path on the right.

"Where are we going?" I ask.

"You'll see."

I scan the hallways anxiously as we pass more rugs over doorways and hear more voices inside rooms—children mostly, pets too. The tunnel branches again, and we turn left this time. I try to keep track of the turns, but this place is a maze. Even though the air is cool, damp spots are showing on my gray shirt. *Tell him!*

"So—"

"Every family has its own room," Rye says at the same time. "Oh, sorry. Go ahead."

"No, it's fine. You first."

"The rooms are called *rukamos*. Most of them are in sectors four and five. There are some in sector three too."

"Sectors?"

"Yeah. Each sector designates a level of the mountain. There are five total. We're in sector four right now. Sector one is the *rukanaga*, the council chamber. It's at the top of the mountain. Sector two is the *rukamura*, the war hangar—where we have the control center and store the weapons and equipment. It also has the biggest doors, so large numbers of people can come and go at once."

"Rye."

But he's talking too quickly to hear me. "Our *rukanu* is in sector three. That's the gathering place, where we have our celebrations and the final Challenge battle. The generator and our storage rooms are in sector five—and the greenhouse. The greenhouse is awesome. It's covered in glass so it looks like a glacier in the winter." He pauses and looks at me. "Is any of this sparking your memory?"

I clear my throat. "Rye, there's something I need to tell you."

Just then we turn a final corner, and the tunnel opens onto a steel bridge decked in LEDs. I take a step back. The bridge spans a huge chasm, and as I look over the edge at the dark ravine below me, I see more bulbs strung down the sides of the cliff. A loud humming echoes through the canyon.

"That's the cistern that holds our water," Rye says. "The water comes from an aquifer. It flows from the cistern and spins the turbines on the generator, providing electricity too. Neat, huh?"

"Is the generator making that noise?"

"Nope. The fans are doing that."

"Fans?"

"I'll show you." He leads me across the smooth, glowing bridge.

The noise gets louder as we move into the center of the gorge, and it's hard to hear anything. Rye points down.

As I look over the edge, I tighten my grip on his hand. At the bottom of the chasm, a giant glowing circle hovers somewhere above the water, and now I can feel the air whipping past my face, lifting up my hair.

"There's one above us too," he yells. "It's how we move from one level to the next."

I look up. As far as I can tell, the shaft continues all the way to the top of the mountain. Directly overhead, another bridge stretches across the canyon. Connecting our bridge to that are two steel staircases, also lit up and circling the shaft like a double helix.

"Do people use the stairs?" I ask. He answers, but I can't hear him. "What?"

"Emergencies," he shouts.

I gape at the starry ravine, the moving air, the twisting staircases, the sleek bridges, the tunnels that lead to more tunnels and to cavern after cavern after cavern.

"Are you ready?" Rye asks.

His voice jolts me back. "For what?" I stammer.

"To go up."

I shake my head. "I need to tell you something first."

"What?"

"I need to tell you something!"

"Hard to hear. Wait." He points to the air, and I nod reluctantly. Then we jump off the bridge into the rising current.

As we rocket past the bridge above us, I see people on the other side of the chasm going down, using the wind created by the fan at the top of the shaft. The LEDs whirl past as the updraft shoots us toward the peak. We go through a large hole in the ceiling and land on another bridge.

There are no tunnels on this level. All sides of the shaft have been hollowed out so that the stone floor, much smaller in diameter than the base of the mountain, fully circles the chasm. The opened walls, lined with huge lighting panels, create an enormous chamber—and it's full of people.

I stare at the windwalkers. They're wearing gray jumpsuits that bulge around their chests, probably covering bullet-proof vests, and embroidered on their backs are large red eagles. The warriors are running around the cavern, stacking automatic rifles and machine guns. And not just that: portable missiles and grenade launchers too.

A thick slab of glass covers the space above our heads, and I can see the feet of the people standing on top of it. Two stone staircases extend on either side of the bridge to openings in the glass ceiling. Rye directs me toward one of them.

"We're going up?" my voice cracks. I wipe my wet palm on my pants.

"Let's go," Rye says. He takes my hand again, pulling me toward the steps.

"Rye, wait," I plead, but he doesn't hear me.

I look back down at the people in gray, the missiles, the deep chasm we've left behind. The whole scene warps, and I trip on the step. Rye helps me back up. I try again to get his attention, but my tongue is stiff and dry, and I can't form the words.

We emerge through the holes in the floor, and for a moment I'm reminded of the testing grounds, taking that first step into the *wakenu*. The rock walls are reinforced with steel, and a large table with the Yakone flag stands in the middle of the room.

But Naira doesn't sit behind the table. A man does. A man with long black hair and a stone amulet around his neck. And instead of the huge windows in the dining hall, there's the glass floor that opens to a view of the mountain's interior. I can see all the way down the shaft, the LEDs directing my eyes to the dark spot that marks the cistern.

There are other people in the room too. Half a dozen men, a few women—all of them in the gray jumpsuits. My heart stumbles when I see the automatics in their hands.

A man with chocolate brown hair is leaning over the desk, talking to the man with the amulet. He goes pale when he sees us.

"Rye?" he whispers.

"Dad!" They look at each other, and then Rye's father moves forward and pulls him into a tight embrace.

"You're safe," the man breathes. "I was so … " He coughs. "Does your mother know?"

"Yes."

"We only just got here. I haven't talked to her yet." Rye's father holds him firmly for a few more seconds before releasing him.

Rye takes a shaky step back and bows to the black-haired man behind the desk. He's standing now, reaching out his arm.

"*Tanaka, Riki*," Rye says, recovering, clasping the man's hand then pounding his fist on his chest. "Your timing is perfect. I have some good news." He turns to look at me. "I've brought you your daughter."

17

Everyone's eyes lock on me as I back away slowly, their bodies listing toward the center of the room. I try to keep my balance, but my mind whirls. *No. No! Did he really just say that I am—that Aura is...? Kava, kava, kava.*

For a brief moment, the chief's eyes light up, and he moves quickly toward me. Then he slows down. When he's three feet away, he stops, stares at me. Frowns. Shakes his head.

"Who are you?" he asks.

"I, um." I continue backing toward the stairs.

In a flash, he's crossed the distance between us and wrapped his iron fingers around my right bicep. "I said who are you?" His brow darkens into a deep burgundy.

"My name is Kit," I squeak.

"What?" Rye says from behind us.

I can't meet his gaze. "I'm sorry," I whisper.

"But ... you had Aura's I.D.," Rye says slowly.

"Did you kill my daughter?" the *Riki* thunders. His grip tightens, and the people around me level their guns.

"No," I gasp. "I didn't. It was the Rangi. I saw them do it."

"Then what are you doing here?"

"I—I wanted her I.D.," I stutter. "Not her real one. There was a fake one. That's what I wanted. Because my fingerprints were on it, and we looked the same. But then I was abducted and taken to the *maitanga* and—"

"What do you mean a fake one?" The chief shakes my arm.

"I sold it to her. So she could ... so she could ... " My voice falters as I try to think of how to tell him.

But I don't have to tell him. He knows what I'm trying to say, and his face blotches into a deeper purple. "Lies!" he roars.

"No, I can prove it. I have it." I reach for my pockets. But I have no pockets. I have no jacket either. The license is gone. "My jacket," I rasp. "It was in there. They took my clothes. Rye, did you see it?"

But he doesn't answer me, doesn't even shake his head. He stares at me with cold, clouded eyes.

"I know what you are," the chief says icily. "You're a Rangi spy. You slit my daughter's throat and stole her identity, impersonated her, so you could inform your people of the location of the testing grounds. So you could murder them."

"No," I cry. "No, that's not true at all. See, I knew you would think that, that's why I couldn't tell … This is all a mistake. I'm not even a windwalker!"

"I expected more from a Rangi. But your cover story is pathetic." He throws me onto the floor. "Jared, Vivian," he commands two of his guards, "Take her to the prison block." He spits at the ground near my hand.

A man and a woman, both carrying automatics, step forward and yank me to my feet. "Wait, please," I beg, "I'm innocent!" They all ignore me. "Rye!" I plead, but he turns away.

My escorts haul me down the stairs and into the war hangar, their guns pressed against my back.

"This is a mistake," I insist. "I can explain everything."

"Shut up," Vivian says as they walk me onto the bridge. Holding my arms, they shove me forward, and we ride the wind down, past sector three and then sector four. We leap off the current at the lowest bridge. Sector five.

Dizzily, I notice that this bridge isn't made of steel like the others. It's made of polished rock. In front of me I see thick, metal beams extending from either end of the bridge and rising up into the shaft above, as if they're supporting the other walkways. I glance over the side and look down at the enormous reservoir, at the water lapping against the stone. But then Vivian pushes me forward, and I cry out as she hits my injured arm.

"What happened?" Jared yells, nodding at the sling.

"I was shot."

"Who shot you?"

"A Rangi scout."

"Who?"

"A Rangi!"

"Liar." Vivian cuffs me over the head, and I glare at her as they force me the rest of the way across.

After we step off the bridge and enter the network of tunnels on the other side, the hallway slopes down, making me feel as if I'm squeezing through the earth's intestines. I focus on breathing normally.

Eventually, the tunnel levels out again, and we enter a large chamber with holes in the floor. Each hole is covered by a grate.

The guards direct me toward one of the cells, and Jared pulls back the iron lattice. He grabs a rope ladder from a shelf in the wall then drops the ladder into the pit, securing the top end onto a metal hook in the floor.

"Climb down there," Vivian says.

I stare at her. "What?"

"You heard me."

"But my arm … "

"Here," Jared grunts. He lowers himself onto the ladder and leans back. "C'mon," he gestures. "Swing your legs over."

I do as he says. I have no other option, not with Vivian's rifle jabbed under my ribs. Slowly, we descend into a deluge of moist air. It smells awful, like we're right next to a sewer. When we reach the bottom, Jared lifts me onto the ground.

As he turns away, I catch a whiff of something that doesn't smell like sewage, a scent I know. *Lemongrass.* I jerk my head back and look at his face. There's something familiar about the curve of his jaw, the shape of his brow.

"Jeremy," I breathe.

"What?" the guard asks.

"Nothing." I look away.

"You called me Jeremy." His tone is guarded. "That's my brother's name. Do you know him?"

"Yes." My voice breaks. "I did."

"You *did*. He's dead then?"

I nod.

"How?"

"When the Rangi attacked the camp."

"Did he die well?"

"He was protecting me."

The silence is thick. "Hurry up, Jared," Vivian calls from above.

He ignores her and moves his face closer to mine. "Did he think you were the chief's daughter?" His throat is taut.

"I—I don't know," I falter. "I guess he did."

He leans back. "Then he thought he was saving her. He died for nothing."

I stagger back. Is it true? Is that why he did it? I press my fist against my forehead.

Jared swings himself onto the ladder. "I hope you rot in Hell," he spits.

I rush forward and grab his foot. "I swear I didn't know. I didn't know who she was."

"That won't bring my brother back." He kicks me away and keeps climbing. When he reaches the top, they pull the ladder up and replace the grille. Then he and Vivian leave.

I crumple to the ground and curl into a ball, stab my fingernails into my palms.

This is worse than anything I imagined. I already knew Jeremy didn't have to die, but I thought he helped me because he liked me, wanted to save *me*. But it's not true. He was trying to protect the chief's daughter. If I hadn't deceived him, he never would have risked his life.

And he's not the only person I endangered.

"Rye," I whisper. I try to ignore the sharp pain in my chest, the way it's moving up my throat. Try to forget the way he looked at me.

Rye thought I was Aura too. That's why he wouldn't leave me in the forest. Why he took care of me. *Is that why he kissed me?*

I hate Aura Torres. I hate her. She's ruined my life, buying her fake I.D., getting her throat slit. If she hadn't been out drinking and partying, attracting the Rangi, she would have gone to the camp instead of me. And none of this would have happened. I never would have heard of windwalking or the Yakone or the Rangi. I never would have watched my friends die. Or killed a person. I wouldn't be in a pit that smells like refuse. Wouldn't be in so much pain.

I scrape my cheek against the rock. *What does he think of me now?* His face flashes in front of me, that look in his eyes, the jumble of confusion, shock, horror, disgust. *He hates me.*

I would hate me too.

Why didn't I tell him when I had the chance? My free hand slides toward my necklace, and I grip the bone pendant fiercely, pressing my thumb into its smooth curves, squeezing my eyelids shut. I don't know how to cope with this throbbing in my chest, the pressure crushing my lungs. I wish I could feel the wind.

An hour passes, maybe four, before I hear someone enter the cavern and lift the grate above my head. It's Vivian.

"The *Riki* has sentenced you to death," she declares.

I stare at her, unable to speak. "But I'm innocent!" I finally splutter.

"You will be executed tonight when the sun has set," she continues.

This can't be real. "Listen to me," I shout. "I didn't kill her."

"Beheaded, according to tradition."

"No!"

Not that. Dear gods, please not that. I see the Shredder running the knife across his thumb, the Rangi plunging his blade into Aura's throat, Holly mouthing *decortication*, the tomahawk flying in the eagle's grasp, flying into the tree at the camp, flying from Rye's hand into his enemy's face. Into my face.

"Wait!" I gasp as Vivian turns to go. She pauses. "Do I get a final request?"

She says nothing. Just slams the grate and walks away.

I smack my fist on the rock then crouch down, tipping from my toes to my heels, toes to heels, numb all over.

They're going to kill me. They're really going to kill me. *Breathe*, I tell myself. I rock back and forth. I was prepared for almost anything but not this! Back and forth. They're going to kill me. *Breathe*.

I can't breathe! Soon I'll never breathe again.

I bury my face in my knees, squeeze my head, rap my fingers against my cheekbone. Again and again. Force the tapping to get inside my brain. Drown out everything else. *Tap, tap, tap.*

Sue and the twins will never know what happened to me. They'll always think I abandoned them.

Tap, tap, tap.

Just like Rye will always think I betrayed him.

Tap, tap, tap, tap.

I keep seeing his face, his cold, green eyes. His beautiful, horrified eyes.

Tap, tap.

I see the sharp edge of the axe. Hear the sound it will make when it …

Tap, tap, tap.

Don't think. *Tap, tap.* Don't think. *Tap.*

Tap.

A grinding sound above shakes me from my trance. The grating is being moved again. *Is the day over already?* I stand up shakily.

The ladder falls into the pit, and a person climbs down. When she gets to the bottom, I make out her profile, the round face and curly hair.

"Lila?" I gape at her, take a step forward. "You're alive!"

"So it is you." Her stiff voice makes me stop short. Her body is stiff too. In the dim light, I pick out the shape of a knife strapped to her thigh.

I stare at the knife, at her clenched fists, and I step back. "Are *you* my executioner?" I ask, reaching for my neck. I had hoped for a bigger blade.

She shakes her head. "I wanted to see for myself. See if it was true."

Neither of us speaks.

Lila breaks the silence first, her voice strained. "Did you do it, Kit? Did you kill her? Coordinate the attack on the camp?"

"No! Lila, you have to believe me." And then I tell her about running away to Winnipeg, about meeting Aura, about Jeremy. But afterward she doesn't look at me, doesn't speak.

Finally, she says, "The *Riki* thought his daughter was at the *maitanga*, so no one reported that she was missing, and the police couldn't identify her body. They didn't figure it out until about the time we were attacked at camp."

I wince. "I know it looks bad, but you have to believe me. I honestly had nothing to do with the attack."

"The chief's wife died when Aura was born. She's his only child. He moved her around a lot to protect her, so few people had ever met her. No one even knew she was in Winnipeg, except your counselor and Naira. You planned it perfectly."

"Lila! You're not listening."

"The tribe is in chaos," she continues. "Not only did we lose the chief's child, but we may have lost our next leader too."

"What do you mean?"

"You were alone with Rye for over a week in the wilderness."

"So? I don't get it."

She lowers her voice. "Did anything, you know, happen?"

"Lila, I seriously don't know what you're talking about."

"Aura and Rye were betrothed."

"What?" My head reels, and I take a step back. "Why?"

"If the chief doesn't have a son then the *Matoa*'s son marries his eldest daughter and becomes the next *Riki*."

"Rye is going to be the next chief?" It all makes sense now—his agitation when we discussed careers, his sudden hostility toward me when he thought I was Aura, his awkwardness when I asked if he had a girlfriend. He didn't want to be chief, didn't want to be told whom he had to marry. And he was forced to travel with me for eight hundred miles through the Canadian wilderness! It's a wonder he didn't kill me.

But then he changed. He started to like me. Maybe he thought marrying me wouldn't be so bad. *I gave him false hope.* "So what's the problem?" I stammer. "He can still be chief, can't he?"

"His reputation's been compromised. Alone with a girl—with a Rangi spy—for so long … "

"Nothing happened! I can vouch for him."

"Who would believe you?"

"Maybe my friends." I fix my eyes on hers.

She looks away. "How do I know we were really friends?"

I search for a way to prove it to her, but I can't find one. "Fine," I concede, "but it still doesn't make sense. If I wanted to upset the succession or whatever, I would have just killed him."

"No—you needed to learn the location of the *Wakenunat*."

"This is ridiculous! Everything I do is twisted, seen the wrong way."

"Because there's no other way to see it, Kit!" Lila snaps.

"What about the truth?" I shout back. "What about what I told you?"

"It's too ridiculous. A normal person would have told someone that Aura had been murdered."

A normal person. Yes, a normal person wouldn't have hidden behind a dead girl's identity, wouldn't have run away from everything, wouldn't have let Jeremy die or lied to Rye. But I did.

"Then I guess I'm getting what I deserve," I mumble.

Lila opens her mouth and closes it again. Neither of us looks at the other. Then she clears her throat. "I should go now," she says.

"Yeah."

But as she steps onto the rope ladder, I call after her, and she turns to look at me. "I know you don't believe me," I say, "but will you at least tell Rye something for me. Please? Tell him I'm sorry."

She bites her lip. "I can't do that." Then she scales the ladder, disappears over the edge of the hole. The ladder is pulled up, and the grate slides back into place.

I drop to the ground, shaking. I find a pebble on the ground and throw it against the rock wall, listen to it clang on the stone floor. I find it and throw it again.

When I lose the pebble, I roll onto my back and look up at the crisscrossed light that spills in from the other side of the grate, high above me. The sun is somewhere above me too, even higher. I try to imagine its radiant beams, floating up there in the sky, try to remember that day at the lake with Rye, when everything was perfect, when I should have told him.

"The wind sings so sweetly and speaks through the night, saying the long wait will shortly be done." I whisper the lyrics, my scratchy voice faltering near the end.

It's almost a relief when they come for me, when Jared climbs down the ladder and makes me go up with him, when Vivian grinds her rifle into my side to shove me through the tunnels and up the current. I keep my eyes lowered the entire time, make myself take deep breaths. *Just a quick drop of the blade, and it will all be over,* I tell myself.

We land at sector three and walk down the right side of the bridge, turning left then right. Then right again. Left once more. Maybe right another time. I stop paying attention.

Eventually, the passageway opens into a massive cavern, and I catch my breath. The cave is like the inside of an enormous seashell. The walls have been carved into huge, sloping ramps that move both vertically and horizontally across the walls and ceiling, the horizontal ridges fitted with tiered seating. Small LED bulbs trace the coiled lines throughout the cavern, turning the chamber into another Milky Way. This must be the *rukanu*, the gathering place.

And thousands have gathered. They fill almost all of the seats, chattering with their neighbors—men, women, children, all come to watch me die. When they see me, they stop talking, and the noise fades to a chilling silence.

On the floor of the room, which has also been sculpted to better catch the wind, stands a solitary stone block. Behind the block, an opening in the wall lets in the outside world, and I feel the wind whip around the curves in the rock. *If I could just grab it, sail out through the door* … Jared must have guessed my thoughts because his fingers tighten around my arm. He and Vivian push me down a ramp and toward the execution block then shove me to my knees so that I'm facing the crowd.

"Try anything," Jared hisses in my ear, "and we'll shoot you down before you can blink."

I don't answer. I just look over my quivering shoulder and watch the purple sun drop behind the mountains.

When the sun has vanished fully, I see the green flash on the horizon, the beacon of life and hope that now signals my death. After the flash disappears, the door to my right opens, and the *Riki* and Rye's father enter the room. In his hand, the warrior captain carries an axe in the shape of a bird, its wings forming the two blades.

I look desperately back at the fading sky, trying to keep my face blank, but my lip is shaking when the chief and Makya reach my side.

"My people," the *Riki* says solemnly, "today we witness the execution of an enemy, a Rangi spy. Her crimes will now be read." He steps aside, and a person moves into the center of the floor. When I see his face, I feel something inside me break.

"Enemy spy," Rye reads from a tablet in his hand, not looking at me, "you are sentenced to death for the following offenses. First, killing the daughter of our chief. Second, assuming her identity.

Third, revealing the location of our tribe's testing grounds and coordinating the murder of hundreds of our youth." The crowd shouts curses at me, but he keeps reading. "And finally, attempting to expose the location of our tribal fortress. As an admission of your guilt, you have accepted your method of execution and will be beheaded immediately."

"Wait!" I cry. "That's not true. I never accepted—"

A bag is thrown over my face, stifling my voice, and someone shoves my head forward so that my neck is stretched over the block. I push against them, but a heavy boot is placed on my back, keeping me down.

I'm screaming uncontrollably now, kicking too. My whole body is convulsing. *Soon it will be over. Soon it will be over.* But I don't want to die. I don't want to die!

A high-pitched wail fills my ears, and I wonder if the axe has done its work, if that's what I hear when I lose my head. But the wail turns into a scream, and suddenly a hot wave of air flips me backward. I hear a clang on the floor, a grinding slam. Then a deafening siren joins the shrieks of the crowd.

With my good arm, I tear the bag off my head. I'm lying on the ground next to the door. It's sealed shut. Outside something collides with the mountain, shaking rocks loose from the ceiling, and as I roll on my side to avoid a falling chunk of stone, I hit something hard. The axe. It landed right next to me.

I look up. Makya is on his back, and Rye and the chief are crouching beside him. Nearby, Jared is holding his leg where he's been hit by some shrapnel, Vivian lies on the ground in a puddle of blood, and those in the crowd who have not been injured are running for the exit.

The fortress is under attack.

Rye raises his head and looks at me. For a full second, we hold each other's gaze.

Then I leap to my feet and run.

I bolt across the floor, up the ramp, toward the tunnel. The sirens echo through the corridors, bouncing off the stone and driving into my brain.

I follow the crowd through the passageways. No one pays any attention to another person in gray, and soon I reach the chasm.

But there's a jam on the bridge. I feel air blowing onto my face and look up. The fan above us has been knocked loose. It's shooting air to the side instead of down.

Everyone is pushing their way onto the emergency staircases. I run for the stairs too, but just as I'm lowering myself onto the first step, Rye bursts out of the tunnel.

"Stop her!" he yells, pointing in my direction. The people around me look at him and then at me. I watch the recognition fill their faces: I'm the one who killed the chief's daughter, the one who must have led the Rangi to their fortress, the one responsible for all of this.

Casting my eyes wildly around the chasm, I look for something, anything, that might help me, but all I see are the stars pointing down into the dark hole.

There's no way out. As the warriors charge toward me, I look back at Rye, feeling the ache in my chest, wishing for the impossible. Then I swing myself over the railing and plummet into the abyss.

18

My stomach rises into my throat as I tumble through the air. Soon I'm falling past sector four. The people on the stairs scream when they see me. I want to scream too, but I can't even breathe. Around me, the stars point the way down, blurring into blue streaks of light as I pass.

I struggle to curl my legs up, press my injured arm close to my chest, wrap my other arm around my knees. I pass the bridge at sector five. Any second now, I'll hit the water. Its dark surface rises up to meet me. Closer. Closer.

Splash! The icy cold liquid stings my skin and knocks what breath remained from my body as I plunge into the cistern's dark depths, flailing my good arm. After several pulsing seconds, my feet touch bottom. I push off the stone and swim upward. My head bursts above the water, and I suck in sweet air.

Gasping and spluttering, I tread water while I look around for a place to exit the tank. I've got to hurry before the Yakone make it down here.

The LEDs shed rippling waves of blue light onto the surface of the pool and into the corners of the reservoir. Rocky walls surround the cistern, random wedges of stone jutting out in all directions. I should be able to climb those, even with a bum arm. I pick the closest one and swim toward it, kicking hard to compensate for my weak paddling.

Suddenly, a strong current in the tank wrenches me under the water's surface, dragging me away from the light. I can't paddle out of it. Can't see a thing. Everything is so dark.

A second later, my body slams against rock and metal, and I feel the crisscross pattern of wire mesh push into my back. The pressure on the other side of the screen slurps at my skin and clothes. I can't move.

Now I remember what Rye said: the cistern flows to the generator, powers the turbines. If I get pulled through the filter …

I place my shoe on the wire netting and push. Hard. I feel a snap, and instantly my foot is sucked through the broken mesh. The pressure pulls the rest of my leg along with it, and I slide through the filter up to my thigh. I shove my elbows against the rock, brace myself against the forceful current. My lungs burn.

I struggle to get the sling off my shoulders then move my hands onto the stone and push against the wall. My left arm wobbles crazily, but I slide myself off the mesh. With a tremendous tug, I pull my leg back through the hole.

Once my foot is free, the current flips me around, and I smack into the wall face first, my stomach stretched across the netting. I feel the sling slip past me into the hole. My brain is humming, lungs blazing.

I push off the wall, angling myself out of the direct flow of the current. Take deep strokes with my quivering arms. The blood thuds in my head. I push through the water. No end in sight. No light. Only never-ending blackness and the current clutching at my feet.

Just when the buzzing in my head has reached an ear-splitting pitch and my lungs are on the verge of eruption, I break through the surface. I gasp in deep draughts of air, but I don't stop swimming. I can't let the current catch me again.

Launching myself at the wall, I curl my fingers deep into the rock, cling to it dizzily for several moments, wait for the oxygen to reach my brain. My breath escapes in staccatos.

I pull my feet onto the jutting stone and relieve the weight from my shaking arms. Then I press down with my legs and continue inching my way up until I've scaled the rest of the wall. I push myself over the final stones and collapse on the bridge.

Whatever painkiller the doctor gave me is wearing off. The veins in my biceps are throbbing. My hands and forearms are too weak to even make a fist. Trembling, I use my elbows to push myself into a sitting position, but I know I can't rest on the bridge for long. Even though I was probably in the water for only a few minutes, that's more than enough time for the warriors to get down here. The mass of people fleeing to safety must have gotten in their way.

Weakly, I stand up and look around. This is the side of sector five without an exit, which means I need to cross the bridge if I want to get out of here. I take a dizzy step forward.

A gunshot cracks in my ears. I spin around and stagger into the tunnel. *Hide first. Then find an exit.*

I careen down the sloping passage, the walls bending in toward me. My shoes slosh, and I know I'm leaving a trail a child could follow.

I duck into the first chamber I find. Wires and meters spread out along the rock, and I hear the thrum of the generator on the other side of the wall. I shudder, thinking of how close I came to getting a view of the turbines.

My vision darkens as I bend over to tear off my shoes and socks. I try to squeeze the excess water from my clothes and hair, but my hands are shaking too much. I feel a stab in my arm. The new bandage is soaked in blood.

I have to keep going. I stumble across the room, heading for the exit on the other side. When I'm through the door, I find myself in a long, narrow chamber. The acrid smell of chemicals assaults my nose. Pipes run from an enclosed steel tank to a larger vat on the other side of the room.

Keep going.

I stagger past the pipes toward a door on the far end, slipping through it just as I hear my pursuers opening the door from the power room behind me, hear their shouts. I have to go faster. My pulse pounds in my ears.

I'm back in the tunnels, at a fork branching out in three different directions. I'm almost certain the passage on the left goes back to the bridge. Should I circle back, try to lose them? *No, they may have left someone to make sure I didn't backtrack.* That leaves the passage straight ahead and the one to my right. But no matter which one I choose the LEDs will give me away. I wish there were a way to turn them off.

An idea surfaces in my foggy brain. I take several steps down the corridor to the left. The blue bulbs wave out in front of me. Then I turn around and careen down the passage that was straight ahead. More LEDs surge on. Taking a few more steps, I spin back and charge down the tunnel on the right. Now stars shine in all three hallways. *That should buy me some time.*

My legs are numb as I escape down the passageway. But the tunnel doesn't curve. If the guards get close, they'll have a straight shot. I try to run faster. My lungs feel ready to collapse.

At last I see a light ahead that's different from the blue glow of the stars, brighter, more natural. I burst out of the tunnel and stumble to a stop. Beside me is a large lamp, and in front of me, a massive greenhouse.

Rows and rows of fruits, vegetables, and grains extend into the dark shadows of the immense cavern. Huge lighting fixtures, shut off for the night, hover over the plants. In one corner of the room, a fence pens in twenty chicken coops. Above my head stretches a carefully crafted glass roof—made to look like a frozen bank of snow in the shadow of the mountain.

The pounding of feet in the tunnel behind me sends me staggering into the rows of crops. I trip over zucchini and pumpkin plants, squeeze between strings of peapods, aim for the orchard, ducking behind the line of trees and racing into the dark.

I drop behind an apple tree and try to control my ragged breathing. Water drips from my hair into my eyes. I clutch the still-bleeding wound on my arm and inhale shakily.

A Yakone soldier enters the greenhouse. He switches on a light attached to the scope of his rifle and, swinging the gun back and forth, walks into the crops.

If I run for the tunnel, he'll have a clear shot. There may even be another person waiting down the passageway. But if I stay here, he's sure to find me.

Moving as slowly as I can, I creep behind the line of apple trees. When I reach the last one, I drop to my stomach and army crawl behind a planter box, ignoring the blazing nerves in my arm. Ahead is the corn. I scoot into the tall dry stalks. Crawl on my hands and knees.

A light slices the air above me, and I drop back to my stomach. I don't move. I hear the guard's shoes rustle the plants. Hear him breathe.

Then he's moving on, and I start crawling again. Clods of dirt stick to my wet clothes, the sweat on my hands, the blood on my bandage. I try not to brush the crackly stalks.

When I reach the end of the row, I pause and look for the warrior. I see his light disappear behind the henhouses. Now's my chance.

I dash out of the corn, the soil slipping away beneath me. I slow down when I near the rock, but my bare feet only make a slight padding sound on the stone. As I reach the tunnel entrance, I glance over my shoulder. He hasn't seen me.

Inside the tunnel, I force myself into a full sprint. Feel the incline in my tense calves and thighs. My straining lungs. The hallway is longer than I remembered. Don't stop. Keep going.

At last I reach the three-way fork by the waste sanitizing plant. I slow down, not sure which way to go.

Blue stars ripple down the hall toward me.

I zip around the corner, taking the tunnel on the right.

There are rooms on either side of the passage. I dash inside the first door, heart hammering against my ribs. When I see where I am, I stop short, shuffle quickly back. It's the prison block.

I run back to the hall. Through the other doorway.

Now I'm in a storage room, like the underground chamber at the *wakenu*, only bigger. It's filled with food. Supplies too. But no weapons.

Something catches my eye on one of the shelves. Painkiller. I stumble toward a bottle and twist off the lid. Toss a handful of pills in my mouth.

A surge of vertigo overwhelms me, and I crouch next to some blankets. That's when I see a door on the opposite side of the room, the side by the hallway. The one that leads back to the bridge. I stand up and lurch toward it.

I push back the animal skin and look in the corridor. The blue lights are still on, but there's no one in sight. No footsteps.

Suddenly, a thunderous roar vibrates through the mountain, up my legs, through my bones. I lean against the reverberating wall and wait for the tremors to die down. I wonder briefly how the battle's going, who's winning.

When the ground is steady again, I dart out of the door and turn down the hall. But then I see movement out of the corner of my eye. A flash of gray. People emerging from the tunnel to my left. Faster! I tear down the passageway.

"There she is!" I hear them call.

I leap behind a curve in the rock. Their footsteps echo through the halls behind me. The only thing protecting me is the twisting tunnel. If it straightens out again, I'm done for.

And then I reach the bridge.

I dash across it, pumping my arms furiously, ignoring the blood that's spurting out of my wound, the black circles in my vision. Any second now, they'll get their shot. The other side of the tunnel is so close. I hear their boots on the stone.

Ratatatat. Ratatat. I hit the ground and cover my head. My elbow slams into the rock, but none of the bullets find me. I get back up and sprint across the rest of the bridge.

Da da da da da. A perforated boom collides with the bursts from the Yakone's rifles, and the clashing gunfire ruptures the air, pounds my brain against my skull.

I dive the remaining three feet into the passageway then leap back up and peer around the corner.

Five Rangi are rappelling down the side of the chasm. On the bridge beneath them are three Yakone. All dead.

I whip my head back inside the tunnel and hurtle down the corridor. How did the Rangi get inside the fortress? Are there more of them? I trip on a rock and stumble forward. Barely catch myself before I sprawl on my face. I've got to get out of here.

I turn right and left at random, cursing the people who built this place for not marking directions to the exit. I hit two dead ends, whirl around and try again. The stars spin out around me.

At last the tunnel ends in a medium-sized cavern. As I stagger toward the far wall, I see a metal control panel with two buttons: green and red. I smash the green button with my fist, and the side of the mountain slides open. At last I step into freedom. Into an apocalypse.

The stars are exploding.

Bright lights streak across the black sky, fiery trails slash open the night, glowing bullets whiz above my head. Scope lamps dance and collide as the owners of the rifles whirl on the wind. Orange bursts of flame spiral through the darkness. It's like fireworks on the Fourth of July.

Until I hear the screams.

The screams. The screams are terrible. Worse than even the attack at the testing center, worse because there are more of them, worse because I can't see who's screaming until their bodies smack the side of the mountain.

The bodies are everywhere. Black Rangi, blending into the sky. Gray Yakone, mingling with the ashy snow. Warriors from both sides lie in pools of blood on the frozen ground, the ice reflecting the blazing explosions above so that the whole world seems an inferno.

A burning torrent of ammunition fans out into the night, the machine gun puncturing the air with its repetitive drilling. Someone falls out of the sky in front of me, bouncing off the rock and tumbling down, down, down to the base of the mountain, disappearing into the blackness.

Two scope lamps interlock as a Rangi and Yakone grapple for the upper hand. A blade gleams in the focused light, and then the knife finds its mark and the rifle lands in the snow, its bulb going out just as its owner vanishes into the night.

It's like the battles in the Aerie, the two sides whirling and diving and spraying their opponents with bullets, but here there's no paint. No mats to land on, no points to be won. Just your life or theirs.

A blast momentarily lights up the sky, and I watch a Yakone twist into a barrel roll and catch a Rangi from behind, like Rye and Lila used to do back at the camp.

The sky plunges once more into night. Then a stream of fire slices the air, engulfs a Yakone warrior, her flaming body the only thing illuminated against the dark backdrop. She shrieks, slapping at her burning clothes and skin and diving into a snow bank.

The red glow outlines the figure of the attacking Rangi, the flamethrower strapped to his back. He pursues the fallen Yakone, but before he can reach her, he disappears—in a roaring blaze followed by deepest night.

The wave from the explosion knocks me back. I cover my head as pebbles from the ceiling rain down on me, bruising my back and hands. Something loud bounces on the ground, and I look over. It's the rifle. I pick it up and slam the butt of the gun into the control panel. The door slides shut.

I lean against the cool rock, panting hard. I don't know what to do, where to go, what to think. I'm trapped inside a fortress under siege, and the people on both sides are after me.

There's nothing I *can* do. They're going to find me. They'll find me and kill me. It's no use. I can't keep running.

I sink to the floor. They'll find me no matter what.

My hand grasps my necklace.

They'll kill me. Like the others.

In my head, I see Aura's purple blood. Jeremy's arching back. Charity's blackened hair. The dead faces at the camp. See the Rangi plowing them down. Those coiling tattoos.

I hate the Rangi. Hate them. Hate them. My pendant digs into my skin.

I see the crumpled Yakone on the bridge. The shell-filled bodies outside. Hear the screams.

Hate them.

The screams. The blood.

No! I push myself up. I'm not going to sit here and make it easy for them. I grip the automatic. If I have to die, I'm taking some of those bastards down with me.

My arms shake as I lift the rifle up, shove it against my shoulder. I clench my jaw and hold the gun in place.

Keep going. Make them pay.

I move across the cavern, staying close to the walls as the blue stars roll out in front of me.

When I reach the tunnel entrance, I peek around the corner. It's empty.

I tighten my hold on the rifle and creep along the passageway. They could be anywhere. I turn right at the first fork, left at the next, the LEDs lighting up the corridor ahead.

Suddenly, the bulbs flicker. A whining clunk shudders through the mountain. Then all the lights go out.

19

I don't move. Just hold the rifle and my breath. Then I fumble for the switch on the scope. My fingers find the small lever. I flip it up … and the lamp turns on.

Except for the muffled booms outside, everything is deadly silent. I walk down the hallway, shining my light in both directions. But there's nothing. No shouting. No crying. No one poking a head out to investigate.

Quickly, I walk toward the nearest doorway. I push back the rug, shine the lamp into the dark room. And then I see the bodies.

Adults. Children too. On the beds. On the ground. Slumped over chairs.

I drop the fabric and scurry backward, slamming into a wall. I cover my mouth, gagging on the acid in my throat. *Did they—are all of them … ?*

I run to the next room. The same horrific sight meets my eyes. I check the next, and the next.

I slam my back against the rocky wall, chest heaving. How many? How many have they killed? Have they found Rye's siblings, Maize and Teff? What about Sarah and that small girl who wanted honey on her bread?

Monsters. They're going to pay for this.

I raise the rifle again, ignoring my trembling arms. At least one of them will pay. I keep walking. Keep going.

A barrage of shells rings through the tunnels.

I throw myself against the wall and cover my lamp, my whole body shaking. I stand as still as I can and listen, but the noise has stopped.

I walk forward slowly, swinging the rifle back and forth, keeping my twitching eyes trained on the swiveling pool of light.

Every time I round a corner, my heart stops beating and my palms grow slicker. I imagine them crouching in the dark with their weapons aimed, just waiting for me to come into view. I grit my teeth. Keep going.

My foot hits a pebble, and the small stone zings against the wall. I freeze, hide the lamp as the noise ricochets down the tunnel. Hold my breath.

When nothing happens, I continue walking, moving slowly, straining my ears to catch the sound of a footfall or the click of a gun, but all I can hear is my raspy breathing and the thudding of my pulse.

Da da da da da da.

Then I hear the screams, and I burst into a run.

As I turn the bend, the light from my lamp falls on a person standing outside one of the rooms. He's dressed in black leather. Raising his gun.

I fill him full of lead.

He slumps to the ground, and another person in leather appears in the hallway behind him. I glue my finger to the trigger, emptying the rest of my clip until the second Rangi drops to the floor.

I lean forward, clutch my head, my raw ears. Wait for the ringing to stop.

It doesn't.

I lurch forward and grab the gun from the first soldier. There's no lamp. I glance at the man's face. He's wearing night vision goggles.

I bend over to grab the mask, but at the last second, I yank my hand back. Instead, I detach the lamp from my old gun and clamp it onto his.

Standing up, I reach for the doorway and pull back the animal skin. Inside, a man lies on the ground, bleeding from his leg. A woman and four children are huddled around him, crying. When they see me, they start screaming again.

"Stop!" I cry hoarsely. "I'm not going to shoot you." I look at the woman. "You know how to use a gun, right?" She nods, face pale.

I go back out to the hallway and scoop up the weapon from the other Rangi. Then I return to the room and hand it to her.

"You're that girl," the woman gasps. "The spy." Her finger moves toward the trigger.

"I'm not a spy." *Kava.* My hand locks on my rifle. "If I were, I wouldn't have killed them." I hold the woman's gaze until she lowers the gun.

"There are night vision goggles on the corpse in the tunnel," I say. "They might help you protect your family, in case someone else comes along." She nods tightly.

I'm turning to leave, when I hear her whisper, "Thank you."

I pause for a moment then duck out of the room, the rifle raised to my eyes once more.

At the next *rukamo*, I stop and look inside. Wide, frightened eyes stare back at me.

"Hide," I tell the people in the room. "The Rangi are inside the fortress."

I keep going. Check other caves. Warn the occupants. At first, they react the way the woman did, calling me a spy, reaching for something to use as a weapon. But when I deliver my message, they don't know what to say. Some say nothing.

Some say, "Thank you."

I stop at every room in the tunnel, the adrenaline coursing through my bloodstream, my finger on the trigger. The next Rangi I meet is a goner.

My muscles are taut as I wind my way through the passages. Taut. Aching. But the adrenaline helps.

Finally, I reach the bridge. The empty chasm is just a few feet away. If I didn't have a light, I might have walked right off the edge. I shine my lamp down the pit and just barely make out the dark water below. It's eerily quiet without the noise of the fans.

I keep walking, but I don't see the rock in my path, and as I stub my toe and stumble forward, my lamp tips down, shining under the steel beams at the edge of the bridge, illuminating something metal. A box. I crouch down, aiming the light directly at the object.

It's a medium-sized container, shoved into the juncture of the bridge and the beams. On the side is a tiny red light. *Holy kava.*

I trace the joists with my lamp and remember the way the entire structure of steel staircases, bridges, and trusses seemed to rest on the huge slab of rock on which I'm standing.

What would happen if it were destroyed? Would the whole mountain collapse?

I look back at the box and feel the sweat adding moisture to my already wet collar. I have a feeling I won't be running into any more Rangi, not if they're going to blow the *Wakenunat.*

The thought sends me scurrying backward.

I should get as far away from the bridge as possible. Maybe if I find a place to hide … No, it won't matter. Nowhere will be far enough. If I don't do something soon, everyone in this mountain will die. And so will I.

I smash the butt of the rifle against the wall, press my fingers against my brow. I don't know what to do! How do you stop a bomb?

You don't. You get it as far away from here as possible and hope it doesn't go off while you're doing it.

Cursing, I sprint back for the box. I unclamp the lamp and pin it to my shirt, carefully scoot the bomb out from under the beams, pick it up, cradle it against my chest.

It's extremely heavy, and I have to lean back in order to support the weight. The veins in my arm bulge.

I'm turning toward the tunnel when the thought hits me: there might be more.

I pivot on my heel and look back across the bridge. If there are, I can't tell from here.

I stagger to the other side, trying to walk as steadily as possible since I don't know what might set this thing off. I bend down to look under the beams. An identical black box greets my gaze.

My heart sinks. How am I going to carry two of them?

I can't. I'll have to remove them one at a time.

Walking as quickly as possible, I enter the tunnel and set the first bomb down on the stone floor—if I don't make it back, at least the charge won't go off under a load-bearing beam.

I return to the second bomb, slide it out from under the tresses, clamp my teeth together as I pick it up. Stabbing sensations shoot from my hand to my bicep.

Where do I go? There's fighting on the east side of the mountain. Maybe the west side will be calmer. But as I look at the endless run of tightly spiraling stairs, I realize I'll never make it out of here in time.

And then I feel something cool sliding across the back of my moist neck. A draft. I snap my head around. A draft means an open door. It means wind.

I shine my light on the swirling air, but it's too hard to catch. I close my eyes and try to calm my galloping heartbeat. Then I turn off the lamp. I'm going to have to do this blind.

Climbing onto the railing, I reach out to the air, feel the chilly breeze brush my arms. It's weak, it's coming from above, and it's moving away from the opening. That means I'll have to ride against the current. I wet my cracked lips. This could be suicide, but I've got to try.

I open myself up and feel the tiny stirring inside my gut. Then I seal the bond and leap off the bridge.

For a fraction of a second, I fall once more toward the cistern below. But the connection holds, and I hover in the air.

It's exhausting—the weight of the bomb wants to force me into the water, and the breeze wants to push me backward. I clear my mind of everything except moving forward, command the current to let me through. And for the second time tonight, I swim upstream.

I move up the current past sector four. Sweat drips from my elbows, but I keep rising, keep straining. Keep going.

When I get to sector three, the draft moves into the tunnels, and the surf becomes stronger. The door must be on this level. I fight the stream into the passageway and then give up and drop to the ground. I almost fall over, but I steady myself and stumble down the corridor.

This time, with the wind as my guide, I know exactly where to go. I turn the lamp back on and move down the hallway, panting raggedly, swaying slightly.

Before long, I reach the gathering place. The door on the mountainside is open again. It must be jammed, unable to close with the power off.

I run into the sculpted cavern. Now there's plenty of wind. I find a current going in the direction I want and reach for it as it shoots off a ramp. I form *honga*, ride out the door.

Fiery bullets still streak across the dark sky, but there aren't as many as there were on the other side. I turn off the lamp. Zip past the glowing shells. Zoom into the night.

Where do I drop this? Into the canyon? I wish I knew how powerful it was, what damage it could cause.

I fly through the air, pushing myself hard, going as fast as I can. My connection wobbles as I strain for every extra ounce of speed, the weight of the box making my arms tremble violently.

I reach more deeply into the air, ask it to propel me forward.

Keep going. Got to keep going.

When I've gone as far as I dare, I dip into a ravine, find a ledge on the cliff, set the bomb down on the rocky shelf. My blood-drenched arms sag at my side, the adrenaline gone.

I hope this is far enough. I stumble to the cliff's edge. Now I have to get the other one.

Suddenly, I stop, look around me. I made it. I'm out of the fortress. I'm safe!

If I go back, the second bomb might go off before I get out. Someone might shoot me. I should leave now, while I have the chance.

What about the people inside?

I bite through the inside of my cheek, jab my fingernails into my leg.

The Yakone aren't my family—they tried to slice my head off. I need to leave. Go help my real family. The twins.

I stand poised on the edge of the crag. I look at the open sky then back at the *Wakenunat*. At the sky, back at the fortress.

I feel the wind beckoning at the fringes of my brain.

"No!" I shout, "I won't! I want to live."

I got one bomb out, that's more than enough. More than they deserve. I'm not a Yakone; they hate me. Why should I risk my neck for them?

"I won't do it."

I have to take care of myself, have to keep running. I can't go back there. Can't throw my life away. I'm free now. Free.

I turn away from the mountain.

And then I see Rye's face, those calm green eyes. See him holding me after I was shot, carrying me through the storm, watching over me while I lay unconscious.

Jeremy too—his strong embrace, teasing laugh. Gone forever. He didn't just save me. He gave up his life for me.

More images now. They swarm my head.

Charity's five dollars.

Aponi's warm smile.

The dancers and painters.

The beautiful testing grounds.

All the people at the camp who were kind to me. Holly, Tornado, Damon, Lila.

No, Lila betrayed me! Rye too. I'm not going back.

But I betrayed them first.

I'm panting, my face drenched in sweat. It hurts to breathe.

I owe them. I owe their families. Those frightened faces in the caves.

My family.

I remember the acknowledgment in the woman's eyes when I stopped the Rangi. The Yakone saying, "Thank you." They forgave me. Accepted me.

My arms are trembling. My heart slams against my ribs.

They *are* my family. I can't abandon them. I have to go back and make it right, prove I'm not a spy. I have to save them.

I have to.

No!

Tears flow down my cheeks.

I won't survive.

I have to. Don't think. Just go, just do it.

I take a deep, shaky breath. Slowly unclench my fists.

"It's okay," I choke. "It's okay." I breathe again, wipe the tears. And when I finally open myself to the wind, my mind is still.

The breeze enters my chest, soothes the pain. I let it fill every inch of my body.

But the current is moving away from the mountain. *This won't work*, I tell the wind. *I have to go the other way.* I immerse myself more fully in the connection, send my mental fingers probing across the sky.

I need an eastward current, I think, repeating it over and over. *Eastward.* And then I feel it, a new wind stream, right below me.

I run off the ledge and hurl myself at the surf before it's gone.

The connection is instant, and I zoom forward, back toward the searing fireworks that twirl around the *Wakenunat*'s peak, driving myself with everything I've got.

When I'm almost there, the fireworks suddenly stop. No more gunshots. No explosions. No screams.

That can only mean one thing. The Rangi have pulled back. They're going to detonate the bombs.

I don't slow down when I reach the door to the gathering place, don't jump off the wind.

I soar through the entrance.

The curving ramps whip me around. The current whishes me through the tunnels. It seems to know right where to go.

We plunge into the shaft. Over the edge.

Hurtle down the chasm.

Will it take me to the bomb?

I feel something in the back of my mind, an inkling, a suggestion. It's as if someone inside of me is asking me to give the command, waiting to obey.

So I give it.

The wind rockets me forward.

I don't have time to think through what's happening. In seconds I'm going to crash into the bridge. I get ready to jump.

But the wind turns. We speed into the tunnel.

There's the bomb. Bend over. Scoop it up. Its weight almost makes me fall. Hold on. Keep going.

Back up the shaft, I try, half hoping. Pleading.

The current whips me around the tunnel. We shoot back out the way we came in. Skyrocket up the canyon walls.

I clutch the bomb. Keep going. Don't let go.

Sector four.

Keep. Going.

Sector three.

Into the tunnel! I give the command just in time.

The wind swings me around the bridge. We dive into the passageway.

To the sky.

We zip through the corridors. Left and right in the dark.

Suddenly, the blue stars come back on. A few moments later, I feel the current beneath me weaken, and then I realize what's happening.

The power's back on.

The door!

If it closes, I'll have no source of wind. I won't get the bomb out in time.

Faster! I scream in my head. *Go as fast as you can!*

The breeze dwindles as I whip around the final bend.

Ahead, the door is closing.

Two feet of sky remain.

I roll on my side and hold the bomb in front of me.

My arms shake furiously. Veins pop out of my skin.

Kava, kava, kava, kava.

One foot of sky.

Go, go, go!

I speed through the opening.

My foot hits the door. I lose my balance. The bomb pulls me into a whirling nosedive.

Honga!

I grab the current.

Keep going.

And then the box starts blinking green.

I shriek at the wind. *Take us now!*

We rip across the sky. Faster than I've ever gone in my entire life. The dark shapes of the mountain peaks race past me.

I thrust the bomb below me. Urge the gale to take us down.

We plummet into the ravine, my heart in my throat, the bomb just ahead of me.

Then I release my hold on the wind. Jump away from the current.

For a few long seconds, the downdraft continues to push the black box into the canyon.

I see its blinking green light move further and further away.

And then it explodes.

Something explodes behind me too.

The other bomb. The sky, the mountains, everything lights up in the blast of orange and red.

The shockwave pounds the air.
Rockets me backward.
I reach for the wind, but there's no wind to find.
I flail my arms.
My body strikes something hard.
And it all goes away.

20

Shink, shink, shink. The sound of scraping metal jars me from my dreamless sleep. That's the first thing I know. The second thing is pain. A deep throbbing ache in my entire body, a splitting pressure on my bones. I can't move.

Slowly, I open my eyes, and the third thing I know is beige polyester. I'm inside a tent, the light fabric peaking at multiple points along the walls and ceiling.

I'm lying on a pad, inside a sleeping bag, and bandages cover most of my body—I can feel the itchy cloth compressing my limbs and torso, my head. When I turn my neck, I discover a person sitting on the floor next to me.

He's a large man, with black hair falling loosely around his shoulders, wearing a dark windbreaker and cargo pants. In his hand is a spear, which he's sharpening with a metal rod. That explains the noise.

"Where am I?" I croak.

The man looks up. He grins, revealing a gap in his front teeth, and my blood freezes. His entire face is covered in coiling tattoos.

I try to sit up, but I can't. I can't even lift my arm.

The man laughs while I struggle uselessly. "Don't try to move," he suggests. "You've broken a leg and an arm, and your back's not in great shape either." He goes back to sharpening his spear.

My tongue sticks to the roof of my mouth. I try to roll over, but a sharp pain shoots up my spine.

"Stupid blighter, I said don't move!" He stands up and walks over to my side. "A bit dense, aren't we ... Kitara Awha?"

My throat constricts. *How does he know my name?* "What do you want?" I wheeze.

"We thought you were dead, you know, when we found you. You were a bloody mess."

"I don't understand—why didn't you kill me? Why am I here?"

The man laughs again and points to my chest. "The only reason you're still alive," he says.

I crane my neck forward, but all I see are more bandages and brown bloodstains on my gray shirt. My pendant is somehow still hanging around my neck, the bottom corner of it chipped off, broken like the rest of me. But there's nothing else.

I look back at the man, the question on my tongue, and he chuckles and removes his windbreaker. He's not wearing a shirt, and I get a view of his bare skin, his tight muscles. A black tattoo spirals across his chest.

It takes me only a moment to recognize the pattern of swirling lines, a design I've seen every day for as long as I can remember. The very design that's hanging around my neck.

"No!" I push myself up. Excruciating pain rages through my arm, my body, my brain, shrouding everything in a scarlet haze. And as the man's distorted face floats toward me, I tumble back into darkness.

END OF BOOK ONE

KOHANGAERE GLOSSARY

Honga: Bond
Kama: Female
Karikara: Wind dance
Kauna: Round (of a competition)
Kohenrehi: Windracing
Koka: You too/ Watch yours
Maitanga: Testing/ Testing grounds
Manewa: Welcome
Matoa: Warrior captain
Muranga: Fire building
Pualani ana: Supplication of the Yakone liturgy
Raiwhapuhi: Rifle shooting
Riki: Chief
Ro: Day
Rukamo: Family dormitory
Rukamura: War hangar
Rukanaga: Council chamber
Rukanu: Tribal gathering place
Taitai: Good luck/ Watch your back
Takaito: Director
Tamo: Male
Tanaka: Hello
Tooka: Winner
Tookakihi: Traditional prize
Tookapuna: Grand champion
Tura: Rules
Waerehi whawhai: Foot racing
Wakenu: Meetinghouse
Wakenunat: Fortress/ Safe place
Wakemo: Bunkhouse

ACKNOWLEDGEMENTS

First and foremost, I am extremely indebted to Jonathon McNey for helping me build Kit's world from day one, being willing to read an extraordinary number of drafts, and in all other ways allowing me to monopolize his time. Some of the crucial details of this story would be missing without the help of my amazing friend and fellow writer, Linda Peterson, and I am so grateful for her keen insights and enthusiastic dedication to this project. Emily McNey, Claire Buys, Jenny Frodsham, Jennifer Shepard, Suzanne Tanner, Susan Bromley, Liz McNey, Kaye Robison, and Kevin Robison, thank you all so much for your encouragement and suggestions. The wonderful feedback you gave me blew me away. Finally, I want to thank my phenomenal husband for being my committed partner in every step of this crazy journey. I couldn't have done this without you. Much love to you all!

ABOUT THE AUTHOR

Katie Robison earned her bachelor's degree in English and French from Brigham Young University and is currently working toward a Ph.D. in medieval and early modern literature at the University of Minnesota. When she's not teaching or doing research, she enjoys running, playing racquetball, inventing new recipes, shooting nature photography, and, of course, writing. She and her husband live just outside Minneapolis.

To find out more about Katie and the next book in the series, visit www.katierobison.com.

CPSIA information can be obtained
at www.ICGtesting.com
Printed in the USA
LVOW03s1151080517
533702LV00005B/1048/P